I0612816

The Wolf
in the Woods

MARTIN ALLISON BOOTH

THE CHOIR PRESS

Copyright © 2024 Martin Alison Booth

All rights reserved. No part of this publication may be reproduced or transmitted in any form or by any means, electronic or mechanical including photocopying, recording or any information storage or retrieval system, without prior permission in writing from the publishers.

The right of Martin Alison Booth to be identified as the author of this work has been asserted by him in accordance with the Copyright, Designs and Patents Act 1988

First Published in Estonia as *Hunt Metsas* by Eesti Raamat.
Cover Art by PiktoGraaf

Published in the United Kingdom in 2024 by
The Choir Press

ISBN 978-1-78963-461-7

Kui hunti kardad, āra metsa mine

Who is afraid of the wolf should not go into the woods
Estonian Proverb

For my family; especially those whose memories and stories
are pressed like Forget-me-nots among these pages

This book is also dedicated to the people of Estonia

Kui hunti kardad, ära metsa mine

Who is afraid of the wolf should not go into the woods
Estonian Proverb

For my family; especially those whose memories and stories
are pressed like Forget-me-nots among these pages

This book is also dedicated to the people of Estonia

Author's note

This is a novel.

I am grateful to my family for all the stories we have shared over the years. Many of them can be confirmed by facts. Many of them are clear memories. Some of them are just vague recollections brought to light after many years.

Despite the fact that many of the incidents in this novel actually happened to my family, the narrative and the substance of the story are therefore effectively my own creation. The thoughts, feelings, behaviour and personality of the characters are the product of my imagination. As such, any resemblance to actual people living or dead is entirely coincidental.

Winter 1940

They left their home, their family, and their country. It was during the first big snow of winter, which by evening had turned to sleet. This, mixed with the wind slanting in from the sea, left the streets slushy and treacherous. They took the sleigh; the car wouldn't have made it down the hill. Pulled by a solemn horse, it scraped through the gates of the dockyard. The iron rails on the sleigh's runners sliced across the snowy cobbles.

A Red Army soldier levelled his rifle's snout.

'Halt.'

The driver hauled on the reins and the horse stopped, cuffing the cobbles with its hooves.

The soldier looked at the passengers submerged by blankets in the back of the sleigh; a woman and two children.

'Papers.'

The woman, Leena, began to rummage in her handbag.

'No. Get out. All.'

Leena encouraged her children out of the sleigh.

The soldier looked at them. Wrapped in their overcoats, mufflers and hats, it was hard for him to tell the children's ages or genders. The bulky coats gave the impression that they were well fed. More rich Estonian pigs trying to skip the country, he thought.

Leena returned his look. How old was he, seventeen, eighteen? His greatcoat hung off him like a tent. His cap was down around his ears. *The Great Liberator.* She could almost put him across her knee and spank him. But he had the rifle. He had the Red Army behind him. She fished out their papers and passed them over.

'Here,' she said. She spoke perfect Russian. She had been born among the Estonian community in St Petersburg; the city known as Leningrad since the revolution.

The soldier slung his rifle over his shoulder. He started to read in the light of the lamp above his sentry post. The papers flapped in the driving sleet. He took his time.

Poor thing, she thought, he hasn't quite learnt to read.

Eventually, he looked up. 'Reason for departure?'

'Visiting family,' she lied.

'What family do you have? Do you know where this ship is going?' He jerked his chin towards the vessel moored not a hundred metres away.

'Yes.'

'Germany.'

'I know. You asked me if I knew. I said yes.' She couldn't curb her irritation; or her growing concern.

The soldier gave her a dirty look.

'Again. What family?'

She hesitated. 'Cousins. We are going to visit my cousins.'

'Running away, you mean?'

'To what? Haven't Soviets and Germans made a pact? If we were going to Britain or America, perhaps you might question us. But, as you can see, our papers are in order. Our purpose is legitimate.' She reached for the papers. 'You have no right ...'

The soldier folded the papers, now as soggy as wet handkerchiefs, and plunged them into his greatcoat pocket. He regathered his rifle. 'I have every right. I have the authority to refuse entry into the port of anyone I suspect. I suspect you. Come. Bring your suitcases.'

He stood to one side and waved his rifle at her. When she looked like she would refuse to move, he jerked it at the two little ones beside her.

She nodded and began to shepherd her children. She knew what would happen to all three of them next. They would be chivvied into one of those sullen office blocks at the top of the harbour. There, they would be made to wait in some cold room without any information for hours; possibly through the night. Certainly until after their ship had left.

'Mother,' the taller child said in Estonian, 'are we not going to Germany now?'

'It's all right, darling. We'll sort it all out. Then we'll be on our way.'

'I don't want to go to Germany anyway,' the smaller child said.

The little party collected their suitcases from the sleigh, one each, and began to move off. The sleigh driver turned the horse around and sliced off into the night. The comforting, familiar scent of wet horse faded on the wind.

Another soldier, sheltering from the filthy night in the sentry post, stepped out to replace his comrade at the entrance to the harbour.

The room was, as Leena had expected, cold. Also, as she had expected, they had been put in there and left. The door was locked. The soldier had taken their suitcases. She could smell boiled cabbage and wet wool. Maret, her ten-year-old daughter, sat on a chair swinging her legs. Her brother, Juhan, lay curled up under a desk by the wall humming to himself and inspecting the lines in the palm of his hand.

'Mother?'

'Yes, darling?'

'Can I take my coat off?'

'No, darling. We'll be going in a minute, I expect.'

'But I'm hot.'

'I know you are, darling. But there's no heating. Take your coat off, and you'll soon want to put it on again.'

'But I'm uncomfortable.'

Leena was uncomfortable, too. The jewels sewn into the lining of her underwear did not take kindly to being sat upon. She'd not been able to take everything from her dresser. The rest she'd taken to her parents' house and buried in the garden against the day when they would be free to come home again.

Home again.

They hadn't even left, yet she sensed that her apartment,

4

her ordered life, her children's happiness and security were already a lifetime away. How long? How long would they have to be gone?

Then she thought of her husband, Hendrik. She hadn't seen him for three weeks. He had, of course, arranged the papers which were still, she imagined, lying sodden in the young soldier's greatcoat. The papers had come by messenger that afternoon. With instructions in Hendrik's handwriting about the need to leave straight away and the ship in which they would be travelling. The ship they could have almost touched, lying by the quayside loading its cargo. The ship that, barely two minutes before, she'd heard sound its whistle; warning anyone within earshot that it would soon be leaving. She broke out of her reverie to see her daughter looking at her. She smiled and blew her a kiss.

Maret was concerned. Even a ten-year-old noticed things. She'd first noticed the rings around her mother's eyes a few weeks before. She'd come to notice that her mother's clothes had started to seem too big for her. She'd noticed that she was not moving as easily as she once used to. She no longer swung her children around by their arms like she used to. She no longer laughed in that sing-song way she had. And now this.

'Mother?'

'Yes, darling?'

'Why does the soldier suspect us?'

'He doesn't suspect us, darling. He just needs to make enquiries.'

'But he said "suspect".'

'He didn't mean it like that, darling. He just needs to check our papers and then we'll be on our way.'

Maret knew Russian. Like all Estonian schoolchildren, she'd learnt it along with her mother tongue. She'd learnt German, too. Her homeland had been subject to one or the other country's rule for hundreds of years. She hadn't encountered many Russians in her short life, however. Not since

Independence. The Independence her father, an officer in the Estonian Navy, had fought for as a young man, twenty years before. She thought again about that soldier. She had heard what he'd said to her mother, what he had meant – whatever her mother had said he meant. She didn't like him. He was nasty. He reminded her of her teacher. Not her old one. The new one. The one who had come to teach them last summer.

Their other teacher would smile all the time. If they fell over while playing, she would hug them until they stopped crying. She would give them boiled sweets to cheer them up. Fruit sweets; raspberry, strawberry. The new one never looked like she would have given anyone a hug, let alone a sweet. Maret thought about that teacher. The new one. The one who spoke Russian. That first day she came to teach them.

Despite the warm weather, back then, this teacher had worn a heavy wool skirt. Taut hair tied in a bun sharpened her cheekbones. She smelled of mothballs.

She closed the door.

She locked it.

She cast a brief, chilly smile around the room.

'Good morning, boys and girls. I am your new teacher. Your old teacher has had to go away. She won't be back. But don't worry. Everything will carry on as normal; exactly as you are used to. Now, I understand that you say your prayers first thing every day. Is that right?'

The children nodded.

'Well, we shall continue to say our prayers. It is very important to say prayers, isn't it, children?'

The children nodded again.

'Good. And, since God can give us everything we could ever possibly want, why don't we ask God for something special today? I know – let us ask God for a piece of chocolate, yes? Close your eyes, children. Keep them tight shut. And pray as hard as you can that God will give you all a piece of chocolate ...'

The children all prayed as hard as they could. They screwed up their eyes. They gripped their hands so tightly together their knuckles went white.

'Now, children ... open your eyes!'

They looked down at their desks. There was nothing there.

'Oh dear,' said the teacher, 'oh dear. God seems to have forgotten you today.' She paused and looked at them with round eyes. Then she brightened. 'I know, let us close our eyes and put our hands together again, shall we? And, this time, here's an idea, let's pray instead to Uncle Joe Stalin for some chocolate, shall we? Come along, children, close your eyes, put your hands together and let's pray to dear Uncle Joe ...'

So the children prayed again.

'Now – open your eyes.'

They did.

There, on every child's desk, was a piece of chocolate.

She'd told her parents this story when she got home. They seemed amused, or concerned; she couldn't tell.

Maret's thoughts wandered from this to the last time she'd seen her father. Or, rather, the last time she'd heard him. It was a few weeks ago in their apartment up on Tõnismägi. Their splendid apartment. Their home. The weather had turned and the heating was on. She was hot in her bedclothes. She'd got up and opened her window. It didn't help. Hot and thirsty, she went to get a drink of water. Her parents were in the living room. They were talking quietly. She stepped up to the doorway in her bare feet to listen without being seen. She did not understand much, but she could tell by the low voices that what was being said was serious.

'They've gone already. It's only a matter of time before we senior officers are taken.' He paused. 'And after they've come for me ... they will surely come for you and the children.'

She heard her mother let out a low moan. 'What are we going to do?'

'Don't worry. I will think of something. I won't let you and the children down.'

She could hear her father get to his feet. She scrambled back to her room. She forgot all about getting a drink of water.

She heard the front door close.

Back in bed, she became aware once more of that underlying unease she'd had in her tummy for many days. What had her father meant? *They will surely come for you and the children.* Who was *'they'*? It didn't take her long to work out. He was referring to those soldiers. Everywhere. Not Estonian soldiers. Strangers. More and more of them, with red stars on their caps. She had noticed on her way to and from school that people were being stopped in the street by these men. There was hand-waving and raised voices. The fluttering of documents produced from inside coats and handbags.

Fluttering of documents. Like the ones her mother gave to that soldier just now.

Maret's quick mind flicked back to that afternoon, before they'd left to come to the harbour. She'd been in the family apartment, not in that stinky, cold room sweltering under layers of skirts and coats.

'Come along, darling, come along. Hurry up. We must go.' Her mother was fretting from one room to the next. 'We must go now.'

'May I take my book?' She had been sitting cross-legged on the living-room floor reading Tennyson's *Idylls* in translation. The one she'd asked for on her birthday. Adrift in the world of Arthur and Guinevere and Lancelot. In turn, comforted and shocked by the emotions they uncovered in her. Courtly love and betrayal. Heroism, idealism and evil. The exquisite melancholy of loss and regret.

'No, darling. Books are too heavy. We'll buy you new books when we get there.'

Her mother took her by the hand; she rose like Queen Guinevere and allowed herself to be led into her bedroom.

Her three best coats were on the divan: her summer one of cotton; her winter one of wool; her red one for parties.

'Put them on, darling.'

'All of them? But, Mother, I am wearing three skirts and two blouses already. I'm very hot.'

'I have told you, we can only take one suitcase each. We have to wear as many clothes as we can.'

As her mother fussed over her with the coats, Maret looked at the already packed suitcase standing beside the bed; almost as big as she was. It was made of a species of cardboard stained walnut, with a brown melamine handle. Its rear hinges expanded to accommodate, at least in part, its bulges.

She turned to object once more but she caught her mother unawares. She could see that the face of reassurance had fallen. Instead, it was drawn and the eyes glistened in the electric light. They were puffy and red.

'Mother?'

'Come along, one last coat, get your arm in here. Push.'

It was a pretend crossness, Maret knew. She pushed and twisted her arm, already bulky with clothing, down through the woollen tunnel of this further sleeve until her shoulder ached. Eventually, the tips of her fingers appeared out of the cuff, followed by the whole hand. Her mother shook and jiggled the coat into some sort of shape around her child's shoulders and body.

'Good. That will do. Now – go and find your brother quickly. I don't know where he's got to, and the sleigh will be here at any moment. Any moment.'

Maret's thoughts were dragged back into that horrid cold room by the sound of the ship's whistle once again.

'Is that our ship, Mother?'

'I don't know ...' Leena said. She had heard it, too; a mournful note like the dying of a Sibelius symphony. It may have been her imagination, but there was something both urgent and final in the sound. They had, perhaps, just a few more minutes and then it would be too late.

There were boots in the corridor. Quick step.

The door was unlocked and swung open.

It was the soldier.

Immediately behind him was another man. In a blue uniform with gold epaulettes. The insignia of a captain third class in the Soviet Navy. He bowed.

'Peeter!' said Leena.

'Uncle Peeter!' said the two children, and ran to hug him; hugs he readily returned.

'Now now,' he said, 'we have very little time, I'm afraid. We need to get you going. The comrade soldier here has performed an excellent task and fulfilled his duty admirably. However, it is clear, my dears, there is no reason to detain you further. I have therefore asked the comrade to escort you with due despatch to your ship. Take your cases – they are here in the hall ...'

As they walked across the sleet-swept dockyard, Leena fell a little behind with Peeter. The children and the soldier continued making their way to the ship. It sounded its whistle one last time; the long note swirling away over the harbour on the winter wind and out into the Baltic night.

'Peeter ...?'

'No questions, dear.'

'But your uniform ...?'

'We make the choices we make.'

'Yes, but ...'

'My ship *Ristna* is in port for supplies. We will be leaving soon after you. You, by the way, will be on the last civilian passenger ship to leave Tallinn. After that – it's all troop ships.'

'How did you know we were here?'

'My dear, how do you think? Hendrik got me to arrange your papers.'

'Hendrik! Where is he? Is he with you? Is he one of you?'

'I don't know where he is. Some fellow came with a note about you from him about three days ago. That's all I know. You know what my brother's like: wheels within wheels. Could be anywhere, doing anything.'

'But why send us to Germany?'

'I know. The last place on earth. Here's your ship ... come, my little ones, give your old Uncle Peeter a bye-bye cuddle.'

The children obliged, with little squeals of delight. They felt his warmth, smelt his familiar uncle-y smell.

The soldier tugged them away and chivvied them up the gangplank. He was keeping his thoughts to himself.

Leena gave her brother-in-law a hug. 'Will you get into trouble? Might that young man inform on you?'

Peeter shrugged. 'It's all about taking chances from here on in.'

'See you again?'

'Of course.'

The dirty Baltic coaster with its salt-caked smoke stack sawed its way through the scrambled seas; beyond the outer harbour and off into the night. The fourth row of portholes, the lowest, dipped itself into the restive sea; sometimes below the waterline, sometimes reaching out as if gasping for air.

There, in that squalid little cabin on board the last civilian passenger ship to leave Tallinn, Leena, her ten-year-old daughter and her six-year-old son shared one of six bunks as they went into exile.

The bunks were lit by the melancholy orange of a single bulb. Had the occupants swung their knees outward into the middle of the cabin, they would have collided with the knees of the other occupants across the way.

The juddering engines, just across the corridor, meant the cabin reeked of grime, diesel exhaust and oil. The air was stale, the floor sticky. The ancient straw mattresses were damp, the blankets dank. Maret wiped the filth from the port-hole with her elbow. She only succeeded in smearing the grease further. Peering into the night, her breath blossoming on the glass, she tried to catch a final glimpse of the lights of the town. Her town. Her home. She could see nothing but the Baltic; a giant's chest heaving and falling.

She only asked two questions of her mother that night: 'When are we going home?' and 'Where's Father?'

'Soon,' her mother replied. 'We'll be together again, soon.'

A few hours later, failing to sleep, Maret whispered those questions again in her mother's ear. Receiving the same response, she knew that she would get no further. So she gave up asking. However, it was those two questions that continued to echo in her mind and her heart every waking day afterwards:

When are we going home?
Where's Father?

Spring 1941

I

'Commander Kotkas?'

'Yes.'

'The Admiral will see you now.'

'Thank you.'

Kotkas stood, tucked his officer's cap under his arm, smoothed his uniform jacket and walked through the door being held for him.

It was an airy office, no ornaments. The desk in front of the broad window was dark oak. On it was an inkstand, two telephones, a lamp. Behind it sat a slight man in his late fifties. His crisp white shirt cuffs protruded half an inch beyond the jacket sleeves. The broad gold rings of his rank flashed in the early spring sun. He screwed the top back on his fountain pen then laid it and the papers he'd been scrutinising aside. He looked up.

'Good morning.'

'Good morning, Admiral.'

'So, let's have a look at you …' he began. The scent of the Admiral's Kölnisch Wasser gave the spartan room a subtle tang of citrus. But before he could say anything further, the door, which had been closed behind Kotkas, swung open again.

The Admiral glared at whoever it was beyond the Commander. 'This is a private meeting. Get out.'

The newcomer wore a field grey uniform with gleaming boots and a silver lanyard. He drew alongside Kotkas. A waft of talcum powder preceded him. He ignored the Admiral and spoke to Kotkas. 'If you would be so kind as to leave us for a few minutes,' he flashed an icy smile, 'we won't be long.'

Kotkas looked at the fellow, a major, then at the Admiral.

The Admiral's shoulders sagged. He waved Kotkas towards the still-open door. 'Apologies, Commander,' he said.

Kotkas withdrew. He heard the Admiral growl to the newcomer: 'Didn't your mummies ever teach you people to knock?' Then the door closed.

He took his seat in the anteroom. Here, half a dozen women sat at their typewriters. Someone had placed a hyacinth in a pot on the window sill. It had blossomed and the office was steeped in its perfume.

A moment later, in the corridor beyond the anteroom, there was a disturbance. The clatter of footsteps preceded a rustling, followed by some species of slapping and stamping. Kotkas suspected that the two navy guards posted either side of the entrance to the office suite had presented arms. Whoever was approaching was clearly someone of significance. The precise significance became evident a moment later. Into the room strolled a short man in a brown jacket with a blood-red armband. Two aides dressed in army uniforms, spattered with red and gold emblems indicating exalted rank, followed him.

Kotkas got to his feet. All the women stood, raising their right arms in salute. The man stalked towards the Admiral's office. One of the aides leapt beyond him to open the door. But then the man stopped. He turned his head. Kotkas became conscious of glacial eyes beneath charcoal eyebrows. The sooty moustache on the upper lip bristled.

'Do you not salute me?' the man said, indicating the raised arms of the women. Kotkas placed his cap on his head and laid the tip of his fingers upon the peak.

'I think,' one of the aides advised, 'the Leader is suggesting you salute him properly.'

'With all due respect, sir ...' Kotkas began.

'That is the problem,' said the Leader, 'you do not offer me *all due respect ...*'

'With all due respect ...' Kotkas continued, 'my understanding is that we in the navy are permitted to salute you in this way.'

'But you are not just "in the navy". You are here in Berlin; at the heart of my intelligence service. Don't you think that this is deserving of a greater sign of your allegiance to me?'

'Perhaps, sir. But ...'

The man glared and spun round to address his acolytes. 'This man dares to give me – me! – "perhaps" and "but"!'

Kotkas continued '... but since I am not a German, nor have I taken the oath of allegiance, and am not a member of your Party, I am surely not duty bound to offer the salute given you by your followers ...'

'You are not German? You speak like a real German ...' The man took a step towards him. 'But he does not behave like one, eh?' he said over his shoulder to his aides. They laughed. 'Where are you from, then, *Mr Ersatz German*?'

'I am Estonian, sir.'

'Estonian, eh? Clearly happy to wear my uniform, take my pay, follow my orders. Yet you deem it acceptable not to fulfil all the obligations that go with such benefits.' He moved so close to Kotkas that the commander could smell his breath; it was sour.

'Sir,' Kotkas said, 'I wear your uniform because we fight on the same side. However, our purposes are different. You wish to win a war. I simply wish to reclaim my homeland's independence.'

The man grunted; the muscles in his jaw flexed. When he spoke again, his voice had the hiss of a bacon slicer. 'Well, thank you so much for your support, Commander. I am sure the entire German nation is honoured by your gracious participation in our little enterprise. Feel free to dip in and out of it as you see fit.'

He turned and stood in front of the Admiral's door, waiting for his acolytes to open it for him. Before they could do so, he swept back to Kotkas. He jabbed his finger at the Commander. 'You think you are fighting for some kind of noble ideal. But, when it comes down to it, you are just a mercenary. A filthy mercenary. Like all the others.'

They went through. The door shut.

Kotkas took his cap off again. He sat.

The women in the office exchanged glances, sat down and got on with their typing.

Kotkas brushed some spittle from his sleeve.

'Excuse me, Commander...'

He looked up.

One of the women, the one who had held the door for him earlier, had stopped typing.

'Yes?' he said.

She was petite; auburn hair in a plait bun. Her eyes were summer blue. She was perhaps twenty, twenty-one. 'Have you any idea ...?' She was looking at him with a mixture of anger and concern. She didn't complete the sentence.

'I have every idea,' he said.

'Well,' she said, 'it was nice knowing you.' She shrugged and got back to her work.

It was over half an hour later that the door to the Admiral's office opened. The four most recent arrivals left. The short man in the mushroom-brown jacket with the bristle moustache stalked past without a glance towards Kotkas. The women had barely time to get out of their chairs and salute before he was gone.

'Miss Meyer ...?' the Admiral called from within.

The woman who had spoken to Kotkas went in while the others returned to their typing. Miss Meyer reappeared. 'You can go in ...' she said.

Kotkas entered. He was not halfway across the room before the Admiral rose from his desk.

'What the hell did you think you were playing at?' he said.

'Sir?'

'Offending the Leader, putting yourself at risk. Putting your whole role ... every possibility ... at risk. Good grief, man. I heard you were headstrong, but *this*...'

'It did not appear to me, sir, that I was doing anything wrong.'

'Did not appear ...?' The Admiral sat down heavily. 'It was all I could do to prevent him from having you thrown out of the window. And, I might remind you, we are on the third floor. Mercifully, I was able to persuade him otherwise.'

'Thank you, sir.'

'Yes, well, it is clear to me from your tone that you are not in the least grateful, let alone repentant. Lord preserve us from the hubris of navy officers.'

*

Outside, in the anteroom, the telephone rang. Miss Meyer answered it. She listened to the person speaking at the other end then took up her diary to consult it.

'Kotkas,' she said, 'Commander H. Kotkas. Why do you need to know?' She listened again. 'Yes, of course, I'm sorry, I didn't mean to question ... if that's all ...? Very well. Goodbye.'

She rang off.

*

'Anyway, I managed to convince him of your value to us ... eventually,' said the Admiral. 'Might I suggest, however, that should you ever find yourself anywhere within a hundred paces of him again, you cut and run?'

'I stood my ground; that is all.'

'Well, stand it somewhere else. And, for goodness' sake, salute him properly.'

'I did salute him—'

'Enough!' The Admiral brought his fist down on his desk, making the telephone receivers quiver in their cradles. He gathered himself. 'My apologies, that was unseemly.' He straightened. 'What's done is done. You may have to face the consequences in due course. In the meantime, we must make as much use of you as we can. Please – take a seat ...'

Kotkas sat.

'So ... why are you here ...?'

'I don't know, sir. I imagine—'

'Rhetorical, Kotkas. Where have you been since you got out of Estonia?'

'Memel, sir. I've been working for your navy up there.'

'Busy place, Memel.'

'Busy place, the Baltic, sir.'

'And, tell me, how do you think you landed up there?'

'You, sir.'

'Me, sir. You are very useful, Commander. And this is the reason I have managed to persuade the Leader to keep you on the inside. My people have sworn you to secrecy, I trust?'

'They have, sir. Signed my life away on your interminable forms.'

'Very well. What I am about to tell you is known by only the highest in the High Command. Not even the security services know about it. They must never know about it until what I am going to tell you takes place. Do you understand?'

'Yes, sir.'

'Well, then ... Britain may not have fallen. But the Leader assures us that the assault on that little island was just a diversionary tactic. He intends for us to keep that upstart Churchill bottled up and occupied with his own insignificant concerns while the eagle's glittering eye turns to bigger prey.'

Kotkas remained impassive. What the Admiral was clearly about to say wasn't unexpected. Anyone in intelligence these days, with even a passing interest in the Baltic region, knew how flimsy the pact was between the two largest totalitarian regimes in Europe. It had in many ways even given Kotkas a glimmer of hope. He would rather not be standing there in that office, in that city, in that country; but if the writing was on the wall, it was as good a place to be as anywhere for the time being.

'The Leader tells us he has planned all along that it is the Communist threat which needs his Iron Heel,' the Admiral continued. 'We are stepping up preparations for invasion – code name Barbarossa; legendary German hero and crusader. The pact just bought us preparation time.'

'Which is why I am here.'

'Your much-vaunted intellect has not let you down. It is the *only* reason you are here. Why you are still alive. As senior intelligence officer in the Estonian Navy, for all your work on communist radio intercepts down the years, your knowledge and insight is second to none. Are you with me?'

'Yes, sir. But, as I suspect you are aware, I am with you only insofar as this all works towards my helping my country return to independence. I cannot guarantee how I will choose to act once we have rolled the Soviets back and my country is freed from them.'

The Admiral shrugged. 'Oh well. What will be, will be,' he said. 'Meanwhile, perhaps it should also be said, I can protect you only insofar as you help us drive the Soviets out of your country and beyond. Once you have outlived your usefulness, who knows what will happen?'

'That is quite understood, sir.'

'Good. Then we are of the same mind.'

'A *similar* mind, sir. For the time being.'

'As you say.' The Admiral took up a pen. 'Then I had better see if we can't find you somewhere to sit here in Berlin. For the time being. Till we've squeezed everything you know out of you.'

'One request, sir.'

'Which is?'

'Before I bend to the task in hand, would it be possible to visit my family?'

'Where are they?'

'I am not sure, sir. I believe they have ended up in Königsberg, but I should like to find out.'

'Very well. You have three days. Including visit.'

*

Fischer had been up half the night. In shirt and braces, he sat working at a desk near the windows. They were dirty. Through them, the weak spring sunlight struggled to pierce the fug of cigarette smoke. The smell of stale coffee hung over the room. He had grabbed a couple of hours' sleep in one of the empty cells downstairs before returning to continue his work. He had slept in his brown pinstripe trousers; the odour confirmed it. He hadn't shaved. Maybe put in an hour or so, then go home and have a lie-down. He was thinking. Say I am going out for a while to follow up a lead or something ...

'Just got a call from the chief.' A man in a blue worsted suit approached him.

'Oh?' Fischer said.

'Seems someone close to the Leader is somewhat aggrieved over some snub the Leader has just endured.'

'What kind of snub?'

'Some uppity naval officer. Refused to salute. Bare-faced insolence.'

Fischer yawned. Blinking the weariness from his sore eyes, he produced a notepad and pencil. 'We can't be having any bare-faced insolence, now, can we? Name?'

'Kotkas. Commander Hendrik Kotkas. Estonian apparently. You've got the Baltics. Do a little digging, would you? Maybe have a friendly chat with the fellow at some point as well, eh?'

'Will do.'

'Soon as you can.'

'Yes, sir.'

His superior left. Fischer threw the pad and pencil down

onto the desk and glared out of the window. *That's the end of that, then. No sneaking off for a lie-down after all. Curse it.*

*

Kotkas handed the Admiral's note to Miss Meyer. She read it. 'You need an office?'

'Yes.'

'And – to arrange the issue of authority from the Admiral to engage in some research?'

'Yes.'

'What kind of research, if I may ask, sir?'

Kotkas looked at her. Was this a trick? Checking to see how watertight he was when it came to confidentiality? Barely out of the Admiral's office and here he was being tested, perhaps. 'Why do you need to know?'

'I don't need to know at all.' She sounded offended. 'However, if you need me to obtain authority for research, I need, do I not, to know what it is you will be researching?' She paused. 'Sir.'

'Just authority to research will do, for now. I shall argue about the particulars when I encounter any resistance from librarians, archivists and pedants.'

Miss Meyer did not move.

'I thought you were very brave ...' a young woman sitting at one of the other desks blurted out.

'Clara. Shh,' said one of the other women.

Clara flushed. She returned to her typing.

Miss Meyer flicked a hand, indicating that the Commander should follow. She led him out into the corridor, beyond earshot of the sentries by the door. 'Only, the thing is, people have been asking about you,' she whispered.

'What sort of people?'

'The kind of people you would be better off not having ask about you.' Her eyes narrowed. Was this man deliberately difficult, or simply another dim-witted gung-ho naval officer?

'Well, thank you for your concern,' he said. 'As you can see from this note, the Admiral has my best interests at heart.'

'That's not always enough.'

'Be that as it may.'

'I am trying to help you. Can't you see that?' She tried again. 'What kind of research? The kind that might get you into further trouble?'

He looked at her. *In this world,* he said to himself, *there are those you sometimes need to trust, if only to discover whether you can actually trust them.* He decided. 'It won't necessarily lead to trouble,' he said. 'Though I don't doubt, bearing in mind my recent interview with the Admiral, *that* kind of research is just around the corner. But maybe you can help after all. I only have three days before I start work in earnest. It might take me that long just to learn the ropes around here. Whereas, I expect you know which buttons to press.'

'If I can help, I will ...'

A truce. It was not ideal that someone else, someone at the heart of the intelligence-gathering community, someone apparently communicating on a daily basis with the secret police, should become aware of where his family lived. But time was, as he had just pointed out, limited. He took the risk.

'I am trying to find out the whereabouts of my family. Surname Kotkas. Wife Leena, children Maret and Juhan. Left Tallinn by ship – must be ... three months ago, now. Last heard of on their way to Königsberg. Some unknown contact of a contact of mine was to find them somewhere to live, albeit temporarily.'

'I'll see what I can do.'

'I will follow things up. I just need to know where best to start, really.'

She started back to the office then stopped. 'You must miss them very much,' she said.

II

There was a noise. The kind found from time to time in any school playground. Not the usual hue and cry of children racing around, playing; it was a commotion. Children cheering, children jeering; at once both thrilled and afraid that something naughty was taking place.

Maret, who had been sitting on the bench under the tree, heard it. She looked up. Across the field, a group of children had gathered. An eddying crowd. They surrounded a core of children who were struggling with one another. A fight of some sort. Despite herself, her vow the day she arrived at the school three months ago never to get involved with anything, she made her way across to the scene. Arriving, she realised she recognised one child in particular among the group that was fighting. Her brother, Juhan. His shirt and jumper had been scragged; a little line of blood was making its way oozily from his nose down onto his upper lip. He was being set upon by others. The children confronting him were older; Maret's age.

Maret launched herself into the fray, threw two children aside and burst onto Juhan's assailants. She clouted each one of them in turn. They recoiled. She turned on the last one, Kurt, still laying into her brother with both fists. Just as he raised his arm to land another blow, she grabbed his wrist and flung him backwards to the ground. The children gasped and the noise abated.

Maret went to her brother. She put her arm around him.

'I'm all right. I'm all right. They didn't hurt me. They are silly and stupid.' He wiped his nose with his sleeve.

Kurt leapt to his feet and hurled himself at Maret.

'You Jew, you filthy Jew!' he screeched, flailing at her.

Maret let go of her brother, fended off the blows, thrust an arm and clouted the boy. The force was such that he was spun sideways and ended up once again on the ground. Maret stood over him, her shadow cast across his face.

'Leave my brother alone,' she said. 'Let me alone. Leave us alone.'

Kurt rubbed the side of his head. 'You Jews. You're both filthy Jews. I hate you.'

'Come on,' Maret said. She led Juhan away to her bench under the tree.

A teacher appeared from around the corner of the school building. It was Miss Sperling; short and slight, big round glasses, nut-brown clothes. From their bench, Maret and Juhan watched the scene develop. Miss Sperling went to the crowd first. It had grown. Most of the rest of the school, older and younger children, had now gathered. Maret and Juhan watched as the teacher quizzed them. They chattered and pointed to Kurt and his cronies. Miss Sperling then turned her attention to Kurt, who was once again on his feet. Kurt pointed; other children pointed. Miss Sperling's eyes followed the direction indicated. Her eyes fell on Maret and Juhan as they sat on the bench across the field. She nodded, made a gesture with her hands for the children to settle down, and set off.

'Maret, Juhan.' Miss Sperling made a point of remembering every child in the school's name. Maret knew her to be kind. Much better than the teacher she'd had before they'd left Estonia. She and Juhan stood up. 'Were you fighting just now?'

'No ...' said Juhan.

'Yes,' said Maret.

'Why?'

'They were hurting my brother.'

'Why?'

'I don't know.'

'Juhan, do you know why?'

'No.'

'You must know why, dear. Boys don't just get into fights for nothing.'

'They were being hateful.'

'Who were?'

Juhan pointed towards Kurt and his friends. But the crowd had dispersed and were back playing at their various games. 'Them,' he said.

'Who is "them", please?'

'I don't know their names.'

'I need to know their names. If they have done something wrong, they need to be told off. Maret, do you know their names?'

'Yes. They are in my class.'

'Ah. And who were they ...?'

'I am afraid, Miss Sperling, I cannot tell you.'

'Goodness me – why ever not?'

'Because it is wrong to snitch.'

Miss Sperling stared at the girl. 'Goodness. But, surely, if the boys have been behaving badly, they need to be punished?'

'They have been punished. I punched them. They won't do it again.'

'Yes, but, Maret, we must not take the law into our own hands. Do you understand what that means, how important that is?'

'Yes, Miss Sperling. But it is over. Next time – if there is a next time – I promise I will not take the law into my own hands. But it is more important I don't snitch.'

'Are you afraid of them, dear?'

'Maret isn't afraid of anything,' said Juhan.

'No, I am sure not.' Miss Sperling looked at Maret. Their eyes met. Maret's at once fierce yet close to tears. After a moment's consideration, the teacher spoke again. 'Well, then, it seems there is nothing more to be done.' Fights in playgrounds were ten a penny. Especially in these profoundly unsettling days. So many fathers away, goodness knows where, doing what. 'I would, though,' she said, 'like to know the reason for the fracas. Do you have any idea at all, Juhan?'

'Well ...' He looked to his sister. 'Maret, is it snitching if I tell Miss Sperling what the fighting was about?'

'I don't know. Was it about something horrid?'

'It was about you.'

'Me?'

'Yes ...'

'What were they saying, Juhan?' said Miss Sperling.

Maret nodded for Juhan to speak.

'They said Maret was Jewish, miss. They said she had dark hair and brown eyes and dark skin and that meant she was a Jew and shouldn't be in school.' He went on quickly, 'But she's not Jewish, miss. She's my sister. And then they said I was Jewish, too, but I have blue eyes and blond hair. I can't be Jewish, miss, can I? And if I'm not Jewish, Maret isn't Jewish, either, is she ...?'

'Dears, dears, dears ...' said Miss Sperling. She took them both by the hand and they sat down together on the bench. 'All this talk of Jewish or not Jewish. You children shouldn't concern yourselves with such things at your age. That is for other people to worry about. Grown-ups. I am sure neither of you are Jewish ...' She stopped and looked at Maret, considering the girl for a fleeting moment. 'Though, it has to be said, you do have the most wonderful brown eyes and dark hair, Maret ...'

'I know,' Maret said. 'My mother comes from Tartu. I'm like her. Juhan's like Father.'

'Tartu – that's in Estonia, is it?'

'Yes, in the south. Mother says we have dark skins because it's sunnier in the south of Estonia.'

'Sunnier? Or a different race, possibly?'

'Race?'

'Tribe, group of people, families. From many thousands of years ago, perhaps. Coming from somewhere else?'

'Maybe,' said Maret, not really sure what the teacher meant.

Miss Sperling took another look at the girl. And wondered. It was her job to advise the authorities should she ever come across anything they might be interested in. No matter how insignificant. It was part of her job. It was not what she went into teaching for. But these days ... these wretched days ... needs must when the devil drives ...

*

Maret and Juhan were walking home from school. The blossom was now out; cherry and apple. The sky was blue, although there was still a chill in the air. In the distance, doubtless from the direction of the station, they heard a train whistle shriek. Some people were leaving on that train. Getting away. People lucky enough to escape that awful city full of strangers and unkindness.

'Hello there,' a voice from behind called. They were joined by a youth in his teens. He fell in step. Maret recognised him as Karl Stieber, the boy who lived across the street from them. Tall, blond, blue-eyed, with an easy loping walk.

'Hello,' she said, without any warmth.

'Quite a to-do at school, eh?'

'What do you mean?'

'You, giving that wretch Kurt what he deserved. I should have done it myself long ago. He's nothing but trouble, so's his gang. But I am so much older than him, it would be seen as bullying. Is it true?'

'Is what true?'

'He was calling you both Jews?'

'It's over and done with,' said Maret, and sought to walk faster to get away from him.

Juhan trotted alongside her. Karl kept pace.

'We're not Jews,' said Juhan. 'What are Jews anyway?'

'Look,' said Karl, 'here's the problem. You two are outsiders, aren't you? From Estonia, that's right, isn't it?' Juhan nodded. Maret kept trudging on. 'You've got to expect people to think you are different if you keep aloof like you do.'

'We do not keep aloof. We just mind our own business and wish other people would do the same,' said Maret.

'These are distrustful times,' Karl continued. 'It doesn't do to set yourself apart. Especially not in a small neighbourhood like this one. I don't doubt Kurt's family are the ones who put the Jew idea into his head. Thing is, you need to try and mix in a little more.'

'I told you ...' said Maret.

'Yes, but it's not helping you. Don't you see?'

'I want to mix in more,' said Juhan.

'Quite right, young fellow. So, tell me, for example, are either of you in the Young People's Clubs? You know the one for boys your age and the one for young maidens? That's a good place to meet people, get on with people better.'

'The school asked us if we wanted to join when we first came,' said Maret. 'We told them we weren't German and wouldn't be staying long. They said we should go anyway. But we never have.'

'Well, there you are, you see?' said Karl. 'If you want to get on with people better and have them stop calling you names, then you need to do the things Germans do. Show them you belong.'

'We don't belong,' said Maret.

'I want to belong,' said Juhan.

'We're going home soon. Back to Estonia. We don't need to be German.'

The three walked on in silence for a moment. Then Karl spoke again.

'I think it's the law that you should go, you know. Your

parents could get into big trouble. I could take you there now, if you like.'

'We have to go home,' said Maret.

'It's just around the corner.'

'What is?' said Juhan.

'The place where the groups meet. It's a big low building on Frederick Street.'

'I know … with the flags outside?' said Juhan.

'That's it. They have great fun, you know. They learn all sorts of things. Fieldcraft, making camp, cooking over open fires. They even go into the forests for adventures. And the girls, well, they … well, I don't know what they do really, but I expect it's great fun, too. I expect they learn to sew and to cook and to make home, and so on. Anyway, it's all great fun.'

'So you keep saying,' said Maret.

'I want to go,' said Juhan. 'Do you go? Will you be there?'

'No,' said Karl, 'I'm in the older group. We learn all sorts of excellent things. Marching, shooting … we go off on manoeuvres, sing songs, wear uniforms. When you're a little older, you could join us there, too.' He laid a friendly hand on Juhan's head. Juhan smiled up at him. 'And soon, I can volunteer for the navy and join the war.'

'What do you want to go to war for?' said Maret.

'All men go to war.'

'Well, I wish they didn't. I wish my father didn't.'

'What does your father do?' said Karl.

'He's in the navy, too. At least, he was when we were home in Estonia.'

'He's a great navy man,' said Juhan. 'He's very brave. He's won all sorts of medals. He let me see them. People think he's the best navy man there ever was in all Estonia.'

'Splendid. I should be honoured to meet him.'

'Hmmph,' said Maret.

'So …?'

'So what?'

'So, shall I take you to the clubs to meet everyone and join in? See what we Germans get up to …?' Karl smiled.

'We have to get home,' said Maret.

'It won't take long.'

'Please, Maret,' said Juhan.

'No. We have to get Mother's medicine and get home so she can feel better.'

'Just for a minute. Please, Maret?'

'No, Juhan.'

'Well, I'm going!' said Juhan, and ran off.

'Come back here!' cried Maret. She and Karl gave chase.

They caught up with him just as they reached the low building with the flags where the clubs met. Maret grabbed Juhan's arm, but he shook it off and ran up the path and inside.

'It's all your fault,' Maret said to Karl, and ran after Juhan.

Karl followed to introduce them to their respective group leaders.

And keep an eye on them.

III

The church bell rang.

There had been so much laughter that Maret barely heard it. But the moment she did, she stopped. They had been playing Cat and Mouse at the end of the afternoon's session. She gasped.

'What's the time?'

The group leader looked at her watch.

'Four o'clock.'

Maret gasped again. 'I have to go. Where's Juhan?'

'Who?'

'My brother – my brother.'

'In the next room, through there.'

'Thank you. I must go.'

'But we have to sing the special song.'

'My mother is ill. I need to get her medicine. I'm sorry. I have to go. When do you meet again?'

'Saturday.'

'Goodbye and thank you.' Maret looked around the whole group, who were waiting to continue their game. 'I really enjoyed myself.'

'Very well,' said the group leader. 'Just this once. But be more organised next time. You should really stay to the end.'

'I will.'

Maret found Juhan and made the same argument that he should leave to the boys' group leader. She grabbed his hand. They ran out of the building and along the streets to the doctor's house.

They thrashed the great iron door knocker with its lion's face until a woman appeared; the housekeeper. She looked down at the two children on the doorstep. Their chests were heaving from running.

'Doctor Paulus?' Maret said, breathless. 'Is he in, please?'

'The doctor is on his rounds.'

'When will he be back?'

'Later.'

'While the pharmacy is still open?'

The woman shook her head.

'Oh, but I must see him. My mother gave me this to give to him ...' She fumbled in the pocket of her skirt and drew out a crumpled piece of paper. She handed it to the housekeeper, who opened it.

'This is a request for a prescription,' the woman said.

'Yes. Our mother needs it. She doesn't have much left and without it she has such pain.'

'Well, I'm afraid there's not much I can do. Come back tomorrow.' She started to close the door. Maret pushed it open again. The woman huffed: 'Young lady, do not be so rude ...'

'I'm sorry, but did the doctor not leave a prescription for us? The name is on that note. Maybe he knew our mother might need some more medicine and filled out a new prescription.'

The woman studied the children's earnest expressions for a moment then said, 'I'll go and see.' She closed the door on them. Maret and Juhan turned and sat down on the doorstep.

'Are we in trouble?' Juhan asked. 'Will Mother be all right?'

'Of course she will,' said Maret.

They waited. Juhan took up Maret's hand and held it.

The door reopened and the children leapt to their feet.

The woman appeared. 'I am sorry, children. I have searched the doctor's desk and his assistant's tray. I even looked on the hall table. But there is nothing for your mother here. I'm sorry.'

'But ...' Maret began.

The woman smiled. 'I'm sure your mother has enough

medicine to get her through the night. I shall let Doctor Paulus know you will be coming back tomorrow and, even if he is not here again, I will ask him to leave the prescription for the pharmacy out for you. All right?' She closed the door.

*

Kotkas could no longer remember how long he had been kept in the cell. It was dark. He'd fumbled for a light switch after he'd been thrown in, but there was none. He was cold; he'd curled up into the foetal position with arms folded, but still he shivered. He dropped in and out of sleep. There was a smell of urine. Vomit. Blood. The only sounds were footsteps beyond the iron door. Those, and the occasional scream; someone being 'interviewed' in another cell. He'd been given some dry pumpernickel and thin vegetable soup once; he imagined it was in the early hours of the morning, but which morning he could no longer be sure.

A key snarled in the lock. The light from the corridor crashed in.

'Right, you. Up.'

Kotkas got up from the mattress, the only piece of furniture in the cell. He put his uniform jacket on and followed the guard. He was brought into another windowless room with chairs and a table. It smelled of disinfectant. The floor was still damp from having been recently sluiced, no doubt. Kotkas noted a man in brown pinstripe trousers sitting behind the table. He wore braces and his sleeves were rolled up. He'd heard that interrogators usually took their jackets off and rolled up their sleeves prior to beating interviewees. That way, if their shirts got bloody, they could just cover them with their jackets, go home, and get their wives to do the laundry. The man was unshaven, his eyes red-rimmed and watery; as if he hadn't slept properly for weeks. Kotkas knew how he felt.

He was told to sit down. The guard who had brought him stood back.

The man took his time. He leafed through a folder containing, Kotkas supposed, intimate details of his life and career back in Estonia.

'Commander Kotkas?' the man finally said, without looking up.

'Yes.'

'You know why you are here?'

'No.'

The man looked up. 'Oh, but you do know. You just don't yet *know* that you know.'

'A further screening process, perhaps?'

'Not so much. More something along the lines of advice, really.'

'Advice?'

'If you wish to stay in the employ of the German Navy. You do wish to stay in its employ, don't you?'

'It depends ...'

The man leant his chair back onto two legs and placed his hands behind his head. Sweat stains on his armpits. 'Ah, now, here, precisely is the problem we need to address. You see how conditional you make things? We don't like the conditional here, do we?' He looked towards his colleague by the door, who, Kotkas assumed, nodded.

'Unwavering, unquestioning obedience, perhaps?' Kotkas said.

The man frowned and rocked back onto four legs, leaning his forearms on the table. 'Commitment. That's the word we like. And yet, sadly, we don't see it so much in you. At present. Which, clearly, is what disappointed the Leader.'

'Ah. That.'

'Ah. That ...' His lips twitched into a smile, which then died. 'Now, Commander Kotkas, we are not unreasonable people here. We understand you come from a different culture, a different context. We understand you don't necessarily – how shall we put it? – fulfil every criteria of commitment to our cause. However, we would like to think you might have the decency to show us a suitable degree of courtesy when you are, to all intents and purposes, a guest in our country. Indeed, in our armed services. Do you understand my point?'

'I understand the point of your argument, yes.'

'Or would you rather we took a little longer to explain it to you?' He smiled again.

'Do I have a choice?'

'We all have a choice, Commander Kotkas. It just depends whether the one you take is the right one.'

It occurred to Kotkas just then that the man was actually beating about the bush. He was offering veiled threats without, it would seem, any real intention of putting them into practice. In short, they were not about to cause him actual bodily harm. It was as if they were acting under orders not to harm him, just shake him up a bit. Someone, somewhere, didn't want him to suffer – just to change his ways a little. Of course, he could be wrong. Certainly, if he went on to not mend his ways, the atmosphere in similar circumstances later might well change. At which point, violence would shoot to the top of the agenda. But, at that precise moment, Kotkas did not feel threatened. Just cautioned. He stood up.

'Well,' he said, 'I take your point and will, of course, bear it in mind. However, if that is all … I'll be getting along, if it's all the same to you. I have much to do in the service of your and the German Navy's cause, and the more time I spend here, the less time available to make sure we hit the necessary deadlines …'

He waited to see whether he would be forced back into his chair. He wasn't.

He turned to leave.

'Kotkas?' the man in the chair said.

'Yes?'

'Sit down.'

There was a silence as the two men looked at one another. Then Kotkas spoke.

'Another time, perhaps. Now, if someone would be so good as to return to me my identity papers, my wallet and my wrist-watch, I'll be getting on with helping you people fight your war.'

He pushed past the standing guard, opened the door and left. No one stopped him. Instead, the guard followed him out and led him along the corridor, up the stairs and, after releasing his belongings to him, out through the main doors.

Back in the interview room, Fischer took out his pen and scribbled some notes on Kotkas's file with savage strokes of the nib. He screwed the pen's cap on and sat back. He looked at the chair the Commander had vacated. Insolent Estonian upstart. He had a feeling the two of them would meet again. In fact, more than a feeling. He would make sure of it.

*

'Mother!'

'Children. Where have you been? I was so worried ...'

It was a small run-down house with a steep tiled roof. It stood on a birch-lined suburban street near the zoo. The animal park had never recovered from its closure during the Great War and now contained just a few abject animals tended by despondent keepers. Nevertheless, the Königs-bergers found some comfort in wandering its paths and peering in at the fretful captives through their bars of a Sunday afternoon. Perhaps they shared a mutual sense of helplessness in these troubled times.

The surrounding streets had caught something of the park's melancholy.

The smell of supper filled the hall.

Their mother was on the verandah. She lay on a steamer chair covered by a blanket. She'd been listening to the traffic rattling and hooting along the distant Hufen-Allee.

The children were close to tears.

'Mother, we're so sorry, we're so sorry,' Maret said.

'What is it, dears?' Leena held her arms out and beckoned them in for an embrace.

The children allowed themselves to be folded in, and related their tale of Karl, the youth group, and the catastrophe of the absent doctor.

Leena assured them she had enough medicine to last the night. 'But, tell me, this visit you made to the youth group. I thought that we agreed you did not need to join them.'

'Oh, but it was such fun!' said Juhan. 'I want to go again. Please, Mother, it is nice, not terrible like you said it was.'

'I never said it was terrible, darling.' Leena stroked her little boy's hair. 'It is just that they will say things that maybe are a little unkind.'

'To who?'

'Not to people ... about them. People that are different from them.'

'But we're different from them and they liked us.'

'Mother ...?'

'Yes, Maret?'

'Are we Jewish?'

'No, darling. What an odd question. Why did you ask it? Did they ask you in the youth group?'

'No. But a horrid boy at school said we were.'

'Well, pay no attention to him.'

'Yes, but I'm afraid that if he keeps saying it, people will start to believe him, and although we will keep saying we're not, they won't listen and then we'll be Jewish to them. Jewish for ever and ever.'

'My dear child, you worry too much. We're not Jewish and that's that. People will know the truth. They won't believe silly gossip and tittle-tattle.'

'Is it wrong to be Jewish, though, Mother?' said Juhan.

'Absolutely not. It's just that, well, some silly people think it is, and they are making an awful lot of trouble because of it. Now – I managed to buy pork knuckle and a little bit of speck this morning, so I've made some lovely pea and ham soup. It should last us two or three meals if we're lucky. Let's go in, and you can tell me about this Karl who brought you to the youth group ...'

*

Fischer came into his superior's office, holding Kotkas's file.

The boss liked Fischer: hard-working, meticulous and often put in far more hours than many of the others. In fact, it was he who got Fischer promoted. If you could call Head of the Baltic Section a promotion. Now that the Reds had swallowed up half of the region, there wasn't much to actually be Head of. Paperwork, mostly: receiving reports, annotating, collating, indexing then shoving into a filing cabinet. Just keeping a steady eye at the Berlin end of things, really. Occasionally, Fischer got to drag someone in, of course. In fact, it was he who had coined the expression they all now used around the office these days: *making Rote Grütze;* red berry soup. Picking up Berlin-based Latvians, Lithuanians, Estonians, East Prussians, Jews ... Communists ... Jewish Communists. It was as easy, Fischer had said, as gathering redcurrants in summer and turning them into red berry soup until they squealed. Good man, Fischer. Diligent, effective, with a sense of humour. Just the kind of fellow a boss with an eye on his own promotion needed.

'Well?'

'Well, I've had a look at Kotkas's background and I've had a little chat ...'

'And?'

'I don't know. There's something I don't like about him. Something of the sea ...'

'The sea?'

'Wilful. Law unto himself. Tidal. Yes, of course we might

expect him to be diffident towards us and our cause. It isn't his, after all. And, by all accounts, we would expect him to be self-serving rather than Leader-serving. People like him in our ranks are, really, ten a penny. That's certainly the part he's play-acting for us.'

'Play-acting? Meaning ...?'

'Meaning there's something he's not telling us ... something that *this* wants us to know ...' he tapped the file '... but we haven't learnt to read it right, yet.'

'What do you think it is?'

'I don't know. His career doesn't add up.'

'In what way?'

'Well, for example, there's this ...' He opened the file and showed it to his superior. 'Spent a couple of years training in Britain with the Royal Navy. Twice; in the late twenties and late thirties. Top class. Top marks. Highly commended. The Royal Navy liked him a lot. And then he acted as liaison for them whenever they visited Estonia.'

'You think there's still a connection?'

'Well, you don't forget those links in a hurry. I know his training was a while ago, but nevertheless ...'

'Yes?'

'If he still were connected to the Royal Navy, why didn't they spirit him out of Estonia? Why did he choose us? Why did he choose Germany to send his family? Couldn't they just as easily have escaped to London?'

'His family are here?'

'In Königsberg.'

'Right. Keep digging. And also have someone look into the family. Have a look at their family tree ... if you understand my meaning.'

'Yes, sir.'

'And Fischer ...'

'Yes?'

'Quickly.'

*

It was evening. Kotkas looked at his watch. Five o'clock. Out on the teeming street, the transition from people working to people relaxing was in full spate. What time had he been dragged from his bed? Maybe five in the morning, maybe a little later. Twelve hours. Perhaps more. He had lost absolutely all track of time in that cell. Heaven knows how many wretched hours for no purpose other than to satisfy a bully's bruised ego.

He went back to his quarters to freshen up. He showered and shaved. He put on a clean shirt and his uniform. He made his way back to 76–78 Tirpitzufer, the home of the German Intelligence Service, where, presumably, he still worked. Though he could be no longer sure.

'Miss Meyer. Is Admiral Canaris in?'

She looked up.

'Where have you been? I have been trying to contact you.'

'You, above all people, should know where I've been, seeing as how you told them who I was …'

'Told who? Oh … you mean … they …?'

'Yes. I should like to see the Admiral.'

'He isn't here.' Her response was as cool as his enquiry.

'When will he be back?'

'I don't know. I have no further meetings booked for him today. He may have gone to the Hotel Adlon. He usually goes there after here.'

'On Unter Den Linden, yes?'

'Yes.'

'I'll see if I can catch him there. Enough is enough.'

'Won't it wait until tomorrow?'

'Nothing these days can wait until tomorrow.' He turned to go.

'Oh, Commander …?'

'Yes?'

'You asked me to find where your family were living.'

'And did you?'

'Yes.' She held a sheet of notepaper with a Königsberg address on it.

'Thank you.' They were just words. After the day he'd just had, he did not feel very grateful towards the young woman standing in front of him. Or the people she represented.

'You are welcome,' she replied, in a similar cool way. She returned to rifling through some paperwork on her desk.

'Commander Kotkas ... I thought you were away visiting family, or something.'

Canaris had walked in.

'I would have been, sir. However – and this is why I am still here – I should like to protest at my treatment ...'

'By one of my people?'

Miss Meyer looked up.

Kotkas looked at her, then back at Canaris.

'No, sir,' he said. 'By the security police in Berlin who seem to treat senior naval officers with the kind of disrespect one imagines they have for drunks and vagrants.'

'They pulled you in, did they?'

'Yes, sir.'

'Sorry about that. Nonsense, of course. I'll have a word; tell them hands off, you're mine.'

'Thank you, sir.'

'Now, if you're to be back at your desk by tomorrow, you had better get going.' Canaris went into his office and closed the door.

It was only after he'd gone that Kotkas realised what had just been said. He turned to Miss Meyer. 'Tomorrow? But, I thought the Admiral gave me three days?'

'You've had two already.'

'Two? But – what day is it?'

'Wednesday. You were here on Monday.'

'They had me shut up in that cell for what ...? Thirty-six hours? *Thirty-six hours!*'

'Didn't you notice?'

'You try it sometime ...'

'Well, if you're to be back here tomorrow, you're going to miss seeing your family. A day's travel, a day with your family, a day's travel back ... I'm so sorry.'

'Oh no. No, I'm not going to let those thugs get in the way of me seeing my family.'

'But the Admiral ...'

'Miss Meyer, would you arrange for a travel permit, please?'

'You're going?'

'Wouldn't you?'

She shrugged; not her problem. If he wanted to make more trouble for himself, that was his lookout. 'I'll arrange the permit.'

IV

The children were laughing as they stumbled over the threshold. They slammed the front door behind them. This afternoon, they had not forgotten to visit the doctor's house; the doctor had not failed to prepare a prescription; and the pharmacy had readily supplied the medicine for their mother.

'Mother?' the children cried down the hall.

'In here, darlings ...' their mother said from the parlour.

They launched themselves into the room with their precious package of something called *laudanum*. Their mother had become very dependent on her medicine, so they were glad, this time, not to have let her down. However, as they approached their mother and presented the package with the bottle inside it to her, Maret hesitated.

'Mother?'

'Yes, dear?'

'There is something different about you.'

'Is there, dear?'

Maret couldn't quite put her finger on it, but her mother had a kind of glow. She didn't dare believe it, but something of her mother's greyness had gone.

'Mother?'

'Yes, dear?'

'Are you feeling better? You are looking, I don't know, *sunny*. Is the medicine making you well again?'

'My darlings,' Leena said, opening her arms so that she might encircle her children where she sat on the couch, 'I have a wonderful surprise for you ... The most wonderful surprise ...'

'You are well again! You are well!' cried Juhan, and, breaking free from his mother's embrace, skipped away to do a little twirl in the middle of the room.

'What's the wonderful surprise, Mother?' said Maret.

But, before Leena could tell her, there was the creak of footsteps coming down the hall stairs. Solid, steady footsteps.

Maret's eyes widened. Juhan stopped dancing.

The footsteps approached the parlour.

Leena beamed at her children. They swung round to look towards the door. Maret clasped her hands.

The footsteps stopped.

A man, clean shaven after a tortuous journey involving hundreds of kilometres, four different trains, and countless hours waiting for points to change – appeared in the doorway.

'Father!' the children cried and, flying across the room, leapt into his arms.

Rejoicing subsided in due course, and the serious business of getting dinner ready, once again as a family, was embarked upon. Hendrik helped Leena in the kitchen. The fragrance of *bockwurst*, potatoes and *sauerkraut* soon filled the home. The children helped by laying the table, skipping as they did so.

*

'Father?' said Juhan, cleaning his plate with a hunk of rye bread.

'Yes, young man?'

'When will we go home?'

Hendrik looked at his son, his daughter, his wife. From the moment his children were born, from the moment he and Leena ceased being simply husband and wife and became family, he had decided always to tell his children the truth about the way the world is. He promised himself he would talk about its failings and foibles as well as its beauties and joys. His own childhood, teenage years and early adulthood had played some part in this resolve. Yes, of course, he should protect them from the vile and the vulgar. He remembered what he'd said to Leena once: he wanted to teach his children from the outset that it was a 'train' and not a *choo-choo*.

'Well, now.' He collected his son and set him on his knee. Maret joined them on the other knee. He gave them a squeeze and Leena a wink. 'Well, now,' he said again. 'We *will* go home – of course we will. But we can only go home when it is safe to do so.'

'What is "safe", Father?' said Juhan.

'Well, in this case, safe is to do with how other people behave. There are people now in our homeland who, sadly, don't like us very much. They are unkind and want to be unkind towards people like us especially. Do you understand?'

Juhan and Maret nodded.

'Like Kurt?' said Juhan.

'Who's Kurt?'

'Someone at school. He's unkind, isn't he, Maret?'

Hendrik looked towards Leena, who nodded, then back at his children. 'How has he been unkind?'

'He's a bully,' said Juhan. He noted his father's face turn grave. 'But it's all right. Maret punched him.'

'You hit him?' Hendrik said to Maret. He found, much against his better judgement, that he was finding it difficult remaining serious. He privately laughed at Juhan's simple statement of fact. He also rejoiced in his daughter's impassive face. So often, as she was growing up, he observed in his daughter his own direct nature: Problem = Action = No Problem. 'Did you know about this?' He looked across at his wife. She nodded again.

'It's all right, though, Father,' said Juhan, 'because we are learning to be good Germans now. So it won't happen again.'

'Good ... Germans ...?' Hendrik looked again at his wife.

'Explain to your father, children,' she said. 'Tell him about the groups you went to the other day.'

So Juhan explained. He told his father about Karl and the songs and the games and the fun they'd had.

'Well, now,' said Hendrik, 'that all sounds just fine. And are you going again?'

'If we're allowed,' said Juhan. 'You will allow us to, won't you, Father? Anyway, it's the law. Everyone has to learn how to be good Germans. My group leader told me.'

'Well ...' said Hendrik '... I don't think it is the absolute law. But, if you enjoyed yourselves, and it keeps you out of fights with the other children, I don't see any harm in you going.'

'Yippee!' said Juhan.

'For the time being, at least. But you must promise me one thing ...'

'What?'

'That you tell me and your mother everything they teach you at these groups. You will do that for us, won't you?'

'Yes, Father. Of course we will. We will tell you everything. Won't we, Maret?'

Maret had noticed her father's tone throughout this exchange. What was it? Worry?

'Father?' she said.

'Yes, dear?'

'When are we going home?'

'Soon,' said Leena.

'Soon,' said Hendrik.

Choo-choo.

*

They lay in one another's arms as the sun rose. Just as they used to when first they had met. Just as they had lain together in defiance after Hendrik had been informed of Leena's father's disapproval of the match. So they lay there, two against the world. They had not made love since Leena had become unwell. As if making love would cause her further damage or drive her illness deeper into her soul. Not that he cared, or needed it. All he cared for right at that moment was to feel his wife leaning against his chest; smell her rich dark hair as it tickled his cheek. As for her breath? Gentle, was it? Or shallow? She was thinner. Her eyes were surrounded by dark rings.

He stroked her hair. He kissed the top of her head. She stirred.

'What's that fragrance?' he said. 'It's beautiful. Flowers? Sandalwood? Vanilla …?'

She laughed. 'Don't you remember? *Vol de Nuit* by Guerlain. You bought it for me three Christmases ago … I still have a little left.'

'Oh yes. Cost me a month's pay.'

They hugged for a moment.

'Hendrik?'

'Mmm?'

'When *will* we go home? Do you think?'

'Soon,' he said.

He thought about how much he would need to do in support of his current employer's invasion of Russia. He thought about the enormous numbers that would be hurled against the German forces. He thought about the astonishing distances needed to travel to make even the slightest headway in such a campaign. He thought about the immense complexity of sea warfare in the Baltic. He thought about all the intelligence he would need to collect and communicate. He thought about all the laborious briefing sessions he would have to mount and endure. He calculated how all this would affect the timing of his and his family's return to Estonia. And then he thought about when he would be released from all his duties with his current employers; or, indeed, if they would ever let him go.

He stroked his wife's hair again then nuzzled her neck to take in her fragrance once more. 'Soon. We'll go home soon,' he said.

He got up.

'Are you going?'

He kissed the tip of her nose. 'Breakfast. I'll make it. For you.'

He took up his underclothes, his uniform shirt and trousers, and started for the bathroom.

'Don't wear that,' she said. '*Their* uniform. I managed to pack some clothes for you. In that chest of drawers. Don't be their creature today.'

He dressed in his familiar old clothes; they still smelled of home. Even, he imagined, the fresh, clean tang of the blue Estonian Baltic. He went into the kitchen. He had used his ration cards to bring the bread, sausage, *sauerkraut* and potatoes they'd had for dinner. He'd also brought sausage, eggs and coffee beans. Coffee was his morning ritual. He roasted the beans himself, ground them and brewed them. It took a while, but it helped him think; took him out of himself. The children were already up and were buzzing around their father. In the midst of his food preparation, he would pat them or give them a little hug. At one point, he noticed Leena had appeared in the doorway and was watching them. He looked across at her and smiled; she returned it. She pulled her dressing-gown cord tighter around her.

'When do you have to be back?' she said.

'Yesterday,' he said. 'No, I lie. The day before.'

'You will get into trouble.'

'Yes, I will.' He reached out to her. She stepped forward and allowed her hand to rest in his; protected. He was still handsome, her husband. As handsome as the day they met. A dinner party with mutual friends. He was tanned, lusty, with the quiet strength earned through years encountering the sea, all kinds of weather and adversity; the adversity that came from long years of active service in the navy. He hadn't said much that evening, but what he said had spoken volumes; deep-rooted experiences of daily challenges ensured his conversation rose above the chit-chat of the others around the dining table. He had walked her home. He had kissed the very hand he was now holding.

Standing there in the kitchen holding his wife's hand and looking at her sad eyes, he felt his stomach convulse at the thought that soon he would have to leave them again.

'I don't want to go back . . .' he said.

The children yelped. 'Yes, Father, yes! Don't go back! Don't go back!'

He didn't reply. He smiled at them and got on with brewing the coffee and making the breakfast.

Hendrik and Leena spent the day in each other's company. Taking a light lunch, drinking coffee. He went out, spoke with the doctor, bought her medicine, and made sure she took it.

The children had gone to their groups.

*

As a young man, Fischer had got a job with a salvage firm, shipping flawed iron and steel to German East Africa for inflated prices. His intelligence and willingness to do what he was told got him promoted to foreman. The Party he saw as an opportunity for further advancement. But it became more than that. Informing on his superiors for their dubious accounting practices meant the authorities took something of a shine to him. Enticed by the thought of wearing suits and proper shoes, he joined the security police in a junior rank. He'd spent the next few years working his way up to the status he currently enjoyed.

Fischer's boss came into his office and floated a message onto the desk.

'What's this, sir?'

'The Estonian. Kotkas. It seems he has blundered. He's in Königsberg. He seems to be wandering around Germany at will – as if he hasn't a care in the world. I thought we'd agreed you'd deal with him, make him toe the line. We don't need this, Fischer. We've enough on our plate, and I have end-of-month quotas to achieve. Straighten him out, have him sent to a camp, or shot. Don't care which. But I don't need this hanging over our heads any longer.'

'I'll go up there.'

'Someone on the ground can do it.'

'I will handle this myself.'

'Very well. But don't take too long. I have the end-of-month—'

'. . . quotas to achieve. Yes, sir. And, as you know, my department is well ahead with ours.'

'Nevertheless. Deal with it.' He marched off.

It was only after he'd left that Fischer picked up the message and read it through slowly. He pursed his lips, and the muscles in his jaw flexed. The message made it very clear it wasn't as simple as his superior had made out. The fat fool clearly hadn't read the message properly at all. Just like him. Podgy-fingered, beer-swilling southern buffoon. He'd clearly forgotten – or had deliberately ignored – Fischer's belief that there was more to this Kotkas than met the eye. Quotas! There was more to security police work than quotas. How that pea-brained lummox had managed to get so high up the promotion ladder was beyond Fischer. Oh well; he laid the message in his Out tray for filing. He'd go to Königsberg all the same. That Estonian upstart could do with a scare – whichever way you looked at it.

*

'May I meet him?'

Juhan and Maret, outside the building where the flags shuddered in the fresh breeze, had joined Karl. He was also on his way home. They had told him about their father's arrival.

'I should like to meet him very much. I shall be going into the navy. It would be interesting and helpful to me.'

'Then come,' said Juhan, taking his hand.

It was spring. Lime, cherry and birch were starting to shoot. Bright green tips pushed out of the winter brown of branches, ready to burst into leaf, spreading their wings. The children sang as they walked; Karl joined in the chorus.

Karl had set his heart on joining the navy ever since his father had taken him to see the sleek grey *Admiral Scheer* slink into Königsberg one hot July some years before. The band had played on the quayside, the waiting crowds cheered, and the noble sailors lining the heavy cruiser's decks in their shining white uniforms returned the welcome. They raised their caps as one person in salute. The rest of that summer, Karl and his friends made battleships out of wood and boxes. They flew a navy flag, complete with its iron cross, made from a discarded pillowcase. Branches served as the great guns. Karl would always insist on being the captain. He longed to hear real naval gunfire. He longed to watch through high-powered binoculars as an enemy merchant ship or destroyer snapped in half under his broadsides, and to be engulfed in a boiling green sea.

When they arrived at Maret and Juhan's house, Karl gave their father a solemn handshake; trembling with a respect verging on awe. He'd never actually met a real-life sailor, let alone an officer. A German officer at that.

Hendrik was amused by the young man's zeal. He made them both a coffee, which thrilled Karl. They sat and talked for half an hour. If Karl had been an enthusiast, by the time he finished his meeting with Commander Kotkas, he had utterly surrendered to the idea that the German Navy was the only place for him. Hendrik, for his part, had not promoted that organisation as such. His encouragement was more for life at sea, active service and the role of an officer generally.

'When are you going back to the Baltic?' said Karl.

'Sometime,' said Hendrik, 'I have work to do in Berlin, first of all.'

'Berlin?' The young fellow breathed the name. To him, it was Camelot: the city of banners, of chivalric ideals and knights errant. 'What do you do there?'

'I think,' smiled Hendrik, 'that's somewhat confidential, don't you?'

Karl flushed and stammered, 'I-I-I'm sorry. Yes, of course. How stupid of me. I am so sorry, sir. You won't report me, will you? It was just a silly mistake. I meant nothing by it. I am not trying to get any secrets out of you, I was just—'

Hendrik stood and rested a hand on his shoulder. 'My dear chap. Nobody's going to report anybody. It was an honest and innocent question. It is quite clear you had no intention of dragging any secrets out of me.' Then, as much to himself as anyone, he said, 'This place. Really.'

'What do you mean, sir?'

'Nothing. Just everybody forced to watch everybody else. Nobody has the freedom to speak their mind for fear of being informed on. It seems to me you've been turned into a nation of sneaks and tell-tales...'

Karl stiffened and got to his feet. He squared his shoulders and stood facing the Commander. 'I'm sorry you feel that way, sir. For me, it is important we cleanse this wonderful country of everything that is holding it back. We need to speak the truth and not sneer and subvert behind our hands. But then, I suppose, coming from a different place, you do not – can not – feel the same.' Then, as if remembering where he was, and who he was talking to, he continued: 'But I am grateful to you for what you are doing on our behalf. The German people are grateful. I wish you a safe journey back to your duties and every success in them.'

Hendrik's face had grown impassive. 'Thank you,' he said. 'Well, now, we mustn't keep you. I very much enjoyed your visit and wish you the very best of luck in your future career.' He held out his hand. Karl looked at it. He hesitated, then took it. He gave it a curt shake and withdrew.

The Commander saw him out. Leena, Maret and Juhan joined them.

At the front door, Karl raised his arm until it pointed towards the ceiling.

'Heil Hitler!' he said.

The children raised their arms in return. 'Heil Hitler!' they giggled.

The Commander gave a nod. 'Goodbye,' he said.

Leena, who had said nothing but was standing leaning against the wall, suddenly gave a little cry and collapsed on the hall floor.

Everyone gathered around her.

Hendrik knelt by his wife's side and loosened her clothing. 'Leena, Leena, what's the matter? What happened? What's wrong?'

'Nothing ... nothing,' she said. 'I'm all right. Just came over a little faint.'

'Children – get your mother some water. Karl, if I may ask you, would you help me get my wife to the living room, please?'

Karl helped. They laid Leena on the couch and covered her with a blanket, and the children helped her take some water.

Hendrik knelt by her side. 'Are you sure you are all right?' he said.

'Yes. Yes. I've got used to them. They're just one of my little "interludes" as I call them. I am sure it's just the effects of the medicine. I feel fine, now. Really.'

Hendrik looked at her. 'I can't leave you like this.'

'What? What do you mean?'

'I am not going back to Berlin.'

'I'll be all right.'

'But you won't be. You aren't.'

'You must go. We need your officer's pay, at the very least.'

'I've decided.'

'Hendrik ...'

'No more argument. I am not German. This is not my fight.'

'How can you say that? Of course it's your fight. It is all our fight. It might not be the way you wish to fight it, but it's all we've got.'

'You are all I've got. It'll be fine. I'll find myself a job here, somewhere. Down at the harbour. There's bound to be something.'

'But, darling. Berlin ... you must.' She took his hand in hers.

'Your husband has spoken.'

'But your wife will have the last word.'

He kissed her. 'I'm staying until I can get us all away from this awful place. Get us home. Somehow. The great War Machine can do its own dirty work. There. That's an end to it.'

The children, who had been stroking their mother's hair as she lay there on the couch, got up and began dancing around the room. 'Father's staying! Father's staying!' they sang. 'We're going home. We're going home!' Then, 'Heil Hitler! Heil Hitler!'

It was only some moments later that the family noticed Karl had gone.

V

It had not been a good Sunday for the duty sergeant at the local police station. If he had thought about it, he would have admitted to himself that he'd been a little short with his colleagues that morning. Overworked, understaffed, underpaid. Moreover, he had not had anything to eat since breakfast and, even then, it was just a bread roll. Standing at the reception desk and setting aside his pen, he sighed. He reached under the counter and pulled, from out of a secret place, a bottle of schnapps. He undid the top and took a swig. That helped.

The phone rang. The bottle was replaced. The receiver was picked up.

When the voice on the phone introduced himself, the sergeant straightened and his manner changed. It was police headquarters, Königsberg.

He listened. When Headquarters called, it was best just to listen. He made notes, nodded once or twice, and grunted at the appropriate moments. The voice on the other end concluded by asking if the sergeant understood what was being required of him. He answered yes. The call was terminated.

'Wowreit!' he called.

A young officer appeared from down the corridor that led to the cells. 'Yes, Sergeant?' He noted the familiar whiff of fresh schnapps.

'Job for you ...'

*

The family returned from the little Lutheran church around the corner. Chestnut, alder and lime swayed spring-fresh with precocious leaves above their heads. Velvety catkins crumbled into yellow dust beneath their feet. Everywhere, Hendrik noted the powdery perfume of an earth rejecting yet again humankind's folly and insisting on pressing ahead with new growth.

At that moment, for Kotkas, strolling with his family along tree-lined streets, Königsberg radiated an air of confidence and permanence. This was freely offered to all those to whom it had given shelter for more than five hundred years. He had visited a couple of times before, as a young Estonian Navy cadet. Nothing, it seemed to him, had changed much in the intervening years. The teeming harbour and old town with its fishmongers, butchers, bakers and grocers. The colourful markets overflowing with produce from the bountiful East Prussian countryside. The horse-drawn trams and coffee shops. The theatres, opera houses and concert halls. The bandstands in the parks with musicians in splendid uniforms *oom-pa-paing* through sultry summer afternoons. Lemon tea on the lawn, coffee and cake in the shade. All of it underpinned the simple yet ample lifestyles of its worthy burghers. Lifestyles that were surely set to continue well into the next century … weren't they?

Somewhere, a magpie cackled. Maret was holding her father's hand; Juhan his mother's. Just before they reached the house, Hendrik stopped. Maret stopped with him. He let Leena and Juhan walk on ahead, watching them, Maret thought, with sad eyes.

'Maret?'

'Yes, Father?'

'You are very grown up. I am very proud of you. These are very difficult times, and you will find them becoming more and more difficult. Do you understand?'

'Yes, Father.'

'There will be times when you will be the one who needs to look after both your mother and your brother. Sometimes, they will *really* need your help.'

'I know, Father ...' Maret was starting to feel anxious. What was her father trying to say to her?

Hendrik looked down at his daughter and gave her a soft smile. He stepped towards a garden wall, of traditional Königsberg red brick, and drew Maret's attention to it. 'See this?' he said, pointing at the moss that was growing in patches there.

'Yes ...?'

He picked a little at the green growth. He held it for Maret and encouraged her to look at it closely. It was like a miniature jungle, velvety as a carpet. 'See how soft it is? See how strong it is? See how beautiful it is ...?' Maret didn't say anything; she just nodded. 'But look how smooth the bricks are. The moss doesn't seem to have anything to take hold of. Yet it manages to cling on for dear life. And it flourishes. It spreads. Humble, unregarded – yet still here. Always here. It will be here long after we're all gone. It will reclaim everything we've built or tried to build in the end. It will win despite all the odds.' He turned again to look at his daughter and stroked her hair. 'Be like the moss, little Maret. Be strong. Hang on. Be strong for me, but especially for your mother and your brother. Be strong and hold on – even when you think you can't, even though there doesn't seem to be anything to hold onto.'

Maret thought he was going to cry. She squeezed his hand. 'I will, Father.'

'Promise?'

'I promise.'

Back indoors a few minutes later, the family set about making their Sunday lunch, frugal as it was, Hendrik's ration allocation having been mostly already used up. Mutton stew made from good East Prussian sheep.

There was a knock on the door.

Maret went to answer. She returned with a police officer.

Hendrik and Leena stopped in the middle of what they

were doing. Potato peeler in her hand, knife sharpener in his; still as statues.

'Yes?' Hendrik said.

The policeman saluted. 'Officer Wowreit, Tiergarten District. Is this the family Kotkas?'

'It is.'

He stepped aside. 'Would you all come with me, please?'

Hendrik put his knife sharpener down. 'May I ask why?'

'Just routine, sir.'

'What kind of routine?'

This question flummoxed Wowreit. Routine was routine. That was it. 'Come along, sir.'

'Right,' said Hendrik to the others. 'Leave this to me.'

'No, sir, all of you, sir. You must all come.'

'These are just children, Officer, and my wife is not well.'

'All of you, sir.'

'Sit down, children,' said Hendrik.

They did as they were told. Hendrik sat down at the kitchen table and Leena joined him.

'Sir ...' said Wowreit. 'Please don't make this difficult.'

'It is not me but you who are making things difficult, Officer. I don't believe there is such a thing as "routine". And I don't believe my family needs to come until I've found out what it is you are hauling us out for, on a Sunday.'

'Are you resisting, sir? That is a very serious matter.'

'Not resisting. Enquiring. And I shall keep on enquiring until I get some answers.'

'Sir. You are being very vexatious. And I should warn you that people who are vexatious are dealt with very straightforwardly indeed. You would not want me to leave here and go back to the station, would you? I would have to bring certain others who, most certainly, would be very straightforward with you and your family. You would not want them to be straightforward with your wife, would you? Let alone your children.'

Hendrik rose and took a pace towards the policeman. Leena rose and stepped in between them. She turned to face her husband. 'Hendrik – no. He's only doing his job. We should go.'

Hendrik looked at his wife. He knew she was right; she usually was.

'Very well,' he said to the policeman, 'I will come. But, as I said, my wife is unwell. I ask that she remain behind and the children with her, to look after her, while I am away.'

Officer Wowreit looked at the woman. A grey face with sunken eyes. He hesitated, then: 'Your wife may stay. We can always come back for her later. The children come with you.'

'Well ...' Hendrik thought about pursuing the argument, but decided against it. There was something in the policeman's eyes that suggested enough was enough. 'Very well. Let me get my jacket. Children, put your coats back on, please.'

They were taken to a fin-de-siècle building, the colour of iron, a few blocks away. It was cold and dark inside. They were led by Officer Wowreit into a room deep within the building. Hendrik noticed that there was a fellow in civilian clothes seated by the door; posted there against the possibility of escape, no doubt.

The room, perhaps once upon a time a ballroom, was barely furnished. Some wooden chairs in a row against one wall. Towards the middle of the room, next to a filing cabinet, stood an august oak desk; master of all it surveyed.

'Sit here, please,' said Officer Wowreit, indicating the chairs. They sat. Duty done, he left, closing the door behind him.

The three of them sat in silence. The dingy room was cold, as if it were disinterested in its occupants. Somewhere, echoing through the building, they could hear voices. These were clearly not engaged in small talk. Rather, the voices were business-like. An enquiry launched, a response returned, silence.

Eventually, a door at the far end of the room opened. A man in a white coat with steel toe and heel plates clacked across the wooden floor towards them. His long face pale and morose.

Hendrik stood.

'Sit down.'

Hendrik remained where he was.

'Sit. Down,' the man said again; slowly, so that both its meaning and the consequences of it not being obeyed could be fully understood. To reinforce the implied threat, the man's cold eyes flickered towards the door. There, Hendrik was aware, sat the man in civilian clothes; undoubtedly armed. Hendrik sat.

The man had a file in his hand. He sat down at the desk, clicked on a lamp. In its mean light, he started to go through the documents page by page; tracking each line with the tip of a pencil. The only sound was the chill rustle of the papers. At length, he stood up. He snapped his fingers at Juhan.

'You. Boy. Come with me ...'

Hendrik stood again. 'Where are you taking him? I'm coming too. So's my daughter.'

'Just the boy. One at a time.'

'No,' Hendrik said, and advanced on the man. He lowered his voice to ensure the man understood what he was about to say was non-negotiable. 'We go wherever you want to take us together. As a family. Or, before that fellow beyond that door can answer your cry for help, I shall have broken both your arms and have commenced work on your neck.'

The man stood there seething. He looked again towards the door, clearly considering summoning help. But then decided in favour of an easier life.

'Very well, come.'

They followed him down a corridor and into a room halfway along. It was a medical room; scales, something to measure height, an examination couch.

'Stand there,' he said to Hendrik and Maret, pointing to a corner of the room. He then took Juhan by the arm and led him to the scales. From a table, he collected a clipboard and into it put one of the sheets of paper from the file he had carried in. He then proceeded to take Juhan's measurements; weight, height. After this, he sat the boy on the examination couch and produced a large pair of calipers. With these, he began to measure the head; front to back, crown to chin. He measured the length of his nose and the distance between the eyes. All the while, noting his findings on the clipboard.

After Juhan, it was Maret's turn.

When he had finished with Maret, he turned to Hendrik and snapped his fingers.

'Papers.'

Hendrik had put his all-important papers in his civilian jacket that morning, in order to leave the house and go to church. He reached into an inside pocket and drew them out. He laid them in the man's impatient hand.

The man unfolded the documents and with his cold eyes began to read.

A moment later, his eyes widened and he jerked upright. He shot a right arm into the air.

'Heil Hitler!' he cried. 'Commander, I must apologise. I had no idea ...'

'No idea as to what?' said Hendrik, collecting his papers and replacing them in his jacket. 'That I and my family are human beings – just like everybody else who comes through your sordid doors and should be treated as such?'

'That you are ... I mean ... you weren't wearing your uniform ... I did not know ...'

'You were not told, you mean? What were you told? A family of Jews have taken up residence in Königsberg? Foreigners? Aliens? Undesirables? What?'

'I was only doing my job ...'

'Then change jobs. Enough. My family and I would like to leave now, if it's all the same to you.'

That evening, in the kitchen, preparing a supper of reheated mutton stew, Leena returned to a question she had asked earlier. 'You really think they were measuring you to see if you conformed to ... a certain racial type ...?'

'Undoubtedly,' said Hendrik.

'But why? And why now? Why hadn't they done it before?'

'Well, as we said, someone probably dropped our name and address into the authorities.'

'Yes, but who?'

'We've been through this. Your guess is as good as mine. It could be a deliberate act by someone. Someone you know or the children know. Someone at school, or a teacher, or someone from the group they've joined. It could be just random. It could just be the system catching up with us. Hard to say.'

'I know. But, well, I don't like to think ... that somebody out there, in our neighbourhood, perhaps, decided to get us investigated in that way.' She shuddered. 'It's sinister.'

'It's the way things are. The good news is that nothing came of it. We've been signed off. I made sure of that. I stood over that white-coated weasel at his desk while he did it.'

Hendrik and Leena did not know, but Maret had been standing in the hall outside the kitchen during this exchange. Though she was not able to understand everything that was being discussed, she knew that the whole episode had left her feeling very uneasy. And, at that moment, to hear that someone her mother or she or Juhan knew might have caused the whole unhappy sequence to unfold made her unhappier still. At the same moment, however, she also decided she had a very good idea who it was who might have done such a thing.

The family settled down and in time made their separate ways to bed.

It was just past midnight when Leena, who had been restless with pain, whispered to her husband: 'What was that?'

'Hmm?'

'Hendrik, are you asleep?'

'What is it?'

'Did you hear that? A noise.' Leena sat up in bed. She gasped. 'Someone's in the room!'

Hendrik sat up. He looked around. There, in the doorway, he could just make out a shape. A wraith.

'Maret?' he said.

'Yes?'

'Are you all right?'

'Yes.'

'What do you want?'

Silence.

'Would you like to get into bed with us?'

Without answering, she padded barefoot across the floor and scrambled in. Hendrik made way for her; she nestled down between him and her mother, who wrapped the covers around her.

Maret remembered the last time she'd climbed into bed with her parents. She was younger then; much younger. It had been a perfect summer's day. They were down in the country near Vasalemma where her mother's family had their big old house. Blue sky, green trees, golden wheat fields. Swallows and swifts swooping among the rooftops and skimming the wheat fields. She'd spent the morning sitting under the ancient juniper tree. It was set, as it always had been, in the middle of the great meadow; an island in a shimmering sea of tall grass. There, she'd read her book. Her body in the shade, with her legs, toes twiddling, in the hot sun. After lunch, she'd gone down to swim in the river beside the woods. It was clear, cold and flowing, as if it were escaping something. Little tiddlers tickled her legs. She remembered watching her grandfather teach Juhan how to fish off the rickety old bridge.

Later that afternoon, old Kalev in his shabby flat cap let her ride one of the farm's horses.

That evening, her legs, arms and face had grown salmon pink and they stung all over. Her mother bathed them in a lukewarm bath then covered them with lotion until the pain subsided. But it returned soon after she'd gone to bed. So she went to her parents and climbed in with them. She felt like she was cooking from the inside out. Her mother cuddled her and sang to her until, at last, she went to sleep.

Her mother cuddled her again now.

'What's the matter, darling? Can't you sleep?'

She nodded.

'Is anything worrying you?' her father asked.

She didn't reply.

'What's worrying you? Do you want to tell us?'

She didn't reply.

'Come on, sweetheart,' he stroked her hair, 'tell us. We're here to help.'

Still, she was silent. Her parents settled themselves down to sleep again. Maybe in the morning their daughter might explain what made her come in to them.

After a few moments, however, Maret spoke.

'Father?'

'Yes?'

'Are you really going to stay with us?'

'Yes.'

'You are not going back to Berlin?'

'Not straight away.'

'Promise?'

'Tomorrow, I shall write to them and tell them I am not coming back for the time being. You can watch me write the letter. You can even post it for me.'

'Yes. And then we'll go home? Back to Estonia.'

'I hope so.'

'Back to the apartment and my school and Vasalemma?'

'I hope so.'

There was another silence.

'But, Father ...?'

'What, dear?'

'The horrible people are there. So we can't go back.'

'Not yet, no.'

'But ... there are horrible people here, too.'

'They're not all horrible, dear,' said Leena.

'But we don't know which ones are horrible and which ones aren't, do we? You said. You said people keep snitching on each other and getting people into trouble. That's what you said.'

'Oh, my poor darling,' said Leena, and gave her daughter a hug. 'You shouldn't be worrying about such things. Your father's here now. I'm here. We'll look after you. We'll sort everything out. You believe that, don't you?'

'Yes.'

'Truly?' said Hendrik.

'Yes,' she said, 'I think so.'

'There's my good girl. You have been wonderful about all this. You've been so helpful to your mother, your brother. You've been helpful to me, too, by helping them. We need you to stay strong. To be the clever, sensible, special *moss-girl* you have always been. It's not easy. It is horrible, like you say. But, if we stick together, if we all stay strong, then, one day, things will get better again ...'

'And we will go home.'

'Yes. We will go home. That's all any of us want and are trying to achieve. All right?'

'All right.'

'Get some sleep now, darling,' said her mother.

It was morning. Maret had gone back to her own bed in the small hours. Hendrik and Leena lay there listening to the birdsong. They watched the curtains' gentle dance before the open bedroom window; the silver birches weaving their shadows beyond. The sun had risen long ago. It had done its work on the dew, which the night had left behind. Somewhere, someone was giving their lawn its first cut of the year. The scent of new-mown grass drifted into the room on the breeze. Hendrik almost shook with fury lying there. How dare the day seem so ... *normal*? he raged. So ... *domestic*?

There came a banging downstairs at the front door.

Hendrik leapt up and looked out. There were two men below in hats and coats. One of them looked up at him and beckoned him down. The other man banged harder on the door.

Hendrik pulled on his trousers and shirt and went down in his bare feet; cold on the carpetless floors. He opened the door.

The two men thrust their identity discs at him.

'Commander Kotkas?'

'Yes?'

'You are to come with us.'

'Why?'

'Now.'

'Why?' Hendrik looked closer at one of the men. 'I recognise you, don't I? Berlin.'

'You have two minutes to pack,' Fischer said. 'If you have not packed in two minutes, we will pack for you.'

'I am not sure I like your attitude.'

'We're not here to have our attitudes liked or disliked. Our orders are to collect you.'

'Whose orders?'

'You are to come with us now. Pack, or we'll pack for you.'

They pushed him backwards into the hall.

Leena was at the top of the stairs.

'Hendrik? What is it? What do they want?'

Hendrik looked at Fischer and his associate; armed, most

certainly. He went upstairs and took Leena into the bedroom. The men followed.

'What is it, Hendrik? Where are you going? What is the suitcase for? Why are you packing?'

'I don't know, Leena. I don't know what any of this is about. But these aren't local policemen. They don't fool around. I'd best do as they say for now; go with them. That's the only way I am going to sort this out, which I will. Then I'll come back. All right?'

Leena sat on the bed, fighting the tears.

'All right?'

She nodded.

Hendrik packed.

He leant down and kissed his wife.

'It'll be all right. I promise.'

'No, it won't,' said Leena. 'I know it.'

They hustled him downstairs and towards the front door, though he tried to shrug them off.

'Where's Father going?'

It was Juhan, in his night clothes, joining his mother at the top of the stairs.

'Where are you taking Father?' Maret appeared with them. The two children stumbled downstairs. They started crying.

'Leena – stop them. Look after them,' said Hendrik.

Leena followed the children and grabbed them as one of the heavies pushed the children back inside and shut the door.

Outside, the unseeing sun shone and the indifferent birches nodded in the breeze. Hendrik could hear the children's howls as they led him to the car.

VI

'Where are we going?'

'You'll see,' said Fischer.

'Why don't you just tell me?'

The car was slipping along at speed through the streets. Past the local police station. Past the building where they took the measurements. They carried on through the Old Town towards the city centre where, Hendrik assumed, police headquarters stood. But they didn't stop. Solid Königsberg's rust-red brick loomed all around them like the walls of a medieval prison. The castle tower poked its head above the shoulders of its huge bulwarks, looking for all the world as if surprised. The car kept travelling. They crossed over the Pregel onto Kneiphof Island, where fishing boats and barges were unloading their produce along the quays, just as they had since Hanseatic times. Then back over the Pregel via Grüne Brucke. Perhaps they were going to some bleak place where the secret police conducted their 'straightforwardness', as Officer Wowreit of Tiergarten District called it.

Down one of the side streets to the left, Kotkas caught a glimpse of what seemed to be the remains of a building.

'What's that?' he said.

Fischer looked, then looked away again, but said nothing.

Instinct told Kotkas that the pile of rubble he'd just seen was probably what was left of a synagogue.

They drove on.

Then, Hendrik started to recognise where he was. He knew the area around the main station. It was where he'd arrived just those few days before.

The car crunched past the trades vehicles, the taxis and the trams and stopped on the station forecourt. The engine was cut.

'Get out,' said Fischer.

'Where am I going? Where are you taking me?'

'I will accompany you. I have your word you will not try to escape?'

'Where am I going?'

'I have your word? Otherwise, I shall have to use hand-cuffs.'

'You have my word. But where—'

'Not seemly for a navy officer – handcuffs. Do you have your identity documents?'

Hendrik fumbled in his jacket and produced them. They walked through the station entrance. With its long marquee and its window resembling the pipes of an organ above, they could have been walking into a music hall. They crossed the bustling concourse onto a platform beneath the extravagant pitched glass roof. A train was waiting; the locomotive grumbling and hissing, impatient to be off. They showed the necessary documents and permits to a uniform at the barrier, and opened a carriage door.

'Thank you, Braun. I shall take it from here. Commander, get in.'

Braun gave a nod and left them. They mounted the steps and found an empty compartment.

The conductor blew his whistle, the assistant stationmaster waved his white paddle, the locomotive shrieked, and with a jolt and a great huff, the train pulled out.

'You are to do everything I tell you on this journey – including when to go to the toilet – do you understand?'

'Yes.'

'To the letter, mind, and no clever ideas. I have a gun, and my colleague Braun back there has an arm with a very long reach. Shall we say, at least as far as your family back at the house? I shall be telephoning him at regular intervals; changing trains, long station-stops; whenever. If I do not call, I am sure you are aware that Braun can get to your wife and children much quicker than you can. Do you understand?'

'I understand.'

The compartment door slid open and a small man with dandruff started to put his case in the luggage rack. Fischer pulled out his identity disc and showed it to him. The man withdrew. Fischer shut the compartment door again.

'Would you please, at least, extend me the courtesy of telling me where I am going?'

'Well, you might as well know now. Berlin.'

'Berlin? Your place or mine?'

'And, on the way, we can have a nice chat. I should be glad, mind you, if you would do me the courtesy of telling me the truth. The whole truth and nothing but the truth.'

'You watch too many American movies.'

'We can start with a little history. Yours. Not the born and bred bit. Though, I imagine, the fact that you are fluent, you were brought up Baltic German.'

'That was my schooling, yes. Though I am not Baltic German, I am Estonian.'

'No German leanings at all?'

He looked at Fischer. 'None.'

Fischer smiled.

'In fact,' Kotkas continued, 'my first encounter with Germans proper was as a cadet. On the gunboat *Lembit*. When we kicked you lot out of our country once and for all.'

'Well, once, at least. The "for all" bit remains to be seen, don't you think?'

The journey proved to be long and tedious. Fischer asking questions. Kotkas providing answers. Answers that he hoped would at least sound plausible even if they were only half true.

'And now, Commander, we come to the Royal Navy. You lived in England for a while?'

'Yes, I spent some time being trained at Greenwich and

Portsmouth. General officer training. Navigation, weapons, tactics.'

'And in the inter-war years, back in Estonia, you acted as liaison for them?'

'I acted as liaison officer for any visiting navy. Swedish, Finnish, Latvian. You name a Baltic state and I liaised.'

'The Bolsheviks?'

'Apart from them.'

Fischer looked at him carefully. 'The truth?'

'The truth, yes. Well, not entirely. Obviously, they dropped in from time to time. But I couldn't describe it as liaison. More a courtesy extended to a difficult neighbour in order to avoid an unpleasant scene.'

'And when they walked into your beloved country without so much as a by-your-leave? You were obliged to liaise then, yes?'

'No. I left.'

'How?'

'You must have that in your dossier on me, surely.'

'Perhaps. But I long to have it from your own lips.'

'Over the years, my country would sail in the great regatta in Kiel. I was selected to be in the Estonia team. It was there I made the acquaintance of one of your navy's officers, Captain Gahlendorf. We became friends. When the Reds moved into my country and, along with thousands of my countrymen, I was on the list to be exiled or shot, I made my appeal to him. He took me under his wing and saw to it that my family were brought to safety. I am enormously grateful to him.'

'I see. And ...?'

'And what?'

'You appear, Commander, to have conveniently left out one significant detail. Or, I should say, person ...'

'You tell me.' *Who did Fischer mean? Tamm?*

'One other member of that sailing team. Someone who shared your training in England. Someone who, indeed, has

72

shared your entire navy career to date from cadet to Bolshevik occupation.'

'Peeter.'

'Your brother, yes. Who is, even as we speak, an officer in the Baltic Red fleet. Now, why, I wonder, did you omit to mention him? Surely, that's one Bolshevik with whom we can assume a significant amount of liaising.'

'I have no contact with him. I lost contact with him the day I left. I don't know where he is, what he is up to. He could be dead for all I know.'

'Hmm. We may come back to this later. Returning to Captain Gahlendorf: he commanded a naval unit in Memel. Which is where you landed on your feet, yes?'

'It is. Until I was called to Berlin.'

'Why?'

'To work in the Intelligence Service.'

'Why?'

'I think, despite your exalted status, it would be treason if I told you.'

'Treason towards what? Who?'

'The German people and your beloved Leader. The people you serve. But you know that. You just wanted to trick me into giving away state secrets. You tease, you.'

'Enough,' Fischer said, glaring. 'You don't seem to realise what a serious situation you are in.'

Kotkas realised only too well, and with every rattle over points, every station-stop, every hoot on the train's whistle, he knew he was being dragged nearer and nearer to Berlin, and whatever awaited him there.

*

'Where the hell have you been?'

All Kotkas could see of Canaris was the top of his head. The Admiral was at his desk looking down at some paperwork. There was a cup of coffee on his desk; clearly untouched, as it had a chalky patina on its surface. He could, however, imagine his superior's expression, bearing in mind the glacial voice. 'With my family, sir. As you know, Admiral.'

Canaris looked up. His eyes locked into a glare that could turn fire to ice. 'I did not know. Oh yes, I knew you had planned to see your family, but circumstances prevailed and you were unable, in the event, to go. At least, that is what I supposed. I thought you were at your desk all last week. It was only when I called a meeting yesterday with all my senior staff that I discovered the truth. What the hell do you think you were doing?'

'Sir – my wife ... my family ...'

'Bah. We all have wives; we all have families. What do you suppose would happen to this war if every one of us went off visiting our wives and children instead of getting on with the fight?'

'There would be no more war. Sir.'

'Don't get smart with me. You are in enough trouble.' He got up from his desk and walked to the window. He looked down at the streets of Berlin; the buildings were grey. The vehicles were grey. The folk streaming to and fro were grey. 'Have you any idea what could have happened to you? Those gentlemen who came to collect you from your little love nest ... if it was up to them, you'd still be in some cellar in Königsberg having the error of your ways being beaten out of you. Or worse. Thankfully, you have friends in high places.'

'I do?'

'Yes. Me. Once I'd found out where you were, I started the process of getting you back again. However, that process involved informing the only organisations with sufficient resources to parcel you up and get you back here as quickly as possible. They, of course, wanted to handle things their way. They wanted me to admit that I'd given you a direct order regarding when you had to be back here. I told them, however, that it was just a request. Open-ended, but that now I needed you back. Had it been an order ...'

'I would have been taken for a deserter.'

'And shot in front of your family, yes.' The Admiral turned to face him. 'And then, of course, they would have turned on your family. The family of a deserter, no less ...'

'I see. Thank you, sir.'

'Don't thank me. Just do your job. Do your job and forget about your family. There will be time to think about families when all this is over.'

'Yes, sir.'

The Admiral returned to his desk. 'By the way ...'

'Sir?'

'How *are* your family?'

'Well enough, sir. Though, having said that, my wife is quite ill. She has some disease of the brain.'

'I am sorry to hear that. Is there anything to be done?'

'We don't know, sir. She's taking medication for it. Our doctor in Estonia said it could go either way. The doctor in Königsberg said something similar. I think that's code for there is only one way it will ultimately go.'

'I am sorry to hear that. And I do understand. Time together is precious.'

'Yes, sir.'

'I will see what I can do in due course. Give you some genuine leave.'

'Thank you, sir.'

'But, for the moment, I need you here. These are impossible times, Kotkas. I'm sorry you and your family are caught up in them. I'm sorry we are all caught up in them. Have you heard of the Königsberg Bridge problem?'

'Sir?'

'Mathematical puzzle; posited by Euler in the 18th century. Königsberg has seven bridges. You need to work out a way of crossing all of them only the once and never retracing your steps. Trouble is – it can't be done. Even the brightest minds in the world have tried and failed. We none of us can cross all the bridges we need to, Kotkas. We just have to make do with the ones we can.'

'Sir.'

'Go back to your quarters, have a wash, get back into uniform and be at the Adlon ...' he looked at his watch '... in an hour.'

'Sir.'

'Oh, and, Commander, be warned, the fellow who brought you back from Königsberg – he has his eye on you.'

'I know.'

In the outer office, Kotkas went up to one of the desks.

'Miss Meyer?'

She looked up. 'Yes? Oh. It's you.' She readied for a fight.

'Yes. May I ask ... did you give my family's address to the Admiral?'

'Yes. I was just doing my duty.'

He took her hand and shook it. 'Thank you.'

She realised he meant it and softened. 'I was glad to help. I was worried.'

'For me?'

'For all of you.'

He nodded. 'Would you be able to get word to my wife and family that I am safe and well and back at work in Berlin, please?'

'I'll see what I can do.'

'Thanks. I'll write a quick note now ...'

*

Karl was preparing to go off to school. As was permitted on days when there was Group afterwards, he had worn his uniform; that was a special pleasure. He always ironed it himself and laid it out on his bedroom chair the night before. Creases knife-sharp. Boots polished into mirrors. Ready to leave, he put his cap on. Until recently, he had placed it so that it was absolutely square upon his head; the peak a straight line with the horizon. It was just low enough on his brow to cause him to tilt his chin upwards, enabling him to look along his nose at everything. But in a recent newsreel, he had caught sight of a young man in uniform like his at a Leader's rally. That fellow had worn his cap at a slight angle, implying sophistication and strength. So Karl's own cap these days was therefore tipped, ever so slightly, over his left eye. As if he'd been on a hundred missions and had emerged a hero in them all.

Maret had been waiting by the school gates. The moment she saw Karl, she marched up to him: 'You!'

'Hello, little Maret. How are you? How are your family?' he hesitated to ask, then, 'how's your father?'

'You snitched, didn't you? You snitched on my father and now they've taken him away. They've taken him away and we don't know where!' She launched herself at him and began flailing with her fists.

'Hi! What's all this about! Hi! Stop it!' he said, and stooped to stop her, but a wild swing knocked his beloved cap flying. He managed to grab her wrists. He turned her round and locked her arms across her body so she could do him no more damage. Or so he thought. But she began to kick backwards with her heels against his shins. 'Stop it!' he said.

Two of Karl's friends came to his rescue. They grabbed the girl, tore her off him and held her tight.

'Now, calm down, Maret, and explain: who told who about what?'

'You. You told the police about my father not going back to Berlin.'

'I did no such thing.'

'Yes, you did.'

'I did not.' He rubbed his arms then his shins. 'But I can't say I'm surprised. I'm afraid you can't go round saying the things he said and get off lightly.'

'You beast!' She tried to break free of her captors. They resisted. She tried to bite one of them. They held her even tighter.

Karl came as close to her as he dared. 'I understand that he's had to go away, now, anyway.'

'How did you know about that?'

'People talk. Everybody talks around here. Everybody knows everyone else's business. They say he was taken away by some men this morning.'

'Do you know where he is?'

'No. I swear.'

Juhan arrived. 'Maret – what's happening? Why are they holding you?'

Karl got down on his haunches. 'Listen, Maret, I did not squeal on your father. All right? It wasn't me. I don't know who it was, but it wasn't me. Yes, I was disappointed to hear him talk like that. About giving up the fight. About running away from his duties—'

'He was not running away. He's not a coward ...'

'Neglecting, then. When everyone else is sacrificing so much for the cause. But, I like you. I like your little brother. I think you are good people. I would never want to hurt you. Please believe me.'

Maret looked at him. He returned her gaze. Her body, which was stiff and straining to break free, relaxed.

'You can let her go,' Karl said to his friends. They questioned him with a look. 'It's all right,' he said. 'She understands. She's fine, now.'

They began to release their grip. Maret shook them off and tugged her clothes back into shape. She took a step towards Karl, who remained where he was, on his haunches.

'All right, I believe you.'

'Thank you.'

'What's going on?' said Juhan.

'Nothing,' said Maret. 'Let's go home.'

Karl watched them go. He then looked around for his cap. It had flown a full three metres away and was lying on the side of the road in the gutter. He picked it up. There was a little grime on the peak. He tried to dust it off, but that only served to spread the grime more widely. So he took out his handkerchief, wet it with spit, and rubbed it on the mark. That only made it worse. A dark grubby smear on the pristine fabric. Karl seethed. He placed the cap back on his head but somehow it wasn't the same. It would never be the same. That stupid little girl had spoiled it. *That stupid little girl with her stupid little family. Stupid little foreign family. Un-German family.* He hadn't informed the authorities. But now he wished he had. *Serve them right if they did get into trouble. Serve them right if he had something to do with it from now on.*

'Come on,' he said to his comrades, and they marched off.

*

Kotkas stepped into the great Adlon lobby. The flamboyant interior mesmerised. It was not so much a hotel as a private members' club. Haunt of film stars and millionaires, foreign diplomats and the Party elite, it was, perhaps, the ideal watering hole for the head of the State's Intelligence Service. Information and gossip hung in the air along with Chanel No. 5 and Romeo y Julieta cigar smoke.

The Commander looked around for his superior. He had heard that Canaris always sat at a certain table in a certain seat in one of the darker corners, where he could see everyone who came and went. It took him a few moments, but Kotkas's eyes eventually caught a glimpse of white hair and white cuffs, and the glint of an admiral's gold sleeve rings.

He set off in that direction.

'Commander Kotkas?'

He looked at the man who had intercepted him. An army captain with the old-Prussian collar tabs of the General Staff on his uniform. He was, Kotkas supposed, a few years older than he.

'Yes?'

'I have been expecting you, sir. May I introduce myself? Captain Ludwig Plötz. Would you join me for something to eat or drink? Come, my table is just over here ...'

'I should be glad to join you. However, I have an appointment ...'

'With me, yes.'

'No, with the Admiral.'

'Yes, I asked the Admiral to invite you here. But it is me you have come to see.'

'I have?'

'You have, sir. Here we are. Please – take a seat. What would you like to drink?'

'A coffee.'

'A coffee you shall have. Good choice. As you can see, I have mine already.' Plötz called a waiter across and ordered Kotkas's coffee. Kotkas considered this officer for a moment. He spoke with a Prussian accent. He had the bearing, diction and self-assurance that suggested army family; probably going back generations. A career soldier, then. If Kotkas were to hazard a guess, also not a Party man. Though relying on such guesses was itself a hazardous occupation these days.

'The thing is,' Plötz continued, 'it would not be – how shall I put it? – *judicious* if you had any kind of conversation with the Admiral here at the Adlon. You are insufficiently high-ranking to be seen at the Admiral's table, do you see? People would talk. Moreover, although the good Admiral may have all kinds of uses for you – I know he values your knowledge and experience highly – I wanted us to have a different conversation. This is my initiative alone. The Admiral did not ask what I wanted to talk to you about. I merely asked the Admiral to invite you here. I mean, if you'd had an invitation directly from me, you might well, with good reason, say simply to yourself: I have no idea who this Captain Plötz fellow is. I have no idea what he wants. Maybe he wants something I am not prepared to offer. Let's face it, Berlin is full of people making demands of people that cannot, in all conscience, be met. Am I right?'

'What kind of different conversation?'

'Excellent. Straight to the point. Just how I was told you'd be. Well, sir, let's see ... It's not so much a conversation as, well, a simple question, really.'

'Which is?'

Plötz straightened his uniform jacket, leant forward, took a sip of coffee and rested his forearms cn the table. When he next spoke, it was as if he was addressing the cup and saucer. He lowered his voice. 'I was wondering whether you were in farming.'

There it was. *Farming.* The magic word.

Only those who knew understood what it meant. An innocent-enough enquiry on the outside but dripping with both meaning and menace on the inside. Significantly, it was a word he had only heard used in such a context on one previous occasion, by one particular person. It was, in many ways, the word that had brought him to that very table.

Farming. Mihkel Tamm had used it. Back home, in Estonia, all those years ago. They were sitting with a beer in a courtyard at the back of a bar on Pikk Street in Tallinn. 'Kotkas, old chap,' he said in his curious Estonian accent, heavily weighted with English inflections. He looked around to check whether anyone was within earshot. They were not. 'Some people I know were wondering if you were in farming.'

'Farming? Well, my father-in-law has a country place about an hour by train west of here. He has some arable, some livestock ...'

'No, no ... I'm talking about "farming". Do you not know the expression?'

'No.'

'Did you not hear it used when you were in England? Perhaps someone mentioned it to you over the years. Here, perhaps? One of the intelligence officers from the Royal Navy you have had dealings with may have introduced you to it.'

Kotkas shook his head.

Tamm looked around and checked the coast was clear again. 'Well, let's put it this way: I am in farming.'

'I thought you were in the lumber business.'

'I am. But I am also in farming. I have certain contacts. In London. And these certain contacts were interested in knowing if you would be interested in being one of *their* contacts.'

'Oh,' said Kotkas. 'That kind of farming. The sort of farming I have been doing officially between my government and the British government over the years?'

'Exactly. You've been linking them with information about the Soviet radio transmissions you intercept in your role as a matter of daily routine.'

'And now the British want me to work with them more closely; albeit covertly?'

'Yes. Through me, that is. I would be your link with the people back in London.'

'No.'

'Why? You'd only be doing what you have been doing these past few years.'

'Yes, but that was on behalf of my government. I would never do anything that would compromise Estonia, her integrity, her sovereignty.'

'Ah. No. You misunderstand. That's not what they are asking. They are simply interested in your passing on information that is only of direct interest to them. Nothing that you might want to keep solely between you and your own government.'

'What kind of information?'

'Anything you might hear from the people you associate with who are linked to a certain other regime.'

'Let's be clear. We are talking about Germany, yes?'

Kotkas's coffee arrived. The hubbub in the Adlon broke in on his reverie. How curious that in a different context and under different circumstances, Tamm and this Captain Plötz had made a similar approach. Kotkas knew there was an important difference, however. What Tamm and he did, back then in Estonia, was simple espionage. Not against the host country but between two third parties; intelligence on German matters passing into British hands. At the Adlon, Kotkas had yet to find out what, precisely, Plötz was asking of him. However, something told him it was to do with working within the regime *against that same regime*. In short, what Plötz was doing right then and there would be instantly deemed high treason should it ever be discovered.

'What sort of farming?'

'That depends on you,' said Plötz. 'Nervous?'

'Yes.'

'Then we can call it off right now. I never said anything. We let it drop. You finish your coffee, thank me for a lovely time and walk away.'

'Or?'

Plötz looked around him. I suppose you are wondering why I asked to meet you here. It's a nice place, this hotel. Bit too swanky for my tastes, but comfortable all the same. And convenient. However, I can see why the Admiral likes it. Notice how there are so many conversations going on at the same time? Seems to mask all the other conversations, don't you think? Listen carefully – can you hear clearly a single word anyone is saying at the table next to us? No, I am sure you cannot. And, just so you know, I checked underneath the table with both hands before you arrived. Nothing. There isn't usually – but it's better to be safe than sorry. Nothing in the lamp here, either. All clear. So you may speak freely. Softly, but freely.'

'I don't know what you want me to say.'

'Are you in farming?'

'I was, yes. In Estonia. But all that is hinterland now, isn't it?'

'I see. Well, then, let me put another question. Can we rely on you?'

'Who's "we"?'

Plötz smiled. 'If we've been in farming, we know better than to ask questions like that, don't we?'

Kotkas sipped his coffee.

'This is proving a little more difficult than I imagined, Commander. I thought you'd be more ready to hear what I am suggesting. My information is clearly wrong. Either that or you are playing me for a fool and I am about to be frog-marched out of here, hung by the thumbs and beaten on the back of my head until my eyes bleed.'

Still, Kotkas said nothing.

'Well, then. Let's go back to plan A. If you are interested in hearing more of what I have to say, please continue to finish your coffee. At the end, remain in your seat. I shall order you another one, and we can continue our little chat. If you do not want to hear anything further, well, then, finish your coffee, we shall shake hands like the officers and gentlemen we are, and you may leave.'

Kotkas took up his coffee cup.

He drained the contents, stood, bowed and left.

VII

She had lied, of course. About there being nothing wrong when she'd collapsed in the hallway the other day. It wasn't just simply fainting. It wasn't just the medication. It wasn't the first time she'd collapsed, either. Far from it. She'd collapsed many times before. Over the past year or so. This was just the first time either Hendrik or Maret and Juhan had witnessed it. Up until then, she'd been able to hold on until she'd got out of the way. *Just going into the kitchen ... Just going upstairs ... Just popping out into the garden ...* and there she'd crumple into a heap, out of sight. That was the first time she'd been caught. Things must be getting worse. Certainly, the pain was greater. Greater? It was at times excruciating. It felt like someone had put her head in a great oaken apple press and was little by little, inch by inch, turning the screw and crushing her skull. A great undertow of discomfort accompanied by sudden stabs of pain. The children hadn't noticed, and Hendrik hadn't known the difference. But since she'd been in Germany, her prescription had doubled. And still it wasn't enough. After a few minutes, thankfully, something of the agony receded. Or, perhaps, the laudanum helped her not mind so much. Either way, the effect never lasted long enough. Within an hour, ninety minutes, she needed to top up the dose; much against advice. But who cared? She'd be out of this world soon enough. What did a little addictive mischief matter in the great scheme of things?

'*How am I, Doctor?*'

'What did they tell you in Tallinn?'

'That it is slow ... but sure.'

'Well, it has become a little faster.'

85

'How long?'

'Hard to be precise. Worst case? Months. A couple of years if you are strong, perhaps more.'

'Thank you, Doctor.'

She was concerned that, from time to time, she lost all hold on reason. Like a switch thrown in her brain, then a whole different area of rationality, or, rather, irrationality, was engaged. At which point, to avoid doing herself harm, she would make herself just sit on the couch, cover herself with a blanket, and let the day slip by. Until the children came home, of course. Then she would try to be as bright as a sparrow. However, even that was getting to be a harder act to put on. She was losing her grip; she knew it. And tired. So tired. And bored. Bored out of what was left of her tiny mind. She'd never get back home, now. She knew that much. She would die here long before the ship that would be allowed to sail back in the other direction. Back north. Back to the place of her birth, her home, her happiness ... but shush ... what was that? The children? Home? Was it that time already?

She carefully arranged the blanket so it draped over her legs and lower body in an *I'm perfectly fine* kind of way. As if she hadn't a care in the world ... Shush ... Here they come ... Smile...

'Mother ... Mother ...' Juhan came running in.

Maret followed close behind. 'Juhan! No! I told you not to tell her.'

'Hello, my darlings.' Although she was able to form her words, her voice was a little slurred. She was very tired. It was only mid-afternoon and yet she wished she could just lie down and go to sleep. *Let it all be over, please.* Yet, here were two pockets of energy bursting in on her.

'You are not to tell her. I'll hit you, Juhan, if you tell her.'

'Maret had a fight with Karl.'

'No, I didn't.'

'He's big and strong, but Maret needed two of his biggest friends to stop her.'

'Juhan! I told you not to say anything!'

'Is this true, Maret?'

'It was just a disagreement, Mother. I thought Karl was the one who told tales on us to the police ...'

'And was he?'

'He said he wasn't. I don't know why Juhan keeps going on about it all. He's just silly and rude and wrong.'

'Was it a fight, though, dear?'

'No, of course not. How could I fight a boy so much older than me? I told you, it was just an argument and he promised he hadn't told on us. I wish Juhan would mind his own stupid business.'

'Don't call me stupid.'

'You are stupid and I hate you.'

'Maret, dear.'

'He is stupid. And so are you.'

'Maret ...'

'And Father. And everyone. And I hate this stupid place and this stupid war and everyone and I wish I was dead!'

'Maret. Stop it. Stop talking like this.'

'Why? Why should I? I didn't ask to be here. Why did you take us away from our home? I don't care if there are horrible people there. I'd rather be there than here. I want to go back to my school. I want to go to Vasalemma. I hate it here.'

Juhan stood staring at his sister. He had never seen her like this and it was frightening him.

'Come here, darling. Come to me. Come for a cuddle.'

'I don't want a cuddle. I don't want you. How will a cuddle help? Nothing will help. Everything's horrible.'

'Darling, you are just angry and upset because of everything. Because Father had to leave us ...'

'Where is Father? Why did he have to go? Why did you let them take him away?'

'I didn't let them.'

'Then why isn't he here? You both just let them take him away. He didn't even say goodbye. He just told you to stop us from going after him. He didn't want us.'

'He didn't want you to get into trouble.'

'He said he would stay with us. He said he would never leave us ever again.'

'No, he didn't, darling.'

'Yes, he did, Mother,' said Juhan quietly. 'He promised.'

'He didn't promise, dears. He couldn't promise something like that. He said that when he was sad and worried about me – about all of us. But he can't stay with us. He knows it now. I know it. If he stayed with us, he would only get into trouble. Real trouble. So would we …'

'He *promised!* He did promise.' Maret was shouting now, and sobbing.

Juhan started sobbing too, standing in the middle of the room.

'No, he didn't, darlings.'

'Yes, he did! Yes, he did!'

'He didn't …'

'He did, he did, *he did!*'

*

It was quiet in his office. Hendrik had gone back to work on Barbarossa preparations. The blackout curtains had been drawn. He sat with a single desk lamp. He could smell cooked meat. His window was open. The building's commissariat was a couple of floors beneath his office. Pork. *Sauerkraut.* Curiously, to him, boiled pork always smelled like laundry. Tasty laundry. It was making him hungry. He didn't have time to be hungry. He closed the window and sat back down to his work.

Someone knocked on his door.

'Yes?'

An orderly entered carrying a pile of papers and folders.

'The files and intercepts you asked for, sir.'

'Thank you. Is this all?'

'No, sir. There are about ten more piles like this downstairs. Do you want me to bring them up?'

'One at a time, I think. Why so much?'

'We've been waiting for someone like you, sir. Nobody else, it seems, knows quite how to analyse and interpret this particular material.'

Kotkas leafed through a wad of flimsies. Some with notes in German attached, some only having unintelligible writing on them; sequences of letters without a single coherent word or sentence. 'These intercepts. Not all of them seem to have been decoded.'

'No, sir. They're working on it.'

'I can perhaps help with that. Would you check that they have the paperwork I left with Captain Gahlendorf in Memel, please?'

'Yes, sir, they have. They are proving very helpful, I understand, in analysing Soviet radio communications. It is just taking time.'

'Fair enough.' Kotkas next picked up a folder out of which fell a couple of dozen sheets of close-typed memoranda. 'And these, what are they?'

'Latest dispositions on ships in the Soviet Baltic Fleet, as you asked for, sir.'

'Fine. I'll start with them. Thank you.'

'Sir.' The orderly stood to attention and saluted. But already the Commander was leafing through the material. So the orderly left and closed the door behind him.

Shortly after, there was again a knock at the door.

'Come.'

It was Captain Plötz. He closed the door behind him. He produced a packet of cigarettes, tapped one loose and offered it to Kotkas, who shook his head, so put it into his own mouth and lit it. It was a de Troupe. He'd liberated a few dozen cartons from French soldiers as he and the German forces flooded across and around the Maginot Line at the start of the war. An intelligence officer, he'd sat with the tanks and artillery outside Dunkirk pounding the British as they drained away across the Channel. It wasn't the blundering failure to destroy that raggle-taggle army that had turned his head. It wasn't even the treachery that the illegal invasion of France symbolised. It was the SS treatment of the locals – the innocents, the women, the children: butchered in bloodlust – that changed his mind. Made him realise he was probably on the wrong side. Started him thinking about how he might do something about it. From the inside. Then he was recalled to Berlin for the same reason Kotkas had been commandeered; preparation for a different adventure. He felt as if Fate had taken a hand; shown him what he needed to do and where he was to do it: at the source of the evil.

'I thought I'd find you here,' he said.

'Did you? And how did you come to that conclusion?'

'I read your file. "Diligent ... Principled ... Problem-solver ..." it said. So ... alone in Berlin, somewhat adrift, probably missing family like hell ... where would I go? To the office. Bury my head in work.'

'What do you want?'

'Why don't we go for a walk?'

'Unfortunately, as you can see by the state of my desk, this Diligent, Principled Problem-solver needs to get on ...'

'Nevertheless ...'

Kotkas paused. He sighed. 'Very well.' He stood, put on his uniform jacket and took up his cap.

They left the Bendlerblock and strolled beside the canal.

'Are we being followed, do you think?' Plötz said.

'No.'

'No, I didn't think so, either.'

The birds were fluting their twilight melodies.

'So, Commander, have you thought any more about what I said?'

'No.'

'Come now, sir. Someone like you. A conversation like the one we had? I find that difficult to believe.'

'All right then, I did think about it, of course. But then I dismissed the whole matter. I thought I had made that clear. Why do you continue pursuing me like this?'

'Because my sources suggest you might have reacted differently to my earlier enquiry.'

'I am an Estonian naval officer in the employ of a German Naval Intelligence unit, invited to participate in assessing and interpreting certain documents. Your "enquiry", as you put it, goes beyond what I have come here to do. It goes beyond what my own ultimate intentions are. Moreover, Captain, should I react in any way positively, it would put me, my wife and my family at a level of risk I deem unacceptable.'

'And your integrity. Don't you think that might be put in service of a greater good?'

Kotkas did not answer. They walked on. Plötz finished his cigarette in silence. He was content to allow the man beside him to ponder further.

Kotkas's mind went back to another conversation, a few weeks before. It had been at the German naval base at Memel, where he'd fetched up after evading arrest in Estonia. He was in Captain Werner Gahlendorf's office. They were smoking cigars and drinking brandy. Kotkas had been debriefed over a couple of days and now he was being interviewed by his sailing rival, skipper of the German boat, and drinking companion at Kiel's Yacht Club of Germany.

Kotkas had already handed over the briefcase he'd smuggled out with him from Tallinn. The case held files with the hard-won methods whereby Soviet radio signals might be decoded. For the past few years, he and his Naval Intelligence team in Tallinn had put them to good use. It was the price he paid for being spirited out of his occupied homeland. The price he was happy to pay to get his family to safety. Not a great price, in the final analysis; after all, his beloved homeland had no need for it anymore.

Gahlendorf had just finished laying before Kotkas the same kind of offer that Plötz implied.

'What are you saying, Werner?' Kotkas asked.

'Simply put, Hendrik, work for us by all means, but let's undermine the Nazis while we are at it. I think, what you have to offer is particularly interesting.'

'Which is?'

'An ability to have a conversation with the British, albeit at arm's length. There is nothing more exciting than having another outlet for our energies, so to speak.'

'Can you say that?'

'I just have.'

'I mean – is it safe to say that? Here?'

Clean cut, charming, privately educated, from a good family, Gahlendorf was self-assured rather than arrogant. However, Kotkas was only too aware that such self-assurance and disregard for the powers that be could ultimately lead to mistakes.

Gahlendorf shrugged. 'I've had a number of conversations along similar lines since I've been here. As you see, I still sit in this seat, sip my Asbach and smoke my Upmanns. This is a secure room in a secure unit.' He laughed. 'The irony is, Bendlerblock commandeered it off an SS unit. There's so much arm-wrestling going on back there in Berlin; it's absurd. If you ask me, it wouldn't take much to topple the whole house of cards anyway, given the right circumstances. It's just up to us to keep poking until it does.'

'Be that as it may, I am afraid my connection with the British lapsed the moment I left Estonia.'

'Ah, well. Disappointment we must learn to live with as a daily occurrence in these straitened times, I suppose.

Nonetheless, it would still be excellent to have you on the strength, old boy.'

Kotkas was still not convinced. 'It seems to me, Werner, that you are appealing to my better nature. The question is, whether better natures have any place in this current context. Or whether simple survival, and the intention to ensure those closest to me survive, is the only course at present.'

'That depends on whether, to survive, the principle method of achieving it involves being complicit in works of evil.' Gahlendorf took another sip of brandy, drew on his cigar and let the cloud envelop him.

He was right, of course. Kotkas liked Gahlendorf and always had; he trusted him. Which was why he'd agreed to think about supporting Gahlendorf's offer. However, he'd left Memel before anything further could be done about it.

Why had he trusted him but found it harder to trust Plötz? Was it something to do with Gahlendorf being a brother naval officer? Was it the shared experience of the great Kiel regattas? Was it the fact that the sealed room in Memel was a million miles away from Berlin, whereas there, with Plötz, he was right in the heart of the beast?

Then again ... It might have been, Kotkas reasoned, Gahlendorf to whom Plötz had been referring, when he told Kotkas about his sources.

'Tell me,' he said to Plötz at last, 'the name of someone that means something to me.'

'In what way?' Plötz was standing contemplating the ripples in the canal water. He lit another de Troupe.

'In a way that puts you and them at risk. Make yourself vulnerable.'

'What would that prove?'

'That you are willing to put your life in my hands. Just as you are asking me to put my life in yours.'

'But, surely, your asking for some kind of proof that you can trust me, trust the people I am with, suggests you are willing to take the step I am offering. Enough of an act of treachery in the State's eyes to have you shot right where you stand and thrown into this canal.

'Perhaps I am on the inside and pretending to be interested. Perhaps I am tricking you into giving me information that you would otherwise never give. Even under torture.'

They walked on a few paces. Then Plötz stopped. He looked around. There was nobody within earshot. Except Kotkas.

'Tamm.'

Kotkas forced himself not to react at the name. His Anglo-Estonian contact. His previous link to the British security services. How did this officer in the Intelligence Service know about him?

'Have I surprised you?' said Plötz. 'Were you expecting a different name? Were you thinking I would say, perhaps, Gahlendorf?' They continued walking. 'Now, I and the people I have mentioned have put ourselves in your hands. Do with us what you will. Look, Prinz Albrecht Strasse is just fifteen minutes' walk from here. Less, if you take a taxi. I will stand here and smoke a cigarette. You may go ahead and talk to whomever you like there. The SS, SD, Gestapo. Take your choice. I'll be here ...' He drew on his cigarette.

Still, Kotkas hesitated. They were just names. They could be on any file in Berlin. Friendly or unfriendly people could have access to them. Once again, he was wondering whether he was being tested. 'Something else,' he said. 'I need something else.'

Plötz gave a little laugh and offered the cigarette packet. Kotkas shook his head again. Plötz took another puff and twiddled his cigarette between his fingers, inspecting the red-hot tip with apparent interest. 'Tell you what,' he said, 'let's go back. I will write down the names and location of a number of files and issue authority to access them. You get them out of the archive, take them back to your office, and look at them.

Give them a good read. When you have examined them thoroughly, we can discuss what it is you have read. How does that suit?'

He sucked the life out of his de Troupe and extinguished it.

*

She knew what to do, of course. She'd known for a long time. Once they'd said. Once they'd told her that it would end. How it would end. Once the pain started to get real.

Of course, the first time she'd started deciding what she would do, Hendrik was still with her, they were still a family; at home in her beloved Estonia, with her family and friends around. But, she told herself, here, now, in this godforsaken country: what was the difference? Hendrik would look after their children. As long as he was safe and alive.

She smoothed out the telegram she'd crumpled in her hand and read it again. But, in doing so, the fury returned.

How *dare* he say he's safe and well and back in Berlin? How *dare* he sound as if he hadn't a care in the world? How *dare* he leave us to face this hell alone? How *dare* he?

She screwed the telegram back up and hurled it across the room.

I'll make him come back. He'll have to. Come back to look after the children. Take them somewhere safe until they could go all home. With me out of the way, it would be easier.

She was only making things easier for everyone. She would be out of the way sooner or later anyway. So what was the difference?

Yes, he'd have to come back. If she got out of the way. He'd absolutely have to.

That was the best thing.

I am so useless. To everybody. My life is over. It's been over for a long time.

Maret has to do most things around here as it is. She's a good girl. Cooking, cleaning. Looking after Juhan. Getting them ready for school. That woman who comes in every morning, to clean, to cook, she despises us. Hates that we are Estonians not Germans; not in the Party. Can't get out of here fast enough. Bare minimum, grabs her money then shoots off. It's only Maret who keeps us going. My darling Maret. I'm so proud of her.

I'm only making things worse for her.

When I'm out of the way, she'll be better off. And her father will come back. She'll like that. So will Juhan.

Once I'm out of the way …

VIII

'Well, what did you make of them?'

Plötz and Kotkas were walking beside the canal again. It was dusk. They had cross-checked with each other that they were not being followed. Cars and trucks with running lights like shooting stars passed. Nothing slowed. Nothing seemed to pay any attention to the army captain and the naval commander strolling under the trees beside the water where ducks swam in the glistening evening.

'I'm not sure. They were just files. Intelligence Service appointments over the past few years. Plus the cities, towns, countries they'd been assigned to,' said Kotkas.

'And sent to.'

'So ...?'

'What about some of the names on the files? What did you notice?'

'Well ...'

'Any common factor?'

'Well, I suppose, if I were to make certain assumptions, I would have said ...'

'Go on. Nobody's listening.'

'... that all the names could be said to belong to people of Jewish origin.'

'Right. And when you perused the files themselves, what did you find was a common factor?'

Kotkas shrugged. 'I don't know. I suppose the only thing I really noticed was that they were dull.'

'Good. Why were they dull, do you think? Specifically?'

'Well, I suppose, because there was very little content.'

'Little content – or no content?'

'Arguably, no content. There didn't seem to be much intelligence being returned to Berlin from them. Any of them.'

'Exactly.'

'You mean to say ... they've been assigned and sent to different places overseas as Intelligence Service agents, but they've never sent back any reports? It's as if they've simply been sent away.'

'Never to return. Never expected to return. Or, put another way, got to safety.'

Kotkas stopped and blew out his cheeks. 'But this is dynamite. If anyone found out what you've being doing ...'

'Which is why I had to arrange special access to those files for you. Only a few, an extremely privileged few, know they even exist. As records of counterintelligence appointments, they are enough, on the surface, to show the casual observer who wishes to make an enquiry. We like making records. But they don't always record what they pretend to record. As you have discovered, they don't warrant closer scrutiny. You asked me to put myself at risk to prove how genuine I am, how genuine is my request that you join us. My life is now entirely in your hands. The only question that remains is – which way will you jump?'

*

'Mother ... Juhan won't go to bed. I asked him three times.'

Leena was in the lounge, sitting in an armchair. There was an occasional table beside her. An empty glass stood on the table.

'Mother?'

Leena looked up and across at Maret, as though trying to decide who was talking.

'Is that you, Maret?'

'Yes.'

'Look after Juhan for me. Look after your father.'

'Mother? Is something the matter? Mother?'

Leena's head lolled.

'Juhan! Juhan! Come quickly! Something's wrong with Mother! Quickly!'

She ran to Leena and grabbed her hands. 'Stand up, Mother, stand up. I don't like it. Stop it. I don't like how you are being. Stand up. Please, Mother, please ... Juhan! Help!'

Leena couldn't be dragged out of the chair, so Maret grabbed her shoulders and started shaking her.

Leena's chin sank to her chest.

Maret started crying.

Leena started crying too.

Juhan appeared. 'What do you want, Maret? What's the matter with Mother?'

'I don't know. Quickly, Juhan, get help. Use the telephone. Quickly!'

Juhan ran into the hall. 'Who shall I ring?' he shouted.

'Mother showed us, remember?'

Juhan picked up the receiver, dialled, and a voice answered.

'Operator. What number, please?'

'Hello. Please, our mother is ill. Please. Help.'

'All right, dear. Who would you like me to connect you to?'

'I don't know. Mother is ill. Help, please. Quickly.'

'Would you like the police?'

'Yes. The police. Quickly.'

'All right, dear. Try to stay calm. Connecting you now.'

'Juhan! Hurry up!' Maret called from the lounge. She was cradling her mother's head on her shoulder.

'Police. Who's speaking, please?'

'Hello. Our mother is ill. Come and help. Please.'

'All right, young man. We'll come. What is your address?'

'Maret!'

'What?'

'What's our address?'

Maret told Juhan. Juhan told the policeman. The policeman said they would come as quickly as they could.

*

Fischer's boss had just finished a meat pie at his desk. The desk light caused his greasy chin to gleam. He was wiping his fingers on his trousers when Fischer walked in.

'I still don't like it,' Fischer said.

'Like what?'

'The Estonian commander I brought back from Königsberg.'

His boss's eyebrows clouded. 'I told you to finish it.'

Fischer shrugged.

'It's late. Go home. We'll discuss it in the morning.'

'The Chief thinks we should dig a little deeper for a while. Maybe the guy's a gateway into something bigger.'

The boss stiffened. 'You've been talking to the Chief?'

'Not deliberately. I haven't been going over your head. We just happened to be in the urinals at the same time. The subject came up.'

The thought of the Chief and Fischer, his underling, buttoning up their flies together galled him. He imagined them laughing together. Laughing at him. His top lip curled. 'Well, then ... if the Chief ...' He took a deep breath to compose himself. It wouldn't do to show that he felt threatened; a sign of weakness. 'You'd better sit down and we'll discuss it.'

Fischer sat.

'So – what's the story so far?'

Fischer told him. When he had finished, his boss sat in silence for a moment, tenting his fingers and seeming to be deep in thought; appearing, he hoped, deeply wise. 'But this Estonian told you on the train,' he said at length, 'that he'd actually thought about staying in Königsberg?'

'Yes.'

'So, if he were in any way a threat to the State, why would he be looking to get himself into the kind of trouble he admitted to you about? He must have known how dangerous it would be to even admit he'd planned to abscond. You could have shot him for that.'

'Had I had orders to that effect, I would have. But that's what's curious – why *did* he tell me? I mean, is he just a risk-taker? Does he put himself in harm's way for fun? For the thrill? What is he – some kind of buccaneer? I don't think so. I think there's a double bluff going on with him.'

'What kind of double bluff?'

'Acting normal. Playing the caring husband and father. Putting the well-being of his family first. Neglecting his duty as an officer. Going absent without leave. Risking imprisonment, or even the firing squad for them. It doesn't make sense. Not now. Not in these circumstances. Who does that in time of war?'

'So ... What ...? He wants you to think he's completely normal so he can bury whatever it is we might suspect him of?'

'Perhaps.'

'Or, Fischer, perhaps you are simply making more out of this than is the case. He's a husband and father. He's an alien in a foreign country basically against his will. I might well think about doing the same thing if I were in his shoes.'

'All right. But, if so, why didn't he arrange things properly? Through the official channels? Why didn't he tell Canaris he was not interested in working for us, hand in his resignation, and seek some kind of acceptable job in Königsberg so he could be near his family?'

'Perhaps he hadn't considered it until then. Where is your wife, Fischer?'

'I don't have one. Not married.'

'Girlfriend?'

'She lives in Dresden, where I come from. Where my folks live.' His thoughts flew to his hometown; his girlfriend's beautiful body, which he had enjoyed so freely, came to his mind's eye.

'Would you like to resign and go back to Dresden to be with your girl and your family?'

'Much as I'd like to ... no.'

'Why not?'

'Because ... because I can't.'

'Why not?'

'Because nobody else is resigning. Because, I suppose, in these circumstances, the best thing I can do for my family is stay doing my job. Until things change.'

'Right. But, if you did go home, without resigning, how would you feel?'

'I don't know.'

'I would suggest one of the ways you would feel is exactly the way our Estonian felt on direct contact with his loved ones.'

Fischer thought about it for a moment. 'All right,' he said, 'so what we see is what we get with him. Is that what you are saying?'

Fischer's boss considered the possibility. Then he recalled the Chief and Fischer's ever-so-convenient conversation at the urinal. Convenient for Fischer, that is. Nevertheless ... if that was the Chief's view ... 'No, I'm just saying – whatever game he is, or is not, playing, drop direct contact with his family into the equation and all bets are off. Navy officer, Intelligence Service agent or double agent ... all of that can fly out of the window when you hit the reality of your family in desperate need. This might simply have been a lapse, nothing more. Back in Berlin, once he knuckles down and resigns himself to getting on with the job in hand, he may reveal more about his true motives. If he has any.'

'So, I continue to keep an eye on him?'

'Certainly. However, I would suggest that, while you are doing that, you might want to get a better idea of his context, too.'

'You mean his family?'

'Yes. When you get the chance, call Königsberg, get someone alongside his wife and children. Get them to wheedle themselves into the family's trust. Start with the children. See if they'll open up and give our man there a little more information.'

'Right you are, sir.'

'And, Fischer ...?'

'Sir?'

'Report directly to me. Only to me. No more "just happened to bump into the Chief" business, if you don't mind. I'm not saying you did it deliberately. But, let's just say, I wouldn't be entirely happy with you if you did.'

'Sir.' *You stupid little man.*

*

Maret and Juhan were standing outside the bathroom, holding hands.

Officer Wowreit stood with them, his hand on Maret's shoulder. He had brought a doctor.

From inside the bathroom, they could hear sounds of distress. They could hear Leena coughing and vomiting. They could hear the running of water and the occasional flush of the toilet.

'Are you sure you don't want to wait downstairs?' Officer Wowreit asked.

'No,' said Maret.

'Come on, let's get you something to eat and drink while we're waiting.' He started to lead them away. Like retrievers waiting outside a house for their owner, they shrugged him off. He tried again. 'Come on ... come on ... you'll feel better with something to eat inside you. I promise.'

From within the bathroom, they could hear the low tones of the doctor. They then heard their mother sobbing.

'I know it sounds worrying, children. It's not nice to think of your mother like this; hear her like this. But the important thing is that she is responding to treatment. It's not good for you to listen to it all. Come on. Let's go back downstairs. Please.'

Maret thought about it. 'Come on,' she said to Juhan. 'Maybe it is best ...'

They allowed themselves to be led downstairs.

Over an hour later, the children were still to be found sitting at the kitchen table. Officer Wowreit was still with them. They sat there in complete silence. Occasionally, Officer Wowreit would offer them an encouraging smile, to which they did not respond.

There was movement upstairs; a creak on the landing.

The children jumped up and ran into the hallway. Wowreit followed.

The doctor was bringing Leena downstairs. She was wrapped in a blanket. The children reached up to help her down the final few steps, and the whole party moved into the lounge. The doctor settled Leena back into the armchair.

'How is she, sir?' asked Wowreit.

'The important thing,' the doctor said, 'is that Mrs Kotkas does not go to sleep. Not for a few hours at least. Perhaps she could have some strong black coffee to help keep her awake.'

'I'll make that,' said Wowreit, and returned to the kitchen.

'Children,' said the doctor, 'let your mother rest. However, if she looks like she's about to drop off to sleep, you must get her to her feet and walk her around the room – can you do that for me?'

'Yes,' said Maret.

Juhan nodded.

'And then let her sit for a while, give her some more coffee, talk to her.'

'What about?'

'Anything. Just so long as you talk – and make sure she answers you, all right?'

'All right.'

He went into the hall and put his hat and coat on. 'I'll be back in the morning to see how things are.'

'You are not leaving?' said Juhan.

The doctor took out a notepad and tore off a sheet of paper. He took out a pen and wrote. 'This is my name and my telephone number. Call me if you need me. All right?'

'All right,' the children said.

The doctor left and they went back to sit with their mother.

'You go to bed, Juhan. I'll look after her,' said Maret.

'No, I want to stay with you. With Mother.'

'All right, then. But go and get a blanket and lie on the couch.'

Juhan got two blankets and gave one to his sister.

Shortly after, Officer Wowreit appeared with a cup and some coffee in a jug. 'Here you are, enough to be going on with. It's real – not ersatz, thankfully. There is a pot on the stove keeping warm if you need more.' He looked down at the children and smiled. 'Don't worry, your mother will be all right, I'm sure. Especially with you two looking after her.' He headed for the hall.

'Are you going, too?' said Maret.

'I have to. I have other things I need to do. Police work.'

'Will you come back?'

'I'll drop by later, when I am doing my rounds. I promise.'

He left them to their long vigil.

For Maret, the night seemed like it would never end. Juhan eventually fell asleep on the couch so she let him rest. She took it upon herself to walk her mother around the room on her own. Round and round on the same stretch of carpet, hour after hour; she got to know the pattern off by heart. She made sure her mother drank all the coffee that was available and scolded her if she refused. She talked to her. About home, about Estonia, about the snow in winter and Vasalemma in spring and summer, when her father took them all sailing from Haapsalu to Saaremaa island. Sometimes, her own head would sag, but she would snap back upright before she dropped off completely. When she wasn't talking to her mother, or forcing her to drink coffee, or walking round and round on the carpet with her, she would say to herself: *When are we going home? Where's Father?*

Just as it was getting light, there was a knock at the door.

'Juhan ...? Juhan ...?'

'Hmm? Yes? I was asleep ... sorry ...' He yawned and stretched.

'There's someone at the door. Go and see who it is.'

Juhan threw off his blanket, stretched again and shivered. He went to the front door and opened it.

'Good morning.' Officer Wowreit was standing there. A woman stood beside him.

'I'm just about to go off shift. I thought I'd stop by and see how things are.' He and the woman, closely followed by Juhan, went into the lounge. 'How is your mother?' he said to Maret.

'We've been walking a lot. She has drunk all the coffee you made. But I've kept her awake.'

'Excellent. Well done, young lady.'

The woman with Wowreit went to Leena's side, took her hand and patted it. 'How are you feeling, Mrs Kotkas?' she said.

'This is my wife,' said Officer Wowreit. 'She wanted to come and help.'

'I think, Erwin,' said Mrs Wowreit, 'Mrs Kotkas is well enough to go to bed and get some sleep, now. Would you like that, Mrs Kotkas?'

Leena nodded.

'What do you think, children? Is it time for her to go to bed?'

'But the doctor said ...'

'The doctor said that you needed to keep her awake for a few hours. It's been all night. I am sure it is safe enough to let her rest, now,' said Wowreit.

'Let me take you upstairs and get you ready for your nice bed, my darling,' said Mrs Wowreit. 'And, children, perhaps you should get to bed, now, too. Don't worry, I'll be here.'

'No,' said Maret.

'Whyever not?'

'It's a school day. We have to go to school.'

'I'm sure school would understand. Erwin – that is to say – Officer Wowreit will go and tell them, won't you?'

'Of course.'

'We don't want anyone to know,' Maret said to him. 'We don't want to be treated differently.'

'I wouldn't tell them exactly why you weren't at school. I would just tell them your mother's unwell and you have to look after her.'

'No,' said Maret, 'the same. Everything must go on exactly the same. Come along, Juhan – let's get ready to go.'

IX

Miss Sperling walked up to the front door and knocked. The door was so old and had been so little cared-for in recent years that it rattled on its hinges. A woman opened it. 'Good afternoon,' Miss Sperling said, and announced herself. Then she asked, 'Mrs Kotkas, I presume?'

'No, I am Mrs Wowreit. Mrs Kotkas is sleeping. Hello, Maret. Hello, Juhan.' She smiled at the two children standing with Miss Sperling on the doorstep. 'Come in.'

Miss Sperling entered along with the children.

'May I ask who you are, please?' said Mrs Wowreit, standing halfway down the hall as if to say to the visitor: *Thus far and no further until I know your purpose.*

'I am a teacher at the children's school.' She took off her hat. 'Are you a relation?'

'No.'

'Housekeeper?'

'No, they've had to let the housekeeper go. Or, rather, I suggested Mrs Kotkas let her go. The woman was precious little use, to be honest. No, I am ... you might call me a neighbour. I have just come to ... help out for a while.'

'Is there a problem?'

'Children – go into the kitchen and get yourselves some milk and biscuits. They are all ready for you.'

The children went. Mrs Wowreit invited Miss Sperling into the lounge.

They sat, backs straight, hands on knees; strangers circling one another, looking for a weakness.

'You asked whether there was a problem,' said Mrs Wowreit.

'I found Maret sleeping at her desk. Three times. On Young Maidens Group evenings, they work and drill them pretty hard, which sometimes has this effect at school the next day, but last night wasn't a Young Maidens night. So I thought I'd bring the children home and see whether ... well, you know the rest.'

Mrs Wowreit considered the rather angular woman opposite for a moment before she spoke. 'May I speak confidentially?'

'Of course.'

'My husband is a local police officer. He was called here last night because the children's mother had ... well, let's say, "some difficulty". I took it upon myself to keep alongside them until things sorted themselves out.'

'Ah. I see. Very kind of you.'

'They have not had a very easy time of things, by all accounts. I don't imagine, as foreigners, they've had much of a welcome. I know they've been investigated thoroughly, for example.'

'And cleared?'

'Yes. Officially declared ...' Mrs Wowreit allowed a satirical note to creep into her voice '... pure Nordic stock.' She immediately regretted it. She hoped the woman opposite hadn't noticed.

'So, they are not ...?'

'They are not anything. Just a couple of innocent children and a troubled mother. Why? Did you think there was more to it than that?'

'No ... I just ... wanted to be sure, like you, that they would not be forced to endure more than they have to date.' *What is this woman hiding? What are the family hiding? It is most unusual, after all, that they are here. Allowed to stay here. And the children? They don't have to do half the things the other children in Königsberg have to do to help the war effort. And as for the mother ... well, yes, she is unwell, but nonetheless, every*

Königsberg mother should do something for the war effort, shouldn't they? She can't be that indisposed, surely?

Mrs Wowreit, still as a millpond, gave a cool smile and held it there. She had learnt from her husband that the children and their father had been informed upon. While, of course, she told herself, such matters were much the case these days, it still seemed sad to her that innocents were caught up in politics in such a way. She also found she was not entirely comfortable with people who took it upon themselves to inform on others. For whatever supposedly righteous purpose. She wondered at that moment whether this teacher in front of her was the reason the children and their father had been summoned to be scrutinised. To her mind, it was unreasonable that friends and families were required to inform on one another. Even children at school, or in their youth groups, were taught to do so. One casual anti-State, anti-Leader remark could turn a person's life completely inside out. Not that she told anyone how she felt. She could not even confide in her husband. He might understand; he might even agree with her, for all she knew. But his job as a policeman meant that she could not risk sharing those particular thoughts with him. And, even if she did, it would either put him at risk or in the impossible position of having to decide what to do with his own wife.

She studied Miss Sperling, who returned the steady look. *She means well, this teacher*, thought Mrs Wowreit. A genuine concern for the children. But over the years she had learnt that the kind-hearted often made the greatest tell-tales. They didn't mean to, of course. They just talked and enquired and persisted in following things up. A lack of simple common sense, perhaps. Eagerness to be nice at the expense of thinking through the consequences. Then again, it could just as easily have been someone else. The neighbourhood was riddled with gossip; such were the times in which they lived.

'Would you like a coffee?' She broke the spell with a courtesy. 'Do you take milk?'

They sat and drank their coffees with a studied formality which neither of them was willing to break.

'You must, of course, inform the father of the situation,' said Miss Sperling. *Can't they see what's going on? The daily influx of wounded and refugees? The increase in rationing? The need for clothes, and especially warm coats, to be sent to the Eastern Front? So much needs to be done and here is this family, somehow immune from anything. Not even the police seem to have done much. Especially not this woman's husband, clearly. Even though I'd given them a good steer in their direction, nothing really has happened. At least, as far as I could tell from what the children said. I couldn't ask them directly, of course. That would only alert them to the fact that I have my doubts about them.*

'I have made every effort to contact the father. But, as you may imagine, since he is on active service, it is a little difficult to reach him,' said Mrs Wowreit.

'Where have you tried? Perhaps I might help.'

'That is very kind of you. However, as you may imagine, my husband, as a police officer, is suitably well connected. I asked him to trace their father's whereabouts and obtain, if humanly possible, a telephone number.'

'Ah. And did he manage this?'

'Yes, about an hour ago. He dropped it off here as he went back to work.'

'Have you tried to call?'

'I have.'

There was a pause.

Mrs Wowreit appeared reluctant to continue, so Miss Sperling said: 'May I ask the result of that call?'

'As their teacher, I am sure it is right and proper that you do. I was just considering whether I am in a position to tell you. He is on active service after all. I am not sure, these days, what would be considered confidential information and harmful to the State if released, and what would be simply statements of fact that would not put our country at a disadvantage.'

Miss Sperling lifted the cup to her lips and held it there while she surveyed the woman opposite. *Every good German needs to be vigilant. Including you. That's what the authorities say. Everyone must play their part. Victory will be ours if we all work together. For the Fatherland.* 'You must do as you see fit,' she said, allowing the cup to clink back into its saucer.

'Suffice it to say, they were unable to connect me with the father directly. He was, they said, engaged on a matter of significance and could not be disturbed. So I spoke with his office. Or, rather, I spoke with the people I was put through to and who answered on his behalf. They did not, I feel, seem very pleased that I had got through to them at all. They were very, well, *cagey*, I suppose is the word.'

'Understandably.'

'Indeed. A strange woman ringing out of the blue and asking after one of their officers on what was, I imagine, a classified telephone line. However, I established that they were in a position to take a message and, importantly, act upon it. As a result, I informed them of the very basic facts of the children's mother's indisposition. I then made it quite clear that, in my view, the father needed to return as a matter of urgency to minister to his wife and family.'

'Ah. I doubt they responded with any great enthusiasm.'

'Why do you say that?'

'Well, if he is engaged on a matter of significance, I can understand that they would be most reluctant to allow him home ... How many others would need to do this?'

'I quite agree, although ...' Mrs Wowreit was about to expand on the nature of Mrs Kotkas's indisposition but decided it was none of the teacher's or the school's business. She veered away from what she was going to say. '... although

112

it is a shame.' She got to her feet. 'But, I have left a message in the right place, and doubtless the father will make his own decision. Now, I am sure you have much to do – these are very complicated times, not least for teachers ...'

Miss Sperling put down her cup and saucer and stood also. She followed Mrs Wowreit into the hall and allowed herself to be handed her hat.

*

'Miss Meyer ...?' Canaris was standing in the doorway to his office. 'Come in here, would you? Right now, please.'

'Yes, sir?' She followed the Admiral and closed the door.

'Did I hear you trying to arrange travel to Königsberg for Commander Kotkas?'

'Yes, sir.'

'But he has been.'

'This is another trip, sir.'

'On his instructions?'

'No, sir. I was arranging this on his behalf. It seemed to be urgent. I have not spoken to him yet. One of the girls took a telephone call from someone looking after his family. As it seemed to be urgent, I thought I would get things ready for him, so as to save time. Apparently, his wife has had some kind of crisis and—'

The Admiral held up a hand. She stopped in mid-flow.

'Miss Meyer. You clearly have not noticed, but the entire world is in some kind of crisis. I recommend you drop the whole matter and get on with the work in hand. I also recommend – no, let us make this an order – I order you not to tell the Commander. I cannot have the man further diverted from his most urgent task.'

'But, Admiral—'

'Have you any idea how much work he has to get through, Miss Meyer? He's a week late starting as it is. Meanwhile, the Leader is quite insistent that his Great Adventure begin as soon as possible. Indeed, the great man is even now sitting at his desk drumming his fingers.'

'But, sir—'

'No, Miss Meyer. It is an order.'

'Yes, sir.'

'Now get back to your own work, please.'

'Yes, sir ... I apologise if I ...'

'It is understood. And the Commander is under no circumstances to be made aware of whatever situation his wife may – or may not – currently find herself in. She is, no doubt, a grown woman and capable of ordering things herself.'

'Yes, sir.'

She turned to go, but then turned back.

'May I speak freely, sir?'

'Always.'

'May I go, sir?'

'Where? Königsberg, you mean?'

'Yes, sir.'

'Why?'

'Well, sir ... I believe in the cause, of course I do. I believe in our country. I am dedicated to victory. But, well, perhaps I can put it this way ... my father was a great and honourable man.'

'Surgeon-general in the Prussian Army, no less. What of it?'

'A decent man, sir. In the midst of the horror and chaos of war, he remembered he was a human being among other human beings. He taught me this. Care, compassion and dignity must be maintained at all costs; even in times when, for survival, we feel we are forced to be inhuman.'

Canaris walked over to the window and looked out. 'This, I, too, was taught by my father. To cling on to humanity even in the midst of madness – this is the real glory of war.'

'If I am able to reassign my work among the others, sir, may I take a few days' leave to go and see this family?'

The Admiral turned and settled his clear blue eyes upon her.

'You've been with me from the start, Miss Meyer. You are diligent, loyal. You are here sometimes before I arrive, and often long after everyone else is gone. I can't recall you having taken any leave ... Very well. Four days. Do what you can.'

'Yes, sir.'

'And not a word to the Commander about this.'

'No, sir. Thank you, sir.'

'No, Miss Meyer – thank *you*.'

*

Officer Wowreit came to collect his wife. He stood in the entrance while she put her coat and hat on. They'd been together five years now; no children. He didn't know whether that was his fault or hers. He tried not to think about it. He loved her and that was that. In some ways, she'd rescued him. Turned his life around. On the farm, out in Masuria among the lakes, he'd grown up fourth of six children. All boys. All he'd known was the dawn-to-dusk labour and the leather-belted thrashings from his father's stubby hands. Bullied at school for being useless at sports. Earning countless beatings from teachers for subsequent mischief, lack of intellectual prowess and rebelliousness. Something about the injustice of it all led him to seek sanctuary in the Königsberg police service, as soon as he was old enough. Something about the uncomplicated task of upholding the law; not having to use his imagination or his initiative too much. Just do the job.

He might still have made a mess of that, too, had he not met her. He was still angry in those days. About anything and everything. She was working in a haberdasher's at the time. He'd been called to a case of shoplifting; a bolt of silk secreted under a coat. Some folk were so poor back then in the Great Depression that they'd steal anything if they could sell it for a crust. She was his witness. But it became more than that. She saw something in him that no one else had ever seen. She had looked beneath the troubled exterior and seen a kind and gentle soul. She'd made it her life's work to bring that out.

He watched her put her hat on. Those pretty slim fingers patting her soft brown hair into place. That one curl that refused to be tamed.

He had no idea what she believed in, though; apart from him, that is. If he could, he would have loved to talk about how he despised the 'other police' as he thought of them. The agents of a corrupt and brutal regime. Not really police. You could get to high office in that lot simply by being a loyal member of the Party. He longed to talk about all that with his wife: the way those awful people went about things, the unlawful things they got away with. But he couldn't be sure how she might react. She might have informed on him. She might have him thrown into prison. Above all, in the midst of all this madness, that would be the worst thing of all – to lose her. They belonged together. They shared everything together. Well, *nearly* everything in these complicated times.

Mrs Wowreit gathered up her basket and called back into the house.

'Mrs Kotkas?'

The reply came from the lounge. 'Yes?'

'I am going now. My husband is here. I will get some shopping for you. Will you be all right?'

Leena came to the door of the lounge. She was wrapped in a shawl and was holding on to the wall. 'Yes. I'm fine.'

'I shall be back in the morning first thing. To make breakfast. Dinner is all washed up and tidied away. You are not to do anything, just rest. Do you understand?'

'Yes. Thank you, Mrs Wowreit. Thank you for all that you have done.'

'We all must muddle through, Mrs Kotkas. What is the point of anything unless we muddle through together?'

'I know.'

Maret came downstairs.

'Are you going?'

'Yes, Maret.'

The feeling of insecurity leapt up within her. She was being left alone with her mother; the way her mother was, how she had been behaving, what she had tried to do. But Maret also knew that Mrs Wowreit couldn't stay, much as she longed for her to do so. She didn't belong there. No one belonged there. Not even Maret, her mother and brother. It was horrible there. It was horrible everywhere.

Mrs Wowreit could see something of the concern on the little girl's face. 'Don't worry. Your mother is fine. And I'll be back first thing in the morning.'

Officer Wowreit, eager for his supper, took his wife's basket and started to lead her away. 'I am so glad you are all right, Mrs Kotkas,' he said. 'And you, Maret, you are a very special young lady.'

The girl could not help herself. 'You are only being nice to us now because you have found out that we're not Jewish,' she said.

'Maret!' said her mother.

'It's all right, Mrs Kotkas. She's upset. Of course she is,' said Mrs Wowreit. She knelt in front of the child and swept the fringe from her forehead with her fingertips. 'You are not to worry, all right? I will be here tomorrow. Everything will be all right, you'll see. Now, make your mother, your brother and yourself a nice warm milk and honey and settle down in front of the fire I lit. Read a nice book. I saw some in the lounge. Soon, you'll be in your nice warm bed and, before you know it, it'll be morning and I'll be back. All right?'

Maret pulled away. 'You aren't my mother.' She took Leena's hand. 'She's my mother.'

'Yes, she is. And she's a lovely mother. You look after her,' said Mrs Wowreit, and she and her husband left.

'Come on, darling,' said Leena, 'let's go back into the lounge and sit by the fire. Where's Juhan?'

'Upstairs, playing.'

'Good. Let's leave him to his games. You can tell me how school was today.' She put a hand on her daughter's shoulder for support, and they made their way back into the lounge.

Maret and Leena sat before the hearth, in silence. Neither felt able to talk about what had happened the night before.

Maret was afraid that whatever did happen might happen again that night.

Leena, if she was honest with herself, was afraid, too.

After a moment, Leena beckoned to her daughter. She stepped across and allowed herself to be folded together with her mother into her blanket. They sat hugging and saying nothing until it was time to go to bed.

*

'Miss Sperling?' The teacher was preparing for the next class.

'Yes, Principal?'

'There's a gentleman here to see you. You may use my office.'

The gentleman was young and thin with a suit that seemed to date from the Great Depression; possibly his father's. He turned a sorry grey hat between bony fingers. He was the best the local security police had available. His carefully manufactured indifferent appearance, though, belied his alert mind. He introduced himself as Ascher.

'How may I help you, Mr Ascher?' asked Miss Sperling, after they had sat down and he had shown her his identity disc.

'Rather – how may *we* help *you*? Since you called us.' It had been convenient that the teacher had telephoned earlier that week. It enabled them to put the blame of instigating this investigation on her. Even though they'd had a similar call from Berlin to look into things with these children and their parents. But they'd been instructed to do it without alerting them – or anyone – to the fact. Here was the opportunity.

'Oh – about the two foreign children?' said Miss Sperling.

'Yes, the Estonians, I think you said. I wondered whether I might have a little chat with them – here – before they return to your classroom from their break.'

She longed for more details. Such visits weren't usually made at school. Usually, she understood, they were conducted at the suspects' home. And not in the middle of the day. At least, initially. She knew only too well, however, that it was best not to question the security police; simply give them what they wanted and do it cheerfully, in the service of the State. 'Of course,' she said, and went off to bring them.

*

There was a tap on the lounge door.

Leena was drowsing on the couch in half-light; the curtains drawn. The wireless was playing Bruckner's *Seventh*. She turned it off, sat up and pulled her shawl further around her. 'Yes?'

'Mrs Kotkas?'

'Yes?'

'Forgive my intrusion. The front door was not locked. I had knocked, but there was no answer, so I took the liberty …' The woman on the couch just blinked at her with drooping eyelids. So she continued. 'My name is Emilie Meyer.' She took off her gloves and held out a hand and shook Leena's, which was soft and quite unresponsive. 'I am from Berlin. From your husband's office.'

'Oh,' Leena said. She dabbed a little moisture from the corner of her mouth with her handkerchief; too much laudanum. 'Is he all right?'

'Yes. He is fine.' She stood looking at Leena. 'May I sit?'

'Oh yes. Yes, of course. Please.'

Emilie sat. Leena struggled to gather her wits.

'Would you like some coffee?'

'That would be nice, thank you.'

Leena tried to get up.

'Please – let me do it. Is the kitchen through there?'

Leena waved a hand. 'No, it is quite all right. I shan't be a moment ...'

She heaved herself from the couch and, steadying herself on the furniture, made her way to the kitchen.

Emilie looked around her. The room was decorated with faded green-striped wallpaper and drooping chintz curtains. Leena's couch needed re-upholstering. The cherrywood dresser and dining table over in the corner, too, had seen better days. There were portraits and silhouettes on the wall of, Emilie imagined, family members belonging to the previous owners of the house or the present landlord. Of personal items connected to Commander Kotkas and his family, Emilie could observe none. A spent lily of the valley sagged on an occasional table in the corner.

In due course, Leena returned with a tray. She handed a cup to Emilie and sat back on the couch. The process of preparing the drinks had helped to lift her from her listlessness. 'Do you bring some news perhaps? Of Hendrik?' she said.

'Not really, I'm afraid. As I am sure he told you, his work is of supreme importance to the State and our Leader. It is consequently highly confidential.'

'Oh. So why are you here?'

'Ah. Well ... as his work is so vital to our undoubted victory, he was unable to come to see you – much as he would other-wise have wanted to. I mean – bearing in mind your indisposition.'

Leena pulled her shawl tightly around her shoulders. 'And ...?'

'I volunteered to come on his behalf. To bring you word of his care and concern for your and your family's well-being.'

'I beg your pardon?'

Emilie was taken aback by this sharp response, but pressed on. 'You see, he really would rather be here, but his duties made it impossible, so—'

'He told you to say this?'

'No. I am just trying to convey—'

'And why did he send you?'

'He didn't send me. I volunteered to come and—'

'He didn't send you? You mean ... does he know you are here?'

'Well, to be honest, no. You see, his duties are such that—'

'Sorry to interrupt ... but are you telling me he doesn't even know you are here?'

'Mrs Kotkas. Please don't exercise yourself. It was just a simple courtesy. He was tied up, you have been in difficulties, I had a few days' leave, so I thought I would come here and see that everything was all right. If there is anything I can do for you and the children.'

She didn't tell her the real reason she had come. She hadn't even told the Admiral. In some ways, she wasn't even admitting to herself why the plight of this family had touched her. Why it had reached down into the parts of her own story she had learnt to bury and keep buried ever since she was eight years old. Even then, at a moment when she could have explained more fully her purpose for being there, she decided such things were better off remaining submerged. She placed her hands on her knees, one on top of the other, and just looked as benign as she could.

Leena broke the silence. 'Who are you? Have you come to spy on us? Are you here to report back to your masters on the condition of the Commander's family perhaps? What is this all about?'

*

'Would you like a fruit bonbon?' The young man offered Maret and Juhan a boiled sweet each from a paper bag. The children took one each. 'Strawberry, I think. They're delicious,' he said. 'My mother made them by hand. Enjoy. Do, please sit. Make yourselves comfortable.'

They sat. He swung the principal's chair round from behind the desk to be closer to them. He sat, leant back, crossed his legs and grinned at them. 'My name's Ulrich. Remind me again, what's yours?'

'Juhan.'

'And yours?'

'Maret.'

'Juhan and Maret. Excellent names. How are you enjoying the bonbons? Delicious, right? Did I tell you my mother made them? She's clever, isn't she? Does your mother make sweets? Does she make them as good as this? I'm sure she does.'

'I don't know if Mother has ever made us sweets, has she, Maret?'

Maret, struggling to keep the large bonbon in her mouth, shrugged.

'Ah, well, perhaps she's very good at other things. I am sure she is. What does she do again?'

'She doesn't do anything, does she, Maret? She's just a mother.'

'No such thing as just a mother.' The man beamed at them again. 'Mothers are very special. They look after you, make sure you are fed and properly clothed, give you cuddles when you are sad, and bathe your cuts when you hurt yourself, don't they?'

'Who are you?' said Maret, pulling the sweet out of her mouth in order to speak, then replacing it.

'I am a friend of the school,' he said. 'I know Miss Sperling and, as you can see, I even know the principal. So you can have no worries on that score.'

'What score? What's a score, Maret?'

'I mean you needn't worry about who I am. I'm a very likeable chap, as you can tell. And as, I am sure, your mother and father are, too.'

'Mother's not a chap,' giggled Juhan.

'Quite right, young fellow. You've caught me out there. So ... if your mother is very busy being Mother. What about your father? What does he do?'

'He's in the navy,' said Juhan.

'Ooh,' said the man, 'I'm very impressed. A hero.'

'Yes.'

'And, what does he do in the navy?'

'We don't know, we just know he is in the navy.'

'Hasn't he told you what he does?'

'We don't see him much,' said Maret, getting the sweet under control. 'And when we do, we just talk about family things. We never talk about his work.'

'Ah. Well, that's understandable. He doesn't want to talk about boring things. He wants to talk about fun, exciting family things. Is he visiting now?'

'No,' said Juhan. 'He had to go away. He went away very quickly. He didn't even say goodbye. Some men came to collect him and took him away. I was very sad. But Mother says she got a message from him to say he was safe and well.'

'Good. Good. Glad to hear it. So, tell me ... when he was visiting, apart from those two men, did he meet with anyone else? Did any of his friends come to your house to see him?'

'I don't think so, do you, Maret?'

'Karl,' said Maret.

'Karl?' said the man.

'Yes,' she said. 'He's at school here. He wants to join the navy, too. He came to meet our father.'

'He told us about the groups we could join. He said we'd like it. And we do.'

'Ah, the Young People's Group and the Young Maidens, you mean?'

'Yes.'

'I hope you are learning lots of good things. I hope you are paying attention.'

'We are.'

'Good. I should like to meet this Karl. He sounds like a fine fellow. Perhaps you could introduce me to him. School will be finishing soon.'

'Of course,' said Juhan.

'Anyone else meet with your father?'

'No. He was only with us a short time. No one else came.'

'I see. Well, I suppose, as I say, he was happy just to be with you.'

'We were happy to be with him, too. We were very sad when he went,' said Juhan. 'Mother was especially sad. She got so sad she was very ill.'

Maret swung a foot at her brother. 'Don't talk about that.'

'Talk about what?' said the man.

'Nothing,' said Maret.

'The doctor came,' said Juhan.

'Oh dear. Which doctor was that?'

Juhan told him.

*

Although it was bright outside, the living-room curtains being drawn meant inside it was in a kind of perpetual twilight. Somewhere, Emilie could hear a clattering of jackdaws as they squabbled and swooped onto the next patch of ground to scavenge.

Leena poured some water into a glass from the jug that was constantly at her side. She took a sip. 'Miss Meyer. You are young and well meaning, I do not doubt. Please do not think that I am ungrateful to you. I recognise that you went out of your way to come here and thank you for your trouble. But, really, what business is any of this of yours?'

'I just thought ... well, I might come and help around the house. For a day or so. Put things straight that you might need putting straight. My father drummed into me the nature of service and the importance of serving others at whatever cost to ourselves.'

'We have someone who helps us. She is the wife of a local police officer. We have no further needs; they are all presently being met.'

'I am very glad to hear it.'

'But, tell me … I wonder … perhaps you have another motive, too.'

'I have not been sent by the State, as you implied earlier, if that's what you mean.'

'I do not mean that. I mean – do you have an interest in my husband?'

'I'm sorry. I don't quite follow.'

'Well, then, let me make it clear. And forgive my directness, but you will understand I have a certain interest in this matter, seeing as how I am the Commander's wife. I am also tired, unwell and in some pain. I therefore have very little time to be subtle or observe social niceties. In short – are you and my husband having an affair?'

Emilie stiffened. 'Mrs Kotkas. I am prepared, of course, to understand fully your unhappy circumstances and the difficulties you, your husband and your children have been forced to endure. I am therefore not proposing to take offence at your question. However, I will assert that I come from a decent German family of great integrity. I can therefore assure you that I have not the slightest interest in your husband. That is to say, other than to show him and you the proper courtesy and concern for his family's well-being. This visit was entirely of my own choosing. If it is not welcome, I quite understand.' She stood. 'And now, I think, it is best if I leave. I offer my apologies if I have in any way offended you.'

Leena studied her for a moment. It was a long searching look.

Emilie felt even more uncomfortable. Yet, she found she was unable to take her own eyes from the deep brown eyes that held her transfixed. There was something in their sadness that told her, despite what had been said, she should not leave. Not yet, at least. This woman was lonely, frightened, adrift. She knew something of how she must feel, from her experiences in her own family history. But still she believed it was not her place to mention this. It was, however, she knew, the real reason she felt moved to come and visit.

'Sit down again, if you will, Miss Meyer, and finish your coffee. And you must forgive me.' Leena smiled. Emilie sat. 'As I said, I no longer have the time or the inclination to observe the conventions of polite society these days. Once, back home in Estonia, perhaps, it was the be-all and end-all of my existence. This vile war, and my vile illness, however, has corrupted any sense of trust or respect for others I may once have held. I should also add that my question was understandable. Not least because, Miss Meyer, you are very pretty.'

Emilie stood. 'Mrs Kotkas. I am not sure—'

'Please. Sit. I mean nothing by it. I simply observe that you have been blessed with good looks. I was pretty once too, you know.'

'You still are.'

'Thank you for saying so, but you are just being polite. My husband certainly did think I was pretty once. I'm sure this was in part the reason why he married me. No – don't say anything … let me continue. There is something about you that reminds me of myself when I was your age.'

'I am sure I am not much younger than you are.'

'Young enough. But there is something in what you said, about your family, about decency and integrity, that chimes very much with my own family, my own upbringing. It is true, is it not, that how we came to be, what we are, is written not just in what we say or do but also runs through our very being like a watermark? I see something of me in your spirit. Yes, on reflection, I think I do understand your motive, your selflessness, in coming here. Would you care for more coffee?'

X

Emilie closed the door on Mrs Kotkas, who had fallen asleep on the couch. She had covered her with a blanket and was just leaving by the front door when the children appeared, coming along the road. They were accompanied by the thin young man with the shabby suit and a teenage lad.

'Hello,' said Emilie on the front step. 'Have you come to see Mrs Kotkas?'

'Yes,' said the young man. 'The children have invited me back to say hello. May I introduce myself? Ulrich Ascher.' He took off his shabby hat and made a stiff bow of the head. 'This splendid young chap is their good friend Karl.'

Emilie looked at the curious group. Something told her this was not really a social visit. Not, at least, from the spare young man.

'Mrs Kotkas is not really up to more visitors,' she said. 'I'm afraid I've rather tired her out.'

'Who are you?' Ascher said. He was smiling, but Emilie detected a little steel in his tone.

'My name is Charlotte Strunck.' She was using her safe name. All of the Admiral's staff were ordered to use one to improve anonymity and security when out and about. 'I just popped in to see Mrs Kotkas, and now I am on my way.'

'Where?'

'Back home.'

'Which is where ...?' Ascher persisted, smiling.

'Oh ... just around the corner,' she said, wafting a hand. This fellow was security police, she was sure of it, now. She only hoped he would not ask for her identity card. The false one; the Charlotte Strunck one. Which, nevertheless would plainly show an address in Berlin, not Königsberg.

Before he could ask a third time, she repeated, 'If you were hoping to see Mrs Kotkas, may I suggest you come back another time? She is really very tired.'

She was glad the children's mother actually was asleep. Too many lies, one on top of another, left too many cracks that could be prised open.

'Well, I'll just be a moment,' Ascher said. He made to go inside.

Emilie stepped across his path.

'I really do think you had best come back another time, Mr Ascher. Not to be rude, but I have just left her asleep. It's best not to disturb her. Really. Is that all right? I hope that's all right.'

Ascher hesitated.

Emilie wondered whether he was thinking about showing his identity disc and revealing who he was. He was perhaps calculating the advantages and disadvantages of doing so. His hesitation suggested that he had not let either the children or the teenager know who he really was, let alone his purpose for coming to the house to see Mrs Kotkas. The silence persisted just a few moments longer as the two of them stood on the doorstep, exchanging constant smiles.

'Oh well,' he said, finally, 'best not to disturb her if she's resting. You are quite right and weren't being at all rude.' He looked steadily at her. 'I can always come back another time.'

'Absolutely,' said Emilie. 'Come on in, children. I'll help you, since your mother's resting, if that's all right. I'll just do that and then get off home.'

The children, by now used to strange women taking charge of them, followed without a word.

Emilie shut the front door. She leant against it and let out the breath she'd been holding in during that confrontation. She went into a front room, pulled a curtain aside and, to her relief, watched as the man and the teenager walked off, deep in conversation.

'Who are you?' asked Juhan.

'Just a friend, Juhan. Just a friend,' she said.

'You don't need to help. I can look after us,' said Maret. 'Anyway, Mrs Wowreit will be coming soon. She said she would.'

Emilie looked down at the serious little girl. 'Of course,' she said. 'I'll just wait until Mrs Wowreit arrives, shall I? Then I'll be getting along.'

Mrs Wowreit arrived shortly afterwards.

'Hello. Who are you?'

'Are you Mrs Wowreit?'

'Yes. And you are?'

'A friend of the family. I came to see them on behalf of Mrs Kotkas's husband.'

'I see.' Mrs Wowreit nodded, then the light dawned. 'Ah! You are the woman I spoke to in Berlin when I called about Mrs Kotkas's difficulties.'

'Not me directly, but the woman you spoke to told me someone had rung.' Emilie smiled. 'So that was you, was it?'

'It was!'

'How wonderful to meet you. The Commander, I know, would be delighted that we met.' They shook hands. 'I hear from the children that you have been very kind. It seems to me that you have helped them and their mother through a very difficult time. I am sure the Commander will be very grateful.'

'Well, we all have to muddle through, don't we? Have you given the children something to eat?'

'No, they told me that you would do this. I didn't want to interfere. I am so glad that people find the time to be kind to one another in the midst of everything that is going on.'

'I agree.'

Emilie considered she could trust the woman standing before her. At least in part. 'May I speak plainly?' she said.

'Of course.'

'The children came back from school accompanied by a young man, rather shabbily dressed, it has to be said, and a teenager called Karl.'

'Ah yes, the children have spoken of Karl. They worship him, I think.'

'Perhaps. But it is the other one, the young man, Ascher, I wish to speak to you about. He is, in my view, security police. Now, I have nothing against him, of course. He is only doing his job for the good of the Fatherland. But I am not sure why he wanted to speak with Mrs Kotkas. And, of course, it is really none of my business. We must support the workings of the State wherever we can. However, I did not believe it was appropriate for him to speak with the children's mother at that time. I just wondered ...'

'Yes?'

'Should he return, which he may very well do, and if you are able, would you sit in with them while he interviews Mrs Kotkas? And, if I might suggest – though it is entirely up to you – would you assist her in her answers?'

'In what way?'

'Well, I doubt she shall say anything untoward, but if you could, would you help Mr Ascher understand that this family are entirely innocent and no threat to the State? Help him see that they are caught up in circumstances absolutely not of their own making. That would be wonderful.'

'I shall certainly try.'

'Thank you. And, one further request ...'

'Yes?'

'If you are willing, would you do the Commander a great service by reporting that conversation to me in Berlin?'

'If I am able to, I shall certainly try.'

'Thank you so much. And now, I think – seeing that the family are in such kind and capable hands – there is no longer any need for me to be here. I had intended staying a day or so longer, in case there was something I could do. But you have everything under control.'

'Please, don't leave on my account.'

'No, really ... I am so glad you are here to help. If there is anything you need, please don't hesitate to get in touch. I know you have the number.'

'I do. Although ...'

'Yes?'

'You still haven't given me your name?'

Emilie paused. Should she be Charlotte or Emilie? How much of a risk was it with this woman? After all, her husband was a policeman. Then again, she already knew quite a lot about her. Besides, whether she called Bendlerblock and asked for Charlotte Strunck or Emilie Meyer, either name would ultimately lead to her. Moreover, if any other person making enquiries was determined enough, and knew which levers to pull, they would track her down eventually.

It was also true, she wasn't sure why, that she wanted this family to know who she really was.

'It's Emilie. Emilie Meyer,' she said. 'However ...' she drew the woman closer to her '... I should be especially grateful if you did not mention me at all. While, of course, the children and Mrs Kotkas are likely to talk about me, I can trust, I believe, that no one outside this house should mention my name. Commander Kotkas is working on some extraordinarily sensitive matters – which is why he can't be here himself. Keeping my name, where I have come from, and where I work out of circulation would add a layer of useful protection. In fact, I suspect it would be best all round not to mention it to the Commander when he comes, either.'

'Really?'

'I am here on his behalf; it's just that he doesn't know I am. I just wanted to keep him from too much anxiety. He has quite enough to worry about.'

'I quite understand. I shall not mention you to the children unless they ask, and they shall soon forget you. Similarly with Mrs Kotkas. Least mentioned, soon forgotten.'

'Perfect,' Emilie said. She took Mrs Wowreit by the shoulders and brushed her cheek with a sisterly kiss. 'Take care.'

'You too.'

Emilie gathered up her things and left.

As she walked down the road, towards the taxis which would take her to the hotel and then the station, she could not help feeling a little regret. It was what that kind woman had said, which, without intending, hurt just a little. *I shall not mention you to the children unless they ask, and they shall soon forget you. Similarly with Mrs Kotkas. Least mentioned, soon forgotten.* For some curious reason, that even she could not at that moment fathom, she did not like the idea of this family so quickly forgetting her.

*

The Admiral was standing at his desk, slipping some papers into his briefcase. He hated the High Command daily briefings in Bendlerblock; they always made him nervous. Everyone was made to feel very stressed, no matter how high-ranking they were. The briefing sessions, without fail, left one afraid of saying the wrong thing; being put on the spot by the Leader; having to justify every last detail of decisions in front of the others; being subjected, almost invariably, to the suppressed sneers of generals who always wanted to give the impression they knew better than the others; competing for the Leader's approval.

'Come into the office, Miss Meyer. Shut the door. How did the visit go?'

'Well, thank you, Admiral.' Emilie recognised the familiar pre-High Command briefing tension in his voice; the clipped way he spoke on those occasions.

'Is there anything you particularly need to tell me?'

'Mrs Kotkas is struggling, but though her body is weak and the pain she suffers is evident, she has a strong spirit.'

'Not so strong a spirit, perhaps ... she wanted to end it all.'

'Perhaps I should have said proud.'

'Forgive me for being direct, but I ask for obvious operational reasons, did she give you any indication of her long-term health?'

'We did not discuss such things, sir. But, if you are worried whether she appeared to be on her last legs medically, I do not believe so.'

'And psychologically?'

Emilie shrugged.

'Very well. Let us hope.'

'For her husband's sake and her children's sake?'

'Of course.'

'There is, though, a matter which you should know about, sir.'

'Concerning the family or the Commander?'

'Ultimately, sir, the Commander. While I was visiting, someone from the security police tried to get in to see his wife. I daresay he was doing a little background digging.'

'For what purpose, in your view?'

'In my view, sir, for the purpose of ensuring the Commander is not a security risk to the Fatherland.'

'And you prevented this investigation?'

'Not directly, sir. Just staved it off.'

'Why?'

'I don't know, sir. I just feel we can trust the Commander to fulfil his duties, despite who he is, where he is from. He is important to the cause.'

'And what cause are we talking about?'

'The Fatherland, sir. Is there any other? Any interference to his work would be detrimental to it. Security reasons are security reasons. I don't deny it. But, surely, he is no risk, and the police should go after other prey.'

'That is your view, is it?'

'Yes, sir.'

'Did you express it to this security policeman?'

'Absolutely not. He did not disclose himself to me as to what he was.'

'And, I trust you did not disclose yourself to him as to who you were.'

'No, sir. According to standing orders.' She thought about how, though, she had introduced herself by her real name to the Kotkas family. She thought she had better not mention that to the Admiral.

'Very well,' he said, and clipped his briefcase shut.

'I thought you ought to know, sir.'

'Quite right.'

'Just in case there were any repercussions.'

'As you say. And, Miss Meyer ...?'

'Sir?'

'I think it best we don't worry the Commander about any of this. Your visit to his family, the policeman, any of it.'

'No, sir. Like you, I had decided that it would be for the best.'

'Very good.' He picked up his briefcase and with a suppressed sigh he left.

She went back to her desk. She hoped the Admiral had taken the hint. If anyone could intervene and squash any sort of investigation into Commander Kotkas or his family by the security police, the Admiral could. He left his office soon afterwards, holding his briefcase with its secret files inside under his arm; as if afraid it might escape.

Back at her desk later that morning, the phone rang.

'Someone called Ursula Wowreit to speak to you,' said the operator.

Emilie took a moment to recall who that was. 'Oh yes ... put her through, please,' she said.

'Hello?'

'Hello, Ursula, It's Emilie. How are you?'

'Well, thank you. You asked me to ring if someone came to see Mrs Kotkas.'

'Yes, thank you. Was it the gentleman I told you about?'

'By the description you gave me, yes. He came yesterday afternoon. Introduced himself as security police, showed me his identity disc, but I didn't see the name on it.'

'Ascher.'

He must have conferred with his superiors thought Emilie and decided that coming clean as to his role was the best option.

'I haven't had a chance to ring you since,' said Mrs Wowreit.

'No problem. Did you manage to sit in with him while he spoke with Mrs Kotkas?'

'No. He shut the door. But I did go in and ask Mrs Kotkas all about it after he left.'

'And?'

'Well, to be honest, I don't think he learnt anything. It was clear Mrs Kotkas was only too aware why he had come to speak with her. It seems she told him about their background, how they came to be in Königsberg, and what little she knew about her husband's work in Berlin. I think he went away basically empty-handed. I am sorry I can't tell you more.'

'That's fine, Ursula. You did very well and you have been very kind. I hope you didn't mind.'

'Not at all. It was all very exciting, really. A little bit of detective work to lighten my dull suburban day. My husband would be proud.'

'You didn't tell him?'

'Of course not. This is between us.'

'Between us. Exactly – thank you so much, Ursula.'

'If I hear anything else ...'

'Of course. Goodbye. Take care.'

'Goodbye.'

Emilie replaced the receiver. She thought she should be

more glad to hear that the security police's visit was wasted. But, somehow, she knew this would only annoy them. Increase their determination to find something – anything. The security police were, to her, the biggest concern. They were capable, if they put their mind to it, of conjuring something out of nothing. If people did something to threaten the well-being of the State, fair enough. However, even if people had done absolutely nothing, they could still be arrested. The sin of omission, the Church called it. And so did the security police.

She looked at her watch. Time for lunch.

She stepped outside the building to go to her favourite café. As she did so, she was stopped.

The man showed her his identity disc. Someone called Fischer of the security police; office address: Prinz Albrecht Strasse.

'May I have a word, please, miss?'

'Yes. What about?'

'Your recent visit to Königsberg.'

Emilie struggled to remain impassive. *How on earth did he know about that?* 'How may I help you?'

'Well, for a start, why did you lie to our officer?'

'Which officer? I didn't speak to any officer.'

Fischer gripped her arm. 'Oh, but you did, and you know you did. You resisted his legitimate request to enter a building and speak to the occupant. I could haul you off for that alone. However, you then proceeded to give a false name.'

'I did no such thing. You must be confusing me with someone else. Or, rather, your officer is.'

'Confusing you with whom? Charlotte Strunck? Which, as we know, was a lie. And, when our officer did finally get to speak with the occupant of the house, she confirmed that you are really Emilie Meyer.'

'Well,' Emilie said, unpeeling the man's fingers from her arm and dropping the hand as if she was discarding a soiled handkerchief, 'if you know my name, you will know where I work. If you know where I work, you will know that it is our duty to use aliases at all times to protect the confidentiality of our work. And, I repeat, I did not know who the man was who I spoke to at that house the other day. He did not identify himself and, I should also say, if he had done so, I would have cooperated fully with his requests – whatever they might have been. I should think, rather than accost me, you should have your officers review their procedures.'

'You should know better than to talk like that to a senior officer in the security police. You are just a secretary.'

Emilie laughed. 'Really? You think that? Well, if that's the level of research you people are capable of, we're in a lot of trouble. I am a little bit more than that. And I don't doubt I have a security clearance far higher than you'll ever have.'

Fischer snorted. Emilie wondered whether he might even be contemplating hitting her. But then he managed to restrain himself.

'So, let us explore those things my officer would have explored with you, had you had the courtesy to allow him a few moments of your time.'

'What things?'

'Let us begin with Commander Kotkas.'

'Who?'

'Miss, I am becoming very irritated. I promise you, if you continue to think you can play games like this, you will see how irritated I can get.'

'And you will see how irritated I can get. Let me make things clear. First, if you wish to interview me, you should go through the proper channels. Second, the proper channels involve applying directly to my boss, whom, since we are in the street among any number of people who have not been – you may notice – security cleared, I refuse to name or even hint at. However, you can be sure he will most probably make life very uncomfortable for you. Third, the reason I "play games", as you call it, is because I was confronted on a door-step in public by some stranger, the identity of whom he chose not to reveal. And now, if you please, I am confronted by you throwing names about on the street with no regard for the risks or security of our country. Fifth, in truth, I can't even be sure you are who you say you are. Those identity discs are notoriously easy to forge. In conclusion, Mr Fischer – if that really is who you pretend to be – it is you who should be reported, not me. And now, if you'll excuse me, I shall go back into my office and do exactly that. How's that for "irritated"?'

She turned around and went into the Bendlerblock. He didn't follow. Even someone like Fischer didn't have the level of clearance that would allow him past the guards. Once inside, and safely through security, she stopped and leant against a wall. She could not stop trembling.

*

Canaris returned from the briefing session an hour later. Emilie asked to see him the moment he appeared. He could see she was agitated, nodded and brought her into his office. She shut the door and, in a few brief sentences, related what had happened outside with Fischer. Expressionless, he picked up the phone. 'State Leader, please,' he said. There was a pause while the Admiral waited to be connected.

'Yes?' A smooth voice answered on the other end.

'Heinrich? Wilhelm. How are you? I just wanted to let you know of an incident that took place concerning one of my senior officers, by the name of Kotkas. Someone from Königs-berg's security unit has been pestering his wife and children. And now someone from my own office has been questioned in a very abusive way. As you know, and have agreed in the past, it is intolerable that my staff, even junior staff, should be harassed by members of one of the departments over which you have control. They are interfering with the work of the Intelligence Service. I request that they are informed as such, and asked to stand down from whatever investigation they have undertaken. Of course, I know, and you know, Heinrich, that it is vitally important for the cause that security police should use their imaginations. Unfortunately, sometimes, they can overexert those imaginations. Chasing shadows that simply do not exist.'

'Sometimes,' said the voice, 'it is a surprise they use their imaginations at all, Wilhelm.' They both laughed. 'I will see what I can do.'

'Thank you, sir.'

'You are welcome.'

*

'Fischer?'

'Boss?'

'Here a moment.'

'Yes, sir. What is it?'

'We've had a "Stop Notice". The Intelligence Service has been on to the State Leader about Kotkas and all he surveys. The State Leader has pronounced himself unhappy with what he hears regarding the way we are conducting our investigation. He has asked the chief to get us to close it down.'

'I see. So, what do you want me to do, boss?'

'Well, we have our orders. Drop the case.'

'Really?'

Fischer's boss gave him a look of irritation; he did not like his decisions being questioned. Fischer took the hint. 'We'll drop the case.'

'Good.' His superior paused. 'Then, open a new one.'

'Concerning what?'

'Concerning why the Admiral is so keen to prevent us from investigating Kotkas. Then … continue investigating Kotkas. Perhaps he is the key to that case. We're no longer investigating him; we're investigating the causes of him.

That is what I shall certainly argue should the Great and the Good get to hear what we are doing.'

'They won't hear it from me.'

'Just, for goodness' sake, keep a low profile, Fischer. It is far better no one finds out, rather than us having to answer a lot of inconvenient questions.'

'Right you are, boss.'

'Oh – and just so you know ...'

'Yes?'

'That's what the State Leader said, too.'

*

Kotkas was walking back from Friedrichstrasse station.

So it has begun, he thought. Reopening the channels of communication with Britain that he had established back in Estonia, through Tamm.

A contact of Plötz had given him another contact, which led to a further contact who introduced him to a dead letter box down by the station. A Swedish tailor who also cleaned clothes: suits, uniforms, evening wear. *The things people leave in the pockets of their overcoats these days. They'll forget their own heads next.*

Kotkas had started sharing information. Tentatively, to see whether the channels were still there at all. But he'd need to get more material to them. And soon.

And then ...? Time would tell.

The only question was – how much time did he have left?

XI

Marjorie Ellis was bored. She often found supper with friends boring these days. Not that she didn't like her friends. They were not dull as such, ordinarily. It was just, simply, since the war began, their conversation left much to be desired.

Their attitude towards her left much to be desired also. After all, weren't they all engaged in perfectly exciting things to do with the war effort? The male friends were all in the services, or the police, or wardens, or, at the very least, in thoroughly important reserved occupations of some kind or another. Her female friends had equally vital roles; working for the Women's Voluntary Service, or the Royal Arsenal, or down at Hawker's in Kingston helping to make Hurricanes.

Yet what was Marjorie? A typist. In a bank.

Money's important too, they would say, it seemed to Marjorie, somewhat patronisingly, though they didn't mean to be like that. *Without money, all our work couldn't go on. Marjorie's typing is fundamental to the success of the war. Outcome assured, thanks to Marjorie.* Or, at least, that's how it sounded to Miss M. Ellis, typist at Glyn Mills Bank, EC3.

She had to admit, she even looked the part. Tweed twin set, hair in a bun, tortoiseshell spectacles. Should any of her friends wish to describe her to anyone, she imagined they would use words like 'harmless', 'unassuming', or even 'slightly vague'. In a kind way, of course. They all liked her. They just didn't place her in the same exciting categories as they, with some justification, placed themselves, now there was a war on.

It was always the same whenever three or more of them met in the West End for supper before a show. Her friends would gather and be nattering in the restaurant, almost before they'd sat down. This would leave Marjorie, usually, sitting at the end of the table, polishing her spectacles. They would include her in the conversation when they could, of course, but she rarely had anything to say. Where the progress of the war was concerned, she was, frankly, woefully uninformed. Indeed, it was rare for her to even express an opinion. This was something everyone else around the table, Miss Ellis noted, was often keen to do.

Which is why she found them a little boring.

As for their opinions as to how the war was progressing and what was most likely going to happen next, they were particularly eager to share their views. Being in privileged positions in their various wartime occupations, of course, they made it clear they were a) extremely well informed and b) unable to speak too much about what they knew, owing to their privileged positions and the very real need for silence. *Walls have ears, you know.*

What little they were able to tell one another, and their views on the various critical events unfolding daily around a war-torn world, often caused Marjorie to twitch in her chair. It was clear, to her at least, that their various roles did not lead to them being as privy to great state secrets as they would like to think, nor as they sought to make out to one another.

Marjorie knew their knowledge and opinions in such matters were flawed for one very good reason. For, Marjorie, despite all appearances to the contrary, was not actually a mousy typist with dusty old Glyn Mills in the City. Far from it. She worked for MI6. Naturally, she could never tell her friends any of this. As far as they were concerned, she was just a minor functionary in a bureaucratic institution with very little to say for herself. Which was the way she liked it.

*

'May I come in, Commander?'

'Come in, Plötz.'

Kotkas was in his shirtsleeves. He was engulfed in paperwork and files. He rubbed his eyes, stretched and leant back in his chair.

'What can I do for you, Captain?'

'How are things here?'

'Getting busier by the minute. You?'

'Ditto. I need a breath of air. Care to join me?'

Kotkas put on his jacket, took up his cap and they walked out.

'Preparations are gathering pace, don't you think? Do we have a date yet?' said Plötz.

They were walking beside the canal.

'No. I can't imagine it's too far away, judging by the material that is being hurled onto my desk every ten minutes.'

Plötz lit a cigarette. 'What sort of material?'

'You know I can't tell you that. "No cross-referencing with other departments unless first passed across senior personnel's desk for approval". *Play by their rules. Their rules are what keep you safe.* That's what Tamm taught Kotkas all that time ago in Estonia.

'Sorry. You are quite right, of course. Protocols must be observed. Perhaps we might approach this matter in a different way. Perhaps, if I suggested something.'

Kotkas kept walking.

'Perhaps the enemy's equipment and deployment are not as ... robust ... as they appear to be on paper.'

Kotkas stopped. Plötz stopped.

Kotkas looked at Plötz. Plötz took one puff on his cigarette.

They both watched the smoke drift up into the trees. Birds sang.

Plötz waited, gazing across the canal as if admiring the view.

Ignore a detachment here; delete evidence of a supply

dump there? One anti-aircraft battery deficient in a given sector? *Could it be done?* wondered Kotkas. Could he give the impression that the Soviet forces ranged across Germany's Eastern front, in Poland, Lithuania, Latvia, were weaker than they actually were? Could he mismanage the interpretation of the intercepts that fell in flurries onto his desk? Or, rather, could he mismanage them sufficiently well that no one would suspect him? Give the impression that the reports he forwarded to the strategic planning groups were absolutely genuine? So genuine that the word mismanagement never entered their vocabulary?

How would he do that?

Why would he do that?

His one ambition was to return to Estonia. The only way he would do that, at present, was to work with the Germans and encourage them to invade Soviet-held territory. Certainly, a seemingly weaker Red front ranged against them would provide that encouragement. However, presenting weaker opposition might mean the German Army, when it rolled across the border, ran the risk of going in under-manned and under-resourced. That ran the risk of the German Army being held, then thrown back. Which, arguably, was Plötz's intention, and that of whoever was pulling his strings. Defeat by Russia at the first cast of the dice would undoubtedly throw the State's ruling elite into turmoil. Weaken their resolve – or, at least, weaken the resolve of the underlings, on whose unquestioning support the elite depended.

He was already trying the information-sharing route with the British – to see if that would work. Wasn't that enough? It certainly fulfilled his own purposes. Undermining the regime while helping him reclaim his homeland.

But to say no to Plötz would put Kotkas in an impossible position. Saying no would suggest to Plötz and his puppeteers that he, Kotkas, was at risk of betraying them. There's no telling what they might do if that was the conclusion they drew. The regime may be evil, but the forces opposing them were not averse to playing dirty, either. This was a struggle to the death for both sides in Berlin's hidden war.

Then, it came to him. He didn't need to say anything to Plötz, either way. All he had to do at that point was nod and tell him he would see what he could do. And that would be the truth. He would definitely see what he could do. *Stick to the truth wherever possible*, Tamm had told him. *And mean what you say.*

Kotkas looked at Plötz and nodded. 'I'll see what I can do,' he said.

*

It had been a good night. They'd had a lovely supper and enjoyed the show. Miss Ellis and her friends were standing outside the theatre in the West End saying their goodbyes.

'See you soon, darling.'

'Stay safe.'

'Don't do anything I wouldn't do.'

They all laughed, kissed one another farewell, and went their separate ways.

Marjorie Ellis walked down Shaftesbury Avenue until she was sure none of her friends were around. She then hailed a taxi. A black cab pulled up and sat there chuntering to itself while Miss Ellis took hold of the passenger door handle.

The British domestic intelligence service MI5 had only recently moved into new premises on St James's Street, which some units of MI6, including Miss Ellis's, had also started to use. All staff were under the strictest orders not to let anyone know their new location, for obvious security reasons. The building was opposite Boodle's, the exclusive London gentlemen's club. If they took a cab to get to the office, staff were instructed to ask the driver to drop them off at Boodle's, pay the fare, then let the taxi drive away before crossing the street and going into the building. Every single member of the security service did as they were told.

'Where to, miss?' asked the cabbie, assuming from the way Marjorie was dressed and her general demeanour that she was a spinster.

'Boodle's, please, driver,' said Marjorie. She shut the door and sat back as the taxi rumbled off.

A few hundred yards down the road, the taxi came to some traffic lights. They were red. While waiting to pull away, another taxi drew alongside. Miss Ellis's driver wound down his window and whistled to attract his colleague's attention.

The other cabbie wound his window down. 'Evening, mate.'

'Evening, pal. Here, I can't remember ... where's Boodle's, again?'

'Opposite MI5,' he said.

*

Kotkas was shown into Canaris's office.

'Sit down, please, Commander.'

Kotkas sat.

'You may have noticed a certain intensity around the department recently.'

'I have, sir.'

'I daresay you are aware why.'

'I am, sir. We're very close to initiating Barbarossa. All invasion units are assembled. Supply lines are just about set. Preliminary briefings are taking place.'

'It felt like this before Poland. It felt like this before France. Sniff the air, Kotkas. Smell the adrenaline.'

'Sir.'

'And you have your part to play in the Leader's Great Adventure, of course.' The Admiral spoke in a matter-of-fact way, as if ordering coffee. 'So let's pop you off to the Baltic, eh? As close as you can get to the Red Army. I need you to plant some facts, for me.'

'Facts, Admiral?'

'The Leader will shortly send a letter to Stalin. He will say that we have categorically no intention of invading. He will swear undying friendship. I need you to use your contacts to reinforce these facts.'

Kotkas took a moment to reply. 'What contacts?'

'Kotkas – this is why I've been protecting you.'

'Sir, you've been protecting me because of my specialist knowledge, surely. My role is to facilitate your Barbarossa preparations. To engage in intelligence gathering and interpretation.'

'That was the easy bit. Anyone could do that.'

'But they weren't doing it very well. I've had to sort out months of inefficiency and disorder.'

'You have been training others up as requested? Showing them your techniques? Creating methodologies?'

'Yes, sir.'

'So, you've created both the means and the momentum. The Leader, the German people and I are eternally grateful. But now we have reached the real reason we wanted you. Your dowry. Your network of contacts and agents back in the Baltic States. Come on, you think I didn't know it still exists? I am in intelligence, Commander. Credit me with a little of it. I've been an agent on the ground, myself. Spain in the last war. I haven't lost contact with my contacts. Neither have you.' He sighed. 'So ...'

'What is it you want?'

'Think of it as influenza. Infect your contacts. Spread the virus.'

Kotkas knew it was the hardest thing about counterintelligence work. Getting the enemy to receive a fragment of information was easy. Making it stick was another matter altogether. The enemy would look to have it confirmed by an independent source. It was therefore necessary to create that independent source. The enemy would then try and find out whether that independent source was really independent or whether the supposed information came from the same original source. To convince the enemy that what you were feeding them was genuine, backed up by a number of different sources, you had to create a labyrinth, then muddy the waters. You had to bury the original source so deep that no amount of digging would help the enquirer discover the truth or who planted the information there in the first place.

Canaris picked up a folder from his desk and began leafing through its contents. 'Well?' he said. 'Do you go, or do I wash my hands of you and leave you to the tender ministrations of our friends in Prinz Albrecht Strasse?'

'I go,' he said. He swallowed and spoke again. 'And then, of course, there's Britain.'

Canaris looked at Kotkas. 'You want to go there, too?' he smiled.

'No, sir. Give them some of the facts, too.'

'Which are?'

'That the build-up of troops and equipment on Germany's Eastern border is to protect them from Allied bombing. It is merely enabling structural and command build-up in safety, prior to the conquest of Britain. They might well pass it on, by whichever means available, to Stalin. What greater corroboration could you ask for than information coming from our Leader's enemies? An enemy with a sophisticated intelligence-gathering service.'

'Perhaps.' Canaris toyed with his fountain pen. 'How do you propose to do this?'

'"Think of it as influenza. Infect your contacts. Spread the virus", sir.'

'And you can do this?'

'Yes, sir.'

'Without compromising us? Without putting the whole of Barbarossa at risk?'

'I think so, sir.'

'You "think so, sir"? You'd better know so, sir. Too many

wars have been lost by people thinking but not knowing for sure.'

'It can be done, sir.'

'All right. But now comes the big question. You know the British better than I ...'

'I am sure, sir, that I do not—'

'Don't play games with me, Kotkas. I am not stupid. I am perfectly aware of your previous life. You know the British better than I. Will they believe what you tell them?'

'If I told them in a certain way.'

'Ah. These channels of communication, are they still open to you, too?'

'Yes, sir.'

Canaris's eyes narrowed. 'How do you know? Have you been using them recently?'

'No, sir.' Kotkas winced inwardly. This was a lie. *Stick to the truth wherever possible. Sorry, Tamm.* 'You are right, sir. I don't know. I only think I know.' *And mean what you say.*

'And how will you find out?'

'By trying them, sir. We'll know if they still exist if they act on any information I get to them.'

'Which we'll find out through our agents in Moscow.'

'Yes, sir.'

'All right. You have my permission to try. The information you are proposing cannot, ultimately, harm our enterprise. If it does harm it, we'll shut it down immediately and throw you into prison for treason.' Canaris said that as clearly as he could, so any listeners-in to the conversation in his office were aware this was not an attempt to betray the State. 'Understood?'

'Understood, sir. For me, however, the question is not whether the British will believe what we tell them, but whether Stalin will. If you ask me, the most important job, in an enterprise such as this, apart from planting the corroboration among people in the Baltic region is, of course, to make sure our own people hear it, think it, and believe it. In this case, the troops in the East.'

'Thank you, Commander. I think you'll find that's my job.'

'Sir.'

Canaris got up and rested on a corner of his desk. He leant forward and spoke in a low voice. The kind of low voice that meant any listeners-in on the outside would only hear a muffled conversation. Kotkas had to lean in to hear him. 'Listen Hendrik, it's not safe for you here anymore. While I appreciate your offer of contacting the British to help our cause, you perhaps do not realise the implications. You are being, and you will be, followed. They are constantly trying to find out what you are about. If you actually do manage to communicate with the British, they shall appropriate that method for their own reasons.' He moved away from the desk to look out of the window. He remained silent for a moment. And then spoke. 'When we first came here, we talked about how your usefulness is limited, didn't we?'

'Yes.'

He turned, and crossed his office, so he might continue to speak to Kotkas in low tones. 'Well, we may well have reached that limit. You have trained up sufficient operatives to learn how to interpret the intercepts. Once you connect certain interested parties also to the British, for their own purposes, that will suffice for them. They might not have even let you get that far, to be honest. Which is the reason I am suggesting you get out of the way, before they get you out of the way.'

'Why are you doing this for me, sir?'

'Because I sympathise with you. This is, as you said, not your fight. You are caught betwixt and between; your family even more so. If I can get you back to the Baltic – right now – you have, at least, a fighting chance.'

'But, surely, if they want me out of the way, they can do that up there just as easily as anywhere?'

'No. Because in the Baltic you might just have a level of

150

usefulness that is still of value to them.' Canaris went and sat behind his desk. His voice regained that ringing clarity that was his trademark. 'You have been to Finland, I assume, Commander?'

'Many times, sir.' Kotkas also lifted his voice.

'There's a unit of your countrymen being assembled there. They got out around the same time you did. As you know, there is no love lost between the Finns and the Reds. These Estonians are being trained up by the Finns. They don't know what for, exactly, yet. Maybe a raid or two into Russian-held Karelia. However, they are also being trained by a unit of our people. The plan is that they return to their homeland the moment we begin Barbarossa. Partisans. In short, they'll need someone to liaise with the intelligence officers. Someone who knows the Baltic and the Soviets.'

'I see.'

'I can argue your case, that you are that man. I can't promise, but it is the best I can do. And, who knows, if Barbarossa goes well, you and your Estonian comrades could soon be warming your toes at your own firesides again.'

'Thank you, sir.'

Canaris returned to his paperwork. 'Very well. That's all. You will stay in contact.'

Kotkas stood, replaced his cap and saluted.

'And, Kotkas ...'

'Sir?'

'No funny business. Remember whose side you are on. Which, I do not need to remind you, is the side keeping your family safe.'

Was that a threat or encouragement – or simply for the benefit of anyone who might just be listening in? Kotkas wasn't quite sure.

XII

In the youth group building, festooned with red, white and black banners, the children had sung their hearty songs and played their jolly games. They were now preparing to go home.

In the Young Maidens group hall, Maret's leader put an arm around her shoulder.

'How are you, my dear friend?' She was a lithe young woman with a milk-and-apples complexion.

Maret looked up at her. 'Thank you, well.'

'And how is your poor mother?'

Maret wished she hadn't confided in her the other day. But at the time she knew she had felt scared and unhappy. Mrs Wowreit was being as kind as she could, and was often 'just popping in' to see them, but she was, after all, a grown-up and a stranger. Grown-ups didn't understand, strangers should not be allowed to understand. And, of course, Juhan was next to useless when it came to discussing such things. Every time each evening, when they'd gone upstairs to their beds, she suggested he might go downstairs at some point and look in on their mother, all he would do was shrug and get on with some drawing, or playing with the soldiers he had made using sticks from the garden. She would have loved to ignore the fact that their mother had tried to kill herself, the way her silly brother did. But what if Mother tried again? She didn't want to think about that. The horrible thoughts came back again and again. Even in the middle of the night. Especially when the wind slammed at the rickety shutters. She hated it.

But she had to be strong. That's what her father had said to her. Practically the last thing he had ever said to her. She would be like the moss. She would cling on, even if there didn't seem to be anything to cling on to. But why did he have to go? Why didn't he say goodbye? *Why can't he be here so I don't have to look after Mother and my stupid brother?* It was hateful. And Mother wouldn't talk. Wouldn't tell her why she did it. Why would she want to die and leave them? Maybe it was her fault. Maybe she'd done something wrong. She had, whether she recognised it herself in her young mind, taken responsibility for the whole family, and her mother in particular.

That's what kept her awake at night: kept her tossing and turning. That's what made her feel lonely; made her want to run away and never speak to anyone again. But then, at least in the early days, after Mother's misery, she told her group leader. Well, her group leader had asked and, since she was really the first one to really seem to care, she felt she could share at least something of her loneliness. The group leader had told her that she would always be by her side; always ready to listen. She should think of her as an older sister, which, as the State was a wonderful family, she really was.

Then, as the days went by and, it seemed to her at least, Mother was not going to do anything again, her painful memories of that terrible night and the daily and nightly worries faded. Now, really, she didn't want to be reminded about it all. No matter how kind the group leader was trying to be.

'Mother's well,' she said.

'Does she still have her headaches? Is she still taking her medicine?'

She wanted to say, *What business is it of yours?* But, after all, hadn't she made it the group leader's business? 'She is taking her medicine,' she said.

'Good. And ... have you heard from your father?' the group leader said, in a way that seemed to her like she wasn't really interested. 'How is he? What is he doing these days? I've forgotten.'

'I told you the last time you asked. I don't know.'

'So you did. Well, I have to say, I quite understand that he is very busy and is doing some hugely important work for the State – you must be very proud of him – but we know, don't we? A good *German* father would keep in better touch.'

She thought of arguing this view with the group leader, but deep down, she felt the older girl had a point.

They had reached the street. A wind had got up. The blood-red banners slapped and tugged at their moorings, as though they were desperate to free themselves.

Karl was there with Juhan. He was waiting to walk them home. He had started to do this the day after their mother's incident; after he had walked off with that thin stranger who had tried to get in and see their mother.

She didn't notice the exchange of looks and the shrug and barely perceptible shake of the head from her group leader to Karl.

*

Marjorie took off her coat and got to work at her desk. Almost the first file she opened caused her momentarily to sit back and ponder its consequences.

At that moment, an army officer entered with a chap from the War Office on a fact-finding visit.

'Hullo, Ellis.'

'Major.'

The officer was a Scot from the Borders who, despite having lived in the grit and grime of London for two years, still managed to exude a whiff of hills and heather.

'This is a Mr Spencer from the War Office. On a fact-finding mission. We're here to show him everything we do, then we shall take him out the back to be shot.' He grinned.

Mr Spencer looked momentarily troubled, which made

Marjorie smile. It was, also, always a matter of some amusement to her that every visitor from the War Office was given a false name. For security reasons. The odd thing was that there were only ever three names used. A kind of private joke. This was, for example, the second Mr Spencer she'd been introduced to over the months they had been in St James's Street. She'd also met three Mr Leonards and two Mr Winstons. She doubted they were all from the War Office, as well. The oddest thing of all, to her, however, was the fact that everyone who actually worked within the department used their own names. Except the very senior chaps, of course, who went, rather grandly, she felt, by single initials.

She stood and shook the visitor's hand.

'Pleased to meet you.'

'And you. I understand you are doing good work,' he said. Marjorie was used to being patronised in this way. She just nodded her thanks.

Mr Spencer's neck was framed by the starched wing collar and stiff tie of an earlier era. He was mindful of his grandfather's half hunter, chained to his lapel, and which was tutting away to itself within the confines of his breast pocket. He needed to be getting along, at the very latest, by five o'clock. He absolutely had to catch the quarter-to-six from Charing Cross. His wife was having an At Home in Tunbridge Wells, and he needed to be there to unstopper the sherry.

'This is Miss Ellis, sir. One of the brightest minds we have. Anything stimulating, Ellis?'

'Well, sir, this has just come in.' She showed the Major and his guest the file she'd been reading.

The Major browsed it briefly. 'The most recent message is about nine months after the previous one. Someone come back to life, have they?'

'It's Kadakas, sir. See the covering message.'

He looked again at the message. 'Kadakas, eh? Now where has he been all this time?'

155

'Well, that's the interesting thing. He didn't use his usual route.'

'Which route is he using?'

'Amber, sir.'

'Amber, eh?'

'What's the Amber route?' said the current Mr Spencer.

'What Amber always means,' said the Major. 'Proceed with caution. It's a shorthand method of identification we came up with in the team. As far as we can ascertain, most Amber intelligence is coming from somewhere within the Nazi system itself. Disaffected Germans working within the regime. They somehow manage to spirit information out to us via third, fourth or even fifth parties. In this case' he looked at the message's first paragraph with its route identifiers 'via Sweden.'

'Is it authentic?'

'That's the problem. It's why we classify it as Amber. Is it designed to undermine their war effort, or ours? And there's usually no way of double-checking. Well – there is one way ...'

'Which is?'

'Wait. If it foretells an event wait until it comes to pass. If it does, well, we know the information was solid.'

'But?'

'But, sir?'

'There's hesitation in your voice.'

'Well, sir, that information may be genuine. But is it just a line with a hook on the end of it? Sprats and Mackerels. Give us two or three nice juicy worms to encourage us to believe the source and then ...' The Major mimed tugging on a fishing rod and reeling something heavy in.

'A great fat false fact designed to send us the wrong way?'

'Exactly – Sprats and Mackerels. Or Minnows and Trouts if you're on the Tweed.'

'So, we're not in a position to act on any information that can't be verified?'

'Not really, unless they coincide in some way with, say, our

Green sources.'

'How often do they coincide?'

'Not nearly as often as we'd like.'

'And who is this Kadakas?'

'Ellis?'

'One of the good guys, sir,' said Marjorie. 'A senior officer in the Estonian Navy. Intelligence. Green for go all the way with him. Until, that is, the Red Army invaded his country and he disappeared. We wondered whether he'd been shipped off to Siberia as were many of the others, or ended up with a bullet in his head and flung into the Baltic … as were many of the others.'

'And his information was classified as Green because …?'

'We've known him for years. He's been over here twice. Training with the Royal Navy in the twenties and thirties. Back home, he often acted as liaison for His Britannic Majesty's Baltic Flotillas. Plus, as things got tense in recent years, and the Soviets started holding their May Day parades in his country, he would get material out to us in other ways.'

'You mean the Reds kept people like him on?'

'Tolerated is probably the word. At least in the early days, when Moscow wanted to give the appearance of a concerned friend. As tensions increased throughout Europe, the Soviets offered to move into neighbouring countries so they could "protect" them. And, what do you think? If a great brown bear wanted to come and live in your house and rummage through your larder, you'd find it very hard to refuse. At first, anyway.'

'And then the hosts started to refuse?'

'Well, they were always very unhappy, but they had no real say in the matter. But then came the *Orsel* incident.'

'Which was?'

'Polish submarine. The Reds wanted it. It was damaged and limped into Tallinn, then a neutral harbour, to claim asylum. The Estonians accepted and followed the international law in such matters – hold the crew, forcibly disarm the vessel, impound it for the duration – that sort of thing. But then, a few days later, some of the sub's crew escaped, and cut and ran with their boat. The Soviets 'blamed' the Estonians and used it as a pretext to occupy the country completely.'

'Though,' said the Major, 'knowing how Ivan works, I wouldn't put it past their own people aiding and abetting the sub's escape so that they could use the pretext.'

Mr Spencer nodded. 'So, how did Kadakas get his messages out before the tanks rolled in permanently?'

'Through one of our Angels,' said Marjorie.

'Angels?'

'People we trust. People who have proved their value,' said the Major. 'In this case, an Estonian-born Brit. Owned a lumber business just outside Tallinn, before the Red Army commandeered it. He still runs the business for them.'

'So, if you could, he'd be the one you'd get to confirm this new intelligence?'

'Absolutely. Nothing more exciting than sitting at the traffic lights, revving one's Bugatti, and having the Amber turn to Green.'

'How hard will it be to find this Angel?'

'Not at all, sir. He's just along the corridor,' said Marjorie, pointing. 'Third door on the left.'

*

He swung the front door open. Someone was in the kitchen.

'Leena? Hello? It's me.'

There was a noise as if someone had dropped something into the sink. A woman appeared, drying her hands on a dish-cloth.

'Commander Kotkas?'

'Yes?'

She put out a hand and shook his. 'Mrs Wowreit. I'm a friend of your wife's.'

'Is she all right?'

'Yes. She's asleep in the lounge. She's often tired. The children are at school. I help out when I can.'

'Thank you.'

'Your colleague told you, then? I thought she wasn't going to.'

'Told me what?'

She hesitated. 'Oh dear. She didn't tell you?'

'Tell me what?'

'Your wife. The other day. Tried to take her own life.'

In a few brief sentences, she told him about Leena, the children; her husband, the policeman; and the doctor.

'Where is she?'

He went into the living room and knelt beside his wife. He took her hand. She stirred. He kissed the hand. Her eyes opened. It took a moment for her to register. Then:

'Hendrik? Oh, Hendrik!' She curled thin arms around his neck and buried her face in his chest. 'Oh, Hendrik. You are here. Thank God.'

Mrs Wowreit returned to the kitchen, finished the washing-up, dried her hands, put on her hat and coat, picked up her basket and left.

*

'So, Tamm,' said the Major, 'we've had this from Kadakas, we think.'

Tamm was short and round, a broad forehead with rimless spectacles. 'Kadakas? Back from the dead?'

'So it seems,' said Marjorie. 'Take a look. What do you think? Is it genuine?'

Tamm scanned the message. 'That's him. Definitely.'

'Just like that? How can you be so sure?' asked Mr Spencer.

'I taught Kadakas to sign all his messages.'

'He signs them?'

'Well, anybody can send a covering message claiming that what follows comes from someone we know. But our contact could have been captured, tortured and his or her methods compromised ...'

'I understand that,' said Mr Spencer. 'Then, if they want to, the enemy could keep the lines of communication open. So they can feed through false information. But you are saying he signs the actual messages. How?'

'He makes a deliberate mistake.' Tamm pointed at the third line. 'There ...'

Mr Spencer and the Major peered at it. It was about a Russian Baltic Fleet convoy.

'I see it: "Convoy out of of Kronstadt",' said Mr Spencer. 'And you taught him this?'

'We were trying to think of ways the recipients of any intelligence might confirm it was authentic. The trouble is, you see, if you put something in the body of the message, like, for example, a code word, anyone trying to replicate it would probably recognise it as a code word and put it in as well. The word may change, but there's a chance it won't, for a while at least, and the people sending the false message might just manage to slip it past us. So Kadakas thought about it, and told me of the time he and his brother were training with the Royal Navy in Chatham. They had an afternoon off and went to visit Rochester Cathedral. The floor in front of the Sanctuary before the High Altar is tiled. However, if you look very closely, every so often, the pattern is odd. A tile is the wrong way round. "Sloppy", you'd think. No. A deliberate mistake. Goes all the way back to medieval times. The workman cannot be perfect. Only God is perfect. Kadakas liked the idea and that's what we agreed would go in his messages. As you know – look at the people here – counterintelligence is all about being methodical. Bad grammar, slipshod syntax, typos, would never be allowed. Perfection is the key. Imperfection is ironed out. Even more so, don't you think, when it comes to the folk in Berlin? Reviewing any of his messages, if they'd got hold of them, they would simply see the two "ofs" as a simple mistake and would not allow themselves as a matter of principle to replicate it in any of their own falsified attempts.'

'So we can act on this information, then?'

'Well, no,' said the Major. 'As we said, this is early days in Kadakas's restarting his correspondence. We need to wait. See whether this information can be corroborated. And also see what else he sends us. We, in counterintelligence, are, indeed, very methodical.'

'Also,' said Marjorie, looking at Tamm to back her up, 'how do we know where Kadakas is getting his information from? He's in Germany. He may be genuine, but we have no idea what is going on there, do we?'

*

'So you are not staying?' Leena said.

Kotkas saw that she already knew the answer; the afternoon light catching the glint of tears in her eyes. 'I can't. I am on my way to Memel. I shouldn't be here at all. But I couldn't miss the chance to see you and the children, could I?'

She hugged him.

He took her by the shoulders and kissed her on the cheek.

'But ... Leena ... Why did you want to kill yourself, my darling?'

'What? Did I?' she said. 'Who told you that?'

'Is it true?'

'I ... don't remember.'

'You won't remember, or you can't remember?'

She looked away, through the window, as if her memory lay out there somewhere. 'I can't remember. When was this?'

'A few days ago, Mrs Wowreit said.'

'She knows?'

'Yes. She's been helping you ever since.'

Leena took a further moment to think. Her brow wrinkled. Then came an intake of breath. A sudden thought. 'Do the children know, do you think?'

'My darling. They found you. They saved you.'

She gasped again then crumpled into sobs.

He let the storm subside, before taking her in his arms.

'I love you, my darling. I miss you. Every minute of every day you are not beside me, there is a deep dark hollow. Even when we were together, as a family, back home in Estonia, when you went out, I immediately began to look forward to your return. Sixteen years of missing you every moment I am not with you. You are not to do this again, do you hear? And if you are finding it difficult to remember or control your feelings, you must write it on a piece of paper and keep it beside you.' There was notepaper and a pen on the table beside the couch. 'Look, I'll write it for you, right now.'

He spoke the words one by one as he wrote them down. *Don't do anything silly. Your husband and children love you. Call for help.* He put the finished note on the table, turning it round so his wife could read it where she lay whenever she needed to.

'You are never, ever, going to leave me. Do you hear?'

He kissed her, but her lips did not respond. He pulled back and looked at her. Her brown eyes were cloudy with pain.

'But, I am going to leave you, aren't I? Some day. Sooner or later.'

'Let's not think about that. Your job is to be here every time I come. And to be ready the day I come to take us all back to Tallinn. That, my darling, is an order.' He smiled, but she didn't appear to be listening.

One rekindled memory dragged another one into her mind. 'Who was that woman?' she said.

'Mrs Wowreit. She is looking after you for the time being.'

'No, not her. The one who came.'

'Who came?'

'The other day. She said she was from Berlin. From your office. She said she came on your behalf.'

'She did? What did she look like?'

'Pretty. Petite. Brown hair. I think she said her name was Meyer.'

Hendrik, who had been kneeling beside his wife on the couch, sat back on his heels. 'Miss Meyer? She was here?'

'Yes. She said she came to see if I was all right. I didn't understand. But now I do ... if, as you tell me, I tried to kill myself ... Who is she?'

'Just one of the people in our department.'

'She loves you.'

'What? Where is all this coming from, Leena? Whatever makes you say something like that?'

'I can tell. She cares a great deal for you.'

'Stop talking like this. This is nonsense. She doesn't care for me one bit. And I feel absolutely the same. I really am quite shocked that you should even think such things, let alone say them.'

Leena took his hands in hers. She kissed both of them, one at a time. 'Whatever you say, my darling. I completely trust you. Nevertheless, the fact remains. At some point in the not-too-distant future, I will no longer be around to plague you. You shall be free.'

'I don't want to be—'

'Shh. You shall be free. And I am telling you that I won't mind one little bit if you decide to remarry. In fact, I insist on it. You need looking after, you poor dear man. You are incapable of doing it yourself. The children need a mother. Goodness knows I have been next to useless to them these past few months, and it is only going to get worse. Remarry, my darling, please. You have my blessing.'

'I shall do nothing of the sort.'

XIII

There was another message, along with the one about Soviet convoy movements that Kadakas had sent.

'This one came a short while ago,' said Marjorie, offering it to the Major. 'There's quite a lot in it.'

The Major read it. 'Monitoring has copied the War Office in on this, too, I see. It has a lot to do with the build-up of troops and equipment on the German side of their Eastern border. We've had most of what this says from a number of different sources. As, indeed, we've had information about a Soviet build-up on the other side. But there's the bit about why the build-up is happening. To protect their troops from us. That's new. Not sure what's going on. Are you, Mr Spencer?'

He handed it to Mr Spencer, who read it and passed it to Tamm.

'Well, back at the department, the thinking was, until this message at least, that they could just be creating some kind of buffer zone. Just to ensure that Uncle Joe keeps to his side of the bargain.'

'Or?'

'Preparations ahead of revisiting the 1812 overture. What do you think, Major?'

'Could be. Could also be, just as it says in Kadakas's message, that the Germans are simply getting all their ducks in a row. Out the way of our prying eyes and impertinent bombs. In advance of their heavily advertised paddle across the English Channel. Having said that, our intelligence from the Soviet side of things seems to suggest Stalin thinks it might indeed be something to do with us. That is to say sending unsettling intelligence just to keep everyone guessing.'

'Really? Why?'

'An attempt to destabilise the pact.'

'Why would we want to do that?' Spencer tried to remain expressionless.

The Major turned and looked at him. A faint smile on his lips. 'You tell me, sir.'

'We have every intention, Major, of keeping a friendly hand extended where Uncle Joe and his comrades are concerned. Their business is their business. Our business is with Berlin.'

'Of course, sir. That's our story and we're sticking to it, right? However, any pact between them and the Germans can, surely, only be papering over the cracks. We've long thought that a rift will appear sooner or later. Isn't that right, Tamm? You're best placed to read the runes in all of this.'

'Two posturing billy goats in the same paddock? There's got to be a thundering of hooves and the clack of horns at some point. The wrangling over who controls Finland – or, at least, who is its best friend – has been going on for months.'

'So ...' said Marjorie, summarising for all in the room, 'we're being asked by Berlin to ignore the fact that the Germans are our enemy, and naively support their fiction that they are merely protecting their troops and tanks. While they are, in fact, we suspect, about to protect their interests.'

'Or are they simply enjoying pulling the wool over our eyes? Confounding their enemies,' said the Major.

'Why now?' mused Mr Spencer.

'Trouble is – why not now? There's never a right or a wrong time to sow general confusion among your enemies, is there?' said the Major.

'So, what are you going to do about it?'

'What does the War Office want us to do about it?'

'Good question. I think, after my visit here, I have quite a number of significant phone calls to make. What's the best guess for me to go back with, Major?'

The Major sat on the corner of a desk and beat a paradiddle on his thighs with his hands.

'Best guess . . .?' he said after a moment, 'invasion East.'

'Miss Ellis?'

'I'm with the Major. The question then is, what do we tell Uncle Joe? What the Germans want us to tell him, or what we think is going on? However, that seems to be a question for you and the War Office, Mr Spencer.'

'Agreed. Though, to be honest, if we can't decide whether this message is genuine or not, neither can Moscow. If we slip it under Uncle Joe's door, it will serve a purpose simply by further muddying the waters. But how about you, Mr Tamm? What do you think? Is it genuine?'

Tamm cocked his head to one side. 'Not sure. My question is different.'

'Which is?'

'Why did Kadakas send us this message? Have we had anything like it from anywhere else?'

'About the troop build-up being simply a protective measure?' said the Major. 'Miss Ellis?'

'No. This is the first we've heard of it. Sounds quite a lot like a party line that they're trying to get us to reinforce; create an independently verifiable source.'

'And so we return to my question,' said Tamm. 'Why did Kadakas send it?'

'So, you mean: is this chap for us or against us?' said Mr Spencer.

'My vote is for,' said Marjorie.

'Reason?'

'Let's look at it the way he sees it. I'm Estonian. What would I want? Get back home. How will I best achieve this aim? Not with the Russians. They kicked me out in the first place. So, then, the Germans are my best option. If they're about to fly like the Valkyrie east, I can hitch a ride back home. Even better if, then, they lose the war. I can be left high and dry in Tallinn, like a crab on the beach as the Nazi tide recedes.'

'How does messaging us help?'

'Maybe he's just doing his job. Whatever that is. But also keeping in touch and letting us know he's alive. One day, even, you never know, he may want us to actually help him get rid of the Germans. He's on our side. No question.'

'Not necessarily,' said Tamm.

They all looked at him.

'I know he's become a friend. Trust him with my life and all that,' he said, 'but we really don't know the full story.'

'What gives you pause, Tamm?' said the Major.

'Well, look at his first message. He's only sent details of Russian ship movements. If he's a "neutral" – why hasn't he sent us something to chew over about German movements?'

'The second message has German troop and materiel movements,' said Mr Spencer.

'Yes, but, as I am sure he knows, we are probably aware of all that already. Or, indeed, anyone with half an ounce of intelligence at the heart of the regime in Berlin would expect us to know already. It's important information, but there's no real detail. And certainly nothing in and around the Baltic generally. In other words, it's safe to send us something like this. It's not anything the regime would actually censure someone for sending, is it? Not least if it is according to their villainous purposes ...'

'You mean our Kadakas has become a Nazi?'

'I hate to even consider the notion – he is a good friend – but ... perhaps. We don't know and can't tell. But here's what concerns me – and why I hesitate to agree with Miss Ellis's analysis. The Reds moved into his country. They needed access to Estonia's seaports in these troubled times, they said. Don't worry, we'll protect everyone, they said. We're your best friends ... and so on.'

'Until the *Orsel* incident ...' said Mr Spencer.

'Yes. Then the velvet gloves come off. Now, one by one, come the purges. Political and military elite. They go into exile voluntarily, involuntarily, or just simply disappear. Kadakas, as you know him, comes to me. He is most definitely on some list somewhere. Only a matter of time. And, we notice, it's not just the elite who are being surgically removed. Their families, too. Pogrom in all its vile aspects. So, we decide I should contact people here, in Britain. Would they be happy to spirit a friend out of a crisis? Someone who is on their side, has been on their side for twenty years, and has a certain knowledge of incalculable value to the war effort? Of course, they say.' He looked at the Major. '*Your* people say. We'll fly a nice little Lysander out to a little field we know, owned by someone in the lumber business. Nice and discreet. Just outside Tallinn. Dead of night. Pick him up and bring him back to safety. Excellent plan, he says. But what about the family? They can come, too, yes? Oh no, comes the reply. We're afraid they are going to have to take their chances.'

Marjorie sat back in her chair.

'Why not the whole family, for goodness' sake?' asked Spencer.

'Lysanders, sir,' said the Major. 'The only aircraft light enough but robust enough to handle such covert operations. Short take-off and landing. Can come to a halt in just about any old field lit briefly by flares. Quick turnaround. Fuel tanks for the distance. Trouble is ... only one passenger seat. Two, if they don't mind being really chummy. Couldn't take a whole family, not in one go. And couldn't risk running a bus service.'

'Why not by surface, then?'

'A week-long train ride all the way across the whole of occupied Europe? Checkpoints every few hours? And ships wouldn't fare any better. Run the gauntlet across German – or Russian – patrolled Baltic? Squeeze through the Skagerrak between German-occupied Denmark and German- occupied Norway? And then the North Sea, teeming with goodness knows who. Meanwhile, no one could justify a submarine for an operation like that. I mean to say—'

'Yes, yes ... I get the idea.'

'So, Kadakas turns to his next best friends. The people with whom he had also been sharing his intelligence on the Soviets in the Baltic. People he spent many a happy week alongside, sailing in competition out of Kiel. The German Navy. Can you take me, please? he asks. Of course we can, they say. And how about my family? Sure, they say. Come one, come all. We'll bring your loved ones safely through our Baltic patrols.' Tamm shrugged. 'Now, tell me, how would you feel?'

'In short, we need,' said the Major, 'to find out which side he is really on. Or, rather, Tamm does. When you are back out in the field, can you try and find out where he is, who he's working for? We will, of course, do what we can here.'

'Of course.'

Mr Spencer walked over to a wall map of Europe. He wafted a hand over Russia. 'Rock,' he said. He then waved a hand over Germany. 'Hard place.' Taking a pin, he jabbed it in Estonia. 'Kadakas. Whichever side he's on, he'll be lucky if he gets out of this game alive.'

*

Coming home from school, the moment Juhan saw his father, he yelped like a puppy and threw himself into his arms. Maret's spirit leapt within her when she saw him. Then almost as quickly subsided. Where was her father when her mother nearly died? she thought. Where had he been, the long nights and the fearful days afterwards? Why didn't he say goodbye properly the last time? Why was he always going away? Why did they ever leave their home? Why didn't he stop all the horrid things?

Why doesn't he make things better?

Hendrik turned to her, still clutching Juhan to him, and gave her a great grin. He held out the other arm, and Maret stepped forward, despite her reservation, and allowed herself, at least, to be gathered in.

'Hello, Father,' she said.

'Hello, my special little girl.'

'I'm not little anymore,' she said.

He looked at her and knew that she was right.

She didn't ask him whether he was staying with them for good. What would be the point? She knew, even then, even at the first moment of reunion, it would not be long before he left them again. Left them alone.

'Aren't you going to give your father a kiss, Maret?' said her mother. Maret didn't reply. 'Not even a smile? Aren't you glad he's home again?'

'Yes,' said Maret.

'Come on,' said Hendrik, heaving the children up, one on each hip, 'let's go into the kitchen and make us all something tasty to eat.'

Maret warmed up a little once she'd got some food inside her. She kept looking across at her father as they ate.

Once or twice, he looked back at her and smiled. A smile that asked unspoken questions. He wanted to get her alone and see if she would tell him why she was so reserved. Though, to be fair, he knew only too well why. But he needed her to open up. To unburden herself. To let him back into her life. It seemed, though, the door was shut for the time being. Bolted from the inside.

'So, tell me, children,' he said, 'how is school?'

'Good,' said Juhan.

'Any more trouble?'

'No, everyone likes us now. I have friends. Tomas and Leo and Kurt. They are very funny. We play all sorts of games.'

'What sort of games? Football? Chase?'

'Yes. And War, of course.'

'War?'

'Yes. Sometimes, I am the good guys and sometimes the bad guys. I prefer being the good guys. The bad guys have to be horrible and cruel. They have to say nasty things and be killed at the end.'

'I see. And who are these bad guys?' Hendrik knew the answer before Juhan gave it.

'The British. They are just gangsters and thieves.'

'Ah.'

Hendrik and Leena exchanged glances. His wife raised her eyebrows as if to say: *What can you do?*

'I'm sure,' said Hendrik, 'they're not all gangsters and thieves, though.'

'Father,' said Maret, who had not spoken a word all dinner, 'you mustn't say such things.'

'I'm sorry – why not?'

'You just mustn't. If you say such things, they'll take you away again.'

'Who will take me away?'

Juhan suddenly sat bolt upright. 'Oh no!' he gasped.

'What's the matter, Juhan?' said Leena.

'Maret. We forgot!'

'Oh no!' said Maret. 'Let's do it now.'

'All right.'

The two children got off their chairs, stood shoulder to shoulder beside the table, looked at their parents, raised their right arms and said in unison: 'Heil Hitler.' They took their seats again.

'We're supposed to do it the moment we come home,' said Juhan. 'Sorry, Father. But we were so excited seeing you that we forgot. I hope that's all right.'

'Of course,' said Hendrik, digging his fork in a potato and trying not to look at either child. 'How long have they been doing that?' he said to Leena.

'A few weeks,' she said. 'They learnt it at Group.'

'Ah. When in Rome, I suppose …' he said. He looked up at his daughter and son. 'Well done, children.'

'We're not in Rome, are we, Father?' said Juhan

'It's just a saying, darling,' said Leena.

'You're supposed to do it back to us …' Juhan said. 'But you probably don't know that, Father. And Mother's not well, so she's excused.'

'Thank you,' said Leena.

'So, tell me, children, who are these people who might take me away?'

'Like the ones who took you away when you came last time,' said Juhan.

'They won't do that again, I promise.'

'You can't promise, Father,' said Maret. 'You can't promise anything. They took Leopold's father away.'

'Who's Leopold?'

'A boy from school. His father didn't behave properly, Leopold said. And someone told on him. And they came and took him away, Leopold said.'

Hendrik wasn't sure he should ask the next question, but it needed asking. 'Did Leopold tell on his father?'

'No,' said Maret. She thought for a moment. 'No,' she said again, more firmly. And then, 'I don't think so.'

'Well, I think that's very sad,' said Leena, to break the silence that followed. 'No one's father should be taken away. We don't like our father taken away, do we?'

'No,' said Juhan.

'But sometimes some people have to be taken away,' said Maret. 'That's what my group leader says. Even if it is sad. It is sometimes the right thing to do. The only thing to do. I asked her about it. That's what she said.'

Another silence followed.

'Let's change the subject, shall we?' said Hendrik. 'What nice things have been happening while I've been away?'

'Oh,' said Juhan, 'I've joined the chess club.'

'Excellent, Juhan. Are you enjoying it?'

'Yes. But I'm not very good at it.'

'Never mind. It's early days yet. I'm sure you'll get better, and I am sure you will become the best chess player in the whole wide world.'

Juhan's eyes shone.

'And, Maret, do you have any exciting news?'

Maret thought for a moment. 'I don't think so ...' then she brightened. 'Oh yes ... you'll never guess ...'

'What?'

'I've been asked to help plan Adi's birthday party. It's coming soon and it's going to be wonderful. All the streets will be closed and the whole of the district will have a big parade. There'll be flags and marching bands and dancing and everything, Group Leader says.'

'Adi ...? Who's this Adi?'

'That's what we call him. We're allowed to call him that, we really are, because he's our friend. He's everyone's friend, especially children.'

'*Adi* ...?' Hendrik looked at Leena.

'Our Glorious Leader,' she said. 'Maret's right. That's what the children call him.'

They finished the meal, washed up, dried the plates and put them away. Juhan went upstairs to play; Leena went into the lounge to rest. Hendrik led his daughter out onto the verandah.

'Let's go and have a lovely talk, shall we, Maret?'

They sat side by side on the steamer chairs, listening to the birds and looking at the birch and alder catkins trembling in the breeze.

'I'm very proud of you, Maret. You know that, don't you?'

'Yes, Father,' she said, more out of duty than belief.

'And you know I have to go away again?'

'When?'

He paused. 'Tomorrow.'

'Tomorrow!'

'It is very painful, I know. For me as well as you. And your mother and brother. It is all very horrible. But I must go. I am not even supposed to be here. I was just very naughty and wanted to see you all, even for such a short time. That's how much you mean to me. I have to go further north and do my job. But you must, please, understand that everything I do, I do for you. For us as a family. Everything I do is to find us a way to get home. To Estonia. To make things the way they were. I know that's what you want. That's all you've ever wanted, all any of us have ever wanted, and that is what I am doing. You do understand, don't you? You must understand. For my sake. For your mother's sake. For Juhan's sake. You are the strongest in the family while I am not around. I need you to stay strong.'

'You told me this before.'

'I know I did. And I am telling you again. Be strong. Stay strong.' He looked at his daughter. 'Being strong, staying strong is how we will get back together again as a family. The only way we will get home. Do you understand?'

She turned to look back at him. There were tears in her eyes, but she refused to let them control her. 'Yes, Father, like the moss; I understand.'

'Will you come here for a cuddle, then?'

'Yes,' she said, and climbed onto his lap.

They sat there for a moment; he stroked her hair.

'My brave little girl.'

'Father?'

'Yes?'

'Is it right that you are a hero?'

'Whatever makes you say that?'

'I don't say it. My group leader says it. Karl says it, too.'

'Karl? The boy I met when I was here last. The one who wants to join the Navy?'

'Yes.'

174

'And they say it about me?'

'No, not about you especially. About all of you.'

'About all of us. Who is "us"?'

'Away in the War. Fighting for the Fatherland. Fighting for the Leader. Fighting for Truth, Freedom and the German people. You are all heroes.' She reached up and held her father's face in her two young hands. She looked intently into his eyes. 'You are one of our heroes, aren't you, Father? Fighting for Victory. Fighting so that our Way will last a Thousand years. Aren't you, Father?'

Hendrik patted his daughter on the head. He kissed her button nose and smiled. Then he looked away.

'Are you crying, Father?'

'There will be enough time for tears tomorrow, my dear daughter.' He took her hand and swung it softly to and fro.

XIV

It was a forlorn band that stood on that Königsberg doorstep the next morning to bid goodbye to one another. The rain dripped off the eaves and bedraggled the catkins. They shared solemn hugs and kisses, as if to show any great emotion would be to betray the desolation they felt. Distancing themselves from the pain was the order of the day.

Hendrik, finally telling himself he really should leave, took each child and then his wife in turn by both hands.

'I'll be back. Soon. We'll go home. Soon.'

Leena could no longer bear the dignified leave-taking and launched herself at her husband. Locking both arms around his neck, she wept. 'I will never see you again, Hendrik. Never.'

'Shh-shh. You will. It'll be all right. I'll be back before you know it. I promise.'

The children were so overwhelmed by their emotions that they had become incapable of expressing them. They looked, to all appearances, unmoved; distant even.

Eventually, their father peeled himself from his wife and, with his battered brown valise in his hand, marched away; the rain pitter-pattering on his uniform cap.

The children looked at one another; both struggling to come to terms with everything that had just gone on. Then, before he was much further along the road, they called after him. 'Father ...? Father ...!'

Hendrik turned round.

The children snapped to attention, threw their right arms into the air and, in voices that echoed down the rain-spattered street, shouted, 'Heil Hitler!'

'No.' He shook his head. 'No "Heil Hitlers". This is not who we are.'

The children dropped their arms to their sides and stared at him.

'I'm sorry, children. I shouldn't have said that. I am upset that I have to leave. Like you. You must do whatever you need to stay safe while I am away. Goodbye.'

There was only silence.

He went.

*

As soon as Karl was able, he made his way to the office of the local security police. He eventually got to speak to the shabby young man in an ill-fitting suit who had taken the trouble to befriend him.

'And you say the Commander's children told you this, Karl?' said Ascher.

'Yes,' said Karl. 'They didn't mean to, but I coaxed it out of them. We were walking home from school as we generally do. As you asked me to do as often as I can. Just in case. And I mentioned that they both looked a little glum. They told me their father had been home, which we agreed was wonderful, but that he had to leave again. They were going home to a house without a father, and that made them sad.'

'And your reason for coming here is …?'

'We talked about how sad goodbyes were. And then the boy asked me an odd question.'

'Which was?'

'Whether they needed to report every instance of people who don't say "Heil Hitler" or if, when someone is sad and doesn't feel like saying it, they were allowed not to say it, once in a while.'

'Who didn't say it?'

'Their father. And, even worse, he told his children off for saying it.'

'Very good.' The man jotted down a couple of notes. 'When was this?'

'Today. Earlier this afternoon.'

'The boy told you this, you say?'

'Yes.'

'And the girl?'

'Said nothing. But didn't stop her brother saying it, either.'

'Did they give the impression they knew that they were informing on their father?'

'I don't think it even crossed their minds. You told me to try and be discreet about it. I was. And remember, they are still relative newcomers to the district, and to the ways of the State. For them, it was an innocent enquiry; a casual chat with their friend.'

'Do you believe the children have been in any way influenced by their experience? Any sign that their father had been indoctrinating them against the State?'

'I doubt it. Many of the conversations I've had with them have been entirely positive towards the State and the Leader.'

'Good,' said Ascher, flipping his notebook shut. 'You've done very well to tell me this. I shall let Berlin know.'

'Berlin?' Karl looked suitably impressed.

This gratified Ascher, as that was exactly the effect he had been going for. 'Now, if you ever have anything you think is worth reporting, you just get word to me and, if it's important enough, I can assure you, Mr Fischer, my colleague in Berlin, will get to hear of it, too. We'll make a security policeman of you yet, young Karl,' he said.

'Oh no. It's the navy for me. Definitely.'

'Ah well, all for the good of the cause, whichever path we choose, eh?' He tousled the lad's hair.

*

'I insist I speak with the Admiral,' Fischer said on the phone.

'And, again, I must apologise, sir,' said the woman's voice on the other end of the line, 'but the Admiral is in a vital meeting and simply cannot be disturbed.'

'Have you any idea who you are talking to?' said Fischer.

'Yes, sir, You told me when I answered the telephone.' Emilie wondered whether Fischer had any idea who he was talking to. She hoped not. 'And I fully respect the importance of your role and the nature of your work. If you could give me just a little idea of what it is that you wish to speak to the Admiral about and I promise I shall let him know the moment he emerges from his meeting.'

'How long?'

'It has just started, so two hours, perhaps.'

'Not good enough. You must break in on him with a message. I insist.'

'Yes, sir. I understand. I am entirely able to do that. But, sir, you in turn must understand, I need to know the purpose of your call to assess whether it is suitably urgent to justify putting my own job at risk.'

Fischer slammed his fist on his desk. *Is she really that stupid, or is she being officious or deliberately obstructive?*

'Are you all right, sir? I heard a noise.'

Fischer collected himself. 'Right, miss, listen ...'

'Sir?'

'I need the Admiral to order that Commander Kotkas does not leave the building. To have security hold him until I get there. I need him, also, to grant me access to your building so I can take the Commander away for questioning.'

There was a silence. 'I see, sir. Well, yes, I can imagine that this would indeed be something I should bring to the Admiral's attention ...'

'Good.'

'However, Commander Kotkas isn't in the building, I am afraid, sir.'

'Where is he then?'

'Well, sir, I am afraid you are going to get a little upset with me again, sir. But, unfortunately, I am not allowed to tell you.'

'What? Why not? If he's somewhere in Berlin, you can at least tell me that, and I can go round and pick him up.'

'No, sir. I think I am allowed at least to tell you this much … in the interests of departmental cooperation, of course … he is not in Berlin.'

'Where is he then, woman, for goodness' sake? Are you being deliberately obtuse? What is your name?'

'Actually, sir, I am not even at liberty to tell you that, bearing in mind the nature of our work. What I can tell you is that Commander Kotkas is currently out of the country on operational service and will be for some time.'

'This is a matter of State security.'

'I am well aware of that, sir. You told me already. I can only apologise profusely. Nonetheless—'

'You are impeding a legitimate investigation. You are obstructing an officer of the State in the course of his duties.'

'*Nonetheless*, sir,' Emilie persisted, 'until the Admiral comes out of his meeting, I have no authority to offer you any more information than that which I have already given you. I can only apologise.'

Fischer felt like slamming the receiver down. Such was the parlous state of the relationship between his department and counterintelligence. That lot seemed to be a law unto themselves. And, even if they weren't, they behaved as if they were above the righteous arm of the security police, the SD, even the SS. He had heard that there were moves afoot to incorporate counterintelligence under a much wider umbrella, which would more closely link his work with theirs. That day couldn't come soon enough, as far as he was concerned. He wasn't sure, but he wondered whether the assistant he was speaking to had been, in fact, that appalling woman he'd tried to speak to the other day. If so, then it would be his particular pleasure to put paid to her, once they all came under the same command structure. He would do a little digging. Get some evidence together. Cite her unhelpful responses as treasonable behaviour. He would come up with something. His department was especially good at that; took some considerable pride in it, in fact.

'Two hours, you say?'

'Sir?'

'Until the Admiral comes out of his meeting. Let him know I insist on speaking with him the moment he does. And, miss …?'

'Sir?'

'If I am not the first person he speaks to, he – and you – will find they shall have to face a very uncomfortable interview with my superiors. Is that clear?'

'Clear, sir.'

He rang off.

'Fischer?' The call came from his boss's office.

'Sir?'

'Are you at last off the phone?'

'Sir.'

'Here, then.'

Fischer went in. The boss closed his office door and lowered his voice. He picked up the dill pickle he'd been eating and continued what he had to say between bites, occasionally dabbing his lips with a grey handkerchief.

'Just thought I'd give you fair warning. I'm going to need you to be packed and ready to leave your quarters at a moment's notice.'

'Boss?'

'No one is to know about this, do you hear? No one. Not even your parents. Not even your girlfriend. At least, until we get the go-ahead.'

'Yes, boss.'

'Something spectacular is about to happen. Something that

will echo in the annals of our Glorious Fatherland for centuries to come. I cannot tell you precisely what. That is just for us senior folk to know. But we have been given permission to alert key personnel. Of whom I consider you to be one.'

'Thank you, sir.' Bearing in mind recent exchanges between the two, and his boss's undoubted jealousy of his subordinate's intelligence, efficiency and obvious influence with the Chief, Fischer found it hard to believe his boss really meant what he had just said. The man's eyes seemed to suggest he was right in this assessment. They were looking past him rather than at him, and there was no warmth in them.

'At some point, Fischer, in the next week or so – maybe a little longer, we'll see – you will get your orders. They will be to prepare to follow the army as it advances. At some point, in the weeks afterwards, you will be required to set up a forward unit, once the army has secured a foothold. I cannot tell you where. However, you are a policeman. I doubt it will take long for you to work things out for yourself.'

Fischer's mind was already working it out. Where else would the officer responsible for the Baltic be sent to? His boss was still speaking.

'Your task is to maintain law and order where your unit will be based. The primary function is to help secure what will be an essential supply chain for the army, provided by the harbours in … that place. The secondary function is, naturally, to re-Germanise and to eradicate any racial clutter. You will be expected to connect with the SS leader there and set up a cooperative liaison initiative. You will need to – shall we say? – *encourage* the local security services and police to collaborate. Though you will find, no doubt, any number of people from that place eager to assist you as well. Experience shows that this is quite usual in countries wherever the State raises its flag. They are quick to see the light, so to speak. Is that clear?'

'Clear enough, for now, sir.'

'Good. So drop everything else, hand any ongoing investigations to other members of the team here, and spend what time is left available to you in working out command structures, protocols and systems for your future posting. Any questions?'

'Yes, sir. Who do I report to at this forward unit?'

'I did not say "help set up", I said "set up". He smiled. 'You will report to no one there. They will report to you. Congratulations on your promotion.'

He held out a hand. Fischer shook it; it was clammy with dill pickle.

'Thank you, sir.'

'Not at all, my friend. You deserve it.' He popped the last of the pickle into his mouth and ground it to oblivion.

It was clear to Fischer that all this talk of promotion, although no doubt genuine, was largely designed to sweep him out of the way. They were just words. This move was designed to prevent him clambering over his knuckle-headed superior to roles above and beyond him in Berlin. Yet, it was also true, he realised, that if he made a good job of the Baltic post, he could leapfrog this clown anyway.

'Thank you, sir. One last thing...'

'Yes, Fischer?' He dabbed his thick lips once more with his handkerchief.

'I just had a most obstructive phone call with counterintelligence. I thought you should know about it...'

*

'Miss Meyer?'

'Yes, Admiral?'

'Close the door, please.'

'Yes, sir.' She closed it.

'You saw this memo?' Canaris held it out so she could read it.

It was one of a number she'd signed for and put in a pile on

183

his desk that morning. She knew what this particular memo contained. There were few secrets between the people of Canaris's inner office and the Admiral. Apart from the direct phone line.

'Yes, sir.'

'This is top secret, but I know and trust you well enough to keep this from anyone else. *Absolutely anyone else.*'

'Yes, sir.'

'We're planning on setting up an office in the Baltic, once the region has been liberated.'

'Yes, sir.'

'I'm going to need someone up there to manage that side of things from an administrative perspective; the procurement of essential office equipment, stationery, communication links with us here in Berlin. The day-to-day running of the place. The support of key Intelligence Service personnel. Someone who is diligent, completely trustworthy, familiar with the labyrinthine ways of the Intelligence Service, and utterly loyal.'

'Yes, sir.'

'So, get ready to leave.'

'Me, sir?'

'You, sir. It won't be immediately, but it will be soon enough. Once the situation becomes clearer. We should hear in the next week or so what timescales we are looking at. I suspect it will be sometime towards the middle of the summer.'

'But ...' Canaris gave her a look; it was, of course, not permitted to argue. 'Yes, sir,' she said. She turned to go, then stopped. 'Actually, sir, may I say something regarding another matter?'

'Of course.'

'I've had a rather difficult phone call. From the security police. They would like to speak to you urgently.'

'Yes, yes, I had a call through on my direct line. I've dealt with it.'

She wanted to ask how it had been dealt with, but knew it

was not her place. What conversations occurred on the direct line was absolutely none of her business. 'Forgive me, Admiral, but I thought you had asked for them to stop investigating the Commander.'

'I did.' Canaris shrugged. 'Perhaps they forgot,' he said, and smiled. 'Be that as it may, and just to reassure you, Miss Meyer, you did the right thing. If they'd asked me, I wouldn't have told them where the Commander had gone, either. But, I have to say, they are very unhappy about it. No matter. Sufficient unto the day is the evil thereof. Is that all?'

'Yes, sir. Thank you, sir.'

The Admiral started to unscrew the cap of his pen in order to get on with the interminable paperwork. He sighed. *People think intelligence work is all about secrecy and puzzle-solving. Ninety-nine per cent of the time, it seems to me, it's about writing memoranda, initialling documents and shovelling files from one desk to the next. And keeping good people from being shot, of course.*

Emilie took the Admiral's sigh as a cue to leave. As she did so, he looked up from the paperwork.

'Miss Meyer ...'

'Yes, sir?'

'I have valued everything you have done for this office. You have been a very special member of my staff, and I really hate letting you go. But, on the other hand, I can truly say I know of no better person I would trust with this huge responsibility. Go with my respect, my admiration and my warmest best wishes for the future.'

'Thank you, sir. But I daresay we shall meet again at some point. When this is all over, sir. When we have won.'

'I daresay we shall. But there's another reason I think you'd be the best person to go.'

'Sir?'

'They are after your blood, I am afraid.'

'Who are, sir?'

'I am sure you can work that out. Just think back to anyone you might have upset today, let alone the past few weeks. People for whom you might have become something of an irritation. An itch that needs scratching, so to speak.'

'I see, sir.'

'In short, it is becoming unsafe for you here. And will become even more so, I suspect. Especially if you maintain the level of loyalty and integrity towards me and our work here that you have done so far. Besides, you know Commander Kotkas better than anyone.'

'Commander Kotkas?'

'Yes, I shall be moving him from wherever he is at the time to the office you will be managing in due course. When everything's in place.'

'Yes, sir.'

'That is all.'

*

A few weeks later, in the Finnish Navy headquarters at Turku, there was a knock on Commander Kotkas's bedroom door.

'Come in,' he said, stirring from sleep.

It was his orderly, Louis. He had come out to Finland with the others in the German Naval Intelligence liaison unit. He was from Kolmar in Alsace. He was also Jewish on his mother's side. But both he and Kotkas kept that to themselves, and hoped no one ever found out. 'Good morning, sir. Coffee. Freshly roasted, ground and brewed as you like it.'

'Very good, Louis. Thank you.'

'Oh, and, sir ...?' He could not conceal his excitement, though he tried to appear unconcerned.

'Yes?'

'Message from Berlin, sir. It's on. Barbarossa. Code word Dortmund. Briefing at zero eight hundred hours. Advance units of Army Group North crossed the Neman three hours ago.'

'Thank you, Louis.'

Autumn 1941

⌘

I

The staff car carrying Commander Kotkas made its way up from the naval base and through the Kalamaja district of Tallinn. The trees were still lavish with leaves; in contrast to the rubble that lay all around. The fall had not yet begun.

'Driver?'

'Sir?'

'Don't turn into the Old Town, yet. Stay on this road and go past the station, please.'

'Sir.'

They drove through this venerable trading crossroads packed with merchants' houses shaded by swaying trees. All around were parks, with their dusty paths upon which children down the years had romped, lovers embraced and the elderly under their parasols had regretted the passage of years. They passed the Baltic station – built in the shape of a formidable manor house, one of which any Livonian duke or German count would have been justly proud – now disfigured by the fire that the Soviets had set as they withdrew. How many times had he and his family passed through its lofty entrance into the high-ceilinged booking hall? Off to Tartu, or the country, or over to Haapsalu on the west coast? How many times especially to Vasalemma, in summer suns and winter snows? Laughing, playing games on the train. Then arriving and passing through the rustic station building. Dusty, rickety; the bare floorboards echoing to their footsteps. Being driven to his parents-in-laws' farmhouse with its pillared entrance and verandah, reminiscent of a plantation home in the deep south of America; the two great limes standing guard at the top of the drive.

The car continued round Toompea, the ancient hill standing thirty metres above all it surveyed, and where the legendary Estonian hero Kalevipoeg's father, Kalev, was supposed to be buried. Here was the solemn Lutheran Cathedral, inside of which Baltic German nobility could once be found at earnest prayer. Here, too, was the opulent Orthodox Cathedral, dedicated to Alexander Nevsky. It had been built at the turn of the century by Tsar Nicholas II to emphasise his dominion over the Estonian people. An authority that was to be shattered by his own subjects just seventeen years later. Here on the hill stood also the great houses of the Hanseatic nobility; indifferent to the struggles of the merchants and peasants toiling beneath their feet.

On top of Tall Hermann, one of the great medieval towers protecting Toompea, Kotkas saw the blood-red flag with its white disc and petulant hooked cross snapping at its mast. Not so long ago, that same mast had carried the flag of the Communist occupation. Then, as the skirmishes turned into savage street fighting, he had witnessed jubilant Estonian partisans shoot it down and replace it with their blue, black and white national emblem of freedom. Shortly after, of course, the German Army had swaggered in ... and replaced it with their own flag.

Before the driver could turn left towards the Town Hall Square, Kotkas directed him past Charles' Church. He and Leena had been married there, and his children baptised. It had struggled to remain upright during the onslaught but, Kotkas noted, there it still stood, resilient.

'Up there, now, please,' Kotkas said, pointing.

The car nosed over the brow of Tõnismägi.

'Stop here a moment.'

They halted opposite an apartment block. He looked up at the window, out of which he, his wife and children would have looked a thousand times.

Their apartment.

The architect-designed two-tone grey building, built after independence as a symbol of the New Estonia, was now draped in red banners. A German soldier in blue-green fatigues emerged and held the door for an incoming colleague similarly dressed. It would seem that the building was being used as a military billet. The outgoing soldier noticed Kotkas in his car and stepped off the kerb to talk with him. Kotkas wound his window down. He made sure the soldier saw the gold rings on his sleeve. 'Yes?'

The soldier saluted. 'May I help you, sir?' Uninvited visitors clearly not welcome.

'No. We're just going.'

'Right you are, sir.' He saluted again.

They drove down the hill and round the corner. They passed his parents-in-laws' former townhouse and grounds. They were both dead now; the immaculate Valter and his staunch wife, Liisu. The first time he had drawn up in front of that house, it had been in a taxi. *If you can't afford a decent car,* his father had once told him, *always arrive everywhere by taxi. It's classless.* Kotkas's brother-in-law, Feliks, had moved in a few years ago; but whether he was still there, or even living at all – since the Soviet occupation – remained to be seen. An image of himself and Feliks in silk top hats, with Liisu and Leena with flowing black veils, solemn behind Valter's cortège, swept all other memories aside.

'All right. Let's go,' Kotkas said.

The car pulled up outside the Town Hall, a stalwart medieval building with a soaring tower. There were four battle-hardened sentries on the door.

The briefing was in the main hall. All the great and the good currently based in the city or at the harbour had been summoned.

Kotkas approached a seat but then noticed someone was beckoning him. It was Gahlendorf. Kotkas shook his hand and sat down beside his friend.

'Look how they repay me for my systematic neglect of duty, my studied indifference to my masters, Kotkas.' Gahlendorf was speaking between puffs on his cigar. 'They promote me. Vice Admiral, no less. Who needs it? What did I ever do to them, to be given all this additional responsibility? Not to mention the bureaucracy. It's a wonder I can get any time off to go sailing these days. And now I've got to organise a whole steaming shooting match here on behalf of our beloved navy. I mean, I ask you.'

Up onto a dais came four men. Three in uniform, one in a suit; all proprietorial.

Gahlendorf stretched out his legs and yawned. 'Looks like we're in for a long morning.' Kotkas joined him and reflected upon what little he knew of his friend. The newly promoted Admiral had been born to inherit the family estate in Schleswig-Holstein, complete with forests full of boar and roe deer. Despite his pedigree, he had the common touch. After a hard day's sailing, Kotkas remembered, he would fling his arms round his younger Estonian opponents and say 'Come!' Bored by the elite of the competition's yacht clubs, he would swing his guests by one of Kiel's harbour bars; windows fogged by the warmth within and the cold night air without. There, he would sup ale with the grizzled sea captains; their Elbseglers battered and salt encrusted, their reefer jackets shiny with the grease and grime of a thousand stormy voyages.

The senior group leader of the SA on the platform did all the talking. He clearly considered the two officers of the SS sitting alongside him his underlings. The fourth one, the civilian, was an Estonian. He was director general of the region and, the Germans insisted, the most important person in the room. Apart from these mentions, though, he took no part in proceedings.

The course of the meeting veered between hubris and sketchy strategic aims. These were mixed with promises of a

191

stronger, independent Estonia – a glittering future under the benevolent patronage of the great German State.

Kotkas kept his thoughts to himself.

The moment the briefing ended, and the echoing *Sieg Heils* had died, Gahlendorf unfolded himself and made for the door. 'Come on,' he said. 'It's got very stale in here.'

As they reached the lobby, someone took hold of Kotkas's arm.

'I thought it was you. Remember me?' said Fischer. 'I wondered whether we'd ever meet again.'

'What do you want?' said Kotkas.

'Oh, so many things … Tell you what, let's go somewhere quieter so we can chat at our leisure.'

'What do you think you're doing?' asked Gahlendorf.

'With respect, Admiral, this has nothing to do with you. It's security police business,' said Fischer.

'Let go of his arm. There's a good chap. And then, as soon as you've managed to accomplish that,' he took another puff on his cigar, 'I shall only take a little more of your precious time. This will involve explaining why, precisely, it is very much my business.'

Fischer held his ground for a moment longer. Then released his grip.

'Name. Rank. Unit. Role here in Estonia, please?' Gahlendorf asked as easily as if he was inviting the fellow to join him for a weekend's shooting on his father's estate.

Fischer recognised authority when he saw it – not that fat oaf of a boss back in Berlin; *real* authority – years negotiating the hierarchy in the security police had taught him this. He duly answered. He then added a little extra information of his own. 'You should also know, Admiral, that I have been given sole charge of the security police here in Tallinn, and that I report directly to my people in Berlin. I do not need to refer my decisions to anyone here.'

'Your mother must be very proud. I shall be interested to

learn what our senior group leader in there thinks about your not needing to keep him informed of your affairs. But that's for another time. For the present, all you need to be clear about is this. We are still in the middle of a war zone. Therefore, the only law that's relevant around here is the law of military occupation. Further, if I find for one moment that you are in any way jeopardising this operation, I can, and shall, have you shot. And, I might add, I shall probably smoke a cigar while they do it. By all means, put my name down in your little black book along with the Commander's here. But if you want this war won, and for you to enjoy anything resembling a glorious future, I suggest you put it away these next few years until our work is done.'

Fischer turned to Kotkas. 'You seem to make a habit of getting your Admiral friends to protect you. Now, I wonder why that is. What makes you so special? So special that you even think it is acceptable to be insolent to our Leader. To encourage sedition.'

'Well,' said Kotkas, 'I imagine it is my ability to get on and do my job professionally, without wasting my time harassing others for no specific reason. I am grateful to the Admiral for his support, but, please be assured, I am quite capable of looking after myself. Now, if you don't mind, while this briefing was of the greatest importance to those people who find these kinds of things important, I need to get back to my office so I can get on with the war. Your war, as I recall.'

Fischer opened his mouth to respond, but the Admiral wagged the wet end of his cigar in his face. 'Tut-tut, my friend. Commander Kotkas is one of the reasons you are even here and able to exercise your ... "ministry". He's undermined the Soviet regime round these parts almost single-handedly, through his intelligence work. He spent some weeks across the water, in Finland, training and equipping Estonian partisans. Then, while you were still on the lavatory in Berlin,

Kotkas and those men came over here, disrupted communications, blew up installations and neutralised key personnel. This was so that our job, when we deigned to appear, was just that little bit easier. I would not be at all surprised if our Leader, far from being insulted, should invite him to lunch and personally hang an Iron Cross around his neck. Now, off you pop. Maybe, if you're lucky, you can find a stray orphan or widow to harass.'

Fischer growled. 'I thought we'd dealt with the Old Boy Network. Back in the bad old days; when we purged your filthy back-scratching systems. It appears some dregs still remain. Not for long.' He left.

Gahlendorf watched him go. 'What's really tragic is that we are on that sea slug's side in all of this. Which makes us evil by association, old man. Backing the wrong horse.' He drew on his cigar. It had lost its taste for him. He threw it down, and ground it with a heel. 'We know which way the wind will blow, don't we? We're going to get our comeuppance, sooner or later. By someone or other. That is, unless our own people don't do the job for them. That's our stupidity. We seem to have a perverse delight in gnawing away at our own flesh. And serve us all right.'

Outside, Fischer, seething, lit a cigarette. He thought about calling Berlin, but as he smoked, he began to calm down. He reminded himself that he'd been put in charge there. How would it look if he went running to his boss after one little spat with a couple of irrelevant naval officers? *Get used to the loneliness of command, Fisher* were his superior's parting words. *Exercise the authority you've been given.*

I can wait, he told himself. *The security police have long memories and long arms. They'll see. Patience is not just a virtue, it's a weapon.* He smoked his cigarette.

'So, old chap,' said Gahlendorf as they walked out, 'what have you done to deserve such close attention? "Insolence", "Sedition", really?'

They emerged onto the Town Hall Square. Cars were pulling up and driving their august passengers away.

'I refused to offer the Party salute in the manner to which the Leader has become accustomed,' said Kotkas. 'And I suggested to my children that they didn't need to, either.'

'Hmm. Impossible, isn't it? Damned if you do, damned if you don't. That just about the sum of everybody's dilemma these days. And we all *have to* make choices. That's the awful thing about this whole tawdry business. Sitting on walls isn't an option. One is obliged to choose. Even if on one side of the wall there's a firing squad. Although there's probably another one on the other side, too. But, it doesn't completely explain this level of interest. Are you up to something?'

Kotkas didn't reply.

'Well,' said Gahlendorf, 'that is a loud silence. If you'll take some advice from not just a friend and a fellow sailor but also a grizzled sea dog in a ViceAdmiral's get-up: be careful.' His ride arrived and swept him away.

Kotkas looked around for his driver, who was just starting his car across the square.

Fischer had finished his cigarette. He stubbed it out beneath his heel.

Kotkas started to climb into his car.

Fischer accosted him. 'You will slip up, Commander. I know it and you know it. You smart alecks always do. And when that happens, you can be absolutely sure I'll be there to grind your bones to make my bread.'

*

'Have you heard from your husband lately?' chirped Mrs Wowreit. She could see Leena was slipping once more into her abyss, and that was the only thing that had come to mind. Juhan and Maret had washed their hands and were helping her get ready for supper.

'No.'

'Oh, well, I am sure you will soon.'

'Are you?'

'Maybe he's dead,' said Juhn.

'Juhan!' said Maret. Don't say such a thing!

'Well, he could be. There was a boy in school, and another at Group. Their fathers are dead. The boy at school was called out of class last week. His mother was crying. She took him home. We watched from the window.'

'I am sure that's not the case with your father, Juhan,' said Mrs Wowreit, already wishing she had not chosen that topic with which to make light conversation. 'There's a saying that bad news travels fast. And you've not heard anything.'

'No news is good news,' said Juhan.

'Exactly, Juhan.'

Maret had fallen silent and was picking at the tablecloth.

'No news is no news,' said Leena from the couch. 'I'm not sure they even know where we are to give us any. They probably don't even know where Hendrik is. How can they send news if they can't get hold of it in the first place?'

'Now, then, Mrs Kotkas. I'm sure enough people know where your lovely husband is, and how to get hold of you, too. You mustn't let yourself get down about all this. You've come this far, I am sure all will be absolutely fine.'

'Like those two poor boys Juhan talked about?' Leena said.

Mrs Wowreit retreated to the kitchen.

'Who's for a nice hot cup of tea?' she said.

Moss, Maret told herself. *Hold on. Hold on like moss. Like Father said.*

*

Kotkas was at work in his office. It was an extensive red-brick building. It once belonged to the Estonian Navy. But now, like most things these days, it belonged to the Germans; so, he reminded himself, did he.

He looked out of his window, which was on the landward

side. Beyond the base, in among the trees, the red, yellow, silver and sage weather-beaten houses of a previous age – the days of the Tsars – cluttered the view. Once, they had been fishermen's, sailors', innkeepers' and sea-widows' homes. Nowadays, they housed the workers who kept the navy base going. Immediately below him, meanwhile, was the service road. Beyond that was the security perimeter and then the public road.

The car was still there.

It was parked outside the base, but very clearly watching. It had been there for at least two hours. At one point, a sentry had crossed over from the main gate to speak to the person or persons inside. After a brief conversation, and what appeared to be an inspection of an identity disc or two, the sentry clearly declared himself content, returned whatever it was, and made his way back to his post.

Whoever it was, were they waiting for him?

If they were, there was one easy way of finding out. He was due to leave in a short while. He would order a staff car and have it take him on an odd route, and then double back on itself. If the waiting car followed, and kept following... well, that would be that question answered.

He finished what he was working on, put the papers back into his desk drawer and locked it. He was about to stand when there was a knock at his door.

'Come.'

A chief petty officer put his head round. 'Message for you from the front desk, sir.'

'Yes?'

'Monika wondered whether you could meet her at the usual place around eighteen hundred hours?'

Kotkas remained impassive. 'Thank you.'

'Sir.' The CPO closed the door.

Kotkas looked at his watch. Twenty minutes to six.

Monika? He hadn't heard that name for nearly a year. He

knew what it meant, however: further complications in an already parlous situation. How on earth did that message even get through to him, though? There, in the heart of a highly secure naval base. Still, Monika always knew how to overcome barriers, get round the rules . . . and people.

He thought about not making the meeting. Then again, he knew it was something he really should go through with. In fact, if he was honest with himself, he always knew there would be a possibility that this was going to happen. Once he was back in Estonia.

The need to check whether whoever it was that sat outside the base was waiting for him took on even more significance.

He picked up the phone and ordered a car to meet him downstairs.

The driver, on his orders, turned right rather than left, once they were through the gate of the base.

The waiting car started up and followed.

They carried on westward and weaved around the Kopli peninsular with its hallowed graveyard for a few minutes. The car remained behind him. Kotkas then ordered that they turn round and head back to the city centre. He looked out of the rear window to see the other vehicle dutifully on his heels. Whoever this was, they were clearly not worried about being seen; not worried about letting Kotkas know he was being followed.

Security police? Or was it Monika? Or was it someone who wanted him to think that the message he'd received had come from Monika? Someone who had a different agenda altogether? Soviet agents lying low after the German advance? Estonian patriots seeking to punish fellow countrymen who wore a hated uniform? It was too difficult to speculate. And no real point doing so. All would be revealed in due course. The first and most important thing was to shrug off whoever it was following him.

'Turn left here, please, driver, then second right.'

They turned into a serpentine street in the Old Town. After a few moments, Kotkas ordered the driver to stop, thanked him, and told him he would walk from there. His car drove off. The vehicle that had been following him was already stationary, a hundred metres or so behind.

A hundred metres was enough. They'd made a mistake. Thankfully.

He walked a few paces then turned towards a hotel doorway. Out of the corner of his eye, he saw someone get out of the car that had been dogging his path. Good.

He went into the hotel, nodded a breezy good day to the woman on the reception desk, and set off down the hall. A quick turn left through one door and a right through another and he was at the rear of the hotel. This was, in effect, another building altogether. It fronted the street parallel to the one he'd been on. The scent of a hearty *borscht* reached him; made him hungry. He continued walking through, nodding another good day to the waiter serving lunch in the restaurant, and slipped out into the street. He ran along it a few yards, turned off down an alley, through an arch, and into a small medieval courtyard. Flattening himself against a wall, he waited in the shadows.

Nobody came.

He would have liked to have been in the room when whoever it was that was following him told whoever it was that ordered them to do it that they'd lost him. But, he realised that pleasure could never be his.

After a few minutes, he made his way to the 'usual place'. This was, unfortunately, on the street where his driver had dropped him off, and where he had last seen his followers. He peered round the corner and along the street. Their car was gone. He stepped out onto the cobbles and, keeping an eye both in front and behind, walked briskly to the rendezvous.

This was a four-storey 14th-century merchant's house. He wasn't interested in the front door; he went instead to a pair of delivery doors at shin level, and which faced onto the street. Through these doors, in former times, and down into the depths of the building, would have been hauled coal, provisions and merchandise. He lifted the ring handle and allowed it to rap on the wooden chevrons. There was a sound of movement from within. The next moment, a latch was lifted, the doors were swung up and out, and a face appeared out of the darkness like a moonrise.

'Come in. Quickly.'

Kotkas clambered down the few wooden steps that led into the core of the building.

The street was checked for watchers, then the doors were shut, and the cellar was once more wrapped in darkness.

An oil lamp was lit.

Both faces now looked like ivory moons against the black depths of the room. The air was thick with the musty smell of centuries. They stood there, looking at one another for a moment. Then, as if on a mutually agreed signal, they stepped forward and gave each other a huge hug.

'Monika!' said Kotkas.

'Kadakas!' said Tamm.

II

'Are you sure we are safe here?' said Kotkas.

'As anywhere,' said Tamm.

They were meeting, Kotkas was only too aware, to begin a thinly disguised interrogation designed to test his credibility. To see whether he'd been turned by his current paymasters. Or, indeed, whether he'd been turned long ago by other agencies, even the Soviets.

Tamm was a friend. A good friend. They'd become very close in the years they had spent in Estonia unlocking Soviet secrets before the war, and forwarding the information to the British. And to the Germans. Yet, even though Tamm was a friend, he still had a job to do. Kotkas understood this. Kotkas also had a job to do, and he hoped Tamm understood that as well. Importantly, Kotkas had decided he could not trust anyone. Not even good friends. Certainly not the British. Not after everything that had happened. Truth to tell, he was worried he could no longer even trust himself. These past few months had been so bewildering, he had simply lost track of who he was anymore. Over recent days, and the latest encounter with Fischer confirmed it, he had had to cut himself adrift from everybody.

'So, what have you been up to, old friend?' Tamm said. 'Coffee?' He went to an alcove towards the back of the cellar where stood a primus stove and a copper coffee pot.

'Yes, please. Where should I start?'

'From the day you left.'

Kotkas outlined his journey. Smuggled out of Estonia through Tamm's contacts, ending up at Memel. Commissioned into the German Navy on Gahlendorf's say-so. Time spent being evaluated by German counterintelligence. Then Berlin, Canaris and Barbarossa. He finished by talking about Finland and his time spent in the wilds of Estonia with the partisans.

'Any problems?'

Kotkas laughed. 'When are there not problems?'

'Berlin, Finland, the Partisans?'

'Felt like one of the family in every case. However ... speaking of family ...' He told Tamm about the close watch the security police were holding over them. Just the facts. No emotions. No speculations. No inner thoughts.

'So, tell me.' Tamm got to the point at last. 'Where are you, as far as we are concerned?'

'Who's "we"? You and me – or the people you work for? Actually, either way, it's not important. For my own safety and sanity, I'm keeping my head down, my nose clean, and adopting an enigmatic profile. I'm back here now. This is where I intend to stay. Digging my heels in. When I think it's safe enough, I will bring my family back. And that will be that. Then, the rest of you can get on and play whatever parlour games you choose.'

'You mean you won't help us?'

'Again – who is "us"? Who's anyone these days? All I can see are various world powers wielding their authority over the heads of little independents like us Estonians. We just want to be left alone. Go and hold your war somewhere else. No one seems to have noticed, but we were neutral at the start of this whole shambles, and even with our government in exile, we're still neutral now.'

'There's a moral imperative in all of this, my friend.'

'Sometimes, we have to prioritise which moral imperatives we pursue.'

'Sometimes, moral imperatives prioritise themselves. The only way to re-establish and keep Estonian neutrality is to side with those who will guarantee it.'

Kotkas shrugged. 'I'll cross that bridge if I come to it.'

'You're not having a breakdown, are you, Hendrik?'

'No. Just keeping myself to myself. It's the only way.'

'And what about those messages you got through to London when in Berlin? Don't they mean anything?'

'To your people, maybe. To me, it was half an idea. Hedging my bets. I had no idea getting back here, getting back home, was going to actually happen. But now I'm here ... well ... new rules.'

'There is such a thing as safety in numbers.'

'I'll take my chances. I'm all right. I know what I'm doing.'

Tamm considered him in the low light from the lamp.

'All right,' he said at last. 'But if you hear of anything you think we might like to know, will you tell us? Some of the old routes are still open.'

'You don't know that you can trust me anymore.'

'No. I don't.'

They fell silent.

Is Hendrik playing a clever game? wondered Tamm. Saying he was out of it, so that London might trust any information he'd give them? And, if so, to whose advantage? London's, Berlin's or, as he professed, his own?

If in doubt, take people at face value. Play them at their own game. What did he once say to Hendrik? *Stick to the truth wherever possible. And mean what you say.* Is that what his friend was doing?

'Isn't this where you say you will trust me anyway?' said Kotkas.

'No. You've made that very clear. Just as you are clear you can't trust me or my people anymore. However, if you feel you could ever get material out through me, intelligence that will help our cause, go ahead. You can leave it up to us to analyse its worth. How's that for a deal?'

'No.'

'Really?'

'No ... if I get anything to you, it will be to help my cause.'

'To bring your family safely home. Here. In a free, independent, neutral Estonia.' Tamm refreshed his coffee. 'Well, good luck trying to keep out of all of this. I give you a week.'

'Before I'm arrested? Killed?'

'Or simply before you're sucked right back into this mess again. War is no place for dreamers and idealists. They only start them. Realists finish them.'

Kotkas smiled. His mind flipped back to the last meeting between him and Tamm.

There was a place where they'd sometimes met, once the Soviets had rolled in. Somewhere quiet. A hidden bay flanked by woodland and a gentle beach, about an hour east of the city.

Hendrik had been first to arrive. He'd come in his old Berliet Dauphine and brought some A. Le Coq beer.

He sat by the water's edge.

There was the sound of an approaching vehicle. He hid until he could see who it was. It was Tamm, who drove up a track into the woods until his car was hidden, at least in part, by the trees.

They'd sat there laughing and sipping beer; the water petting the foreshore. The conversation conducted against a caprice of gulls' cries.

Then they lapsed into silence and watched the restless sea.

'If you want to get out – from under the Soviets – I could arrange it,' Tamm had said. 'Or, we could find a way of keeping you here in Tallinn. Undercover. I could get some papers.'

'Stay?'

'Yes, it's okay here.'

'And what do I do when they find out who I am?'

'They won't do that. I'll fix it ...'

Hendrik thought about it; considered the risks. 'How about the British?'

Tamm looked at his friend. 'I'll see what I can do.'

In the event, Tamm couldn't quite do enough, couldn't rescue both Hendrik and his family. So, Hendrik turned to Gahlendorf and the Germans. He remembered how, even then, Tamm had helped. Had spirited Hendrik out from under the Soviets, just as they were starting to haul off the senior military and naval personnel. It was also he who had got messages to Hendrik's wife and brother.

Hendrik, back in the cellar, drank some more coffee. 'Where's Peeter, do you know?'

Tamm shrugged. 'Last I heard, enjoying the hospitality of the Soviet Baltic Fleet. Whether he's gone over or just playing both sides against the middle, we can't tell.'

'There's that We, again. Which one is it this time?'

'There's a few of us left here. Estonians. Gone to ground; not associating with either of the monsters. You could join us.'

'We've had this conversation. Just before I left. Someone is bound to recognise me.' Though, to be honest, the thought of lying low, and leaving it just at that, was achingly attractive to Hendrik. He was tired. He was lonely. Yes, he was even scared. The longing for it all just to go away was very strong. He wondered again, as he had done these many confusing weeks, whether all the decisions he'd made would ever make sense; should he at some point in the unforeseeable future ever be granted the luxury of looking back. Maybe that was what history was. Real life was a sequence of vaguely connected ideas made in the frantic moment. History was a rationalisation of ideas that, at the time they were being made, were simply not connected in that way. Life was the doing of things in the here and now. History was the undoing of them, and their reshaping in a way that suited the narrative of a different time, a different place, and in a different context. By people who simply didn't, could never, and would never understand. Because they simply weren't there. 'I'd better get back,' he said.

'Okay.' Tamm stood. 'So … to be clear … you're dropping us? You're dropping everything?'

'I have to.'

Tamm shrugged. 'Up to you, dear boy,' he said. He inspected the street through the delivery hatch. 'All clear.'

Hendrik began to clamber out of the cellar. He turned and shook his friend's hand. Perhaps for the last time. Millions of such handshakes were taking place all over the world these days, he thought. Between parents and children. Lovers, wives and husbands. Brothers and sisters. Friends and enemies. Captors and captives. Executioners and condemned. The living and the dying.

This one was no different. It contained both a forlorn hope and a final farewell.

*

Kotkas made his way along the road that led to the medieval city wall at the northeastern end of the Old Town. There, the great tower Fat Margaret had stood for centuries, presiding over the harbour. He felt along its broad walls until he came to a stone that shifted with a little pressure like a loose tooth. He fiddled with it for a moment and it gave way. Inside was a little crevice. It was empty. Kotkas replaced the stone. *Good – it is still there. Just in case.* He started back towards the centre of the Old Town.

'Hendrik!'

He stopped to see who was calling him. It was an SS officer.

Kotkas cocked his head; he recognised the voice, but the man's eyes were in shadow beneath the glistening peak below the death's head cap badge. The officer closed on him and reached out a hand. All became clear. It was his bother-in-law, Feliks.

'Wonderful!' Feliks gripped Kotkas's hand as if it were a lifeline. 'I'd heard a rumour you were back. That you'd grabbed a berth with the Germans like me. Still in the same game, though, I hear. Intelligence? Come. Here's a café. Let's sit down and you can tell me everything ...'

'Sure. But I had better warn you, it's not safe talking with me ...'

'Really? Why?'

'Best you don't know.'

'As you wish.' He patted Kotkas's hand. 'You're safer talking to me in this get-up, though, eh? Ah, Hendrik! What days are these, eh? Where have the golden summers gone? I still mourn our beautiful racing yacht. Our yacht club. Don't you? So – tell me – what have you been up to?'

Kotkas told his brother-in-law the minimum needed to satisfy the fellow's curiosity. Until he knew Feliks's motives better, it was right to be cautious. Not least, bearing in mind the fellow's SS insignia.

Yes, as far as he knew, Leena and the children were perfectly safe.

Yes, he was working for the Intelligence Service.

Yes, he was currently billeted in Tallinn, though goodness knows where next ...

When Kotkas sought to learn more about his brother-in-law's circumstances, however, he found that this was also somewhat edited. Perhaps for similar reasons. Not that, Kotkas realised, Feliks had ever been one of his closest friends. He was his relative by marriage. A strong enough bond, for sure, but not a blood tie. Not a chosen friendship. Feliks was, after all, only related by marriage. On his father's death, Feliks had inherited his considerable textile empire. Wealth and breeding, right school, Tartu university, superior social circles; they all provided boundaries, Kotkas felt, even if he and Feliks had sought to disregard them. Feliks had, for example, never agreed with his parents' resistance to Kotkas and Leena's union. Moreover, they had spent many hours sailing together in Feliks's bright new six-metre. Racing in all kinds of weathers meant they developed at least a bond of mutual respect and trust. They had spent even longer in the Tallinn Yacht Club bar afterwards. But there was always difference. This meeting was different again, Kotkas felt. Nobody knew whose side anyone was on anymore. War brings many things: change, death, dismay, the agony of parting ... all permeated by mistrust.

'No, my dear Hendrik,' Feliks was saying, 'my membership of the SS is simply a matter of convenience. A temporary measure in times of difficulty. Just like you, I am sure.'

'But ... Feliks ... the SS?'

Feliks lowered his head. 'I know. What could I do? I was an officer in the Estonian Home Guard. I had a certain background, one might say, not least because it was a Baltic German upbringing. Once upon a time, not so long ago, an elite – all that nonsense. When I transferred from our Home Guard, you might say, they transferred my status, too. I told them I wasn't actually Baltic German but pure Estonian – we just went to those schools, moved in those social circles, didn't we? I said I was happy to be a simple soldier. But they insisted. And when the Germans insist ... well, I don't have to tell *you*, do I ...?' He looked at Kotkas.

Kotkas tried to read those eyes. The fellow wanted reassurance where there could perhaps be none. Not while they both wore those particular uniforms. And he was only too aware that not everyone in the SS there did so because they felt obliged. There were plenty of Estonians, he knew, who couldn't wait to climb into the uniform and goose-step around the country as if to the manner born. 'Why did they insist?'

Feliks shrugged. 'Why do you think? Elite with elite? Officer class with officer class? But also something a little more subtle. Fold us in. Expose us to their guilty secrets. Make us complicit by association. So we can't turn on them.'

'This is dangerous talk, my dear chap. How do you know you can trust me?'

Feliks smiled. 'If I can't trust you, Hendrik – of all people – then the whole world really has gone mad.'

'Thank you.'

'I mean it.'

'In which case – may I speak frankly?' Feliks nodded, so he continued. 'They might try to move me on in due course. Insist I follow the flag. But I intend to stay here. What's your plan?'

'Stay, too. Whatever happens. The way I see it is this ...' Feliks drew on the café table with his forefinger. 'The Reds turn and start to push back. We have the most modern arms and equipment now, thanks to our current employers. We are better trained, better organised. We can give a better account of ourselves as Estonians than we did before Ivan occupied us the first time.'

'We did not give any account of ourselves the first time. We just rolled over and let them tickle our tummies.'

'A political decision.'

'Foolishness.'

'So, we stand and fight the next time. There are already thousands of men gathering in the forests. They are ready to rise up and see off the next invasion. Working together with us, we might, like the Finns, give Ivan such a bloody nose that they could just decide to leave us alone.'

'Or ...?'

'Or, they don't come. The German advance succeeds, and we are left being run by the Nazis.'

'In which case?'

Feliks lowered his voice. 'There are already thousands of men gathering in the forests – for whatever eventuality ...'

'Plus you?'

'Plus me.'

*

Kotkas returned on foot through Kalamaja. Approaching the navy yard, he saw the car parked across the road from the gate. He thought about turning around but decided to try and make it past and into the relative safety of the base. However, as he approached, one of the men got out and started towards him. The car coughed into life and drew up alongside. A rear door flew open and Kotkas was hurled inside by the man who'd got out, as if he was a sack.

'Big mistake – walking,' said the man, who clambered in after him. He drew a pistol out of his pocket and held it on his lap.

'I should remind you that I am a navy officer.'

'I deduced as much; there's very little escapes us. Though the uniform's a big clue. But wearing one and deserving one are two very different things.'

Kotkas was taken back into the Old Town. At one point, the driver parked beside a telephone kiosk and made a call. He got back in, drove a few more blocks, and pulled up at the top of an alley.

'Out we get,' he said.

Kotkas was pulled along into the darkness between the buildings. And then the two men proceeded to practise their boxing skills on various parts of his body. Soon, he sank to his knees from the sustained blows and the pain. So the men moved from pummelling to kicking. He finally collapsed into the foetal position on the cobbles. They landed two more blows with their government-issue steel toecaps then stood back to admire their handiwork.

Kotkas looked up; heaving, nauseous, and with blood oozing from a cheekbone.

Someone emerged from the shadows and lit a cigarette.

'Ah. Fischer. Good afternoon,' wheezed Kotkas. 'Lovely day for thuggery.'

'You either allow us to follow you or you allow us to beat you up,' Fischer said. 'Feel free from now on to choose which form of entertainment you prefer. We are happy to provide both. And don't go running to your guardian angels, or we'll double the dose.'

'You mixed your metaphors.'

Fischer sneered and left.

Kotkas struggled to his feet with no assistance from his tormentors. With one hand holding his stomach and the other bracing his ribs, he tottered out into the street. Pulling himself up to his full height, he set off; wincing with pain at every step. His two assailants followed.

He made it into the town centre and went into a café. One of the men followed him in and sat across the room. Kotkas downed a beer and a vodka in quick succession. Somewhat revived, he set off again; the fellow barely twenty paces behind.

He went into a tobacconist's to buy cigarettes. Leaving again, one of his escorts took up the shadowing while the other went into the shop. Doubtless, he was going to question the proprietor to find out what Kotkas had said, what he had bought and, most probably, inspect anything that might have been handed over.

Despite the discomfort from his beating, Kotkas continued to meander through the Old Town. He took some delight in having no object in mind other than to keep his followers trudging after him. He would go into this department store to browse, then that tailor's to feel the texture of some suit cloth. He would leave again having purchased nothing. One of his attendants would nonetheless have to dutifully go in afterwards and question the staff: *What did he do? Nothing. What did he say? Nothing.* Kotkas allowed himself a wry smile at the thought of the futility of their assignment.

While arbitrary and mindless, the beating had achieved one significant thing, Kotkas realised, however. He now longed for the ability to send new information across to the British. Even if only to spite Fischer and his thugs. But how? It was too risky. Not just for him but for anyone with whom he came into contact.

Perhaps, instead, he might, after all, take Tamm up on his offer. Was Tamm really able to help him stay in Estonia this time? Get him some papers; help him disappear? That loose stone in Fat Margaret could be useful after all. Putting messages in for one another had been how Tamm and he had communicated in the past.

What would that mean, though, putting himself back in Tamm's hands? On the run from the Germans as well as the Soviets … and goodness knows who else?

Either way, he might at least be able to bring his family back. Send them to Vasalemma, to stay at the farm, out of harm's way. Maybe he could join them. Hide away with them.

Was he the hiding type, though?

Why didn't he just simply stay in the German Navy? Lie low, wait, like Gahlendorf appeared to be doing?

Wait? Unthinkable. He'd never waited for anything in his life. Wasn't his way. Wasn't the navy way. What was it the British Admiral Nelson once said? *Our country will, I believe, sooner forgive an officer for attacking his enemy than for letting it alone.*

He even toyed with the idea at one point of asking Emilie to help in some way. He only wondered this for the briefest of instants, however. It would be callous to involve her; besides, she was on the 'other side'. And, of course, far away in Berlin.

Kotkas realised that it had become a challenge; a puzzle. Intelligence officers liked nothing better than to have a problem to solve. Nevertheless, while engaged in the daily round of his intelligence work, something would, he knew, continue to nag at him. It wouldn't be enough anymore to be working towards his ultimate goal of helping return his country to the independence it all too briefly enjoyed. He knew now he would absolutely have to do more. To contribute in some other way.

Tamm was right. He'd been drawn back in.

After a couple of hours, he made his way to the relative sanctuary of the navy base; waving goodbye to his chaperones at the gate. By then, he had already begun to form a plan.

He made to step into his office. But was brought up short. There was someone in the outer room.

'What are you doing here?'

Emilie turned. She still wore her travelling clothes. A small fore-and-aft maroon felt hat with a pheasant feather. A trim sea-green cotton tunic with matching pleated skirt. Sensible shoes – she had walked from Baltic Station. She was holding a carpet bag; her trunk was being taken straight to her quarters. She had refreshed her lipstick. 'The Admiral sent me to help.' She gave a tentative smile.

'I don't need any help.'

The smile fell away. She let the bag drop to the floor. She was angry with herself for even allowing the thought that he might be pleased to see her. Had she not been ordered by Canaris to come, she would not have stayed one moment longer. 'The Admiral thinks you do.' She started to pull her travelling gloves off, a finger at a time. This appeared to need her undivided attention. 'Where shall I sit?'

'Please yourself.'

He brushed past into his office and closed the door. There he sat engrossed in paperwork for more than an hour. Just beyond the door he could hear desk and chairs being moved and muffled conversations.

A little later, Emilie knocked on the door.

'Yes?'

'I brought you a coffee.' Her tone was brisk. 'Your fellow, Louis, says you have it about now. He tells me you haven't heard from your family. Would you like me to try and find out where they are, how they are doing?'

'As you wish.'

'Why are you being so frosty with me?'

'Why did you go to Königsberg? What right do you think you have to concern yourself with my personal business?'

'The right as a good German to support those fighting on our behalf, by ensuring those they love are secure and cared for. You could not go. I could.'

'Well, thank you for being a good German. I am sure the Leader and the State applaud you. For my part, I'll thank you never to involve yourself in my family's affairs again ... do you hear?'

They looked at each other. He at his desk, she in the doorway.

Emilie broke the silence. 'Do you want me to try and contact your family or not?'

'Yes.'

'Please.'

'Please.' He stood up and walked out.

'What about your coffee?'

'I didn't ask for it.'

He set off down the corridor, knocked on Gahlendorf's door and went in. 'Once I've set everything up here,' he began without preamble, 'for you, for Canaris ... Once I've put the team together, got everything working properly and the interception system working well ... how about I go back to who I really am?'

'And who, really, are you?'

'Just a navy officer. A seagoing commander. Give me a ship.'

Gahlendorf laughed. He couldn't help himself.

It stung.

'Can't do it, old chap. Estonians in charge of one of the State's precious warships? Whatever next?' He paused. 'Sorry for laughing, but ... Well, there is one way, I suppose ...'

'Which is?'

'Join the Party. Pledge allegiance to the Leader.'

'No.'

'Come on. A little arthritic salute once in a while. For the right reasons. What harm could it do?'

'All the harm in the world.'

'I see. Listen ... you know me. I've made it clear what I stand for. But we are never really sure which side you're on, are we? That's half the problem. Well, let me help you. Come over to our side. And by "our side", I don't mean what you might think I mean. One day, this will all be over, one way or another. You know it. I know it. One day, our great Leader will be no more. The world will revolve on its axis again, and Germany can go back to its old ways. That's what I'm fighting for. True independence and hope for the future. Come and join this kind of Germany. Not the one that's here – the one that is to come. Think of your German roots. Your German heritage. Your German future.'

'I have no German roots.'

'Are you not Baltic German?'

'No. Estonian. I just grew up in the Baltic German culture. The one left behind by former overlords, before the Tsar took an unhealthy interest in my country.'

'Nevertheless, we are a club within a club, so to speak. German naval officers. Honour, integrity, fighting for a good future. A true future. Not the future those boobies in Berlin want. But one we can be absolutely proud of and sure of.'

'I'll think about it,' said Kotkas.

'What happened to your face, by the way?'

III

Marjorie walked into the Major's office with a slip of paper. He was enjoying a brief respite with a cup of tea and a digestive biscuit.

'Message from Monika, sir.'

'Saying …?' He placed the cup in the saucer with a clink, finished his biscuit and dusted the crumbs from his uniform jacket.

'He's re-established contact with Kadakas.'

He looked up. 'Any view as to whether our friend Kadakas is still feeling kindly disposed towards us?'

'No, sir. It's a bit confusing really. Monika seems to be saying Kadakas is no longer working for us.'

'So who is he working for?'

She reviewed the message. 'It doesn't say, sir. He does say Kadakas is now sailing under a flag of convenience, as he puts it.'

'Meaning …?'

'Well, I imagine, if Kadakas really did send those messages from Berlin, then he now wears that uniform.'

'Makes sense. The Germans are back in Estonia. Could easily have gone there with them.'

'We just need to know how convenient is this flag of convenience.'

'Right. So be it. Either way, tell Monika to drop him or, if needs be, neutralise him. We can't have someone like that roaming around knowing what he knows. Especially if he's had a change of heart. Voluntarily or enforced.'

'But, there's more, sir. Monika says, however, that we can trust anything Kadakas sends us unless or until proved otherwise.'

'What does that mean?'

'No idea.'

'Right. Watching brief, then, please, Marjorie. And alert me the moment Monika gets in touch again. I do hope it's soon. No telling when the great Russian Bear will get tired of running and turns on its tormentors.'

'Sir.'

And, Marjorie …?'

'Yes, sir?'

'Tell Monika – one sign of tomfoolery or double-crossery from Kadakas and he is to finish him …'

'Yes, sir.'

'… by whatever means he deems necessary. If he's lost interest in us, well, then, we can just as easily lose interest in him. He can fight this war on his own. Or he can be dead. Either way, we'll want him off our hands.'

'Sir.'

'Any more tea in the pot, by the way?'

*

In her more lucid moments, Leena found that her memory of things long past was clearer than remembering what she'd done that morning.

She had stopped looking at herself in mirrors. She had stopped bothering with make-up, lipstick, because that would have meant looking in mirrors. She didn't want to be reminded of her younger self, let alone the self that was once healthy and happy and flushed with the vigour of life. A life that had gone. A life that would now, she knew, never return. Why stare that in the face?

What a youth! What a life! The thrill and expectations of future promise that danced around all privileged young women. Promises once, it seemed, that were entirely likely to be fulfilled. A wealthy family, a grand home. And what an adventure! At one time, even, to have been brought to

England, to St James's Palace in London for her Coming Out. To be presented as a Debutante at the Court of King George. Draped in silks and pearls; like a princess.

Unbelievable now, of course, sitting there, bones aching, head throbbing and heart broken on a chaise longue in some squalid house in a foreign country surrounded by strangers. How high she had flown. How low she had fallen.

Where is Hendrik? Why doesn't he come? Why doesn't he take us out of this horror?

Hendrik. Her darling Hendrik. Handsome, elegant young naval officer. Her hero. Everyone's hero. Never quailed before her father. Stood up to her mother. But constantly courteous. Born to command. Commanded her parents. Not by confrontation but by personality and will.

She'd been in the hall, listening at the door.

Her father had not been unsympathetic to him, though her mother was. The meeting had not gone well, Hendrik would tell her afterwards. Liisu had nodded to him upon entering the parlour but did not add a smile. She sat observing him throughout the interview. Leena's father stood, or, rather, loomed with the light from the French window behind him; his watch chain restless across his circumference, rising and falling with every breath. Hendrik's request to continue to court their daughter was noted. No more than that. Valter made a few cursory enquiries after his family and circumstances, then Liisu rang the bell that sat on the occasional table beside her. A servant entered to escort the young naval officer out. Hendrik tripped as he left.

Leena had stepped back from the door as he came through it. She was about to go to him, when her father appeared. He gave his daughter a look then turned to Hendrik.

'Make something of yourself, my boy. Do your best,' he said.

Valter made his way back into the parlour. But not before giving his daughter a sly wink.

Hendrik took his hat and coat from the servant. As he put

them on, he turned to Leena. 'I will respect your parents,' he said. 'I will respect their views. But, nonetheless, I shall have it my way in the end. Don't worry, my darling, I always get what I want.' He pecked her pretty nose before slipping out into the night.

Gone eighteen months. Eighteen long months. Training with the Royal Navy and then back to sail the Baltic on active service. He was promoted, assured a future, given a pay rise. Then, at last, he returned to her, and to meet again with her parents.

They were persuaded.

Had father done some mining into Hendrik's past and prospects in his absence? Of course he had. Everything he quarried, it seemed, had come up silver and gold.

She listened again at the door. Her father knew she would; he raised his voice that she might be included.

'Well, my boy. It seems you have made something of yourself.'

'Are making something of yourself,' her mother had corrected.

'Well done. I am happy – rather, that is to say, Liisu and I – are happy to consent to your marrying Leena.'

'Thank you, sir. Madam. You have made me the happiest man alive.'

'Glad to hear it,' Liisu had said. 'I should be concerned if you were in any way unhappy about it.'

And they all laughed, and called Leena in, and there was more laughter and hugging and a little champagne.

'Of course, my boy,' Valter had then said, 'we shall settle you in one of our houses. I have one in mind. A most suitable residence for my daughter and son-in-law, once you are married.'

'Most suitable for a young family,' her mother had added.

That was where a little frost descended.

'Thank you, sir ...' Hendrik said, 'madam ... that is most generous and kind. However, I am proposing to find an apartment of our own. My navy pay will stretch, I am sure, to something entirely comfortable and suitable for me and my new beautiful wife, once we are wed.'

She squeezed his hand.

'Really?' her father had said. 'Are you sure?'

'Quite sure.'

Silk and pearls and a society wedding had followed.

Oh, the music. The dancing. The long sultry wedding night!

Leena took up again the message from Hendrik saying he was in Tallinn, safe and well. *Safe and well.* It had come that morning. She had read its contents to the children when they came home from school that afternoon. All three danced and hugged each other. For the first time in goodness knows how long, Leena had danced with Maret, who shone. Just for a while, until Leena had fallen back onto the couch; after which she just sat there laughing and clapping as the children continued singing: 'We're going home, we're going home!' Home to their apartment; something entirely comfortable and suitable for a young naval officer's family. *Safe and well.*

But now the children were fed and in bed, and Mrs Wowreit had gone home, and the night had fallen, and the window shutters were closed, and the vodka was finished, and she was left alone with her thoughts again.

Safe and sound in Tallinn?

Don't worry, my darling, I always get what I want.

But there was no mention in that brief note of sending for them. Not even the implied hope of sending for them in the near, or further, future.

Safe and well.

She screwed up the message and threw it onto the floor.

Why did he not send for them?

She reached for her laudanum.

*

Fischer was enjoying a cigarette. He stood looking out of the window of his vast office on Toompea Hill. Below him lay the city and its populace, over which he was pleased to have some significant control and influence. The phone rang.

'Yes?'

It was a call from one of his colleagues in Berlin. 'You know your idea about getting someone into Canaris's office?'

'A lifetime ago, yes. Don't tell me you finally managed it. Well, better late than never, I suppose. Doubt I'll get any credit for it, either. Well ...?'

'Well, thought you'd like to know our girl took the place of someone you had a particular interest in ... As I recall, you fancied your chances with her.'

'I never did.'

'Yes, you did. You said that, with your girlfriend all the way down in Dresden, you thought you might—'

'Yes, yes. Get on with it. What's so important?'

'Well, our girl's got word to us that the pretty little bird you have had your eye on has made her nest in your part of the forest.'

'Estonia?'

'Yes. Tallinn, to be precise.'

'Really? Who's she with? Who's she working for, then?'

His colleague told him.

Fischer stubbed his cigarette out and smiled to himself. *Two birds; one stone.* Bait and prey.

*

Kotkas was crossing the Town Hall Square, looking for lunch. The tall merchants' buildings with their pastel-coloured walls and their steep red roofs provided an almost fairytale backdrop. Kotkas thought of the bedtime stories he used to tell his children. Princes and dragons and damsels in distress. Wicked witches and greedy goblins. Gingerbread and marzipan. The essence of childhood. The stories of innocence. The ache returned; the longing for everything to be the way it was: his wife and family back at home and him just out to pick up some freshly baked bread from the baker's. At that moment, he might almost have imagined things were indeed the way they had always been – if it wasn't for his two guard dogs as ever in tow. As they had been for the past two days.

He was brought further out of his reverie when he noticed some people being herded into some trucks. A German SS officer was standing nearby.

'What's all that?' Kotkas asked.

The soldier scrutinised the German naval officer before deigning to speak. 'Just rounding up a few Communists, Jews, troublemakers ...'

'... and Estonians?'

The officer shrugged. 'They're all scum.'

So it had begun. Kotkas had heard a rumour in the mess a few days before that they had even started exporting Jewish families from Germany to Estonia. And now this. An independent nation under the benevolent eye of Berlin, or some kind of glorified internment camp? So much for treating Estonians with respect. Undesirables being herded together in a corner of the world where they could be discarded ... or worse.

His mind worked its way back to Plötz and that day in Berlin when he had been shown the list of so-called Intelligence Service agents. Jewish people being given an escape route out of hell. And now hell had come to his homeland.

Desperate affairs require desperate measures, as Nelson had once said.

A woman and two children – a young girl and a little boy – were now being loaded onto one of the trucks. The girl, beautiful dark skin and rich black plaits, looked like Maret. He looked closer; it wasn't. Neither was it Leena and Juhan. But the momentary resemblance left him with a stabbing unease. What if it had been?

He returned, accompanied as ever by his two ugly bookends. He was glad to leave them to go beyond the navy yard's secure perimeter fence.

He worked long into the night. At about a quarter to ten, he picked up his phone and dialled Gahlendorf's extension.

Gahlendorf was still at work, too. 'What is it, Hendrik?'

'Best not on the phone. Who knows who's listening? I just rang to see if you were still around.'

'Always around. Cursed promotion. Pop into my office; we'll chat.'

Kotkas outlined the concerns that had grown while working through the latest material gathered in from various intelligence sources. He illustrated them with the paperwork he'd been poring over.

'... so, you see ... the trouble is – it's very clear the army needs to slow down its advance. The Soviets intend to draw them further and further in. Stretch their lines of communication until they creak and crack. Build up their confidence so they start making mistakes. Then, of course, there's Tsar Alexander I's dictum ...'

'Which is?'

'It was his army that defeated Napoleon ... Alexander said once that he had every confidence in his generals. Especially, he pointed out, generals *January* and *February*.'

'So – tell Army Group North. Tell Berlin.'

'Would they listen to me? Past evidence suggests they don't take kindly to negative projections. It's all hubris: *forward to glory; it is our destiny; ignore the misery guts, the nay-sayers, and devil-take-the-hindmost!*'

'That's their problem, not yours. Your job is to simply give them the intelligence. Not your job to tell them what to do with it. Just tell them. It's best you do, rather than them finding out later that you kept such information from them. That would, surely, go much worse for you. Keep your nose clean.'

Hendrik returned to his desk and composed his intelligence report. He included his views that the Soviets appeared to deliberately be drawing the army further and further into the cave of the Bear.

He then made a full copy of everything.

Hendrik, not for the first time, was grateful that every good sailor, whatever their rank, had a *hussif*. Back in his quarters, he rummaged around in his bedroom drawer and pulled it out. Leena had given it to him once for his birthday. A folded leather wallet. Inside were needles, pins, cotton of various colours, darning yarn, a foldable pair of scissors, a thimble.

He slit open the lining of his navy greatcoat, placed the copies of his report to Army Group West inside, and spent the evening sewing the lining closed again.

*

Maret and Juhan wandered back from their respective Group meetings. Karl Stieber had left them at the top of the road, as he did most times nowadays, to make his own way home. He still enjoyed Group but was growing increasingly impatient to get on with the real war. Unfortunately, it would still be nearly two years before he would be able to finally leave his dull little hometown and these silly foreign kids for good. He longed for the day when he could offer his service to the State in a different way.

The children were singing songs that celebrated the vigour and supremacy of the Fatherland.

They reached the house. Mrs Wowreit would arrive shortly to make them their evening meal. She had increasingly reduced her attendance, having her own home, her husband and her own life to look after. In any case, Mrs Kotkas was able enough at least to open the door for her own children and make them a snack or something to drink until they could be properly fed.

So Maret knocked and waited.

She knocked again.

Something about the silence, the way the door knocker trembled and stopped dead, disturbed Maret.

She knocked once more. Harder.

Still no response.

A tremor of unease shot through her. This was not right.

'Juhan, go around the side. Look in through the living-room window. See if Mother is asleep.'

He did so.

A moment passed.

Then Juhan let out a cry. 'Maret! Maret! Quickly ...'

Maret ran round to where her brother was standing. His eyes wide. His hands spread in alarm.

'Mama! It's Mama! Look ...' He jabbed a finger at the window.

Maret, just as Juhan had just done, gripped the window sill and levered herself up to look in. It took a moment to make out in the darkness what was there. It took another moment to work out that the feet that were dangling there, seemingly from the ceiling, belonged to their mother.

She didn't quite comprehend what it was she was seeing. She just knew she had to act. She spun round, found a rock in the garden and hurled it through the glass. The window shrieked as if in pain as it shattered. Then, wrapping her cardigan around her fist and forearm, she crashed away more shards until there was space enough for a child to clamber through.

'Help me in, Juhan. Help me.'

Juhan bent down, hands braced on knees, and allowed his sister to tread on his back. She hauled herself through the window, cutting her arms and legs on the teeth of glass which had refused to leave where they were embedded in the frame. She then turned round and, reaching out, pulled her brother in behind her.

They ran to the legs.

'Lift her up, Juhan, hold her. Hold her.'

Juhan, with the effort and strength only given to terrified children, clamped himself onto his mother's calves and lifted. She swung, bent and buckled, but the strain on the neck had been eased momentarily.

Maret climbed up onto the table beside the couch. Reaching up, with fingers she could barely control, she worked at the knot of the dressing-gown belt which was connecting their mother to the cord of the ceiling light.

'Keep still, Juhan. Keep her still.'

'I'm trying! Hurry up!'

Once upon a time, a few birthdays ago, Maret had begun scrabbling at the string that had tied the brown paper around one of her birthday presents. She had reached for the scissors, as the knot was so tight it seemed there was no way to get at the mysteries within. 'Never cut a knot,' her father had said to her. 'Always take the time and trouble to untie it. You never know when you will need that string again.'

Despite the panic and terror she was experiencing, this injunction by her father had returned to her now; as had all the times she had patiently untied every knot she had encountered ever since.

At last, with one final tug, her mother was free.

Leena tumbled to the floor, with Juhan collapsing underneath her in the process.

'Juhan, Juhan ... are you all right?'

'Yes,' he said, dragging himself out from under.

'Quick, telephone the police ... the doctor ...'

Juhan ran to the hall.

Maret knelt down beside her mother, unsure now what to do.

'Mother? Mother?' she said. She tried to pull the woman's head round to look at her, but it just lolled back onto the carpet where it had lain.

Maret remembered something she'd been taught at Group. How to tend to an injured soldier or civilian. She took her mother's wrist. Making sure she was not placing her thumb on it, where her own pulse was strongest, she felt with the tips of her fingers. Was there something? A little give, a little pressure down there beneath the thin white bare flesh? Or was she imagining it?

She could hear Juhan shouting breathlessly down the telephone.

'Mother …?' she said again. Then, 'Hurry up, Juhan! Tell them to hurry!'

Hendrik's message, the one he'd left those months ago on the table beside the couch, the table that Maret had scrambled onto to untie her mother, lay on the floor. It had been kicked off.

Don't do anything silly. Your husband and children love you. Call for help.

*

It was dusk. Kotkas had sauntered down to the quayside within the navy yard in his greatcoat. The launch he'd ordered to be made ready for him was there. It was nodding in the swell. A sailor undid the ropes tethering it to the land and, alone, out on the water, Kotkas chuntered off into the deepening evening.

The dark sea rose and fell; inhaling, exhaling. The wavelets toyed with the spangled reflection of the setting sun. He approached the Old Town harbour as the sun finally turned its back and sauntered off. He tied the painter to a mooring ring and made his way up the dripping steps, which smelt of salt and seaweed. The stairs were set into the granite blocks that made up the harbour. Little pools of seawater had formed on each step where they'd been worn down over the years by the tread of countless sea boots.

Tugging his coat around him and turning up his collar, he pulled the wool hat down further onto his head and hurried to a bar he knew. A bar he'd known since, as a young man, he started out to make a life working with and on the sea.

The room was fuggy; loud with drinkers. Fishermen spending a little of the proceeds from the day's catch before taking the rest home to their families. He looked around. He tapped a fellow on the shoulder.

'Yes?'

'Does Nils still come here?'

'Nils? Yes – he's over there.'

The informant waved his beer across the room. Kotkas's eyes followed and settled on a short dark fellow with a face as wrinkled as the waves of the sea he'd spent his life upon.

'Nils?'

'It took the fisherman a moment to recognise who was speaking. 'Hendrik?'

'Yes.'

Nils grabbed Kotkas's hand with both of his and pumped it up and down a dozen times.

'Well, well, well. There was a rumour you were around. I didn't believe it, because there are so many rumours these days. Ghosts and other sightings of days long past, never to return. How are you, my lad? How are the family?'

'Well,' said Kotkas, allowing the word to suffice for both parts of the question. 'And you? How is your mother?'

'Mother's dead these three years. Just me now.'

Kotkas knew the sea had taken both Nils's brothers and his father over the years. The only human left to sustain him had been his mother. 'I'm sorry,' he said. Though he also knew that what would still give his old friend and mentor purpose would be to kick off from shore and trawl the fishing grounds of the same sea he had tangled with all his life.

'Working for the Germans, are you?' his friend asked.

Kotkas shook his head. 'Working for Estonia. Just happen to wear, once in a while, a German uniform.' He looked down at his greatcoat. Although it was clearly navy issue, he'd removed the gold rings and the brass buttons with the scissors from his *hussif* to keep recognition down to a minimum. This had not fooled Nils, however.

'Are you here for long?' Nils asked. 'Beer? Answer the second question first.'

'I should love to have a beer with you, my old friend.'

They drank, and spoke of people long gone. They reminisced over adventures shared. It was Nils who had taken Kotkas out in

228

his first sailing boat, piloting the channels and rocks off Tallinn Harbour. It was Nils who had advised on the plans for, and construction of, Kotkas's brother-in-law Feliks' new sailing boat. It was Nils who had taken charge of the six-metre when the Soviets invaded, putting her into storage until she could be sold; the world having no use for leisure pursuits anymore. It was Nils who had sold it to his cousin Jan over in neutral Sweden. It was Nils who had put the money into Feliks' bank account.

Then, as long as Kotkas would have loved to put the inevitable off further, he came to the point of his visit. 'How is your cousin over in Sweden?'

'Jan? He is well.'

'Do you still see him?'

'Once in a while. We speak on the wireless. Arrange to meet on this or that fishing ground.'

'I'm glad.'

Nils looked at him. 'There are two kinds of glad, my friend. Glad for the other, or glad for oneself. Which is it here?'

'Sadly, the self part is the reason I have come. For which I apologise.'

'Friends need never apologise. What can I do for you?'

Kotkas lowered his voice. 'When are you likely to meet up with Jan again, do you think?'

'Probably next week.'

'Any way of guaranteeing this?'

'Depends.'

'Do you think, as well as coming *back* with a catch, you might actually *leave* with a full load?'

'I don't understand.'

'I think you have a pretty good idea, though.' Kotkas took out a slip of paper he had prepared in his office. It was a line of text; the attribution showed it was from the Bible. Mark 1.17. Nils took it. *And I will make you fishers of men.*

'Can I leave you to think about it? Get a message to me at the base if you and your cousin decide you are happy to go ahead with things, and I'll arrange the rest ... another drink?'

They sat, drank beer and shared more stories. Then it was time for Kotkas to leave. He took off his outer layer to reveal, underneath, civilian clothes. 'Now, do you think Jan would like a lovely reasonably new navy greatcoat?'

'How much?'

'Free.'

Nils looked again at Kotkas and understood. 'I am not sure Jan would be terribly interested in a navy greatcoat. It is too cumbersome for fishing. Can you think, instead, of someone who might make better use of it, perhaps?'

'Well, yes ...' said Kotkas, and lowered his voice again, though the raucous atmosphere in the bar had not subsided for one moment. 'I wondered whether Jan, or perhaps someone he knew and trusted, might be able to get this to the British Embassy in Stockholm. Perhaps someone there could do with a good quality overcoat.'

Nils nodded, took the coat and folded it up into as tight a bundle as he could manage. He ignored the strange sensation of rustling paper. 'I'll see what I can do.'

'One last thing ...'

'Anything.'

'If you and Jan are happy to go ahead, would you make sure this goes along with the greatcoat?'

Kotkas handed Nils a further folded slip of paper.

'Sure,' Nils said.

He opened the message and read the single line written there. *Tell Monika Maret happy to spirit the disenchanted.* A broad smile grew on his face. 'I understand,' he said. 'And yes.'

Back at the navy base, Kotkas secured the launch and climbed up onto the quayside.

It was only then that he noticed the two navy police sailors and a lieutenant.

'Are you here for me?' he said.

The officer nodded.

IV

The navy police took him into the guardroom and sat him down in one of the cells. The officer did all of the talking.

'We had a call.'

'Oh yes?'

'From our colleagues in the civilian security police.'

'Ah.'

'It appears they have officers on permanent duty outside for you.'

'So I have learnt.'

'They saw you go off in the boat, sir. They tried to follow your progress from the shore in their car but lost you when the road veered inland. They went to a lot of trouble, they tell us, searching for you everywhere in the town but could not find you. They were very ... disappointed ... sir.'

'Please offer them my apologies. However, truth to tell, I grew somewhat weary of their company and felt like having a little time to myself...'

'I see, sir. We will set aside why you are wearing your civilian clothes and not uniform while at the base and on duty,' the lieutenant continued. 'The ordering of a naval vessel for personal use without following the strict protocols is a more serious matter.'

'Indeed.'

'However, the main reason we have detained you is that we have been asked to.'

'By the civilian security police?'

'By them, yes, sir.'

'Because ...?'

'Because they claim that you were technically absent

without leave. Absconded. They could make a case that they can find no orders, nor any reason why you should have left your post at this time ... This is an extremely grave matter and one which, you understand, people here are taking seriously. Unfortunately, Commander, as a result, we have been asked to hand you over to them for further questioning.'

'I see.'

'However ...'

'However?'

The lieutenant and the sailors broke into grins. 'We look after our own. Those pigs have no jurisdiction here, and we won't let them have a look-in, sir. They can ask and claim and stamp their little kiddy feet until they are blue in the face. We uphold law here. Not them.'

'Thank you.'

'Nevertheless, sir, you do seem to be in a bit of a difficult situation. While we do not accept their position in all this, they still wait over there for you and will probably arrest you the moment you step outside the base. Your movements at present appear to be very limited. That can't help you, or the German Navy, or our war effort.'

'I wonder, would it help if they believed you had interrogated me yourself? The conclusion being that you have established beyond all reasonable doubt that mine was simply an innocent trip, a compulsive sailor taking to the sea for some thinking time. Something like that?'

'It's possible. The Admiral could pass that on to whoever regulates those buffoons beyond the gates.'

'Good. I think it would also help if you thumped me, just to illustrate the point. Raise a bruise or two, somewhere where it can be seen when next I go out and about.'

'It's against the law to strike a superior officer, sir.'

'Would it help if I made it a direct order?'

'Left or right eye, sir?'

'You choose.'

*

Emilie was still orientating herself. She was out among the cafés and shops. It was dusk; the shops were just closing, the cafés and bars preparing for the evening. The lights were coming on, making every window and every entrance a place of welcome. Music, both classical and popular, spilled out onto the streets. The aroma of coffee and beer and evening meals accompanied her as she wandered the cobblestones of the Old Town. She might almost be in turn-of-the-century Vienna, she thought. Was there really a war on? But then she recalled what had happened to the capital of the Austro-Hungarian Empire after the last war had rampaged through it.

She had just turned down another narrow street when she felt someone come up behind her and press her close. She was about to twist round and say: *Do you mind?* when the person appeared before her and leered into her face.

'We meet again,' said Fischer.

'What do you want?'

'Ah, now that's quite a long list. How long have you got? Never mind, I know where best we might start. Come with me.'

'Where?'

'Where I tell you. And, not to put too fine a point on it, I am easily offended if people do not do what I ask of them.'

'I have to get back,' Emilie said, and made to go. He stepped in her way.

'I am sure you do. And you will, absolutely, be allowed to do so in due course. But first I need you to come with me. Or would you rather be arrested for obstructing the police in their lawful business?'

She considered a number of possible responses, all of which would ultimately fetch her up in either trouble or a dead end. Or simply dead. 'All right. But this had better not take too long.'

'It will take as long as I wish it to take. That's the beauty of my work.'

*

'I'd like to indent for a new greatcoat, please.'

Kotkas was speaking to the quartermaster in the stores. The warrant officer was beyond retirement age but had volunteered to serve again, once war broke out. His round ruddy cheeks were set off by a full Bismarck moustache.

'A new one? What happened to the old one, laddie?'

'I lost it.'

'Lost it? Well ... people like you usually go to posh tailors.'

'I'm not people like me.'

'It'll cost your department.'

'Fair enough.'

'Greatcoats don't grow on trees.'

'No, they don't.'

'Right – let's get you measured up. You need to be more careful in future, laddie.'

'I will.'

*

Fischer and Emilie reached a tall building in the Old Town. It was over five stories high and had a Dutch gable. The door was thick and heavy but otherwise nondescript. Fischer opened it and drew Emilie in.

A woman came out from one of the downstairs rooms. She smiled. 'Welcome back, sir.' Fischer grunted and led Emilie through another door. There was a hubbub. Emilie noted a dozen or so senior German officers; army, navy, SS. They were either sitting at tables or at the bar at the far end. They were all drinking and smoking. A gramophone was playing Horst Winter's *Ich nenne alle Frauen 'Baby'*. Emilie also noted the waitresses. All about her age. All had smiles locked into their lips.

'I have applied for you to be seconded here.' Fischer spoke without looking at her. 'I think you'll agree it is a much more agreeable task than the rather dull administrative one upon which you are currently engaged. The role is very simple: supply these brave fellows with what they need. They are weary from combat, lonely and ... they miss their wives and girlfriends. To that end, there are any number of rooms upstairs, should any of the gentlemen require a little privacy in order to get to know you better.'

Emile fought hard not to slap him and run. 'Thank you for thinking of my welfare and seeking to remove me from the pressure of administrative work,' she said, 'but I am quite content with my mundane tasks.'

'Ah. You see, my dear, here is the difficulty. You seem to be under the impression that this is a somewhat sordid affair. Far from it. Come.' He took her back through the house and into the street. 'You see, Miss Meyer, this work I am asking you to do is highly specialised, sensitive and of great importance to the war effort. The fact that you are Intelligence Service means you are particularly qualified. As you may imagine, relaxation, alcohol and ... companionship ... is a very potent alchemy which often leads fellows to speak about things they would otherwise be better advised keeping to themselves, or not think it at all. These things, however, the State finds very interesting and is always eager to hear. Especially if, for some reason, these gentlemen are being less than loyal to the State in their purposes. If so, we would be particularly keen to hear about it. And that would be your vital job – reporting what you hear.'

'By "the State", you, of course, mean you?'

'I am the State, the State is me. Just as you, too, are the State, I trust. Because, my dear, if you are not – well, we would need to have a completely different conversation than this one, wouldn't we?' He liked the idea of her being in this place entertaining all those men. He'd even spent some time earlier that day imagining it. It excited him. He might even enjoy her himself sometime. She couldn't refuse him or he'd have her arrested. But that wasn't the main reason he'd brought her to the House. He was after Kotkas. If he had read that Estonian weasel correctly – and he undoubtedly had – the Commander wouldn't be able to sit idly by while one of his counterintelligence colleagues was subjected to this humiliation. Then he'd have them both: the Estonian in front of a firing squad, the girl tied to the House. He took out a cigarette and lit it. 'I'll give you a little while to think about it, my lovely. Consider your options, so to speak. As I said, I've already applied to have you seconded to this vital work. So now it's up to you. Off you pop, back to your office. Gather up your dainty little lady's things. I shall send a car in an hour or so.'

'And if I decide I don't want to do this?'

'I shall send a car in an hour or so. Either way.'

*

'What's the matter with your eye?' Gahlendorf had come into Kotkas's office and was leaning against a wall with his arms folded. 'This is getting to be a bit of a habit.'

'Tell them, not me.'

'Who?'

'Germans. Any of them. All of them.'

'I'm German.'

'Then you'll have a go at me too at some point, I expect.'

Gahlendorf smiled for a moment then took a chair and sat. His tone changed to one of concern. 'Listen, Hendrik, I am afraid I have some troubling news for you.' Kotkas laid his pen and the intercepts he was working on aside. Gahlendorf continued. 'I wanted to come and tell you personally, rather than let anyone else do it.' He paused. 'It's your wife.'

Kotkas sat back in his chair.

'It's all right!' Gahlendorf continued. 'She's all right. She is being looked after. Your children are being superb. But, I'm afraid she tried to take her own life.'

'Again?'

'*Again*?'

'Yes. She is so ill. She takes so much medication. She loses perspective ...' He subsided into silence, trying hard to control the howl that echoed around the hollows of his life.

Gahlendorf gave him a moment. Then, 'I am so sorry.'

Kotkas gathered himself. 'May I have compassionate leave, please?'

Gahlendorf gave a deep sigh and looked steadily at his friend. 'I'm afraid that is not possible.'

'Why not?'

'You know why not. You've seen what's needed here. The pace things are running at. The immense importance of your contribution.'

'What about the importance of my wife, my family?'

'My dear fellow, I sympathise, of course, but—'

'Sympathy. What kind of sympathy is this?'

Gahlendorf stood. 'It should be plain to you, as it is to everyone here – everyone on active service anywhere – that one simply cannot allow everyone who has some kind of personal crisis to go running off home willy-nilly when the mood takes them.'

'When the mood takes them? My wife just tried to kill herself. Are you saying my wanting to be beside her is some kind of selfish whim?'

'Of course not. Listen. I know you are upset. I would be too, if—'

'Upset? You don't know the meaning of the word. Upset to you is spilling your brandy or letting your cigar go out. That's just about the sum of your experience of personal tragedy. You people make me sick!'

Gahlendorf went to the door. 'You will remain here, at your post. That is an order.'

'Orders! You know where you can shove your orders.'

'I shall ignore that, Commander. Your request for

compassionate leave is regrettably refused. I suggest you take the rest of the evening to compose yourself. Then I shall expect to see you back at your desk tomorrow morning and fulfilling your duties. And, my friend, a little advice ... you may wish to lash out. I don't even mind you lashing out at me. But if you want to help your wife from here on in, control your temper and for heaven's sake keep your nose clean ...'

Kotkas watched him go. He sat for a moment. Then, getting to his feet, he flung his uniform jacket on, took up his cap and left.

He roamed the base in the twilight, ending up down by the harbour. He stood staring out to sea. The sea he and Leena had gazed at together all those years ago, arms around one another, the day she told him they were expecting their first child.

He recalled the day and the long night that Maret was born. It was at home. There had been complications. The doctor had come out into the living room to see him in the middle of the crisis, to prepare him for the worst. The doctor had suggested it might be a question of either saving the baby or saving the mother.

'Both,' Hendrik had said.

The doctor laid a hand on his forearm. 'I promise to do my best,' he said, and went back into the bedroom.

Hendrik had looked down at his sleeve; his wife's blood was on his arm from the doctor's hand.

Both Leena and Maret survived, though his wife had to go immediately into hospital where she convalesced for over two weeks. In time, they had taken the risk of trying for another child. Juhan was delivered safely and speedily. They had thought their troubles were all over. All they had to do from then on was to play happy families. The dashing naval officer, the beautiful heiress; the golden couple. Their two lovely children.

Now look at them. He stared at the heaving water; a wind

had got up, fretting the surface. He felt like yelling. Yelling at the waves as they mindlessly pushed in and sucked backwards again interminably. Yelling at the broken clouds, silver against the closing night; unaware that he even existed; unaware there was a war on. Yelling at the stars staring down at him with heartless eyes. He kicked at a stone; it plunged into the sea and sank to the bottom.

It was beyond suppertime, but he was not hungry. He made his way back to his office block; caught between not wanting to enter that hell-hole anymore and knowing that he probably at that moment had no choice. He wanted to run. He looked up at his office window. The lights were on. Emilie, in silhouette, was looking down at him. She waved a shadowy hand, making clear he was needed there urgently. He went.

'What is it?'

'I heard,' she said. 'I am so sorry. If there's anything I can do ...'

'Thank you.' He took his seat. She didn't leave. 'Is there anything else?' he said.

'There's a message on your desk.'

He took it up and read it, then laid it down again. 'They want you to work for them in that house?'

'Yes. As my direct manager, you have to sign the authority.'

'On secondment?'

'Yes.'

'Do you want to go?'

'What I want is unimportant. It is my duty as a German to go where I am told. Do what I am told.'

Kotkas walked across, guided Emilie further into the room and shut the door. 'Do you know what they want you to do?' He folded his arms.

'Yes.' She looked up at him.

He saw dismay in her eyes. 'And you're happy with this?'

'My happiness doesn't come into it.'

He looked at her a moment longer, unfolded his arms, took

239

the note and tore it in half. He took the two halves and tore them in half. He kept tearing until they were snowflakes which he then trickled into the wastepaper basket beside his desk. He looked up. Her blue eyes were misty. 'I'll fix it,' he said.

'No, sir.'

'Yes, sir.'

'You'll get into trouble. I'll get into trouble.'

'We're all in trouble, all day every day while this war continues. It's not about avoiding trouble. It's about making the best choices we can under the circumstances. It's about not letting others make those choices for us as often as possible.' He put a call through to the government building, spoke to the senior group leader's office, then rang off. 'It's done,' he said.

'You will get into trouble.'

'More than I am already?'

Emilie looked at him; something of what she had come to recognise as his quiet determination had left him. 'Are you all right, sir?' She sat down in the chair opposite his desk.

'Stop calling me sir. My name is Hendrik.' He stopped. He looked at her. How could such an honest face be caught in these appalling times? Surely all the Miss Meyers of this world deserved to know the truth, so they could make their own choices rather than being forced to live off the sour milk they'd been fed on these past ten, fifteen years. They'd been turned into these mechanisms of a depraved regime because they didn't know any better. If they knew better, then maybe there could be hope for them. For everyone.

'May I speak frankly?' he said.

'Of course.'

'No, I don't think you understand. When I ask to speak frankly, I am about to tell you something you will not want to hear. You may well decide to pass on what I tell you to the authorities. You cannot afford to know what I will tell you without knowing the risks attached. Once told, it will change your perception of me. Are you prepared for that? Are you prepared for something that will either put you at risk or, indeed, cause you to hate me and have me thrown to the wolves?'

'You are frightening me.'

'The truth is frightening.'

'You may tell me what you wish. Everything you say to me will be kept in the strictest confidence.'

'You cannot make such a promise. You really have no idea what it is I might tell you.'

'May I be the judge of that?'

Kotkas paused. Then: 'Right,' he said. 'Get your coat.'

'Why?'

He gestured around the room and tapped an ear.

She nodded. 'I'll get my coat.'

They went outside and made their way along to the navy yard's quay. The sea was treacle-black; the night air was both salt and fresh. The off-shore wind ruffled their hair and brushed their cheeks with chill fingertips. The lamps cast their pools of ochre light on the cobblestones.

'I am an Estonian patriot,' Kotkas said.

'I know.'

'You may know, but do you understand? The point is: this is everything to me. My beginning, my end. I worked with the British before the war, on behalf of my country. When the Soviets came, I tried to get to England, but they couldn't take me and my family, so I ended up in Germany. I use the expression "ended up", you understand, not "chose". While they couldn't get me to England, and since I had to go to Germany, I never thought I would stop working for the British.'

A gull broke into a lament. They stopped at the end of the quay. They looked into the night, across the water towards the outer harbour wall. It was not possible to tell where the black of the sea ended and the black of the horizon began.

'So what happened?'

'I chucked it all in. Chucked in working for them, for your people, for everyone. I was going to disappear from view in Königsberg, hide away with my family. But the security police dragged me back to Berlin. I took some persuading, but eventually I agreed to pick up where I left off.'

'I see.'

'My plan was, and always has been, to get my family back here. Home. But it's still not safe. The Soviets will come back. You know that, don't you? So it seems that they have a better chance in Germany; in Fortress Königsberg, no less, one of the safest places on earth, as far as anyone can tell. Therefore, I continue.'

'Your family are not safe anywhere. Who is?' said Emilie.

'One thing I know. Where they are better off. Which is with me.'

'Then that is what we must try to achieve.'

'We?'

'Well, it is one thing to fight for a cause, to pursue an ideal and bring it to life. It is another thing to try to help people who need your help.'

'But you still believe in the cause?'

'Yes. Even if you don't.'

'I don't have to.'

She turned and looked at him, lit by the pallid light of one of the harbour lamps. 'No, I don't suppose you do.'

He paused. 'Neither do you. Have to, I mean.'

They started walking back along the quay.

'It's every German's duty,' she said. 'We've made a vow to fulfil our destiny come what may. Vows must be kept. It's the foundation of civilisation.'

'Do you really think that, though?'

'What do you mean?'

'You've worked at the heart of Berlin. You've seen the secrets. You can't be blind to everything that's going on there ... everywhere ... surely?'

242

'Like what?'

'Like the deportations. Tearing families away from their homes, their loved ones and incarcerating them. Expelling them to countries like this one. And worse. You don't really think you should be loyal to that, do you? The life you are living, you must surely realise, is a false one, since much of the truth has been withheld from you, deliberately, by your country, your State and your Leader ...'

She stopped and turned on him. 'You come here, your family comes here. We rescue you from persecution, imprisonment, probably a firing squad for you ... you receive our help, our protection, you wheedle your way into the highest echelons of our security services ... And then you have the effrontery, the arrogance, the insensitivity, to throw all this back in our faces. How dare you!'

'Don't play that game. The *We gave you refuge when you were in greatest need* rubbish. You know as well as I do that my being here is a mutually convenient arrangement; no more, no less.'

'A mutually convenient arrangement? And I suppose that your telling me all this, trapping me in your subterfuge, is your way of including me in your own special little mutually convenient arrangement. Just so we are clear. Is this what you really think? Is this what you've thought all along? You have been happy playing us for fools?'

'If I have been playing you for fools, it is because that's what you people are. You must be to support this ... disease.'

'Well, this is easy for you to say now, isn't it? Now that you have this hold over me.'

'What hold?'

'I'm at risk now, just like you. Thanks to you very conveniently tearing up that secondment request. Convenient for you, that is. Now that I have nowhere to turn, you can admit your treachery openly because you know there's very little I can do about it.'

'But you can do something about it. You can do your patriotic duty. You can turn me in. You might not be their favourite person, but they'll surely look kindly on you when you hand me over to them.'

'You're naive if you think they'll just say thanks and not drag me down with you.'

'Don't be so sure. Think about it. Think back to the conversation we've just had in the office. I made sure I did all the running. All you talked about was doing your duty; whether you liked the idea or not. Were you to have started saying anything else, I would have stopped you. You can very easily put all the blame on me.'

They started walking again. 'Why wouldn't I?' she said.

'You have just said it: *It is one thing to fight for a cause, to pursue an ideal and bring it to life. It is another thing to try to help people who need your help.* I need your help, Emilie. My family need your help. I've placed myself, my family in your hands because I trust you. I need you.'

'How can you do this to me? How can you force me to make such a choice?' She fell silent. In the distance, she watched half a dozen fishing boats, lights fore and aft, heading out of the civilian harbour for the night's work, pursued by keening gulls.

'Say something,' he said.

'What can I say?'

'Anything – even if it's just: *I'm calling the security police.*'

'You joke about this?'

'I'm not joking. Miss Meyer ...'

'Don't ... Don't speak to me ... Don't say another word ... You have just asked me to betray my own country, the country my father served with honour. The country thousands of young men are putting themselves in harm's way to protect – to keep you and your precious family safe.'

'Your father served a vastly different country. I think even you are serving the country you wish it could be. Not the one it has become.'

'Yes, this one!'

'Why fool yourself any longer? You know as well as I do – even though you refuse to admit it – those young men you mention are putting themselves in harm's way by liars simply in order to justify their lies ...'

'Not. Another. Word.'

They walked on. The noise of the waves competed with the whimpering gulls. The wind continued to tug at their hair.

Kotkas stopped and grabbed her arm. Beneath the light of another streetlamp, he turned her towards him and looked deep into her eyes. 'Pack,' he said. 'Go and stay with my family wherever they are now. I'll send a car. I'll get you travel papers. You'll be away from here before they notice. Let me get you away before things get worse for you.'

She levered her arm from his grip. 'For me? Or to get me out of the way while you save your own skin?' She returned his look. His eyes were not those of a traitor. They were the eyes of a human being. Desperately in love with his wife. Devoted to his children. A man who just wanted to be with them; care for them. She could understand this kind of loyalty, too.

They began walking again.

'Why the British?' she said. 'And, come to that, why not the Russians? Surely, if it protected your family, you would make a pact with the very devil himself if it meant they could carry on living in Estonia safely?'

'I suppose that's what we are all doing ... making pacts with the one slim chance we have of emerging from this madness alive. Even you. But I couldn't trust the Russians to treat me or my family with any decency. Not after all I'd done to them; against them.'

'Why didn't you escape with your family to Sweden when you had the chance?'

'I'm a naval officer. First rule: stick to what you know; it's your only chance. Second rule: if you have no other orders, then sail towards the sound of gunfire. I'm not in the habit of running away.'

'Is there a third rule? There's always a third rule. Everything comes in threes.'

'Trust no one.'

'You're trusting me.'

'You're not "no one".'

Despite being upset, she couldn't help the smile that danced across her face. But then she continued. 'You could have sent your family to Sweden, at least?'

'The last ship out of Tallinn carrying civilian passengers wasn't going to Sweden. And I wasn't about to send my family across the Baltic in midwinter in anything smaller than a cargo vessel.'

'You could send them to Sweden now.'

Hendrik waved a hand seawards. 'Have you any idea what it's like out there now? Destroyers, dive bombers, minefields, torpedo boats, submarines. I'll keep them as near to me as I can, thank you. Königsberg's as safe a place as any, don't you think? The safest place I could think of anyway. The great Prussian fortress city; impregnable, unassailable – that's what you Germans believe, don't you? The first chance I get, of course, I'll get them home. The only question is when.'

'When? seems to be the only question for everybody these days ...'

Hendrik nodded. 'There is no other question.'

She turned away and looked once more across the sea, as if towards that safety they'd just spoken of. 'Let me think about it,' she said.

'Don't take too long. The knock on the door could come at any time.'

'I am only too well aware of that.'

V

'Just in from Monika, sir.'

It was deep into the night. The office reeked of the Major's favourite tobacco, Rattray's Old Gowrie. Marjorie smiled to herself. Lit by a low light and full of pipe smoke, it was as if someone had tried to recreate Charles Dickens's foggy London backstreets right there in the dingy corners of St James's Street.

'Thanks,' said the Major, taking the file. 'Which reminds me ... any news on Kadakas?'

'Yes, surprisingly. Something came through via Stockholm. If not via Monika directly, via his connections.'

'Concerning what?'

'Russian intercepts, sir. And some German dispositions in the Baltic region. Looks authentic.'

'Let me see ...' He puffed away on his pipe as he read. In Marjorie's mind's eye she could see him in happier days, striding across the Borders with his pipe, kilt and wading staff. She knew, however, that his comfortable 'Scottishness' was, in many ways, something of a refuge from the awfulness of military conflict. She'd learnt from a colleague that he had been a Subaltern during the wholesale slaughter that was Passchendaele in the last war. He'd been invalided out. His purpose now was to prevent bloodshed or, failing that, bring the conflict to as swift a conclusion as possible. He spoke at last. 'The Germans are overreaching themselves, it seems.' He looked away into the distance as if trying to visualise the violence and shattering of human lives that was surely about to follow. He blinked, as though snapping himself out of it. 'The Russian counteroffensive can't be too long in coming now,' he said, 'but why is he telling us this?'

'Because we need to know? Because it helps us?'

'Or … because he wants to get all pally with us again, now he's seen the writing on the wall.' He handed the papers back. 'Write it up for tomorrow morning's briefing. Don't tell them it's Green. Could have been compromised.'

'And Kadakas himself?'

'Pinch of salt.'

'As you say, sir.' Marjorie started to leave but then turned back. 'One odd thing, though …'

'What's that?'

'Another message arrived via the same route. I put it at the end of the report, even if it clearly doesn't belong there. A curious message, just one line.'

'Let's take a look.' The Major leafed through to the back.

Tell Monika Maret happy to spirit the disenchanted.

He took his pipe out of his mouth.

'Do you know what it means, sir?'

'Damned if I do. Monika will know, though. See if you can get a message through to him.'

'I have already.'

'Good lass.' He clamped the pipe back between his teeth and let out such a billow of smoke it would have made *The Flying Scotsman* proud.

*

'Come!'

Kotkas had returned from the harbour, absorbed in thought. He stepped into Gahlendorf's office.

'How are you doing?' the Admiral said. Kotkas shrugged. 'Well, I can't promise things will look better in the morning, because they won't. But I am glad you are here. For a while, I wondered whether you might just skip. Grab one of our launches and head out to sea; Finland, Sweden, somewhere.'

'For a while, so did I. But when it comes down to it, there is so much I have yet to do here.'

'Good man. Now,' he waved a memorandum at him, 'look at this ... it is as you said. The High Command are paying no attention to any warnings of overreaching themselves. There's a big push before winter. The fools. They should be consolidating. Digging in. Take Leningrad, by all means, while digging in along the Ukraine border. Over winter, resupply, and push again in spring ...' He tossed it onto his desk. 'They think there's a great beginning in all of this. Instead, it's bloodlust, vainglory. A rush – straight into the abyss ... Damn their stupid mindless arrogance. Millions, Hendrik. Millions will die, will suffer. All those wonderful young men. All those promising bright futures. And the women, the children. Monstrous. That's what it is – monstrous.'

Kotkas wondered whether his friend was drunk. He knew he loved his brandy, but never had Kotkas seen it have such an effect on him. 'Sir, might I suggest you lower your voice?'

'I told you before – we can't be overheard in my office. Let us consider for a moment the end game.'

'Of all of this?'

'Yes. You are aware of how things will most likely turn out?'

Kotkas nodded.

'Now consider, for a moment, how long that is likely to occur and what kind of damage will be done – on both sides of the encounter.'

Kotkas nodded.

'The question is, do we need the whole Third Act, or can we continue to seek to conclude matters at the end of the Second? Don't say anything.'

Kotkas looked at him.

Gahlendorf, with his left hand, rested the tips of two fingers on his top lip to mimic a certain moustache. He raised his right hand in a discreet Party salute. 'Are you interested in being part of the Act Two finale? Or would you rather hang on for the Third Act? That is – if any of us get there.'

Kotkas considered for a moment. 'In my view, there is no Third Act,' he said. 'It's a two-act play and the Second Act is well and truly here. It will take care of itself. We would only make it worse for too many people by poking the sore; making it bleed.'

'No, then?'

'No.'

'So be it. I was just asked to sound you out.'

The phone rang.

'Yes?' Gahlendorf said. 'Right. Yes, I'm available.' He put his hand over the mouthpiece. 'They are putting some SA group leader through. That was quick. Place must be bugged after all.' A smile flickered and died. 'But what can the SA want with me, I wonder?' He returned to the phone. 'Good morning, Group Leader. How are you ...? Who? They've got orders for what? Who are they after?' Gahlendorf's eyes looked directly at Kotkas. 'Well, the Commander's not here at the moment. Yes, I'll let them in. Have them call me with their names and I'll alert the guard at the gate. What ...? Yes, if I see him, I'll hang on to him. And who as well ...? What ...? I see. Yes, sir. Understood.' He replaced the receiver thoughtfully. 'Seems, old man, like you've become very popular. Not just with our security police but the little cherubs running the show here as well. They pine for your company, long to see you, and promise to hang on every word they extract from you ...'

'They want to arrest me?'

Gahlendorf shrugged – as if to say it would actually make it true.

A deeper silence fell.

'I see.' Kotkas considered for a moment. 'Sir. If I surrender myself into your custody, would you put me in prison? Better still, would you have me put in prison in Königsberg?'

'Perhaps. Perhaps not.' Gahlendorf, if he were honest with himself, was not clear which was best from that point. 'Maybe we could still make a stand. After all, they've got nothing on you as such. Just, it seems, a bit of insubordination. You gave them the slip or something, I think they said. Can't be trusted. You've become a security risk. That sort of thing.' He looked at Kotkas, who clearly wasn't convinced. Neither, he admitted to himself, was he. 'Trouble is, whether you've done something or nothing, legally speaking, won't matter a jot once they've got you in their claws. They mentioned Miss Meyer, too. They think she's somehow mixed up in all of this. They think you conspired to snub the security police. Preventing her doing her duty as a woman and a German or something.' He paused. 'It's bad, my friend.'

Kotkas nodded.

'So we have a number of choices. We could fight and drive them off...' His voice faded to silence, recognising the futility of Plan A. He opened a cabinet and drew out a bottle and two glasses. 'Or, we ...' he said, and tailed off again.

He poured, deep in thought.

They drank and savoured in silence.

For a moment, Kotkas wondered whether Gahlendorf might next pull a pistol from his desk drawer and offer it to him. The honourable way out.

The thought had also occurred to Gahlendorf.

In his drawer was indeed a loaded pistol; there for any eventuality. In his mind's eye, he could see it lying inert and oily black in the darkness among the papers. To all intents and purposes, it was harmless; until. that is, it was called to speak with its savage voice. It would be the work of a moment for him to unlock the drawer, take the weapon out, lay it quietly upon the desk blotter and vacate the room; closing the door behind him. Nothing need be said. Ninety percent of all communication was, he understood, non-verbal. Outside, he would light a cigar, lean against the wall in the hall, wait for the brief yet definitive crack from within then calmly ask his duty officer, lolling even now in the office along the hall, to send for the medics. He would ensure his great friend, sailing companion and Estonian patriot would receive a burial with full military honours.

He would insist upon it.

But then he shook his head like a wet dog shakes off seawater. He downed the rest of the contents of his glass. 'What am I thinking?' he said. 'You know what – let's just get you out of here ... right away. Make you disappear. Get you so far out of their clutches, they'll give up and pick on someone else. How about getting you well out to sea? As you said: in command of a ship where you belong. We can pretend you've sworn allegiance, can't we? It's all made up in the end, isn't it? This whole absurd farce.' He picked up the phone. 'I'll fix the paperwork.'

'What about my work?'

'You've done enough. There's plenty of bright enough folks to pick up where you left off. You've trained them well.'

'Then what about you?'

'Me? I'm big enough and ugly enough to look after myself. Don't worry, I'll go and speak to the senior group leader. He's a ninny, which makes him easily swayed. I'll convince him that this is just a petty vendetta by the security police over some imagined slight. Once he realises it is interfering with the smooth running of his precious administration ... But you can't stay. Let's face it ... it *is* some petty vendetta, and you'll never be free of it here. Make yourself scarce. At least for a while. No telling what that slug will do to you if he gets what he wants now.'

'Thank you, sir.'

The two men stood. There was something final attached to that moment. Gahlendorf poured them out another glass each. They looked one another in the eye, knowing they might never meet again.

'To full tides and fair winds,' Kotkas said, and toasted his friend.

They clinked glasses.

'Till we round the final buoy and hear the finish gun,' Gahlendorf replied.

Kotkas returned to his office.

He began stuffing a briefcase full of papers.

Emilie knocked and entered. She was pale. 'What is it?'

'Oskar?' Kotkas called the chief petty officer in from the outer office.

Oskar entered. 'Sir?'

Kotkas turned his wireless on and the volume up loud. He spoke in urgent whispers.

'Send a couple of men. One to Miss Meyer's quarters. One to mine. Tell them not to speak to anyone and, if asked, not to tell a soul what they are doing. That goes for you, too, my friend.'

'Sir.'

'My suitcase is on top of the wardrobe. Emilie – where's yours?'

'What's going on?'

'Get the men to pack both our suitcases, Oskar. Throw everything they can find in them. Then get back here as soon as possible. Emilie, where's your suitcase? What's the address of your quarters?'

She told Oskar. He left.

'But what's going on, Commander?'

'Neither of us can leave this place, it's become too dangerous. Unfortunately, we're not safe inside the base either, now. The security police are getting authority to enter. Gahlendorf can hold them off, but not for long. He's got us transport out of here in two hours. Supply ship to Memel. There, he's arranging for me to take command of a ship.'

'And me?'

'You need to disappear. I want you to go to Königsberg as

we discussed earlier; gather my family and get them and yourself away somewhere. Lie low until I can come for you all. Do you think you can do it?'

'Yes.' She started to go then turned. 'And, just in case you were wondering … I had already decided to do this.'

*

Fischer had returned to his office from the navy base in the early hours of the morning. The birds had flown. He had shouted at anyone and everyone he came across. The next day, first thing, he had rung the base and demanded to see Gahlendorf. *Regrettably, sir, the Admiral is not available at the moment.*

A thundercloud enveloped him for the rest of the day.

The following afternoon, he was summoned to SA headquarters to meet with the group leader. He knocked and was admitted.

The group leader was leafing through a memorandum marked, as all of them were, with a hooked cross clutched in an eagle's cruel talons. The group leader looked up and with a sharp gesture of his head encouraged his visitor to sit down. In silence, he took a corner of his shirt out of his trouser band and cleaned his rimless spectacles with it. When he had finished, he tucked his shirt back in and put his spectacles back on.

He'd left his wife of eight years half a dozen months ago, before being posted from Bavaria to this godforsaken hole on the Baltic. *Irreconcilable differences*, he would tell his comrades in the Officers' Club. As a result, and with great regret, the marriage foundered. Now he was quartered in a house built, he imagined, in Frederick the Great's time, when Germany owned half of Europe. Something he and his colleagues intended by force or favour to own again.

Schnapps and fantasies of the potential availability of the widowed owner of his building sustained his cold evenings, alone in the high-ceilinged master bedroom, chewing on his particular favourite titbit, *Bierwurst*, by lamplight. *A drunkard and a pig* was his estranged wife's verdict on her husband. In the past, she had frequently expressed such opinions in front of his lofty Party colleagues. This became a painful embarrassment for him. So she had to go. Or, rather, he had to take the first posting that was subsequently offered to him. The Party did not look kindly on members who were divorced. Not the image of the perfect Aryan lifestyle they wished to present to the world.

'So ...' he glanced at the name at the top of the report '... Fischer. Welcome.'

'Thank you, Group Leader.'

'Cigarette?'

'Thank you.'

'Now, I suppose you are wondering why I asked you here,' he said. 'Well, let me explain. It is my understanding that, in your view, you have no need to report to me or my colleagues anything of what you are doing, who you are investigating, or why. Furthermore, it seems that, while I don't doubt the efficiency and efficacy of your methods, from time to time, you – perhaps through naivety or ignorance of the subtleties of managing affairs in an occupied country – inadvertently tread on people's' toes. Including – and this is of particular importance, as you will no doubt understand – the senior group leader's. Sometimes, it seems, even using my own people to do it. Through not having consulted with me or my colleagues, you have actively put at risk policies and agendas we have painstakingly been putting in place.'

'The thing is, Group Leader—'

'Please do not interrupt while I am explaining matters for you. In short, we cannot afford loose cannons. We do not need cavalier approaches. The left hand most definitely needs to know what the right hand is getting up to. We need coordinated and efficient approaches to the management of affairs in this part of the world. How would it be if I trampled all over your well-laid plans? No, do not answer. It was a rhetorical question. Now, listen very carefully, Fischer. Doubtless, used properly and in conjunction with my other services and departments, you are a very useful tool of the State. However, I insist – and do please note my use of the word *insist* – that you and your office remain in daily, and if necessary hourly, contact with my office. I have a very efficient team and I shall make them available to you at all times. But we cannot have any further disruption to the progress of our creation of a well-run, loyal and resilient satellite state here in the Baltic. Is that clear?'

'Yes, Group Leader. However, I was given to understand by my superior that I was to have a completely free hand in everything that directly concerned me and my men in this area of operations.'

'Yes, well, I have spoken with your superior and, indeed, his superior and, not to put too fine a point on it, your superiors have the same superior that I have. And my superior is very clear that what I have outlined to you is the preferred arrangement from now on. In short: that you will report to me and I give you your orders. As you are no doubt aware, back in Berlin, there is a clear intention at the highest level for my superior ultimately to oversee all related offices and departments. And that includes yours. Which is why I called you here, and why I am very glad we have had this little chat. I trust all is now clear, and that we shall have your total and undivided cooperation from this moment on.'

'Yes, Group Leader.'

'Good. See how easy it is for us all to get along? Now, I have a lunch appointment. Do feel free to close the door on your way out. You may finish your cigarette outside.'

'Yes, Group Leader.'

Summer 1944

⚮

I

'Marjorie. Where are we with the Soviet push in the north?'

It was the daily routine. The Major with his pipe, Marjorie with an armful of files which she placed one by one on his desk as the subjects came up.

'I've just compiled this briefing note for you to take to the War Office, Major.'

'Good. How's it looking?'

'A lot of wireless traffic, as you would expect from a concerted advance. Plenty of confirmed reports from our people. The further west Stalin drives, the more visible he becomes to us, as it were.'

'Indeed. Have we had anything of late from Kadakas, as far as you can tell?'

'No, sir. It's gone quiet again. A few came in from Monika and his people.'

'Fair enough. Any more news from sources about the rumours we're getting through from our colleagues the Berlin watchers about a failed assassination attempt on the Evil One and the attempted coup?'

'The bomb? Not much. Only that, as you say, it's not worked.'

'Yes, more's the pity. Still, probably just some twitchy generals seeing writing on the wall and understandably keen to get into our good books, eh? What with Uncle Joe in the north, and now our people about to push on from Normandy, it probably won't be long before the Evil One's been put paid to anyway. Why are you smiling?'

'Sorry, sir. It was just your mention of Normandy.'

'What about it?'

'I was out with friends for dinner a week or so before D-Day. Playing the silly filly of a secretary as usual. I listened to all their absurd theories of when and where and how, in their view, the proposed invasion would happen. And I couldn't help thinking to myself: *I could tell you, my darlings, what's actually going to happen ... but then I would have to arrest you.*'

*

'Alarm!'

The klaxon howled around the minesweeper, setting everyone's stomachs convulsing. Sailors ran to their posts, pulling on life preservers and struggling with the chinstraps of helmets.

Kotkas looked out through the greasy windows of the bridge with his binoculars. A sailor stepped up and offered him a helmet. He waved it away. This did not go unnoticed by the men around him. Estonian or not, they liked that in their officer.

The M35 heaved in the long Baltic swell. The grinding of the engines and the smell of diesel a backdrop to the shouted orders outside, beyond the relative calm of the bridge. The sky was grey but the clouds were not so low as to prevent aircraft sorties. Half a dozen dots appeared through Kotkas's binoculars heading straight towards him from the east. He kept his glasses trained on them until he could make out the type. They looked like MiGs; the sort that had blood-red stars on their wings.

'Starboard ten,' he said. 'Fire when ready.'

The ship swung round, bringing the anti-aircraft guns to bear. A moment later and the familiar *pom-pom-pom* of the ship's protection rattled the windows. The other ships alongside Kotkas in their little flotilla began similar manoeuvres. Soon, a curtain of anti-aircraft rounds was arcing its way towards the oncoming aircraft.

Kotkas let his binoculars drop to his chest on their strap. Terrifying as it always was, it had also become routine. Sometimes, five, six times a day the klaxon would scream and the ship's meagre defences would be deployed. He felt the usual rising anxiety, the prodding doubt, the ice in his gut. But ever since his time as a cadet on *Lembit* all those years ago, he'd learnt that panic and fear offered unhelpful counsel. One whispered in one ear, one whispered in the other, and neither gave the kind of advice one really needed to survive.

He took a sip from the coffee on the sill beside him and pulled a face. He would never get used to ersatz coffee – but that was all that was available from navy stores these days. At least for minesweeper crews.

He glanced at the man standing beside him. His first officer, Busch. He could see his face was shiny with sweat. The fellow gripped and regripped his binoculars.

'Here we go again, eh, Busch?'

'Here we go again, sir.' Busch forced a smile.

'Thankfully, we're not alone.' Kotkas nodded at the other minesweepers. 'Five determined little ladies like us, intent on defending their honour, should scare those suitors off, eh?' Taking another sip from his ersatz coffee, he sat down in his commander's chair as if to enjoy the show.

The raid lasted two and a half minutes. A tapestry of bright tracer across the grey; punctuated by gouts of water and thuds from bombs pocking the lurching seas.

And then it was over.

'Casualty and damage report, please, Mr Busch.'

'Sir.' Busch wiped his hand on his trousers, pulled the handset from its hook, and relayed both the request and then its response. 'Some light bullet damage, repairable, sir. One buckled plate from the bomb that fell a few metres amidships, repairable,' Busch reported.

'And …?'

'*And*, sir?'

'Casualties?'

'A few grazes, sir. All being tended by the medics.'

'Thank you, Busch. Make sure we have extra eyes on the horizon, would you? Those aircraft may have been acting independently. Or they could be trying to soften us up for an attack by a surface vessel.'

'Sir.'

Kotkas took another sip of his ersatz coffee. It was disgusting. He thought about Louis. He missed his orderly; not least because he made proper coffee. Louis, coming from Alsace, had that French touch with coffee. More importantly, he also knew where to get hold of the real stuff. Goodness knows how he did it. And it would probably have cost the earth, too.

The last thing Kotkas had done before leaving the navy base at Tallinn was to take his orderly to one side and tell him about a certain fisherman down in the harbour; where to find him, what to tell him. Kotkas had jotted a quick note explaining who Louis was, how he had his complete confidence, and the fact that it was imperative he was taken to Sweden and safety.

When they said goodbye, they hugged and thanked each other for their friendship which, they swore, would never die.

Kotkas took another sip, winced, and set the mug down.

They waited a further tense twenty minutes, scanning the horizon around the minesweeper. Kotkas had been up seventeen hours already. His head throbbed and his eyes felt as if they'd been plucked out, rubbed in salt and put back the wrong way round. He stretched and was just thinking about taking his leave, when one of the lookouts cried out. Binoculars swung to focus on the direction he was pointing. It took Kotkas a moment, then he saw it. A faint pencil scratch on the horizon; carbon grey against the dove grey of the sky. The tell-tale streak of smoke from the stack of a warship.

It was a lone Soviet destroyer. The flotilla, though five in number, were not as well armed as the warship that had clearly decided to engage them. The officers turned their binoculars towards the lead minesweeper; waiting for orders to be flashed across to them by a signal lamp.

'What do you think, eh, Busch?'

'I think we'll be told to run.'

Their flotilla commander, younger and a less experienced naval officer than Kotkas, was known for being especially cautious.

'Me, too. Pity. I should think we had a better chance of doing some damage by meeting the threat head-on. Surprise Boris by not turning tail but by showing him our teeth. Doubtless he's hoping to scare us off, give chase and spank our backsides as he does so. Five against one? Good odds. If we came at him from different points of the compass, his guns wouldn't know which way to swivel.'

Busch leant more towards the flotilla commander's point of view. Especially since they'd had to leave three other of their ships in port for repairs. But Kotkas, Busch knew, was highly respected by the men. Something about the way he made war gave them confidence, helped them find the courage to do everything he asked. If Kotkas said they ought to attack ... well, attack they should.

However, Kotkas's, or the flotilla commander's, tactics were not put to the test. At that moment, the grey sky briefly bloomed orange then returned to its original complexion. Seconds later, a loud *crump* was heard, followed by the unmistakable shudder of an explosion. Two more concussions were felt as, clearly, the Soviet ship's magazine exploded.

'Mines,' said Busch unnecessarily.

Kotkas nodded. 'We hadn't got to that area yet. Signal our commander: we're going to pick up survivors.'

'Save them?' said Busch. 'They're the enemy, surely?'

'Have you got a wallet, Busch?' said Kotkas.

'Sir?'

'I don't doubt that in it, you have a photo of your wife and children. I dare say, if you asked those terrified fellows out there, thrashing about in the water – if any are left, that is – they would show you the photos in their wallets, too.'

'But the mines, sir ... should we be putting our ship at risk like that?'

'Busch. We are a minesweeper. If we can't tippy-toe through them, no one can.'

Two hours later, and the last man was pulled from the water. He was dead. He lay face down on the curtsying deck of the minesweeper. Kotkas looked at the poor fellow. All of a sudden, he felt cold. He realised what it was. For the first time that day, he actually experienced a sense of dread. By the braid on the dead man's epaulettes, this was an officer; captain, third class. The last he had heard, this was his brother Peeter's rank. He didn't want to, but he knew he had to give the next instruction.

'Turn him over,' he said.

*

Emilie paid her weekly visit to Leena and the children. It was evening. The bats were swooping amid the trees across the street. The air was full of the scents of the hot summer day that was just ending. Emilie hoped to catch the mother before she went to bed. She was feeling particularly uneasy these days, not least with the news that a group of German officers had tried to kill the Leader, take control in Berlin and, presumably, sue for peace. They hadn't succeeded, and now the whole world was being turned upside down in purges. She only hoped Commander Kotkas had not been involved.

Maret opened the door. 'Why do you keep coming around?' she said. 'We've told you, we don't need you.'

'And as I've said, Maret, your father asked me to keep an eye on you all. And that is what I am doing. May I come in, please?'

Maret hesitated before stepping aside, barely holding the door wide enough for Emilie to pass through.

'How are you, Leena?' Emilie settled in a chair beside the couch.

Leena turned her eyes towards the visitor.

'Same as yesterday. And the day before. And the day before that.'

'It can't be helping you being here.' Emilie looked around the room, dingy in the dusk. 'Why don't you let me get you away from Königsberg, like I've been asking? Take you to my hometown. Well away from all this, where I can look after you properly.'

'You are very kind,' said Leena, 'but the children are happy here. They have their friends. They have a life here, now.'

'We like it here,' echoed Juhan.

Emilie sighed. 'Then I'll stay around and do what I can for you.'

'You don't need to,' said Maret. 'Mrs Wowreit comes.'

'Yes, and is it fair to keep asking her to come? She has her own things she needs to do. I'm happy to help.'

'Why didn't our father come instead of you?'

'He couldn't. He has to stay where he is for the time being.'

'In Estonia. Without us.'

'We've been through all this, Maret. No – he's not there anymore. And it wasn't safe for you there. He couldn't get you back, and then he had to leave himself.'

'Where is he?' said Juhan.

'We don't know. Have you heard from him?'

'No,' said Leena.

'Well, the post just isn't working very well these days. There's so much disruption with the way things are. He could have sent you a dozen letters and none of them have got through.'

'Or he hasn't sent any,' said Maret.

'He'll get through to you one day. I'm sure of it. In the

meantime, please, let me help. I can help you. All three of you, if you'd only give me a chance.'

'Why don't you go away? To your nice house far away you keep talking about?'

'Maret!' said Leena. She tried to raise herself up on her elbows where she lay, to admonish her daughter further, but grimaced and flopped back down again. 'Don't speak to our guests like that,' she said to the ceiling. 'Miss Meyer is only being kind. Emilie, please, you are welcome to come anytime you like. It's just – until we hear from Hendrik, I don't think we should go anywhere. Here is where he knows we are. Here is where we stay. We'll hear from him sooner or later, and when we do, then we'll decide what's best.'

'Unless he's dead,' said Juhan.

*

The flotilla had pulled into its current base at Libau, on the west coast of the Kurland peninsula. The city, with its villas, parks and lakes, gleamed in the sunshine. Its cafés and – even in those straitened times – its baroque-fronted shops selling quality produce gave it a personality that the locals maintained rivalled even Paris.

Kotkas was getting ready to leave the ship. Despite the little gem of a city's attractions, however, he never liked going ashore. That was where the real risks were, as far as he was concerned. Or, rather, where the risks he had no control over were. At sea, he knew where he was, what he was doing. Safe; although 'safety' in wartime was a relative concept. All of this was made especially worse by the fall-out from the attempted assassination of the Leader a few weeks ago. Already, he'd heard two or three fellow officers had been spirited away in the dead of night.

He looked across at the survivors from the Soviet cruiser's crew being shepherded off his ship by soldiers. He thought back to their officer, lying dead on the minesweeper's deck.

Thankfully, when his men had turned him over, he had not recognised him. He wondered where Peeter was. Then he wondered where his family were. Hopefully now safe somewhere in Emilie's care. How long had it been since he'd heard from them? Months. He'd sent a message before he'd left for sea on this latest tour of duty. Perhaps there'd be a reply waiting for him ashore. Even if there wasn't, he'd resolved to get down to Königsberg on this occasion to see if he could find them, or at least get an idea of their whereabouts. He wasn't supposed to leave the base. In fact, he wasn't supposed to have any time away from his ship at all – not now the Allies had landed in France. Everyone on constant alert. But that was a thousand kilometres to the south. They were a Baltic outfit. He'd announced to his crew that they deserved three days to themselves, and he required them to report back to the ship at the end of the week. Busch could manage things until he got back. He'd ring in twice a day while away to check there was nothing critical. If they were ordered to put to sea, Busch was instructed to argue that they needed repairs, and at least thirty-six hours. That should be enough.

He slung his kit bag over his shoulder and stepped onto the gangplank.

There was indeed a message waiting for him at the port office. It wasn't from his family, though. On the front of the telegram was officialdom's eagle and the savage slash of a cross. He opened and read. It was a summons to Berlin signed by some colonel or other. No reason; just a command to be there by the next day. What was it? A trap? He had to go, of course. Which meant, of course, that it was the end of getting to Königsberg for him. He might be able to squeeze a visit there on his return from Berlin. If he ever did return.

Later that day, he gathered his crew on the deck of their ship and let them know he had to go to Berlin and might be away a while.

'How long for, sir?' one of them asked.

'I don't know. Could be just a couple of days, could be a little longer. Look after yourselves. Take the time off, as I said. Play nicely.' Despite the fact that they were Germans, they were good men. Excellent sailors. He would miss them and it was clear they would miss him. They gave him a brisk, seamanlike *hurrah*! as he stepped off his ship. Which they'd never done before. Why? Was it a final farewell? Did they know something he didn't?

He arrived in Berlin the next day. He had telegraphed ahead. A staff car had been sent to collect him from the train at Ostbahnhof.

It was raining heavily. The car lurched through the traffic, its windscreen wipers slapping. The streets teemed with military vehicles splashing hither and yon. The storm engulfed Berlin in a deluge. Eerie slate-black skies tinged with maroon light. It felt like the end of the world. Even if it wasn't, Kotkas thought, one day, this self-obsessed city was bound to disappear up its own fundamentalism.

They pulled up outside one of the many heavily protected buildings in Berlin.

'Leave your bag, you won't be needing it,' the SS officer who had met him said. He trotted Kotkas through the rain, up the steps, past the guards, and inside. Kotkas could not help thinking about the pistol that nuzzled in his escort's burnished holster.

Shaking the rain from their caps and brushing down their uniforms, they entered what was once most probably a ballroom; a hangover from Prussian glory days. Chandeliers and mirrors; sombre portraits of august military heroes from the distant past. A number of other officers from various branches of the German military, aviation and maritime war machine were standing around. The SS officer clacked his heels and left.

Before Kotkas could sidle up to another naval officer and ask why they were there, a colonel with gleaming black boots, extravagant lanyard and the red flashes of a staff officer strode into the middle of the room. He ordered all of them to assemble and to make a neat line along the far wall. Kotkas joined the others. He looked around in case there was a soldier with a machine gun ready to redecorate the wall with their blood. But he could see no one armed in that way.

They waited in a long, straight line just a moment longer. Then the Colonel called them to attention with a bark.

There was a pause; a silence.

This was followed by the sound of boots marching down a corridor just off the ballroom.

A group entered. The line of officers bristled even further to attention like the hackles of a wolfhound.

The Leader appeared. One arm hung down by his side. There was a tremor in his other hand. He was pale as a bone.

One by one, he went down the line of officers. At each, he stopped and looked into the fellow's eyes. An aide read out a commendation. The Leader took a presentation case, held by a second aide, opened it to reveal the Iron Cross on its cream-coloured pillow within and handed it to the officer. They shook hands, after which the officer either saluted in the Party way, or the Prussian way, or simply bowed with a stiff nod of the head.

Kotkas realised why his crew had cheered him when he left the ship. Someone had obviously told them why he was going to Berlin. That realisation didn't help Kotkas feel any better about where he was and what was about to happen.

As the Leader drew nearer, Kotkas found himself needing to keep himself from trembling. Not from excitement, at the thrill of being at such a prestigious occasion, but from anxiety. He was sure he would be recognised, and then what? Hauled out of the line? Accused of being a traitor? Dragged headfirst downstairs into the courtyard and shot?

The Leader arrived toe to toe with him.

The Aide read the citation. 'Commander Hendrik Kotkas,

Minesweepers. Three successful tours of duty, outstanding record on active service. Two commendations for bravery in the face of the enemy. Award: Iron Cross, Second Class.'

'Well, Kotkas,' said the Leader, 'a good man. I notice you already have the Minesweeper award.' He indicated the oval decoration with the gout of water depicting an exploded mine pinned just below Kotkas's left breast.

'Yes, sir.'

'Good work. Keep it up.'

The Leader gave Kotkas the open presentation case with its medal inside; then smiled. A cold smile, with dead fish eyes. To Kotkas's horror, the Leader followed this by holding out his hand for it to be shaken. Kotkas hesitated; he couldn't help it; *the thought of touching that man.* The temptation to refuse the gesture was powerful. But then he overcame the urge and reached out. They shook; the hand was clammy and surprisingly limp. Kotkas's own hand trembled. He couldn't pull it away quickly enough, as if the other's hand was diseased and Kotkas was likely to catch something. To cover this swift withdrawal, he saluted; as if that was what he'd planned all along. He was glad that it had not been mandatory down the line to offer the Party salute.

The Leader made as if to move on. Then stopped.

He gave Kotkas a searching look. Kotkas kept looking straight ahead. The Leader narrowed his eyes as if trying to remember something. Kotkas felt like he wanted to explode or, worse, blurt out what he was dying to say: *Yes, I am the one who offended you in Canaris's outer office. Yes, you disgust me. Yes, I wish that bomb had put paid to you.* It would be worth it, Kotkas thought, if only for the satisfaction of having said it to his face. Especially in such company. But was it worth it for the summary firing squad that would follow? No. He kept his counsel.

The Leader gave a little twitch of the head, as if realising to dwell any further on this insignificant fellow would be a waste of his valuable time, and, moving on, addressed his attention to the next in line.

A tedious reception followed, once the Leader had departed. Kotkas took his leave as soon as was diplomatic. Outside once more in the rain, he hailed a taxi. He took it to Tirpitzufer. Inside the Bendlerblock, he showed the duty officer, a member of the SS, his identity card. The officer appeared unimpressed. He scanned a list on his desk.

'I don't have your name here, Commander.'

'Perhaps not. I am based in the Baltic. But I have worked here in the past.'

'Perhaps, sir. However, security has doubtless changed since you were here last. Got a little too soft. We had to step in. So, unless your name is on my list ...'

'If I found someone to vouch for me ...?'

'Perhaps.' The duty officer picked up his phone. 'They would have to come and collect you, of course, and stay with you all the while you are in the building.' The officer's index finger was poised over the dial. 'If you would care to give me a name?'

'Admiral Canaris.'

The finger was withdrawn. 'Perhaps another name?'

'Not sufficiently senior for you?'

The officer looked at Kotkas as if to say, *One more crack like that, and I'll have you thrown into the cells.* He repeated his last sentence, but slowly. 'Perhaps ... sir ... another name?'

'How about Captain Plötz?'

The officer paused then prodded his finger into the dial at *zero* and turned it with an efficient flick of the wrist. '*Major* Plötz,' he said to the operator while looking at Kotkas.

'Kotkas, welcome.' Plötz trotted down the main staircase into the lobby like a dancer in a Hollywood musical. 'Don't worry about issuing a pass,' he said to the duty officer, 'the Commander and I are going out.'

'They stood on the street, rain finding its way down

between Kotkas's collar and neck, while Plötz looked to hail a taxi.

'Congratulations on your promotion, Plötz,' Kotkas said. Plötz grunted.

They climbed into the back of a taxi and Plötz told the driver to take them to the Adlon. He lit up a cigarette and offered one to Kotkas, who shook his head, so snapped his silver cigarette case shut.

Kotkas opened his mouth to speak, but Plötz indicated the driver and held a finger to his lips. When Kotkas was last in Berlin, everyone had to exercise caution as to who could and could not be trusted. Now the rule of thumb seemed to be: trust no one. The rain drummed on the taxi roof.

They arrived and dived through the rain into the hotel. Kotkas, half expecting to see Canaris, looked across towards the Admiral's table but he was not there; surveying all who came in and went out. His absence added a greater sense of foreboding to that which Kotkas was already experiencing. The smell of damp officers' uniforms pervaded the room.

They ordered coffees. The Adlon, naturally, still had the real thing. Though it was, perhaps, a little thinner than before. And twice the price. A drop of rainwater formed at the end of Plötz's nose. He swatted it off. 'There's been something of a purge, as you might imagine,' he said. 'Canaris is gone.'

'Gone? Where's he gone?'

'Well, initially, he was encouraged to consider his advanced years and took the hint. He retired. But, subsequently, word has it, he was implicated in the July bomb and has been arrested and thrown into prison somewhere. It seems they've had their eye on him for a long time but could never prove anything. Then, the day of the bomb, someone rang him at home. They said something like, "We've done it!" Canaris, I hear, said, "Put the phone down, you fool," but too late. There was an echo and a click on the receiver – listeners-in – and it was all up for him. Naturally, it was really all about the SS always wanting to get overall control, which they now have. Don't they just love pulling all the strings! A pity – but, as they say, all's fair in war and war.'

The casual way the Major related what were starkly unnerving and dangerous events was clearly forced. Kotkas wondered why he was making light of such things.

'How have you been? What have you been up to?' Plötz said.

Kotkas gave him a brief outline of his work in intelligence in the Baltic, his brush with the security police, and his transfer onto minesweepers.

'Still think you can keep yourself out of it?'

'Keeping myself out of things that I don't need to be involved in? Certainly. I am working through my own agenda, you might say.'

'Minesweepers, though. You know why you're there, don't you? Best chance of getting blown up in the whole navy. Happy to sideline you, I suspect. And, of course, there's the fact that you are still a commander.'

'What does that mean?'

'Well, let's look at the evidence. Life expectancy on active service, not least in minesweepers, means that anyone who manages to survive a few months automatically rises to higher things. How long have you held your rank?'

'Since the beginning of the war.'

Plötz spread his hands in a gesture which said: *There you are, then.* 'They don't trust you. At the very least, they hope you'll go out in a blaze of glory.'

Kotkas looked at him. 'What's all this leading to?'

'What do you mean?'

'Your running me down like this. Softening me up for something? Let's turn to the last page.'

Plötz nodded, took a sip of coffee and lit another cigarette; one of his last de Troupes. He twirled it between his fingers and inspected the smoke as it curled. 'They'll come for me, too, soon. They're making connections with the attempt on the Leader's life everywhere. People hauled in and systematically brutalised until they talk. They're getting whole lists of names. Sometimes, people talk just to stop the pain. They say any name that comes into their heads that they think their tormentors want to hear. Remember the conversations we had?'

'Of course.'

'I didn't have that kind of chat just with you. Most of the ones I spoke to have already disappeared. Can't be long before one of them tries my name on for size.'

'Why are you telling me all this?'

'Well, in the first place, a warning to you. Who knows when or where your name might come up? Keep your head down for as long as possible.'

'And in the second place?'

'We need to keep the work going. We need anyone who is not yet caught up in this tidal surge to carry the fight to them, by whatever means necessary. You might think of this not so much as a request as a bequest. Your inheritance.'

Kotkas looked at the man. The uniform was still as clean and as neat as it had ever been. The hair was still immaculately trimmed. But, now that he looked properly, Kotkas could see the sleepless nights in the other's face; the endless pacing of his quarters, filling the place with cigarette smoke, waiting for the inevitable knock on the door.

Kotkas thought about Tamm. About the message that he hoped had got through to him: *Tell Monika Maret happy to spirit the disenchanted.* If it had reached him, Tamm would have understood what it meant. He would know that *Maret* was the name of the family's 6-metre yacht. He would know that Nils the fisherman was the one who had got it out of Estonia. He would work out that 'Maret' was Nils and put that together with the expression *spirit the disenchanted.* In his mind's eye, Kotkas saw Tamm spiriting away men, women, children – whole families like Kotkas's own – people who no longer wished to stay in Estonia under any kind of evil regime – now the Second Act was coming to its unavoidable conclusion. He imagined Nils getting them onto his fishing boat under cover of darkness; taking them to the fishing grounds where they would be transferred to the boats of his Swedish cousin and, from there, to safety.

Kotkas spoke. 'One thing I don't quite understand. Why did whoever it was ring Canaris? Why did they choose to tell him about the bomb?'

'Why do you think?'

'They wanted to implicate him, deliberately?'

'No. They thought he'd be glad to hear the news.'

'Why?'

'Why do you think? Who do you think actually authorised all those Jewish agents and had them sent overseas to safety? Why do you think so many British intelligence tricks and deceptions succeeded?'

The truth dawned on Kotkas. 'Because they were allowed to. Because they were believed by Berlin. Because the Admiral said they should believe.'

Plötz nodded and puffed on his cigarette. 'It was Canaris who set up your meeting with me here, all those years ago.'

'But, if he was … doing all that … why didn't they suspect him earlier? How'd he keep himself out of the cells?'

'None of us really know. That was his particular ability: to present a blank face to everyone. One rumour I did hear, though, was this. Imagine, if you will, how much information the head of a secret intelligence service can obtain. Not just about your enemy but about everyone on your side, too. What dirty secrets might everyone around you be hiding? Who's to say what the Admiral had on everyone? For example, what if the one person who had the power of life or death over you knew you had something over them, and wouldn't hesitate to use it, if ever you felt threatened? What would you do?'

'Like, for example, you had discovered that your superior had a mother or grandmother who was Jewish?'

'Exactly. It is amusing, is it not, to think of the all-powerful State Leader acting as the Admiral's guardian angel? At least until the evidence against Canaris became so damning that he could argue that any "revelation" by the Admiral under duress was forged.'

Kotkas spent a moment taking this in. Then he spoke. 'When last you and I were here, we discussed the method whereby I would indicate my interest in becoming involved. If I were indeed interested in being involved. I would ask for another cup of coffee; if not, I would leave.'

'I remember.'

'What I can do, you should know, I am doing already. I have been doing it for some while. Doubtless, I will continue to do even more now, until they stop me.'

'Thank you.'

'It would be a privilege to have another coffee with you.'

II

Maret had experienced an air raid before; earlier that week. The bombers had concentrated on the centre of the city. There had been any number of air raid alerts up to then, but all but that one had been a false alarm. The reality came as a shock. It was scary but at least it hadn't lasted long.

Miss Meyer had come round the next day to see if they were all right. Of course they were. She didn't need to ask. She had said they shouldn't stay in their rooms if another one came, but, when the sirens sounded, they should go into the shelter at the end of the street. Juhan wanted to go, but Maret said he was just nosy and that they were perfectly fine staying in their own home. Besides, Mother was not feeling very well and they couldn't usually move her from her bed. If Mother couldn't go, then Maret wouldn't go. If Maret wouldn't go, Juhan wouldn't go either, he said; albeit a little reluctantly.

And here they were again, three days later. That horrid loud, heavy, throbbing noise; like monsters rattling the windows, trying to get in. She covered her ears with her pillow and wished they would all go away. But they didn't. Miss Meyer had told them to at least get under the big old kitchen table if a raid came again. Maret would have liked to, but Mother was very asleep in the next room. She had taken her medicine, and when she did that, it was hard to wake her again. The doctor had given her lots more medicine since that horrid time when Mother had tried to hang herself. It had made her very tired, and very hard to understand when she spoke. But at least she was quieter these days.

Now, in her bed, next to her Mother's bedroom, Maret

tried not to listen to the latest raid. She hated the way the bombs banged like great hammers on the houses and the streets, making the ground shiver. Even the guns of the local air defence artillery barking in reply made her clench her fists and clutch the pillow tighter around her head.

The hammering on the streets got louder; a giant with iron boots getting closer and closer. Maret felt like she wanted to scream but knew she was far too grown up for that. So she stuffed the corner of the pillow in her mouth and screwed her eyes tight.

Then came the greatest noise of all; a blast which took out the house next door and half of Maret's home. The whole earth seemed to heave and the back wall of Maret's room came crashing down; letting the night, smoke and tumult in. She screamed and leapt from her bed. She ran onto the landing. Another blast sent a gout of flame up from the ground floor. It seemed to have come from the kitchen. The gas had exploded. Maret screamed again. Fire started to take hold everywhere. She looked down towards the lower level. It had already begun to take hold of the staircase.

Maret, horrified, broke into her mother's room. Leena's bed had been tipped up by the blast. She sat dazed on the floor, blood streaming from a cut on her forehead.

Seeing her mother's incapacity, Maret realised she had to do something. If she didn't, no one else would.

'Hurry! There's fire! We must get out!'

She took her mother by the wrists. Leena allowed herself to be pulled to her feet and led onto the landing. The flames started to creep up the staircase like a murderer in the night.

Maret was now a section leader at the Young Maidens Group. She had, just weeks earlier, led a session on how to escape burning buildings. Now she knew why she had been asked to teach such things. She also now knew why the sirens had been repeatedly tested around the same time.

'Wait there!' she said to her mother, though Leena was so

dazed she wasn't about to go anywhere. Maret ran back into the bedroom and dragged a blanket off the bed. She leapt into the bathroom, hurled the blanket into the bath, and opened the cold tap as far as it would go. She plunged the wool under the water until it was soaked through, then dragged it, still streaming, back out onto the landing. She flung it around her mother and herself and started off down the stairs.

'Quickly, Mother, quickly …'

Tented in the sopping blanket, they pushed down through the fire, flames snatching at their legs. At the bottom, coughing uncontrollably, Maret jostled her mother out through the front door and into the street beyond.

It was only when they had got about twenty metres away from the burning building that Leena forced her daughter to stop.

'We must keep going, Mother. In case the building falls down on us. We must get far away.'

'Juhan!' Leena cried. 'Juhan's in there!'

To Maret's horror, she realised her mother was right. She looked back at their home. The whole front was already ablaze. As she looked, one of the upstairs windows burst with the heat, and part of the chimney fell down.

Leena tore herself away from her daughter and started to stumble back towards the building. Maret seized her arm and clung on.

'No, Mother, no … you can't go back in!'

'Juhan!' she cried, and started to beat her daughter's hands to make her let go. Maret scrabbled at her mother and managed to get her arms around her. For a woman now so weak and unwell, Leena's terror and desperation for her son gave her an eerie strength. She wrenched herself away from her daughter again.

'Juhan!' she screamed.

Maret ran after her, and began wrestling with her. 'You mustn't go back in. You can't go back in. You can't.' At which point, the front of the house caved in and the roof crumpled down on top of it.

Spent, Leena fell to the ground and lay there. Maret joined her. They both began sobbing.

'Juhan ... Juhan ...!'

'I'm sorry ... Mother, I'm sorry ...' cried Maret.

*

Emilie had been bombed out of the house where she'd been staying. At least the bombers seemed to have gone for the night. She wandered through the streets, heading towards where Hendrik's family lived. She wanted to see that they were all right.

It was pandemonium. All around, there was the clanging of bells and the crying of sirens as ambulances and fire engines chased through the devastated streets.

A few blocks from where the Kotkas family lived, Emilie came across a small town square at the centre of which was a patch of grass no bigger than a soccer pitch. Here, people, now homeless, were being gathered by the authorities. A church had set up a trestle table and were already handing out soup and sandwiches of bread and cheese.

People were wandering around shocked, lost, distressed. Some sat on the grass and cried; others sought to put their arms round loved ones to console them. Medically trained people were seeing what they could do to help. There were those who had been injured by bomb blasts, flying shards of glass, or from having leapt out of first-floor windows to escape certain death in what were once their homes.

Charred and incinerated corpses lay around, too. Unattended. The urgent need was first to attend to the living.

As much as Emilie wanted to help the injured, she told herself her first priority was to find out how the Kotkas family were doing. So she hurried past. But then someone called her.

'Miss Meyer?'

Emilie stopped and looked around. There were no street-lights but people were using torches, while vehicles had positioned themselves so their headlights might assist those helping others in the square. No need for blackouts now; all any new aircraft would have to do was drop their bombs in and around the burning buildings that now lit up the streets of Königsberg.

Emilie couldn't see anyone she recognised.

'Miss Meyer?' The voice called again.

It was a young voice, she realised. She looked down, and there, sitting cross-legged right by her feet, was a barefoot boy in his pyjamas, shivering.

'Juhan.' She knelt down and held him in her arms. 'You must be freezing. What happened? Why are you here?'

'A bomb fell. I ran. As fast as I could,' He said. 'Do you know if my mother and sister are all right?'

'I'm sure they are,' she said. 'We'll go and find out, shall we?'

Wearily, Juhan stood, then wobbled.

'But first,' Emilie said, realising he was in shock, 'sit down for a moment and let's see if we can't get you a blanket and something to eat. Have you had anything to eat?'

'No. I just ran. Then I got here, so I sat down.' He started to cry. 'I didn't know what to do.'

'I know, you poor dear, I know ...' She held him while he sobbed.

About an hour later, Juhan and Emilie made their way to the house. Emilie had found the boy a blanket and something to eat. She'd even acquired some shoes for him. These had been provided by a woman whose son was in the army and did not need them anymore. Because he'd been killed in Russia.

The street where Juhan had once lived was nearly all rubble and flames. They went up to a policeman who was picking his way through the clutter of wood, bricks, glass and personal possessions down the street.

'Anyone from this zone has been taken to the school,' he said.

Emilie and Juhan found Maret and Leena being looked after by an elderly woman in one of the classrooms. Leena cried and clutched her son to her breast the moment she saw him. Maret wanted to cry, too, with relief, but forced herself to remain in control of her emotions; as she had been taught at Young Maidens. The family's joy at being reunited went largely unnoticed by the rest of the people in that room. Emilie stood to one side She did not expect thanks; neither did she get it. There seemed no room for thankfulness at such a time; just shock, desperation and occasionally relief. She waited for her chance to speak. Eventually, it came.

'I am so happy you have all found one another again. But we must think about what to do next. Now that it is clear you can't stay here.'

'What do you mean we can't stay here?' said Maret.

'I mean, your house has gone – we saw. I am not sure whether we will find another place to stay around here – so many people have lost their homes – there's bound to be great difficulty for many people to find somewhere to live, even if only for a while.'

'We'll find somewhere.'

'Perhaps. Perhaps not. The simple solution, though, would be for you to come with me as I have been suggesting and find somewhere to stay in my hometown.'

'No. Father won't know where we've gone. We will wait here.'

'I quite understand your reasoning, Maret. But what does your mother think?' She placed a hand on the woman's shoulder. 'Leena? What do you think?'

Leena looked up at Emilie. It was clear she did not recognise her. It was clear she had been so overwhelmed by everything that had just happened that her mind, perhaps in self-preservation, had simply closed its shutters for the time being.

'We are staying,' said Maret again.

'Then I'll stay with you,' said Emilie.

*

Hendrik arrived at last in Königsberg. He stared at the torn buildings and debris-scattered streets. The city reeked of smouldering piles, raw sewage and charred corpses. Some were still lying like grotesque toppled statuary among the clutter of bricks and mortar. The Pregel still flowed, but now the turgid surface was littered with the remains of boats, timber and decomposing flesh: human beings, horses, cats, dogs, fish, vermin. *The British have at least solved the Königsberg Bridge problem*, he thought. All the crossings he could see had been blown to fragments and now lay in tumbled heaps among the putrid waters.

A surge of despair suddenly overcame him. This was accompanied by fear. It was a different fear, however. This was not suppressed by adrenaline and elbowed aside by the challenges of combat. He was in the chasm of helplessness and dread.

His taxi couldn't get him close enough to the road in which, the last he knew, his family lived. So he paid the driver off and walked. His fears were confirmed when he turned into the street and saw shattered buildings and buckled, leafless trees. All the houses had been damaged in some way by the firebombs and the subsequent inferno. He had seen all of this elsewhere recently and with increasing frequency. Once or twice, he even thought, *Serve them right. They've brought it on themselves, reap the whirlwind.* But compassion always over-ruled, and a sense of the agony of human suffering would emerge. *Why do we do it to ourselves? Why do we let fools and monsters into our lives and give them the freedom to destroy everything we hold dear?* There were, however, no such thoughts as Hendrik surveyed the wasteland where his wife and children had once lived. There was only despair. He went up to the house and saw it had collapsed in on itself. The raid, he knew, had been a couple of days ago. But still parts of the house smouldered, and the stench of burnt wood and fabric hung overall. In there, somewhere, was the couch on which his wife had once lain. He only hoped that his wife had not been on it when all of *this* happened ...

'Do you know where they went?' He had found an elderly lady to ask. She looked at him with haunted eyes and shook her head. 'Where did they all go from here?' She didn't know. 'Do you know the Wowreits? He's a policeman. I think he and his wife live locally.'

'Policeman?' she said. 'Well, there is one lives around here. With a wife. I don't know their name, but they live two blocks that way. I don't know the house. They live near the grocer's. Do you know it?'

'Yes.'

Hendrik found the grocer's. Unlike much of that whole area, it was still standing, as were the houses immediately nearby. The door was locked. Peering through the window, he could see the shelves had been stripped of all their produce. He knocked. Eventually, a thin man in brown overalls came to the door. 'Yes, we deliver to the Wowreits. Number 20,' a bony finger pointed.

Hendrik knocked on the front door. Mrs Wowreit answered. Her eyes were red. She took a moment to recognise him.

'Oh, hello,' she said, without any warmth.

'Do you know where my family have gone?'

'No. I'm sorry.'

'Do you know if they are all right, perhaps?'

'I don't know anything, I'm afraid. It's all just terrible.'

'Do you know how I might find out where they've gone? How about the police station? Where is it, please?' She told him how to get there. 'Thank you. Will your husband be there? Perhaps he'll know where they've gone.'

She looked at him, expressionless. 'My husband was on duty, helping older folk to the shelters. He was killed in the raid.'

'I'm sorry. I'm so sorry.'

He wanted to thank her for all the kindness she'd shown his family, but it seemed somehow inappropriate. So he took her hands in his and they stood, silent, for a moment. Then he raised one of her hands to his lips and kissed it.

'I'm so sorry,' he said again, and turned away.

'I hope you find your family,' she said, and closed the door.

At the police station, the desk sergeant ran a finger down the casualty list, his lips formed Kotkas's family name as he did so; the scent of fresh schnapps wafting from his mouth. No such surname was found. Hendrik wondered where else he might ask. The sergeant said he could try the Town Hall.

He thanked the policeman. 'If you track them down,' he said, 'I'm presently with the navy at Libau. If you could get word to me there.'

'Of course, sir.'

After he had gone, the sergeant drummed his fingers on the counter for a moment. The sergeant didn't like the fact that this officer had given out where he was based, even if it was to him, an official of the State, and even if it was for a very valid reason. But this wasn't what gave him pause. *Something about that surname 'Kotkas'...* He opened a file containing the list of people wanted for questioning.

There it was. Hendrik Kotkas. He thought it had rung a bell.

He picked up the telephone.

*

Hendrik scoured Königsberg for a further two days, sleeping in doorways as there were no rooms available; all taken up by the dispossessed. Finding nothing, he considered staying on but realised there was little point. His family could be anywhere by now. Or nowhere. If they were trying to get in touch, as he had indicated to the desk sergeant, they would be doing it through the navy or the Intelligence Service. That's where he needed to be. Rather than him finding them, they had to be able to find him. He made his way back to the station and caught the first train north.

In a strange way, despite the desperate circumstances, he found he was actually looking forward to rejoining his ship. He even took some comfort in imagining the cheers and grins of the crew as they welcomed him back on board his command. He knew there would be demands to inspect his medal; they would even pretend to polish it. The medal, he would tell them, was not just for him – but for all of them.

Which was troubling.

There are enemies and there are human beings, he thought. *One has difficulty, sometimes, remembering that they are actually the same thing.*

*

Emilie had found Leena and the children a disused office to shelter in. She had scavenged a couple of old mattresses and three blankets for them. She slept, herself, in her coat on the floor.

Leena lay on her mattress, wrapped up. Occasionally, she let out a low moan. There was no more medicine. The doctor's house had been destroyed in the raid; the pharmacy had closed down. She tried to take her mind off the pain and the cold. She thought of Estonia – home – and, curiously, she thought about the trees. The pines and the spruces, the aspens and the alders. Tall and proud. *They will be there long after I've gone*, she thought. Long after. And then there was her favourite. The silver birch, waving its wand-like branches at the clouds. The pretty little leaves;

silvery-green in the spring, almost jingling like bells in the light Baltic breezes. It would be hard to leave them especially; they'd been her friends, her comfort, her joy for as long as she could remember. From what she had seen, there were few trees now, there in the centre of Königsberg. The shattered buildings, like broken teeth, had nevertheless retained a certain dignity, despite their battering. The kind of noble dignity of a wounded, dying stag. The people of Königsberg, too, clung on to such dignity as they could. But it was draining away by the day, through hunger, illness and fear as to what was coming next.

It was nearly dark before the children came back. They were bright with triumph. Juhan waved half a chunk of bread.

'An old lady gave it to us!' he exclaimed. 'She saw we were hungry and tore it off the bread she'd gone to find for her husband. And guess what ...?'

'What?' said Emilie.

'Maret found some coal!'

Maret held out a hefty lump. It needed two hands to hold it.

'She had to fight a boy for it,' Juhan said. 'He was tough, but she won!'

'Well done, Maret,' said Emilie. 'See if you can't chip about a third off of it, and we'll put it in the stove with what's left of the wooden chair and some newspaper. You'd like a fire, wouldn't you, Leena?'

Leena didn't answer. She was still remembering silver birches. She shivered, and pulled the blanket closer around herself.

The stove was lit and half the bread was shared among them.

'My turn to go out tomorrow, children. I'll get some more food and coal then,' said Emilie.

Leena moaned again. Emilie got down beside her, lifted her up to a sitting position and cuddled her as best she could.

She looked at the two children sitting across the room in the light of a pilfered oil lamp. She held out one hand towards them, inviting them to join her and their mother.

Maret shook her head. Juhan followed his sister's lead and shook his, too. He nestled closer into her. But his sister was a bit lumpy and fidgeted. After a couple of minutes, he got up and went across to fold himself into Emilie and Leena's embrace.

Maret stared across at them, hugging her knees.

'Come on, Maret,' said Emilie, 'let's keep each other warm.'

'I am all right here, thank you.'

'Leena?' said Emilie.

'Come on, darling,' Leena whispered; her mouth dry.

'All right, Mother, if *you* say so,' said Maret, and joined them.

Enough was enough, thought Emilie. She needed to get these poor things right away from there. Get them to relative comfort and safety as quickly as she could. She also had to let Hendrik know his family was safe.

The next day, she tried again at the post office to put a call through to anyone who might be able to contact Hendrik. Any lines that were still operational, however, were restricted to people on official business only. They were doing all they could to restore communications to the general public, the person behind the counter assured her, just as he had been assuring everyone who had come in over the days since the raid.

'But this *is* official business,' said Emilie. I am trying to put a call through to the Marine Regional Command.'

The post office worker shrugged. *They all say that.* 'Then try the harbour. Speak to the navy's shore office there. They might be able to help.'

The navy's shore office. Of course. Why didn't I think of that? Emilie told herself.

'Regional Command?' said the petty officer at the desk.

'I'm afraid I can't do that just on your say-so, madam. Do you have any written authority, or some such, that might help?'

Emilie thought about producing her Intelligence Service ID but then remembered the security police and her need to keep a low profile, even in those desperate times. In any case, it was unlikely that would make much difference without some kind of signed paperwork authorising her to send the message. Moreover, she wasn't sure she wanted to mention Commander Kotkas's name in such a context, either, for similar safety reasons. 'Is there no way I can get a message to them?' she pleaded one last time.

Another petty officer had come into the office.

'Message to who?' he said.

'Regional Command. I wanted to ring them, try and get through to an officer. I don't know where he is, but they are sure to know, and could arrange for him to get in contact with me.'

The man exchanged a smile with his colleague. 'They are not necessarily "sure to know" anything, ma'am. Not these days.'

'Nevertheless, I need to try. But I can't, unless I have some kind of authorisation.'

'Well, that's right, yes. However – here's a thought ... We're just about to send half a dozen midshipmen up that way. They've just finished training and will be deployed to various postings. I'm sure you could ask one of them to take a message if you want to write it. Here – you can use this pad and these envelopes ...'

*

Kotkas surveyed the horizon with his binoculars. The coastline swayed with the gentle nudging of his ship to starboard. The towers and spires of medieval Tallinn sat in the circle of his lenses like a magic lantern show. In under an hour, the flotilla would be snubbing its way past the breakwater and into the familiar sights, sounds and smells of his beloved hometown.

Home.

He lowered his binoculars.

It had been nearly three years since he and Emilie were bundled into a navy launch and taken out to a troop ship headed for Memel. The pang of loss returned. An emptiness deeper, crueller than hunger.

They came alongside, and, having secured his ship, Kotkas left Busch in charge.

He found the port and town seething with troops and vehicles. He made his way to the harbour office to make his report.

'Ah, Kotkas...' It was the port commander. A lean man with a scar on his top lip; earned during the invasion of Norway at the start of the war.

'Sir.'

'You speak Estonian, don't you?'

'I do.'

'Come with me.'

As they walked, Kotkas noticed three midshipmen mustered on the quayside.

'New intake?'

'Yes,' said the port commander.

'I think I recognise one of the fellows. May I go and have a word with him, sir?'

'If you are quick.'

They went up to the group. The petty officer addressing them stood to one side. Kotkas approached a tall slim fellow with blond hair.

'Karl?'

'Sir?'

'Don't you remember me? Hendrik Kotkas. You know my family in Königsberg. Or, rather, you know my children,

Maret and Juhan. I believe you introduced them to their groups.'

'Oh, sir, yes. Apologies, I didn't recognise you.'

'We're both out of context. It's normal. So you've made it into the navy? Well, congratulations. How are you? How's your family?' He paused. 'How's mine?'

'My family is well, sir. As for yours, I don't know, I'm afraid. My mother, before I left, said she had seen them once recently.'

'Before or after the air raid?'

'After, sir.'

'So you think they are all right?'

'As far as I know, sir. Oh, but, sir ... I have this for you. Not sure who it's from. An officer gave it to me before I left Königsberg.' He dipped into his breast pocket and pulled out a slightly crumpled envelope. 'Sorry, it's a bit battered ... I took it to Memel, then we were moved to Libau, then we were sent here to join the fleet supporting the evacuation. Everywhere I went I asked after you. Nobody really knew where you were, what ship you were on. So I just kept it.'

'Quite understood. Thank you, Karl. That was very kind of you.'

The port commander checked his watch.

'Come along, Kotkas,'

'Right away, sir,' said Kotkas, then to the young midshipman, 'got a berth yet, Karl?'

'Not yet, sir,' said the petty officer on the midshipman's behalf. 'They've only just arrived. Port Office is assigning over the next two or three days.'

'Very good,' said Kotkas. 'I could do with another pair of hands. If it's at all possible. I'm Commander H. Kotkas, minesweepers ...'

'I'll see what I can do, sir.'

'Come along, Kotkas,' said the port commander, and drew him away.

They reached a building which, it was clear from the crowds and the guards, was some kind of clearing house for refugees and other people the authorities weren't sure about.

'Recent arrivals from all parts of Estonia,' said the port commander. 'All sorts. Military, civilian and, doubtless, some undesirables. See what you can do over the next few days to help the processing detachment, would you? Interviewing, translating, screening.'

'Yes, sir. But my ship …'

'… will still be there when you get back. Your first officer can look after things while you're here. I understand Estonian is a ridiculously difficult language to learn.'

He left Kotkas to it.

The afternoon wore on into the evening with Kotkas assisting an SS officer; checking out the ragged folk who stood in front of the processing desk, one after another, with their various stories of disaster, escape and eventual arrival in Tallinn.

Kotkas translated every tale faithfully. At least for the first couple of hours. But then, once he had established that no one on his side of the desk understood a word of Estonian, he started to take little liberties. Simple little sentences seemingly of no significance. *I, too, am an Estonian*, he would say, once he felt he could trust an interviewee. *I am a patriot like you*, or *I will try to help*, and *I will see if I can get you away from here*. If any German had asked him, he would have said he was just offering a word of encouragement, of hope, of a wish for better days; which, in many ways, he was. But nobody did ask. The SS officer was just as irritated by this tedious task as Kotkas was, and clearly couldn't wait to get it over with.

In fact, it wasn't until the early hours of the morning that the SS officer finally decided they needed to get some rest. Kotkas returned to his cabin on board ship.

Back on board, he sat with his lieutenant over an ersatz coffee.

'So, what's going on, sir?' said Busch.

'The Reds are pushing hard in the East.' There was a catch in Kotkas's voice; he could hardly bring himself to say the words. 'Estonia's likely to fall.' *Not again. Not all over again.* 'So High Command have decided to consolidate round the Kurland peninsular. Pulling all troops back from the East.'

'All troops?'

'Yes.'

'And civilians? The government in Tallinn, the whole regime structure being torn down and ferried in trucks and ships back?'

'As far as I understand it, yes.'

'I see ...'

'Some Estonian recruits to the army are staying on to resist, along with their partisan comrades. But that's about it. We're in for a sticky time, it seems, Viktor.'

'It does indeed, sir.'

'No one's safe. And, apparently, the purge is still going on, following the attempt on the Leader's life. Poor people ... they'll be after anyone and everyone. And if they don't have any evidence against them – they'll make it up. It's a complete mess.' Kotkas looked through his cabin window at the organised chaos portside. 'The dragon may be dying, but it's still thrashing its tail.'

'You really think it's all over?'

'Don't you?'

Busch shook his head, not to disagree: 'Too dangerous to even think it. Defeatism is treason.'

'Perhaps, but the alternative is unthinkable, too. The word is that the general order from High Command – apparently coming down from the very top – is: no surrender – fight to the death. Which is encouraging ...' Kotkas paused. He looked at the young naval officer beside him. 'How do you feel about that?'

Busch shrugged. 'I took an oath.'

'All right. But if, in the next few weeks, we have an opportunity to help the cause in different ways – other than fighting to the death – how would you feel about that?'

'It would depend on what those different ways entailed.'

'Naturally. How about the crew? Do you think they'd be up for, how shall we put it, creative ways of engaging with the situation around us?'

'If you led them, sir ... they would probably follow ...'

'Depending?'

'Depending.'

'Very well. Would you do me a favour?'

'Of course, sir.'

'Sound the crew out, would you? Quietly. Just prime them for the possibility of some –unconventional – warfare, so to speak.'

'I will, sir.'

It was only after Busch had left, when Kotkas was taking off his uniform jacket with a yawn, that he noticed the envelope Karl had given him earlier. He sat down on his bed and opened it. It was from Emilie, dated a week ago. *Family is safe. Leena very poorly. Going to the station to see if we can get a train to Hannover and ultimately Lehrte, where my family live. The address is ...*

Kotkas gripped the note as if he would never let it go.

III

'Sit down, Maret, Juhan ...'

Emilie Meyer had sat with the family at the railway station in Königsberg for almost two days. Every train that departed east seemed to be a troop train carrying men – increasingly younger men – to the front. There were thousands of others in and around the station. Civilians, refugees, homeless, all trying to find a way out of the nightmare; struggling to reach family and friends around the country. Despite her misgivings, Emilie eventually showed her Intelligence Service ID to station staff. She hoped that they weren't as directly connected to the powers that be. It did the trick. The next train that would allow civilians on board found the four of them squeezed into a compartment with half a dozen other anxious and weary passengers.

And now they were in Lehrte, with Emilie's two stepsisters, in the family home. It was a pretty little town just a few kilometres beyond Hannover. It was a key north-south, east-west junction for the railways. There was a vast sugar refinery which occasionally filled the Lehrte air with a heady bittersweetness. It had a sleepy main street with the usual doctor, post office and *bierhof*. Each summer, the locals held their extravagant *schützenfest*, with its brass bands, beer tents and shooting competitions. This gave an opportunity for men in antler-buttoned Loden jackets and feathered caps to get drunk, and for women in *dirndls* to get kissed. The town centre was surrounded by comfortable suburban homes, many in their own grounds. There was the occasional Gothic villa. Nodding trees were everywhere.

Emilie had been to the family plot in the Lutheran

cemetery off Iltener Street. She had been putting forget-me-nots on her father's grave. Twice a widower, including Emilie's own mother, he had been a much-respected if austere Prussian surgeon general. He had died just over five years earlier. She arrived home and stepped up to the front door. As she did so, an army motorcyclist pulled up and handed her a message. She read it on the doorstep, smiled, and went inside.

'Children ... children ...' she called. Maret looked out from the living room; Juhan looked through the upstairs bannisters.

'I have heard at last from your father.'

'Father!' cried Juhan.

'Shh,' said Maret, 'you'll wake Mother.'

'But Father ... He isn't dead ...!' he said again in a shrill voice, barely quieter than before.

'Now then,' continued Emilie, 'tomorrow, your father has arranged for a navy ambulance to come. It will take your mother to Groß Rhüden military hospital in the Harz mountains. The air is clean, there is fresh water, good food, lots of medicine ... she will be very well taken care of.'

'They are taking her away?' said Juhan, clambering downstairs on his behind.

'No,' said Maret, 'I won't let them.'

'Maret, she will be much better off there with proper care. She can be much better looked after than we can here.'

'You have arranged this,' said Maret, 'deliberately. You want her out of the way ...'

'No, I don't. It is your father's idea.' She held the message up again. 'It is his wish that your mother be taken somewhere where she can be properly looked after.'

'You're glad she is going.'

'Not glad, no. But I am positive it is the right thing.'

'Then we should all go with her.'

'Yes,' said Juhan, 'let's all go to the mountains. I've never seen mountains. I've read about them. Seen pictures in books.

They look wonderful. We should all go to the mountains.'

'Maret, Juhan. Listen. This is a military hospital. Besides, you two children have had far too much to cope with. We're just managing to settle you down again here in Lehrte. You start school the day after tomorrow. We'll try and make things as normal and as comfortable as we can here. Don't you see? This is all for the best.'

The children fell silent.

Then Maret spoke, quietly at first. 'If Mother goes, I'm going with her.'

'Sorry, Maret ... what did you say?'

'I said,' now she raised her voice, 'I'm going with Mother and you can't stop me. Someone has to go. Mother can't be left all alone like this. It's not right, it's not fair. She mustn't be thrown away like this. I am going with her.'

'No one's throwing her away, Maret.'

Maret repeated herself in words of one syllable, so that the stupid woman could understand. 'I will go with her. You can't stop me. You're not my mother. You don't own me.'

Emilie looked at the girl. *Girl? No ... young woman. She's seen so much that a child her age should never have seen. She's had to do so much. She's had to grow up too fast. She's carried her family on her shoulders all this way. Perhaps it's right she sees this to the end where her mother is concerned. Her mother does not have much longer. A few weeks, perhaps? Then Maret can come back and the three of them try to get back to as normal a life as possible. She can restart her schooling then.*

'All right, Maret. You go with your mother to look after her. Like you've been doing so well all these years.'

'Can I go too?' said Juhan.

'No, you're staying here with me and going to school.'

*

Kotkas left by the main gates of the naval base. He'd been back and forth between Tallinn and the western Baltic over the past few weeks. Shielding convoys; ferrying troops, civilians and even Estonian refugees to the rear. Every time he returned to the navy base in Tallinn, he half expected to see a car once more parked outside, with men waiting to follow him. There never was. He wondered where Fischer and his thugs had got to. Did they know he'd been back in their sphere of operations a good half-dozen times? Clearly not. Or they were simply too preoccupied with tormenting undesirables to notice.

The previous week, he'd made his way to the fishermen's drinking hole down by the harbour. He had enquired after Nils and was told that he had gone. Now that it was all up for Estonia, Nils had taken one last cargo of half a dozen families and gone to find a new life with his cousin in Sweden.

Kotkas had also gone to the ancient city wall, to the fortress tower known as Fat Margaret. She had suffered some blast damage but, solid and indomitable, it would clearly take a lot more than Soviet bombers to bring her to her knees. He clambered over some low-lying rubble and approached the substantial walls. He located again the loose stone on the northern side. He had left a brief scrap of paper in it before his most recent escort duty; a note to Tamm asking for a meeting. He went there again, now. He pulled the stone out. There was a slip of paper. He recognised Tamm's handwriting. It was dated a couple of weeks earlier.

My dear brother-in-arms, it read, *it has been murder here. The SS up to their old tricks. Anyone and everyone they take a dislike to, they arrest, hang or summarily shoot in the back of the head in the middle of the street. It's as if they blame us Estonians for their abject failure at Leningrad and are somehow trying to shore up their defences from Ivan with our dead. You and I know that in terms of sheer numbers, Uncle Joe will be enjoying pork,* sauerkraut *and blood sausage in Kadriorg Palace at*

Christmas. We don't have much longer, that's for sure. And, if you are reading this, you will know what the March bombing did to our beautiful city. Whole neighbourhoods obliterated. What the future holds for Tallinn and Estonia once this madness is all over is anyone's guess. We won't be able to meet, sadly. I need to carry on the fight elsewhere, now. But I trust and pray that you keep safe and we meet again somewhere, sometime and – pray God – soon.

Yours aye,
Tamm

There was a PS.

That fisherman friend of yours gave me a note to give to you. I'll put it with my note. I don't think it's from him, though.

Kotkas closed Tamm's note and opened the other one. It consisted of just one sentence.

Leaving tonight for Sweden with the fishing fleet – a thousand thank-yous, my dear commander, comrade and friend.

Louis

Kotkas tore the notes up and cast the fragments to the wind. Just a little more debris to mingle with all of the rest that was lying around his beloved hometown these days. There was nothing of significance to anyone else in those notes anyway. He replaced the stone and moved off.

He wanted to go for a walk.

He was saying his goodbyes; he knew it.

He ambled down the streets that he'd known as a boy, as a young man, as a husband, a father, a naval officer. He looked in at windows where once he'd sat with friends; for dinner, for a coffee, for a beer.

The wind chased itself around the Town Hall Square. It

slapped Kotkas on the cheek and flew off, tugging swirls of litter along with it. The evidence of the Soviets' bombing earlier in the year lay all around. Debris, dust ... stench. Old Thomas, legendary guardian of the city, who had once swung on his perch atop the spire, had crashed to the ground in one of the raids. Even he was unable, it seemed, to help his people in those desperate times. Mangled beyond repair, what was left of the proud weathervane figure, with its moustache like swallow's wings, had been borne away in solemn ceremony. It was as if he'd been real; as if he'd died.

Kotkas continued his walk. He rounded Cathedral Hill. The devastation beyond never failed to stagger him each time he'd encountered it. As Tamm had mentioned in his note – whole streets, whole communities had been completely obliterated by the Soviets in their March bombing. There was just pile after pile of rubble now. Jagged pinnacles that had once been shops and factories; craters that had once been homes. And the stench. Always the stench of death and destruction; even so many months after the catastrophe. A volcano's crater.

Kotkas stood silently for some minutes surveying the scene. One question swam round his mind as he looked at the desperate scene: *Why?*

Shaking his head, he eventually forced himself to move away. There would be time for grieving later.

He made his way to Charles Church. Here, he had been married. Here, his children had been baptised. He went inside. Four years of conflict raging around it had not been kind to the old place. The latest assault on its lofty walls even more damaging. The plaster was covered in cracks like cobwebs. Great chunks had come adrift and had shattered where they had fallen. He pulled a bench upright, wiped the debris off it and sat.

He prayed.

When he was ready, he stood up, dusted himself off, bowed to the outstretched arms of the Christ over the altar, and left.

Up and over Tõnismägi. To the apartment, where he stopped once again.

Though it had escaped the worst of the bombing, the building was empty now, the jetsam of a retreating army strewn across the entrance. The windows out of which he would have looked a thousand times were shattered. The curtains Leena had ordered from her father's factory on Väike-Karja flicked shredded ends in the breeze. They waved their farewell to him.

He wandered down to his father-in-law's house and clanged the front door bell. There was no answer. Feliks had either left already or was away fighting a rearguard action, perhaps as a patriot, not as an SS officer. Or had died.

A thought caught him by surprise. Why not visit his own family home in Nõmme?

He hitched a ride on a grubby army truck which was headed south; full of shocked, wounded and weary young men grateful to be leaving the hell of the Eastern front. He leapt off a few metres from his parents' home. His mother and father were dead now; had been for many years. He thought it a mercy. They would have been devastated to have witnessed all that was now taking place. He went up the short drive and rapped on the washed oak door. He didn't expect anyone to answer. But then he heard movement.

He waited.

A bolt was drawn and a latch turned. The door swung open.

'Hendrik! My dear brother!'

'Peeter!'

They fell on each other's necks and wept.

*

The ambulance came the next day. Emilie, her sisters and Juhan were there to see Maret and her mother off.

No tears, Maret told herself. No need for them. I am doing

only what a good Young Maiden has been taught to do. Be strong, be reliable, be brave. But she couldn't help feeling just a little sad as the ambulance drove away. Those they were leaving behind dwindled to nothing in the dust of the road out of the rear window. *Moss. Remember the moss.* She could just make out Juhan still waving vigorously as they turned the corner out of sight for good.

Juhan. Her dear brother. Aside from the air raid, they'd not been apart since this whole awful thing began. How she would miss him. Even if he was annoying.

She recalled a hot July day, the summer before the war started, back home. Back in dear Vasalemma. They'd walked through the meadow, swathed in cornflowers, marguerites and poppies, down to the stream. The sweet smell of hay and the warm remembrance of dusty Estonian farm tracks. They'd swum, then lay on the rough grass to dry off in the sun. Juhan had dug around in the earth with his fingers, eventually surfacing a worm.

'Maret?'

'Yes?'

'I dare you.'

'You dare me to do what?'

'To bite this worm in half.'

She got up on her elbows and looked at him. 'Yuk,' she said, 'no, I will not.'

'But I've dared you. It's a dare. You have to do it if it's a dare.'

Maret thought for a moment. 'Tell you what,' she said. 'I'll do it if you do it. I'll bite it in half and you have to bite the other half.'

'All right.'

'Right.' She took the worm from her brother's grubby fingers. She watched it coil as she held it in her pinch. Then, steeling herself, she opened her mouth, placed it on her tongue, and bit down hard on the cold squirming flesh. She nearly gagged and spat the severed half out of her mouth. 'Yeuch!' she said, and spat again. Then she held the still-twirling remainder out towards her brother. 'Now you,' she said.

Juhan took one look at it, leapt to his feet and scampered off laughing.

'Come back!' Maret called. 'You have to take your turn.'

'No, I don't!' he called back. 'You never dared me.'

While the memory gave Maret a sense of warmer, better days as she sat there in the back of that cold ambulance, it also gave her a sense of what she had lost. Gone, probably for ever, she realised. She looked down at her dying mother on the stretcher, covered in blankets.

It's all over … it's all gone. No home. No father. No mother.

She was sure that Emilie had arranged to have her mother taken away.

Yes, that horrible woman has probably made up that whole message from Father. Just to get rid of Mother. Probably couldn't be bothered to look after her anymore. Maybe she thought our father was already dead. And soon Mother will be too. And that horrible woman doesn't want the bother of having to make all the arrangements. In fact, that horrible woman will probably manage not to bring me back afterwards, either. Maybe she'll even find a way of getting rid of Juhan. Why should she care about either of us? We don't belong to her. And I've been just as much trouble.

She felt like crying again but shook herself out of her melancholy.

Young Maidens do not cry. They are never downhearted. Courage and Determination are the Order of the Day. Victory is assured if we are resolute. Adi will still win, she told herself. *Look at what he's achieved already. It's his destiny. It is Germany's destiny. Of course …! Adi …! He's my father now. And isn't that what we call our country? The Fatherland?*

She began to hum one of the inspirational songs she'd learnt at Group, and started to feel a little better.

'So, tell me, Peeter,' Kotkas said, as they sat in the kitchen drinking Russian State vodka, 'the last time we spoke you were an officer in the Red Fleet.'

Peeter shrugged. 'They threw me out. Guess they could no longer trust me. Too many questions – why had I let your family go free down at the harbour? for one. But they didn't shoot me, thankfully.'

'I can see that.'

They chinked tumblers.

'Far too useful, what with my navy training, especially with torpedoes. So they put me to work in a munitions factory down by the harbour. Civilian. Gave me a two-room apartment and everything. I only managed to get back here in our parents' home when your boys in field grey turned up.'

'They are not my boys.'

'No. Did you hear about the port commander? Admiral Gahlendorf, I think his name was.'

'You remember Gahlendorf – we sailed against him at Kiel. Drank with him in bars.'

'Oh! That Gahlendorf.' Peeter rubbed his chin. 'Never made the connection. Admiral, eh? Nice fellow. Good company.' His hand stopped stroking his bristles. 'Poor chap.'

'Why – what's happened?'

'Strung up from a lamppost down by the harbour somewhere. Poor beggar.'

'Who by?'

'Which group and for what reason doesn't seem to matter anymore, does it?'

Hendrik tried to let the news sink in. It was hard to believe his old friend, his sailing companion, his mentor and protector had gone. All the man had really loved was brandy, cigars and the sea. It was absurd: dragged into a war he had no interest in, promoted into a role he had no need for, and murdered for reasons unknown and which would probably never be known.

'God bless him,' Hendrik said, and they toasted their absent friend.

Remembering Gahlendorf made him realise something else. 'But, you mean to tell me, when I was here last time, you were working for the Germans in the same factory?' He sounded almost indignant.

'That was just about the size of it.'

'And you are working for them again?'

'I am in the business of making torpedoes, not making friends.'

'But, I must have passed that building a hundred times while I was based here. Why didn't you try and contact me?'

'Why didn't you try to contact me?'

'I didn't know you were here.'

'There you are, then.'

'Someone must have said something, somewhere. It was the whole reason I decided not to go to ground here because I knew some day someone – the wrong someone – would recognise me and the game would be all up.'

Peeter took a thoughtful sip. 'It may be a small city, but it's plenty big enough, it seems. And remember, you are far more notorious than I am, big brother. After all, it was you that ran the show at the harbour in the last days.'

'I suppose so.' Hendrik laid his glass on the table and turned it round. It made a rasping noise on the wood. 'You know Feliks was still here?'

'No. I never bothered with that part of the world much. They were your in-laws, not mine.'

'Well, what are you going to do, now? You could come with me. I could vouch for you. Get you into the navy with us, if you like?'

'No, thanks. I like it here. I was born here, grew up here, and this is where I will die.'

Hendrik looked at him. 'And you think I should do the same? Should have done the same?'

Peeter laid a hand on his brother's shoulder. 'Far from it. You had a family to protect. You have done the absolute best you could in these impossible circumstances. I would have done the same. Besides, knowing you, that uniform you are wearing isn't half the story, is it ...?'

Hendrik drained his glass but didn't answer.

'And, you? When the Soviets come back?' he said at length.

Peeter shrugged. 'I still have the credentials the Russkies gave me. Most likely carry on making torpedoes. Listen, Hendrik, promise me something.'

'Anything.'

'When this is all over, when the beautiful Baltic breezes have blown all the filth and stench and garbage away, promise you'll come back? Promise you'll move heaven and earth to find me?'

'I promise. If it is in my power, I promise. But we don't know how this will end. No one does – not even those fools in high office who pretend they do. But if I can get back, by God, I will do it. And we'll make a new home here. My family, you, me ... A new Estonia. Bigger and better than ever before. Never say die.'

Peeter refilled the glasses from the bottle, and they toasted their hopes in the soft light of a fading day.

'Never say die.'

*

After their goodbyes, Kotkas made his way through the confusion to one of the buildings near the harbour. Here, he knew, civilians were being held. There were a couple of SS guards on the door.

'What's happening, Sergeant?'

'Don't know, sir. Been here most of the day. Orders just to keep this place locked up.'

Kotkas could imagine what the plan was now. Evacuation of anyone and everyone had been the order of the day up to that point. His ship had even taken part in these operations the previous few weeks. Germans, Finns, Latvians, Lithuanians ... Estonians, all shipped out to the relative safety of Libau, Windau, Memel and other ports. In the dying moments of what was left of the German Baltic regime, however, there was no time for such luxuries. The authorities needed to keep the undesirables out of the way. Prevent them from interfering with as orderly a withdrawal as possible. Any interference by panicking locals would impede progress. Military men and machines, they would look after. German civilians, they would also preserve. Which meant they would intern anyone who made trouble, or seemed likely to. The SS would leave them to the Soviets to deal with after they had cleared off. Or worse – set fire to those places where they were being held as they left.

'Open up,' he said.

The guards looked at one another.

'Come on. Open up.'

'But, orders, sir.'

'What orders? Everyone's moving out. Go and join your unit. Get out of here before you miss the bus and they push off without you.'

'But—'

'That, too, is an order. Tell them Commander Kotkas gave you permission. On my head be it.'

The two guards hesitated a moment longer, then buckled.

'Sir.'

They unlocked the door, slung their rifles over their shoulders, and trotted off.

Inside were about a hundred people; men, women, children. Huddled, confused and afraid.

Kotkas spoke to them in Estonian. 'Is this all of you?'

'All that they've left. They took everyone else. We're mostly

Estonians, but there's some Latvians and Lithuanians here as well,' a small balding man with a torn suit and gnawed fingernails said.

'We were only trying to get on a ship. Get away. Save our children,' said one of the women. She had the berry eyes and sinewy hands of the southern country folk.

'Come on, let's get you out of here,' said Kotkas.

Nobody moved.

'It's all right. Don't be fooled by the uniform. I'm an Estonian naval officer. Follow me.'

They looked at one another, then, one by one, they joined Kotkas, who led them out of the door. They made their way, a string of civilians among the melee that was a retreating army, towards the quayside. Nobody challenged them; too busy saving themselves.

They reached the ship.

'Busch?'

Busch's face appeared around a door on the M35. 'Sir?'

'Get these people on board. See if you can find somewhere for them to settle below. And get them something to eat and drink. I daresay they haven't had anything hot for days. How quickly can you get us ready to leave?'

'A couple of hours, sir. Finished refuelling. Just getting the last of the supplies on board.'

'Very well. Keep these people out of sight.'

'Sir.'

The crew on deck doing the loading watched as the raggle-taggle men, women and children, with few or no belongings, clambered up the gangplank and were escorted below.

It was well after dusk before the M35 slipped her moorings and slid out to sea. As they passed the lead minesweeper, Kotkas's flotilla commander came out onto his flying bridge. His own ship was getting ready to leave Tallinn for good, too. With a hailer, he called out to Kotkas. 'Where are you headed?' The words, like starlings, swirled then took wing on the evening breeze.

A seagull cried.

Kotkas took his hailer and called back. It was in Estonian: 'Helping my people escape their tormentors' filthy clutches.' He backed it up with a smile and a cheery wave.

It was gobbledygook as far as the flotilla commander was concerned; he cocked his head and cupped his hand to his ear. 'What did you say? I didn't catch it!'

Kotkas said something further in Estonian: 'Taking them across the sea to freedom.' He waved more vigorously and ended by saying, but this time in German: 'See you in Libau,' which he made sure the commander heard.

'Ah! Libau!' The commander waved farewell. 'See you there!'

The reply floated over the water to Kotkas. He gave the helmsman an order, and the lean grey ship turned into the swell and headed across the harbour bar.

Heavy artillery fire could be heard from the east.

A blood-red sun was setting.

Kotkas, on the flying bridge, looked back at the battered but unbowed city; his home.

He saluted.

Winter 1945

I

The room was quiet.

Outside, people spoke with soft voices. Leena had not been put on a ward with the soldiers. Soldiers died where they lay; next to their comrades. Leena was a civilian. And a woman. Her curtains were drawn. She was alone.

Maret was still asleep in a room across the road.

There was a sea mist that often would close in on Tallinn from the Baltic in the summer. As everything became indistinguishable, the foghorn of the lighthouse in the bay would commence its low haunting moan. It would echo across the water every two minutes like a Viking ram's horn; calling the spirits of the dead to rise again.

The haar rolled in over Leena's memories now, obscuring much. But through it rose the ghosts of her family and their story, the story that had brought her to where she lay.

Though the medication had rendered her nearly immobile and unable to utter, her mind still functioned. Like a seashore, memories would wash in and out of her thoughts. There was no structure to them, however. Just a rising and falling of images.

Her family's venerable wooden-shuttered villa. The maroon Chinese broadcloth curtains and Isfahan rugs. Comfort, security. Her grandfather. She sitting at his knee by the fire in the vast inglenook as he prodded it with a poker, causing sparks to dance upwards like fairies.

The tales he told her of his life.

As a young man, he had been conscripted into the Tsar's navy and spent thirty years on the Caspian Sea.

Then, at the age of forty-six, he had been given a bounty

and a handshake and turfed out into the tangled streets of Petrovsk. Left to his own devices, he wondered what to do; an Estonian all the way down there at the outer edge of Asia? But the Caspian was a crossroads for silk and linen and astounding Persian rugs. So he spent all his bounty on every bolt of fabric and textile he could lay his hands on. He then strapped them to a train of camels and walked them back up the length of the continent of Europe to his homeland.

Wealth and comfort followed.

The wealth and comfort Leena enjoyed throughout her childhood and young adult life.

Privileged? No – blessed.

Born amidst the splendour of St Petersburg; where all the best Estonian families spent part of their year in those days.

Dinner parties and summer balls in Estonia.

Mingling with the elite at the top of Tallinn's Cathedral Hill.

Coming out as a debutante in London at the Court of St James.

Meeting a dashing young naval officer.

Hendrik. Hendrik. Hendrik.

She could no longer pull his face into view.

She knew she cared for him, and he profoundly cared for her. That was what comforted her most as she lay there.

She moaned.

Well, at last, she would get her wish. To get out of his way. Get out of everyone's way.

Now that the moment was actually here, she wasn't sure she really did want to go after all.

But she knew she had no choice. She was being dragged out of this life.

Before, she had made the choice; sought to take control of her own death. Tried to make sense of all that had happened to her and her lovely family since the day the Red Army oozed in.

Then, through the sea fret in her mind, she realised that she had never really had control of anything.

Ever.

It had all been done to her. For her.

Her only choice, the only thing she had really done by herself, and for herself, was her wonderful marriage and her beautiful children, Maret and Juhan.

Those were good choices.

The best she ever made.

But there was one choice yet to make.

One thing she could still control.

She could let go.

She turned her face to the wall.

*

They had endured nearly three solid weeks of alerts, alarms and extreme moments as the sea war in the Baltic grew in intensity. The minesweepers had been out in force, on general convoy escort duty. Fending off raids by air and sea. Both troops and refugees were being moved further and further west as the Red Army and the Red Fleet snapped at their heels like a wolf pack.

There was now a general order to evacuate even Libau, Windau and Memel – and consolidate around Königsberg.

Each time the M35 had sailed south, Kotkas had looked longingly north, towards Sweden, and safety. How many times had he wondered whether he might just make a run for it? Jump ship. But he had known he couldn't do it. More – he needed most of all to be reunited with his family. The death throes of the war had swept all means of communication away. He hoped the children were still there in Lehrte; Leena in safe hands in the military hospital. That they were being looked after. That they were waiting patiently until they could all be reunited. That was the only real plan he had left. To somehow get to them. Protect them from the maelstrom that was closing in both from the West and the East.

The almost continual need to be at battle stations ground the crew down. Sometimes, he could see, they sagged like damp washing at their posts. The incessant routine of one watch on, one watch off, meant that there was time to rest physically, but never time to relax. A state of heightened anxiety was the norm, and there was nothing Kotkas could do to alleviate it. Stalin made sure of that. His admirals and generals continued to inflict a combination of sleeplessness, fear and nasty surprises on their enemy with malevolent skill.

Kotkas looked round at Stieber, standing on the bridge behind him. The young fellow's confidence had been drained in the first action he experienced at sea. It was a sudden submarine attack. Its torpedoes narrowly missed hitting the minesweeper aft. There had been many such moments of terror since. Day and night. The night watch seemed to have got to the young man worst of all. The lad never seemed to have recovered. Even now, he was pale and drawn.

Although Kotkas had first gone to sea at roughly the same age, the context was different. As a cadet, he had been fighting for his country's independence. There was a sense of pride, of inevitable victory, in every action the *Lembit* had engaged with. There was a meaning, a purpose, which the crew in those days could almost touch. Stieber's purpose was far more abstract these days. Fighting for an ideal with little evidence that it would come to pass. It may have been treason still to even consider the possibility of defeat. Yet the prospect of defeat was clearly all around them. One did not continually accompany cargo and troop ships west – never east – and not realise why that was so.

If Stieber was nonetheless still filled with the ambitions of a glorious future for the Fatherland, Kotkas reckoned he was about the only one on board the ship that did so. Not that the crew didn't conduct themselves with the greatest professionalism and integrity. Of course they did. Kotkas was very proud of them for that. But it was the professionalism of accomplished sailors. It was upholding the integrity of the navy, not of the State.

He took up his binoculars and scanned the horizon.

He recalled, not for the first time, the night the ship had left Tallinn all those months ago. The time they'd brought those poor refugees he'd stumbled upon to freedom – the freedom he was even now denying himself.

*

He had invited the officers who were not on watch to join him for dinner in the officers' mess. Stieber was among them. They had finished their meagre rations and were drinking ersatz coffee.

'Sir?'

'Yes, Busch?'

'The men want to know what we are doing, where we are going.'

'I'm sure. However, we are operating under sealed orders. You know as well as I do that it is a court-martial offence to reveal the contents of sealed orders, until the time or the location assigned by Marine Group Command.'

'Yes, sir.'

'Well,' Kotkas had stretched, 'I am going to try for an hour or so in my cot. I suggest those of you not due to go on watch do the same. Goodnight, gentlemen.' He had gone into his cabin and closed the door.

A short while later, there had been a knock.

'Come.'

Busch had entered and closed the door behind him.

'Take a seat, Viktor.'

'I will stand, sir. If you don't mind.' He paused. 'May I say something?'

'Of course.'

'The men trust you. You know they will do anything for you. But if you are putting them at even greater risk, don't you think they have a right to know what they are doing and why they are doing it?'

Kotkas surveyed his lieutenant. He knew him to be navy first and foremost; not a Party man. 'You say the crew trust me, Viktor?'

'Yes, sir.'

'But do *you* trust me?'

'Absolutely.'

'Then I will trust you. I will tell you what I propose to do with those poor folk we have down below. And then I will leave you to decide what you do with that information. Is that acceptable?'

'Yes, sir.'

'Then here is my plan.' He had then leant over his chart desk and drawn a line with his finger on the map of the Baltic that lay there. 'We are here ... I propose we keep behind this rough line of longitude which, as far as any of us know, is still behind most of our minefields. Essentially German waters from there all the way back to Denmark and Norway, so to speak. Screened within reason from significant elements of the Red Fleet for the time being.'

'Yes, sir.'

'I propose shortly turning north-north west and heading towards Sweden.'

'You are not surrendering, are you?'

'Tempting, Viktor. But, as you say, the men trust me. They're good men, I would not betray them. I daresay they would rather go down fighting or until they are ordered to surrender. I may disagree, but I respect it. I am not selling them into slavery. I am just hoping – sooner rather than later – that we bump into a neutral Swedish ship where we can hand our passengers over to them.'

'May I sit down, sir?'

'Please.'

Busch had sat and rested his chin in his hands. 'So, let me get this straight. We are ferrying some people across the Baltic instead of following orders?'

'There are no orders, Busch, not yet. It is every ship for itself, with instructions to rejoin our flotilla, probably in Libau, when able.'

Busch had stood again. 'Well, sir, I am surprised and disappointed. You are telling me that we are taking around a hundred undesirables – including women and children – out of a war zone to a place of safety ... illegally?'

'I would call them refugees, but if you want to put it like that ...'

'And you didn't think we'd agree to it?' He paused. Then: 'Of course. It is exactly the right thing to do.'

'You think that's what the men would think?'

'Of course they would. We're human beings.' Busch took his wallet out of his pocket and showed Kotkas the photograph of his family. 'You taught us that much, at least.'

A couple of hours afterwards, Kotkas had been unable to sleep with the tossing of the ship. He had left his cabin and gone on deck to look at a writhing sea. Every crew member he encountered turned to look at him and had given him a knowing grin. Kotkas had smiled back. Busch had clearly told them.

He had then gone onto the bridge. Busch was there with Stieber.

Kotkas laid a hand on his lieutenant's shoulder. Busch did not turn; he kept his eyes fixed upon the horizon beyond, but he nodded.

Stieber's expression, however, back then, had been unreadable.

*

It was unreadable even now as the minesweeper escorted its latest convoy towards Königsberg.

Kotkas lowered his binoculars.

The sea was skittish and pounded on the hull; an unruly child clamouring for attention.

Although the transfer of the precious cargo to the neutral Swedish coastal defence ship had been successful, and they'd returned to Libau unscathed to rejoin their flotilla and carried on with their duties as if nothing had happened, he could tell that Stieber still continued to harbour resentment. Or was it something else?

Kotkas took a couple of paces closer to the midshipman, so that the crew on the bridge could not hear them above the thrum of the engines and the slashing of the sea.

'How are you, Karl?'

'Very well, sir.'

'Rough sea this morning.'

'Sir.'

'You've got your sea legs, though – I noticed that the other day. Just remember, keep your feet slightly apart, bend a little at the knees with each roll, and ride the peaks and troughs like you are at a fairground.'

'Sir.'

'How long have you been on watch?'

'Three hours, sir.'

Too soon to tell him to go below. But the strain in the young man's eyes showed that, even should he go below, he would be unlikely to manage more than a few fitful minutes. It was not too soon, however, to break the fellow's fixed look and the tight grip on his binoculars.

'Busch?'

'Yes, sir?'

'You have the ship. I'm going below with Midshipman Stieber a moment.'

'Yes, sir.'

'Come with me, Karl.'

Kotkas had the officers' mess steward bring them both an ersatz coffee to his cabin.

'So, tell me, Karl, what made you want to go to sea?'

Stieber shrugged. 'It was all I ever wanted to do.'

'Very good. Hold on to that. When things start to get tough again, remember why you wanted to come to sea. Let that be a little light in the darkness for you.'

Stieber stiffened. 'I am not afraid, sir.'

'No, of course you aren't. But just in case you ever feel like you might become a little afraid, that's my advice. And here's another piece ...'

Stieber looked down at the deck, trying to appear as if none of what Kotkas was about to say was of the least interest to him. 'What?' he said into his boots.

'Look around. Everyone else feels just like you. Don't judge your inside by their outside. It's all right to be afraid, Karl. It's okay to show your emotions.'

'No, it isn't. Courage, determination and faith in the ultimate victory is the order of the day.'

'Now listen here, my friend ... if I can teach you one thing while you are under my command, it is this. Throw all that youth group drivel overboard. Treat it like the poppycock it is. Slogans and ideals don't get a ship sailed or a battle won. Out here, only the sea teaches us what really matters. Learn from the sea, not from a bunch of clowns who send young men to war, while they themselves stay at home with their women and their cocktails watching Rome burn.'

Stieber glared. His jowls moved as though wrestling with what he was longing to say. Eventually, he decided he must say something. 'Why are you always so bitter, sir? Why do you hate Germany so much?'

'Bitter?' Kotkas thought about it. 'Yes, I suppose I am. I suppose I have been bitter for a long time. Certainly for the

318

past four years. Bitter at my country being overrun time and again by people who don't understand us and have no interest in trying to understand us. Bitter at their own boorish obsessions. But bitter, too, I think, by the way we have allowed ourselves to be overrun. That is why I took the decision to rescue those refugees and hand them over to the Swedes after we left Tallinn.'

'Allowed yourselves to be overrun? Estonia is a weak nation. You needed our German guts and know-how.'

It was Kotkas's turn to bristle. 'You clearly don't know the background. How we let the Soviets in. the first time. No, I don't suppose you do. You are German. That's all you care about.'

'That's unfair, sir.'

'Nationalism is unfair by definition. Let me, in any case, tell you what happened back then. Back in the good old days before we Estonians were swamped by other people's greed. There was no doubt war was brewing. We knew that. As an independent state, barely twenty years old, we had decided we really did not want anyone else to come running our lives for us. So we declared ourselves absolutely neutral. Threaded an army across our borders to show we meant it, and positioned artillery in and around every island we could think of in the approaches to the mainland.' He drew an invisible map with his finger on his chart desk. 'Tallinn ... Tallinn Harbour ... Tallinn Bay ... Guns ... guns ... guns ...' He drew intersecting arcs beyond the invisible gun emplacements all across the invisible Tallinn Bay. 'There was not one centimetre of the approaches to our harbours that could not be covered by coastal artillery. What with that, our ships, and our men, there was nothing we wouldn't do to fight for our freedom. We'd done it before. We'd thrown out the German Landeswehr and the Russians at the end of the last war. We'd broken free. Little Estonia had taken on the Eagle's talons and the Bear's claws and won. If we did it then, we could do it again. We believed it.'

Despite the obvious insult to his country, Stieber couldn't help himself but ask: 'So why didn't you this time?'

'We wanted to. God knows, we wanted to. The navy were certainly up for the fight. Like the Finns, we thought if we gave that big bear just one hefty rap on the nose, it would decide we weren't worth the trouble, and lumber away to pester some other poor nation state. But that was the navy. The government, at the first sign of the Russians wanting to come in and use our ports for their ships, welcomed them with open arms. A mutual assistance pact it was called. Though what the Soviets meant by "mutual" was not necessarily what others understood it to mean. The navy was beside itself with fury. We senior officers marched to the government building up on Toompea and demanded to see the President or the Prime Minister. But they were nowhere to be found. Left us to it. So we marched back to our posts and made the best of it we could. One by one, those in high office sidled out of the door or were spirited away by the Soviets. For about six days, I was even left in charge of the whole port of Tallinn. Me? Can you imagine it?'

Stieber shrugged.

'Then a Polish submarine sought sanctuary. I followed all the correct protocols with regard to receiving a warship into a neutral port. I had all the armaments removed and was busy tying up loose ends, and maintaining the diplomatic initiative, when the beggars slipped their moorings and sailed off into the night. That was enough for Uncle Joe and his thugs to warrant a full-scale invasion. Bitter? Too right I am.'

'So,' Stieber turned, his eyes kindling with something that wasn't understanding, 'you mean to tell me, you joined the German Navy just because you had to, not because you wanted to?'

'That wasn't the point of the story, Karl. You asked me why I was bitter, and I thought—'

The klaxon sounded; urgent in that little cabin. Stieber grabbed the chart table, his knuckles white.

'Stations,' said Kotkas. 'Come on, Stieber. To your post.'

The midshipman was locked onto the table. Kotkas prised the young man's fingers off. He gripped him by the elbow and led him through the door into the passageway. 'Quickly now, your comrades depend on you.'

Stieber started to move. Then, eventually, caught up among other members of the crew as they raced to their stations, he ran.

*

The nurse brought Maret into the room. The clock had been stopped.

Her mother lay there, peaceful now, her hands folded across her chest.

The nurses, once they'd found her, had observed the tradition of opening the window and leaving the room for a couple of hours, to allow the soul to depart. Only then had they laid her out and gone to fetch Leena's daughter from where she was staying, in the nurses' quarters across the road.

Maret still refused to allow herself to cry. She remembered an earlier time. When she had been brought into the presence of the dead like this. When she was a little girl. Her mother had led her into the parlour of the Great House in Tallinn, where Maret's grandmother Liisu lay in an open coffin, surrounded by freesias.

'You may kiss Grandmama,' Leena had said.

Maret didn't want to. The horror of looking at a real dead person, let alone touching one, let alone kissing one, made her recoil. Leena knew what her little girl was going through; she'd gone through it herself. It was the custom. She led her daughter forward.

'Just kiss her on the cheek, darling,' she whispered. 'It isn't anything. It won't hurt. Don't be afraid. Be brave ...'

So Maret kissed her dead grandmother's cold cheek.

The cheek hadn't always been cold. Maret remembered the days she and her grandmother sat together in the sauna at Vasalemma; draped in loose clothing, with their unbleached linen hats that looked like they were made out of newspaper. Lovely, friendly Grandmama. Born a peasant, now a millionaire's wife. Those big pudgy fingers that would pod peas in the garden. The hefty forearm that brought the hatchet down on the chicken's neck in the farmyard, leaving the poor headless creature to flap high over the roof of the barn. The treble chins that would wobble when she laughed. In order to show one's wealth, a businessman had to have a well-fed spouse. One day, Maret hoped she, too, would be plump. Not thin like her mother.

She stepped up to the bed. Took her mother's hand in hers. Cold, like her grandmother.

She rested her other hand on Leena's forehead and brushed a wisp of black hair to one side.

She leant over and kissed her mother goodbye.

II

The flotilla was a day out of Königsberg, which had become its home port for some weeks. As ever, the ships were interminably engaged on escort duty; evacuating an ever-diminishing army and as many desperate refugees as they could manage – which was never enough – deeper and deeper into the Fatherland. The air raids, minefields and torpedoes tormented them with greater and greater frequency. Death and dismemberment on one ship or another was almost a daily occurrence; sluicing blood into the scuppers and over the side with seawater a common task.

In the middle of the night, Kotkas found Stieber looking over the aft rail. It looked to Kotkas as though the young man was contemplating throwing himself overboard. 'Are you all right?' he said.

Stieber turned at the sudden voice. He wavered and steadied himself by holding onto the ensign staff. He mumbled something which Kotkas could not hear. The sea breeze captured the whiff of alcohol from the young man's breath and wafted it towards his commanding officer.

'Are you drunk, Karl?'

Stieber shook his head, which made him need to hold onto the staff even tighter. He mumbled again.

'What? What did you say?'

Stieber mustered all his faculties to speak. 'It's unbearable. All of it. I can't take any more,' he slurred.

Kotkas stepped towards him. Stieber pushed him away with both hands and in a moment had clambered up onto the aft rail. He teetered at the top, staring into the stern water churning below.

'Oh no, you don't ...' Kotkas reached out, grabbed the young fellow's waist and threw him backwards onto the deck. Stieber landed on his side, rolled over, buried his face in his arms and began sobbing. 'Leave me alone ... let me go ... let me finish it ... I can't stand it. I can't stand it anymore.'

'Come on, let's get you down below.' Kotkas helped the boy to his feet. 'We can talk about it in my cabin. Come along. One foot in front of the other ... that's it ... steady now, young fellow. We'll soon have you safe and warm. It's all right ... it's all right ...'

Kotkas didn't blame the poor child – for he was still really just a child. Though he'd had any chance of a real childhood torn from him by the propaganda machine. He'd been raised on a diet of lies, disguised as the promise of glory and heroism. Yet all the lad had known since he joined up, Kotkas realised, was defeat and ignominy, underpinned by an interminable round of constant anxiety, interspersed with bouts of fear, and the occasional squall of terror. There was no glory in running away. There was no heroism in day after day, week after week, evacuating a decimated and demoralised army in a full flood of retreat.

Approaching the door that would take them below, Kotkas and Stieber were met by the petty officer of the watch on his rounds; a machine gun hung on a strap from his shoulder. He shone his torch briefly on the two faces, lingering on that of Stieber's. The young man winced in the sudden glare. Despite his groggy state, he knew that being drunk on duty was a punishable offence; one that might even lead to the firing squad.

'Are you all right, sir?' said the petty officer, still scrutinising the young man.

'Yes, thank you, Fessler. Carry on,' said Kotkas.

'Yes, sir.' He clicked the light off again and saluted.

Wrapped in a blanket and drinking coffee in the skipper's cabin, away from prying eyes and difficult questions, Stieber had sobered up enough to make some kind of sense. 'Mines. They're the worst. Ours ... theirs ... British bombers dropping them in our rear, now. No such thing as safe waters anymore ...'

'Are there ever safe waters in war?' Kotkas said.

Stieber paused. 'Are you going to report me?'

'For what? To whom? Report you to myself?'

'To the authorities – once we're ashore?'

'How long have you been drinking, Karl?'

'Since I was about fifteen.'

'No, I mean secretly drinking. Hiding the booze away somewhere in your cabin. Taking little nips when you get the chance. To ease the pain, blunt the fear ...'

'Do you do it?'

'No.'

'Have you ever done it?'

'No.'

'Are you going to report me?' he said again.

'Will you stop drinking; at least, whenever we are at sea?'

'I'll try.'

'You'll need to do more than that.'

'Then I will, sir, yes. I swear on the Leader's life.'

'No need to go that far. I shall be glad to take your word as an officer.'

'You have it.' He took a corner of the blanket in which he was wrapped and twisted it between fretful fingers.

'Good. When you are ready, we'll go to your cabin, search out all your little hiding places and throw everything overboard. Is that clear?'

Stieber looked at him without responding, so Kotkas repeated himself. 'Is that clear?'

'Yes, sir.'

'Then there is no need to report you, is there? No harm done. This time.'

*

They slipped into Pillau, Königsberg's port, in the early hours of the next morning, while it was still dark. The icy black waters of the inner harbour swirled around them. It was one of the coldest, bleakest winters anyone around there could remember. As they came alongside and secured the ship, Kotkas became aware of a deep silence. There was a weird glow in the eastern sky. On the flying bridge, Kotkas raised his binoculars. It wasn't dawn – that was the silvering to be seen higher in the Prussian blue sky – this other glow, immediately above the tree line on the horizon, seemed to tremble. He noticed the vague outlines of other humans on ships and on the quayside, standing equally still. And underneath all that stillness was the silence. He realised that it was the silence of people; alert, tense, listening. And what Kotkas and all of them heard – as it were, beyond the silence – was a distant constant rumble. So faint. So barely discernible. But it was there. They all knew what it was. The sound of a vast bombardment; a thousand Soviet guns perhaps fifty kilometres from the city, softening up exhausted soldiers among the outer defences before the final push for Königsberg.

For those poor souls, this would be a different kind of dawn, Kotkas knew. It would be a daybreak without mercy and would be followed, as night follows day, by the remorseless reaping of human lives.

Someone blew a whistle and challenged some work detail to stop their idling and get on with it; whatever it was. It was as if that whistle was a general order. People everywhere shook themselves out of their reverie and stirred. Pillau was soon once again all noise and confusion. Besieged on three fronts by the Red Army, there had been a desperate evacuation for weeks. As daylight grew over the next few minutes, it lifted the curtain on a scene that was even more chaotic than Kotkas or his crew had witnessed in Tallinn. Although Pillau was similarly bustling with vehicles, soldiers and sailors, here there was an increased sense of urgency verging on panic.

Last autumn, the grey storks, as they did every year, had hauled their long, lean bodies into the air, flapping their wings like blankets, and wheeled southwards. This time, though, it had left the people of Königsberg with a profound sense of loss; as though they were being abandoned by even the storks, who, some said, might never return.

Stieber, pale and morose, stood on the bridge alongside Kotkas, transfixed by what he saw of the harbour. There was rubble and debris everywhere; the result of pitiless Soviet air raids. Across the black and brackish Friches Haff, the Vistula Lagoon, could be seen plumes of smoke; rising from what was left of the city itself. A crater on the moon could not have looked more desolate. There was the unmistakable smell of burnt buildings, equipment, spilled petrol, and even gas. And underneath all that was another, unholy, stench: incinerated or rotting human flesh.

'Invincible bastion of the German spirit,' Kotkas said.

'Sir?' said Stieber.

'Isn't that what your beloved Leader called this city, in one of his broadcasts?' He mimicked the Leader's hectoring style: *Königsberg could never fall. It is far too German.*

Stieber gave Kotkas a baleful look. Was it because of what he had just said? Kotkas wondered. Or was it because the boy had been prevented from killing himself? Or discovered to have a secret drink problem, or been treated with compassion by his commanding officer, despite his guilt? Or was it the shock of the sights and smells before them? Or all of the above?

'Family come from here, don't they?'

'Yes, sir.'

'Manage to get to see them?'

'I got ashore about four, five weeks ago.'

'Are they all right?'

327

'I don't know. I was told they escaped to Danzig.'

'Well, I hope they are safe,' said Kotkas.

Snow began to fall again, as it had done practically every day for the past few weeks.

After a while, he patted the young fellow's shoulder. *Still only a boy, for goodness' sake.* 'If you want to go and find them, you can,' he said.

Stieber looked at him. 'Find them …?'

Kotkas nodded. 'I'll sign you off the ship's muster. Get you some papers so you can travel. Rejoin your family. Where you belong. Where we all belong.'

'This is where I belong. Defending the Fatherland with every last drop of my blood.'

'The Fatherland's got nothing to do with it. All you are doing from now on is defending the cowards and bullies cowering back in Berlin. The wretches who hurled us all into this abyss in the first place. They're deceiving you so that you might save their sorry skins with every last drop of your blood.'

'That is defeatist talk. You could be shot for it.'

'So shoot me.'

Stieber glared at the Commander and marched off.

Kotkas left the bridge. Still in his sea boots, he jumped onto the quay and made his way through the shambles and the slush to the port office.

He found the port commander packing a briefcase. The staff were throwing things into boxes and flinging confidential papers into an incinerator in the middle of the room.

'As you can see, we're pulling out,' the officer said. 'We're reorganising our defences around Kiel. They're hounding us on all sides. Look out of the window. Most of the city bombed out of existence. The rest about to follow. It's a mess. You need to get your ship out of here tonight. No orders, just get yourselves to Kiel while the waters round here are still German.'

'What about the evacuation? There must be hundreds of

thousands out there needing to get out. Not only soldiers but also wounded, refugees ... men, women, children, the elderly, the infirm ...'

'They will have to take their chances.'

'But—'

The port commander put his briefcase down on the desk with a thump. 'Look, Commander, I hate this as much as you do. But they do have other ways to get away. On the roads. Across the ice of the Haff. And the main station may be lacking a roof, but there are still trains; for the time being at least. If you see a troop or cargo ship, act as escort. Otherwise, just preserve yourself. Or, rather, preserve your ship. You, we can replace. And that, if you'd prefer, is an order.'

'As you say, sir.'

The port commander looked at him. There was something in the fellow's response that suggested, if he got the chance, he wouldn't be obeying that order for very long. He didn't blame him.

Kotkas saluted, turned, found a spare desk and took up a pen and some paper.

My darling Leena, he wrote.

> *I hope you are feeling a little better. I have written to you via Lehrte so often these past months. I have tried so many times to get letters through to you. I have had no reply, so I assume you didn't receive them. Or you have moved. Or you have written back and they have not got through to me. I only hope you realise how much I love you and long to be with you and the children. This awful conflict is nearing its conclusion. What that will look like, and how it will affect us, remains to be seen. I shall strain every nerve to get back with you as soon as I can. As soon as this is all over. Then we will see what we can do about getting us all home again. Home to Tallinn.*

Of course, we must be realistic. Who knows what will happen?

This may end up being the last letter I ever write to you, the way things work out. Be strong. Be brave. I know you are, my darling. If we had any possessions left, I should attach a last will and testament. But since we have nothing, I have nothing to leave you. Except my love.

If you never hear from me again, know this. I do love you. I have always loved you. I will always love you.

I miss you and send you kisses. I send our darlings, Maret and Juhan, kisses, too.

Please pass on my great thanks to Emilie for everything she has done, if she is still with you.

Until we meet again.

Your loving Hendrik

*

Emilie tapped on the bedroom door. 'Maret? Come and have something to eat.'

Maret did not reply. She had spent much of the time since she'd returned from Groß Rhüden, three days earlier, in her bedroom.

Emilie knocked again.

The postman had brought the telegram from the military hospital at the beginning of the week. REGRET MRS LEENA KOTKAS DECEASED YESTERDAY. PLEASE COLLECT DAUGHTER. It had come via military channels to Lehrte's telegraph office. The town postman had brought it to the house, since all the messenger boys had been called up. He had insisted on driving Emilie the four-hour round trip to collect Maret.

Emilie became firmer. 'Maret. Come along. You haven't had anything to eat for hours.'

Still, Maret did not respond.

Emilie called downstairs. 'Juhan. Come and speak with your sister.'

Juhan left the kitchen table, where three meals sat growing cold, and knocked on the bedroom door.

'Maret. It's meat. We have meat today.'

'Pork,' said Emilie.

'Pork,' Juhan repeated through the keyhole. 'Please, Maret. I am very sad, too. But you are my friend and friends have to be together. They have to help each other. Please, Maret. Please come.'

There was movement within, a metallic click, and the door opened.

'I am coming because of Juhan. Not because of you,' Maret said to Emilie.

'Understood,' said Emilie.

They went downstairs and began to eat. Halfway through, Maret happened to look out through the kitchen window. There were clothes on the washing line, flogging in the stiff east wind.

'Is that my skirt?' Maret asked.

'Yes,' said Emilie. 'I thought I'd give it a nice wash, it was so grubby.'

'No!' Maret cried. She leapt from the table and ran outside. She dragged the skirt down, sending pegs flying like starlings, and began scrabbling around in the still-wet pockets. She drew out a sodden scrap of paper and howled. 'No!'

Emilie and Juhan had joined her.

'What is it?' said Emilie.

'Mother. Mother's address. Where they buried her. They wrote it down for me.' Maret tried to undo the note. It fell apart in her hands. The ink had been washed away.

'Don't worry. We'll go again, sometime. When we get there, we can ask them, and they'll tell us.'

'I hate you!' Maret cried, and ran back upstairs to her room.

It was late afternoon when Fischer finally arrived at the office of the security police in Königsberg. It had been a gruelling four-day haul across the region from Memel by boat, train and army lorry; barely evading the Soviets. He was hungry, he was tired. He would have settled, however, for a bath and a shave; to wash off the stench of retreat. But duty, as he always insisted, came first.

Voigt, a burly detective superintendent in a rumpled suit with a greasy collar, greeted him. 'Welcome. Not quite Berlin, Fischer, but near enough all the comforts of home.'

'Thank you. Where shall I put my things?'

'That desk there will do you. It was Ascher's but he got killed in a raid.'

'Fair enough. Are we staying put or moving out?' He gestured out of the window at the long line of carts and barrows, with the elderly, women and children muffled against the cold. They were slogging along the slushy roads out of the city; passing the incinerated corpses still lying in the streets from the latest air raids as they went. 'All those feeble-minded peasants running away.'

'Regional Party Leader Koch has not given the order to evacuate. The cowards are taking it upon themselves. If we had more men available, we'd have orders to go out there and shoot them. But we'll leave the spineless rats to their stupidity. In this weather, they won't last twenty-four hours. And even if they do, Ivan's waiting for them out there somewhere. Our job is to stand fast. We will win in the end if we stick together, shoulder to shoulder. Koch has promised it.'

'So, tell me, what is the main task these days?'

'Same as it's been for months. Rounding up the criminals involved with the attempt on the Leader's life. Funny, with everything else going on, you'd think Berlin would give us other things to do. But, apparently, it is the Leader's personal orders. Also, if we catch any particularly big fish, they want us to film the interrogations and executions and pop them up to Berlin. It's certainly a foul nest, I can tell you. You pull out one loathsome creature and it becomes clear, after a little persuasion, that they know any number of other slimy characters that we need to talk to.'

Fischer laughed. 'When I was a young man, I worked for an iron and steel company. Once in a while, I got to accompany a load on our African routes. It's a long way to Tanganyika, I can tell you. Sometimes, we'd come round the Cape and up the west coast. One Christmas, we did just that and put in at some godforsaken African backwater. The place was filled with the sound, my friend, of the squealing of piglets. They were lashed onto the backs of bicycles as the men of the house came home with Christmas dinner. The air is even now filled with the squealing of piglets, is it not?'

Voigt grinned. 'So, tell me,' he leant back in his chair, 'what's this all about then? Weren't you some kind of station chief up there in the Baltic? What's happened that you're back mixing with us hoi-polloi? I'd have thought they'd have found you something else worthy of your rank.' Fischer's silence suggested this was not a subject he wished to continue. Voigt took the hint. 'Oh, by the way,' he opened a drawer and pulled a message out of it, 'this came in from the port office today, asking if it could be sent on to you. We took a look at it, couldn't make head or tail as to why he wanted to contact you. We were going to forward a copy of it to you in Memel. But, well, you're here now, aren't you?'

Fischer read the signature at the bottom of the message. 'Stieber ...?' He shook his head.

'A young midshipman apparently, on minesweepers. He claims he met you, or got hold of your name through the local office, at least, a year or so ago ...'

'Ah, yes, I remember now. Young Stieber. Helpful little snitch. I wonder what he wants with me.'

He read the message.

He sat down and read it again. *So, that pig Kotkas is here?* To his surprise, he realised that the message filled him with a species of righteous indignation. Before he'd finished reading, however, he was already planning an outlet for it. The thought of spilling blood excited him. He had not felt this way since Kristallnacht. He looked again at the message in his hand and crushed it. 'The pig,' he said, and picked up the telephone. 'Get me the port commander.'

*

'Glad you made it out safely, Monika. What's it like over there?' said Marjorie.

'The Soviet advance?' Tamm sat on the edge of her desk.

'Yes.'

He twisted a paperclip into grotesque shapes; struggling with a way to describe what he'd seen, and what he'd subsequently heard from his sources. The murders, the rapes, the torching of entire villages, the nailing of living human beings to barn doors, the eviscerating of children, the strafing of refugees by aircraft until not one in a thousand souls survived. 'Well,' he said, 'you know that day in high summer when, for some reason, the atmosphere is such that from under your feet – in the gardens, on the streets, out of drains and pavements, and from every nook and cranny – hundreds of thousands of ants, and especially flying ants, start seething; bubbling up like a boiling broth; Dante's *Inferno* ...?'

'Yes.'

'It's worse. Tell me, is it true what I'm hearing – that whatever Uncle Joe conquers, he gets to keep?'

'I'm afraid that's classified information, my old darling, even for you.' The Major had appeared behind Tamm.

Tamm stood and drew himself up to full height, which wasn't much. 'Did you hear what I just said to Marjorie – about what's going on over there? It's evil, Major. No matter what name you give it … liberation, strategic necessity, right-eous vengeance … it's the wholesale and wilful massacre of human beings. I thought that's what our going to war was supposed to stop.'

The Major stood for a moment, studied Tamm, then spoke. 'You weren't in the last unpleasantness, were you?'

'The war to end all wars? No. But that didn't work, did it? Because of the stupidity of politicians. Mediocrities sitting around in their gentlemen's clubs with other mediocrities; smoking their cigars and dividing up the world with fictitious boundaries to appease this one, or buy off that one. That's why this one started. And these idiots are about to do it all over again.'

'Not our problem.'

'But it is. At least – we can't let them go round slashing and burning every man, woman and child in their way just so they can get to keep what they've stolen. We can't.'

The Major paused again for a moment. 'When you need to get rid of gangrene, you have to amputate the whole limb, old son. Even if that means taking some of the healthy flesh with it.'

He reached down and with his knuckles rapped his left leg. It was tin.

*

It was approaching dusk; a sallow light. Kotkas was leaving the port office. He had asked the staff inside to find some way of sending his final letter to his family. He happened to glance across at the harbour gate, thirty or so metres away.

A car had pulled up.

Cars were pulling up at port gates all the time. But there was something about the man, sitting next to the driver, that made Kotkas feel uneasy. Something far too familiar as he sat there in the arc of the security light; the hat, the rounding of the shoulders, the snub of the nose … Fischer? It couldn't possibly be the same car that had plagued him all those months ago in Tallinn. The same make and colour, though. Standard issue, probably. But it could, perhaps, be the same man. It certainly, even at that distance, looked a lot like him, albeit in that failing light.

The passenger got out and walked towards the guard at the gate. Kotkas felt a sense of dread; there was that stalking tread with which he had become familiar over time. Fischer had some piece of paper in his hand. An authority to act, details of a particular ship or person, a request for assistance from the navy police? Some instinct told Kotkas that this was not something he should waste time finding out. The guard had taken whatever papers there were and was headed with Fischer into the guardroom, where the officer of the watch sat. It wouldn't be too long, Kotkas supposed, until Fischer was permitted free access to the harbour itself.

Kotkas's intention up until that moment had been to see what he and his ship could do to rescue further wounded and refugees. But what use would he or his ship be if he was dead? Keeping the port office between him and the gate, Kotkas ran.

Reaching the ship, now heaving for breath, he called up to Busch on the flying bridge to start the engines and get ready to cast off immediately.

'But, sir,' Busch said, 'we are still completing loading supplies.'

'No time. We have to get away. Now!'

Busch ducked back inside the bridge and gave the order to start the engines.

Kotkas's alarmed voice had rung around the whole ship. Crew members stopped what they were doing and looked across at their skipper. In between sucking in lungsful of air, Kotkas continued. 'There's a car at the gate … it is the security police … if I am not mistaken … and, if I am not further mistaken … they have come for me … at least, I am not about … to wait to find out.'

Stieber was on deck, supervising loading a hold.

Kotkas gathered himself and stepped onto the gangplank. He noticed the midshipman. The fellow's expression was not the same as that of the others. What was it? It was more than curiosity. Expectation, perhaps? Anticipation? Gratification? *The Germans have a word for it,* Kotkas thought. *Schadenfreude:* Pleasure in another's misfortune. 'Is this your doing?' Kotkas said.

'What if they have come for you? About time, too, if you ask me. I've been wondering when they would act.'

'What have you done?' Busch called down to Stieber.

'He deserves it,' the young man called back. Then, noticing other crew members looking at him, explained further. 'Don't you see? He's as much an enemy as the rest of them. He's betrayed us all. He has helped enemies escape. He has put us all at risk. He is full of defeatist filth. He deserves to be arrested and tried for what he has done.' Failing to get the response, especially the approval, he was expecting, he tried again. 'He is an enemy of the State, an enemy of the Fatherland. An enemy of the Leader.' He turned back to Kotkas, who was now on the deck. He had regained his breath. 'I sent a message,' Stieber continued. 'I told them you were mixed up in the bomb plot. I told them you have misused your authority with this ship to assist the enemy. I told them what you said about defending the Fatherland.'

'You fool. You stupid young fool! What has he ever done to you?' Busch shouted from the flying bridge, and dived back inside to chivvy the chief, down in the engine room, on the voice pipe.

The crew scattered to their various stations, racing to cast off and put at least a few metres between the ship and the quayside before whoever their skipper needed to avoid got close enough to make it on board.

'Car's coming!' said one of the sailors of the watch, looking across the port with his binoculars.

So this is how it ends? thought Kotkas. The engines shuddered into life. *Too late. Too late.*

Stieber looked around; any smile of triumph fell away. All around him he could see nothing but contempt.

'What have you done?' snarled one of the crew, heaving on a hawser.

Stieber shot a panicked look at Kotkas, who shrugged. 'Leave the lad,' he called to the seaman, 'it's too late …'

'What do you mean, *What have you done* …?' Stieber said to the sailor, who glared back. 'I thought …' Then, to no one in particular, he whimpered, 'I don't know … I don't know anymore … I don't understand … what have I done?'

'Let go Forward. Let go Aft!' Busch ordered from somewhere above them.

There was a sound of lines splashing into the water as the ship was untethered from the quayside.

The light was fading from the sky. Snow whirled round in wraiths.

'It's too late,' another sailor said. 'You've done for him, you've done for our skipper, you little monster.'

'I'm sorry. I'm so sorry.' Stieber looked dazed.

Only the aft spring line now held the ship to its berth. The engines were grumbling, the whole ship was juddering and the sea was beginning to churn as the screws started to bite.

The car was approaching fast, its headlights full on. It had taken some time to force its way through the melee in the harbour, but now people were realising that, if they valued their lives and limbs, they needed to get out of this maniac's way as the car lurched at them. The driver, sensing a break in the press of humanity in front of him, pounded the horn with the heel of his hand and pumped the accelerator. Soldiers, sailors and harbour workers scattered before him like shrapnel.

'Stop!' Fischer wound down his window and leant out. He waved his pistol at the ship and shouted. 'Stop! By order of the State. You are forbidden to leave this harbour!'

Stieber stared at the shouting man and the roaring car. Then, before anyone could stop him, he flew across the deck, vaulted the aft quarter safety rail and leapt onto the quayside. He landed heavily, rolled, surged back to his feet and ran pell-mell towards the onrushing vehicle.

The car didn't stop.

Neither did Stieber. He hurled himself onto the bonnet, smashing the windscreen.

The driver, in horror, stamped on the brakes. The vehicle slammed to a halt, as if it had hit a brick wall.

Stieber's body fell off the bonnet and rolled beneath the front wheels.

He was still breathing.

Fischer, incensed, wrenched his door open, ran round, pointed his pistol at the writhing form of the young navy officer and fired. Once, twice, three times.

Stieber shuddered with the impact of the bullets, then lay still.

Utterly still.

Fischer gave the corpse a kick, and spat.

Then, as if realising for the first time why he was there, he looked up and across at the M35.

It had slipped its aft spring line and was already nosing away from the quayside. There were now maybe five metres of icy black water between ship and shore. Kotkas stood midship, silhouetted by one of the bulkhead lights on the minesweeper's superstructure. He was staring at the dark mound of the young man lying inert beneath the car's head-lights on the quayside.

Fischer raised his pistol and fired half a dozen frenzied shots at him.

A machine gun, from somewhere above Kotkas on the ship, clattered a cruel reply.

Fischer was dead before he hit the ground.

His unseeing eyes open to an infinite sky.

'Self-defence,' said Busch on the bridge, handing the machine gun back to the petty officer of the watch. 'In this light, it was hard to know who was shooting at us or why.'

'I'll make a note in the ship's log,' said Kotkas, his voice empty of all emotion. In a daze, he continued to gaze at Stieber's lifeless body onshore. A pile of rags, now. It, and the rest of Pillau, began to dwindle and merge into the night.

The ship continued through the blackness towards the other harbour wall. Soon, all that remained of her was the swirl of disturbed water she left behind, and the gentle nudging of wavelets upon the dank stones of the quay.

By now, people were gathering around the car on the quayside.

The car's driver got out. Shocked, he had sat there while all the shooting had been taking place. He had not been able to see what had gone on through the shattered windscreen.

'What's happened?' said an army major, elbowing through the crowd and taking charge. 'Who's this?'

'Senior Security Police Officer Fischer,' said the driver.

'Who shot him?'

'I don't know.'

A sergeant arrived. He prodded Karl Stieber's corpse with the toe of his boot. 'And who shot this young fellow?'

'I didn't see that, either. He was crazy. He just ran at me. I didn't have a chance to brake.'

'Why are you people here? Civilian police, I mean?' said the Major.

'I don't know. The boss hadn't told me what was going on; why he wanted me to drive to the harbour, or drive so fast once we were here. Something about some Estonian is all I know.'

'Well, no doubt it'll all get sorted out in due course.'

'Fat chance anything will ever get sorted out nowadays, sir,' said the sergeant. 'Not with the unholy mess that the whole place is in.'

'Mind what you say,' said the Major. 'But, to be honest, you're probably right. Much more important things to think about. Like saving our own skins. Get this lot tidied up, Sergeant ...'

'Yes, sir.'

'And you ...' he said to the driver.

'Yes, sir?'

'Take a look at what's going on around you. There's no law to uphold anymore. Ivan will be here in the next few days, without a doubt. Go and pack. Tell your people to get the hell out of this town. Make your way to Kiel, or Berlin, or anywhere you like. It's every man for himself. That's the only law that has any clout these days.'

*

Maret was woken by a noise. It was a coughing, rasping sound. This was soon accompanied by a curious metallic squealing. It took her a moment, and then she realised what it was.

She got out of bed and, in her nightdress, stepped to the window and opened the shutters.

There was a full moon set in a raven-black sky shimmering with stars. From her window, she could look towards the woods a hundred or so metres away. In a clearing, she knew there were tanks. Because of the night, she couldn't actually see them. However, she'd come across them a couple of days previously. A Panzer company of around twenty of them with their support vehicles. They had been there for some days. They had given Maret a sense of comfort and security. The Fatherland's guardian angels.

She heard her door open and looked round. In the moonlight, she saw Juhan, barefoot. He pattered across the wooden floor, rested his hand on her shoulder, and joined her in looking out.

'Did you hear them?' he breathed.

The light of the moon made their faces precious.

'Yes.'

'What are they doing?'

'I don't know.'

Then, across the meadow that lay between their house, the wood and the clearing, Maret and Juhan heard voices. Orders being called. All at once, the noise of engines rose. The clatter of caterpillar tracks, and the squealing of the bogies around which they revolved, rose with it. With a jerking and a juddering sound, one tank was obviously moving off, followed by another and yet another. Maret's and Juhan's mouths fell open.

The Panzers were pulling out.

'How can they do this?' said Maret. 'They have to stay. We need them to stay.'

'Has Adi betrayed us?' said Juhan. 'He promised to keep us safe.'

'He will, Juhan, he will,' said Maret, and patted her brother's hand. It was still resting, warm, on her shoulder.

But she wasn't so sure anymore.

*

'Signal sir,' the wireless operator had informed the officer of the watch. 'It's from the flotilla commander.'

Here it is, thought Kotkas. *A message to have me arrested and brought in for court-martial*. He had been wondering for the past few hours when they would catch up with him. He wondered whether Fischer was dead. Or, if alive, what he had said. 'Read it out, please.'

'Message reads: *To Commander Kotkas. Am about fifteen nautical miles behind you. Reduce speed to five knots. Will be with you approx. sixteen hundred hours. Stop engines when in sight. Meeting on board me.*'

So, he has given chase, Kotkas thought. By the expressions on everyone else's faces on that bridge, he could see they were thinking this, too. What should he do? Run, or follow what were quite explicit instructions? He'd planned, depending on the outcome of the Fischer matter, to get back into Pillau or go on to Kiel and see what else he could do; who else he might rescue. This message changed all that.

It didn't take him long to consider these new options, and a further moment to come to a conclusion. It was not their fault his crew were in this situation. He would take full responsibility, deny any of them had anything to do with it, and go quietly. Who knows? Perhaps the war would be over before they had the chance to put him up against a wall.

'Reduce speed to five knots.'

'Five knots, it is, sir.'

At just before 1600, the flotilla commander's minesweeper could be seen approaching at speed. Kotkas ordered his ship's engines to slow and his launch to be lowered. Soon afterwards, he found himself on deck, shaking hands with Busch and returning the crew's salute. They had lined the side of the minesweeper to wish him well. He climbed down the boom ladder and stepped across the gunwale onto the launch. It puttered off across a choppy grey sea to the other ship, which had slowed to a crawl as well.

Kotkas's flotilla commander's cabin was bright and warm. He was offered ersatz coffee and a cigarette, both of which he welcomed.

'I suppose you know what this is about, Kotkas?'

'The incident in Pillau.'

'What incident in Pillau?'

'Is that not what you wanted to talk to me about?'

'Not as far as I know. Not heard anything of that nature. I left for Kiel soon after you did. Not had anything over the wireless to that effect, either. What was this incident?'

'Well, sir, if that's not why I'm here, I shan't burden you further with it.'

The Commander gave Kotkas a curious look, but continued. 'We're to turn around,' he said.

'Sorry, sir? Go back to Pillau?'

'Do stop going on about Pillau, please, Kotkas. No, but we're not to go to Kiel, either. We're to head for Libau again. High Command has issued a general evacuation order for the whole region. Our part in it is to escort any and every ship from the Kurland peninsular to Denmark.' He paused, then, getting no response, continued. 'Well, off you go, then, Kotkas. No time to lose.'

Kotkas replaced his cap and saluted. 'Thank you, sir.'

'Thank you, Kotkas, and,' his commander stood, 'who knows how this will turn out, so here's my hand. I would be honoured if you shook it. It has been a privilege serving with you.'

'And you, sir.'

'Good luck and good sailing.'

Spring 1945

I

With the trees budding, the birds singing and the sky blue, in ordinary circumstances, Emilie might almost call the morning idyllic. At breakfast, however, she and her sisters, whose house it was, were forced to speak in low voices, so the children would not hear. The radio, which was usually on from the start to the end of day, was switched off.

The children came down soon after to eat their stale pumpernickel with its single slice of sausage. The sum total of their breakfast these days.

'No school today, children,' Emilie said. 'The police came round this morning and told us we all need to stay in our homes.'

Then the firing started.

About a kilometre away to the west, crackling rifle and machine-gun fire, with the *whump* of the occasional mortar, could be heard. The children's eyes grew wider and wider.

'Keep away from the window, children. Sit down on the floor in the middle of the room,' one of the sisters said.

The fighting, for Maret knew this was what it was, lasted perhaps an hour.

It appeared to get closer.

Then it stopped.

Then nothing.

Not even birdsong.

*

'It's a mess.' The Commander was briefing Kotkas in his cabin. The Baltic's heavy swell caused them to sway as they spoke. 'Königsberg, I hear, has been razed to the ground.

346

Refugees destroyed as they escaped; especially over the frozen Haff. The Russians bombed the ice beneath their feet, just like Napoleon did to them in 1805 at Austerlitz. Anyone left behind in the city ... well ... let's just say, we're reaping what we sowed so freely the day we stepped across the Neman in '41.'

Kotkas knew only too well the catastrophe that had been unleashed as the once all-conquering army, metre by metre, lost its grip on East Prussia. He recognised, also, the need for people in deep shock to go over such events again and again. He let the flotilla commander run through his litany of dismay.

As he did so, Kotkas's mind wandered. It settled like a stork upon one strange incident among the many and harrowing events they'd encountered during the endless days of evacuation. It was a week or so earlier. A woman had somehow got wind of his name while they were yet again alongside at Libau. Moreover, she had learnt that he was the skipper of a ship; escort to a convoy bound for Denmark. She had tracked him down. A half-starved woman swaddled in a heavy coat; a thick woollen shawl pulled tightly around her head against the Baltic squalls. A refugee among the tens of thousands of evacuees, from Königsberg and elsewhere, somehow miraculously fetching up at Libau – desperate for onward transport.

'Captain Kotkas?' she had said, calling up from the quayside to where he stood on the deck, overseeing embarkation. His armed crew was holding back the crush of humanity on shore that appeared close to panic. 'Don't you remember me?'

He did not.

'It is true, we have never met,' she continued, 'but my name is Sperling. I was your children's teacher at their school back in Königsberg. Teacher, and protector.'

Ah, yes.

Miss Sperling went on to plead with the undoubtedly kind, compassionate captain to take her on board and carry her to safety. As a special favour to one, such as she, that had always had his children's and his whole family's well-being in mind.

Kotkas took pity on the poor woman. He ordered his crew to let her come on board.

So the ship had brought her and the many others on the minesweeper, and in the convoy they were escorting, to Denmark. There, hopefully, they could begin their new lives once the war was over.

And then Kotkas remembered seeing Miss Sperling hurry down the gangplank to the relative safety of a new homeland. He recalled that she had failed to look for him at any point during the crossing. Let alone thank him. And on arrival, she had simply disappeared into the harbour throng.

He shrugged the memory off and returned to the present.

The two minesweepers were all that was left of their eight-ship flotilla due to the attrition of war and the extremes of the endless evacuation. Both officers were exhausted, unshaven and, Kotkas felt, one air raid away from a complete nervous breakdown. He had lost count of the number of times they'd left Libau like this with another full load of soldiers and other personnel – Estonians among them – every face empty, bewildered.

He thought back to when he'd found young Stieber, drunk and ready to commit suicide. Kotkas remembered how he'd reflected, then, that there was neither glory nor heroes in retreat. Yet over the recent weeks, he had witnessed courage. Great courage. Courage in defeat, courage in refusing to succumb to the inevitable.

The State, the absurd folly of one little man's warped imagination, was imploding.

'The wolves are at every door.' The Commander was still speaking. He had finally reached the reason he had summoned Kotkas for a briefing. 'Our orders are that we're to head north.'

'North?'

'Yes. To Norway. High Command has decided to concentrate all available forces in that region. Gather and resist. Regroup, recover, then continue the Thousand-Year Empire from there.' Even though he was a loyal German, the flotilla commander, Kotkas noted, could not keep a hint of irony from his voice. 'So, this is our last cargo of evacuees. Back to your ship, and plot a course for Norway. We'll maintain radio silence until we are there. Communication only by lantern.'

Kotkas saluted.

So, he thought, *it's all change yet again*. Which, as any sailor knows, is better than nothing.

As he made his way back on deck, he couldn't help thinking that his superior officer, ever cautious, had perhaps grabbed the Norway option rather than argue for further perilous evacuation work. But then again, he told himself, there was danger everywhere. Norway at least offered something he hadn't experienced for many weeks.

Hope.

After all, if they did manage to make it to Norway, there was the possibility of escape over the border into Sweden.

Wasn't there?

*

At two o'clock on the afternoon of the day after the fighting, the knock at the door that Emilie was dreading came. She took a deep breath and went to open it.

Maret and Juhan peered out from behind the living-room door.

'Go back inside, children,' she said, and turned the latch.

Maret and Juhan didn't move.

Framed by the doorway stood a lean long-legged man in a strange brown uniform, wearing a dark green helmet with a small white stripe on it.

'Good afternoon, ma'am,' he said, and saluted. He spoke in a language Maret had only just begun to learn before she had to leave Estonia. She recognised it as English, even though it had a curious twang, but that was about all she understood.

Emilie, for her part, knew more than enough to get by.

'Good afternoon.'

'Lieutenant Stewart, US 9th Army. I am here to inform you that we have liberated this district by force of arms and that, effective immediately, the laws of military occupation are in effect.'

'Meaning?'

'Meaning: we are enforcing a curfew from seventeen hundred hours to zero nine hundred hours. Identification papers to be carried at all times. No gatherings of three or more people. And the orders of any member of the US armed services or its allies are to be obeyed directly and to the letter.'

'Thank you for advising us, Lieutenant. You will find that we are entirely content to cooperate.'

'I'm glad to hear that, ma'am. There is one further stipulation that I need to make clear to you at this time, however.'

'Which is?'

'My commanding officer has identified your premises as of sufficient size and quality as to be suitable for the temporary billeting of a number of our men, until it is time for us to move on.'

'I beg your pardon?'

'Ma'am, ten of my men are to be stationed here in this house. That's an order.'

The lieutenant stepped aside and beckoned a group of men forward. Emilie hadn't noticed them until that point. They had been hovering a few metres away, waiting for their lieutenant's instructions.

Maret and Juhan, seeing the lieutenant's gesture, stepped further into the hallway to look at what or who it was he was waving to. Emilie's sisters, who had been in the kitchen, also appeared.

The soldiers approached the house. Maret could see that they were heavily armed; rifles, pistols and even machine guns. Their skins had the olive hue of people who had grown up in a sunnier climate. They were festooned with gold and silver: chains around their necks, bracelets, watch straps, rings. One or two of them even had gold teeth.

'Pirates!' whispered Juhan.

'No, Americans,' said Maret. She had worked that much out.

Emilie raised a hand. 'Stop, please. No further. I cannot allow this.'

'I beg your pardon, ma'am?'

The soldiers, now gathered around the lieutenant, peered into the house, One of them saw the children. He grinned, unbuttoned a breast pocket and drew out some chewing gum. He offered it to them. Juhan reached out but Maret slapped her brother's hand aside. She couldn't help but notice, though, on the soldier's wrist was a watch. It wasn't an ordinary watch. It had the image of something she recognised from a few years ago, when her mother had taken her to the cinema in Tallinn. On the watch was a little picture of Mickey Mouse.

'I am afraid, ma'am,' said the lieutenant, that you cannot refuse us permission to billet men here.'

'And I am afraid, Lieutenant, that what you say I can or cannot do is of no interest to me. Occupation or no Occupation, I am not permitting even one of your men to step over this threshold, let alone ten. I have a teenage girl here. Plus, there are my sisters and, of course, myself. I am only too dreadfully aware of what conquering armies are capable of doing to the women and girls of a defeated nation. And I can assure you that this will not happen here.'

'Ma'am. I must insist.'

'Insist as much as you like. Take your men away.'

The lieutenant squared his shoulders and, for a moment,

his hand twitched towards the pistol in his holster. But the woman who stood in front of him was clearly resolute. The trouble was, he realised, she had a point. More than once in recent months, he had needed to prevent one of his men giving a German woman what would best be described as unwelcome attention. The man had been drunk with either alcohol or victory, or both. Thankfully, he'd stopped anything more serious happening. But even such coarse behaviour, in his eyes, a good Baptist boy from Jonesboro, Arkansas, was serious enough.

He took a step back.

'Very well, ma'am. I shall report your refusal to my company commander.'

'Please do. And I shall give him the same answer as I have just given to you, should he decide to come to this door.'

'Yes, ma'am.'

The lieutenant saluted and shepherded his men away.

*

The two minesweepers, with their final cargoes of exhausted troops, had sailed south-west through the night. They were side by side, protecting each other's flanks. They'd negotiated a minefield, endured three attacks from the air, and evaded at least one enemy ship which had appeared on the eastern horizon at dawn. But now, late afternoon, they were pressing on towards Copenhagen, looking to slip through any further enemy patrols under cover of night. Once in Danish waters, they should be safe. The last they heard, Denmark was still under German control. It would be a simple matter from there to sail through the Kattegat and make for Norway.

Every member of both ships' crews were on deck, with eyes strained to see even the slightest fleck on the horizon, in the air, or under the water. The sea squirmed blue-grey as if trying to escape the sky's leaden attentions.

Kotkas had just dared to let himself believe that they might just make it to Denmark when yet another alarm was raised.

It was a hunting pack of three Sh-4 Russian torpedo boats. They came from the south, almost from nowhere, and hurtled towards the more cumbersome minesweepers.

Immediately, the two ships opened fire, but little could prevent the narrow razor-snouted boats closing in on their prey.

All at once, as if choreographed, the boats loosed their torpedoes. These leapt like fish from the tubes on the decks and plunged into the water. Kotkas and his flotilla commander separated, as previously agreed. One to port, one to starboard. However, the flotilla commander's ship turned too slowly and two torpedoes were too quick for him.

She was hit aft. The concussion of the resulting explosion rocked Kotkas's own ship.

The torpedo boats swarmed around the injured mine-sweeper like wolves around a wounded elk. All the ship's guns were firing at her tormentors.

Kotkas had the crew swing their M35 around and close in on the three smaller but more agile vessels, firing whatever weapon the minesweeper was able to bring to bear. It was enough. Evidently, the Russian boats had been prowling around the Baltic for some time. They did not loose off any more torpedoes. The moment it was clear Kotkas was not about to run anywhere but would stand up to them instead, like confronted bullies, they turned and ran. Soon, they had vanished completely over the horizon. Doubtless, they would report Kotkas and his commander's location. Doubtless, some other Red Fleet vessel would be upon them in the fullness of time.

'Damage too severe. Taking on water. Cannot make much headway. Go on. Save yourselves.' The flotilla commander flashed a message across the water.

'I shall take you in tow,' Kotkas replied.

'Too far. We won't make it.'

Kotkas turned to scan the chart spread out on the table behind him, then looked up. 'Reply,' he said to the signalman, 'Bornholm. Still under German control. We can tow you there.'

There was a pause as if the floundering minesweeper across the water was thinking.

Then its lantern flickered and flashed. Kotkas's signalman called out the response: 'They say "very well", sir.'

So, one behind the other, united by hawser, they limped towards the island of Bornholm: fortress; bastion of the Western Baltic. She was queen of all she surveyed – from Sweden to the north, Germany to the south, and the Danish mainland behind her, due west.

*

'When are we going home?'

'I'm not sure you ever will be, Maret,' said Emilie. 'We don't know where your father is. We don't even know if he's still alive, I'm afraid.'

Juhan couldn't help it; he let out a sob.

'I know, Juhan, it's hard, but we have to face facts. It looks like I shall have to be your family from now on.'

'No, you will not!' cried Maret. 'You are not my mother. You never can be my mother. You never will be.'

'I know that, Maret. I'm not trying to be. But your father asked me to look after you. Don't you think we should honour that? At least until we know what has happened to him.'

*

Dusk was falling as Kotkas brought his binoculars to bear on the first lighthouse of the Bornholm coast. Seeing it, identifying it, meant he and his crew could breathe just a little easier. There were big guns on that resolute little island. Pursuers simply wouldn't come that close.

They were soon intercepted by two German fast attack

boats, who proceeded to escort them to the island.

Through the night, the two ships crept ever closer to relative safety.

They rounded the island's northern headland, at which point their guardians left them to pursue other duties.

They slipped quietly into Rønne Harbour shortly before dawn.

Kotkas could not believe it: despite everything, they'd made it.

Taking his leave of his commander, who set about organising some makeshift repairs to his damaged vessel, Kotkas made his way to the harbour office to give his report.

'Papers, please, Commander,' the lieutenant behind the desk said. Kotkas handed them over and the officer spread them to read. He looked up with something approaching suspicion in his voice. 'What's an officer in counterintelligence doing in command of a minesweeper?'

'Long story.'

'I'm in no hurry.'

So Kotkas gave him the gist, without touching on the Fischer element.

It seemed to satisfy the fellow. 'Well,' he said, 'owing to the situation in Berlin, there are no orders at present, so—'

'What situation in Berlin?'

'You haven't heard?' The lieutenant's eyes widened.

'We've been at sea. Radio silence.'

'The Leader ... he's dead.'

'How?'

'Killed himself, by all accounts. Bullet or poison. Or possibly both.'

'But he's definitely dead?'

The lieutenant nodded. 'Admiral Dönitz is in charge. We had official notification a couple of days ago. Everyone is in shock.'

'I can imagine. So what happens now?'

'Well, as I said, there are no orders at present. You'll have to wait for them like the rest of us. However, the island commander has said that any ship not under his direct control is relatively free in this constantly developing situation to make its own decisions for the time being. In short, if you wish, we can offer you what limited provisions are available for a ship your size, let you take on some water, refuel, and head out to sea again.'

Kotkas returned in something of a daze to the M35. He made his way to his cabin. Shortly afterwards, Busch knocked on his door.

'Come.'

'Just wondered whether there were any orders, sir?'

Kotkas had been expecting this perfectly legitimate question. In fact, he'd been thinking about it on the way back to the ship from the harbour office.

'Sit down, please, Lieutenant,' he said. He outlined the situation regarding the Leader and Dönitz and the subsequent absence of direction in a few sentences.

Busch sat shaking his head until his skipper had finished.

'So. It's over,' he said.

'Just about.'

'So, what do you suggest, Commander?'

'Well, we appear, at least for the moment, to be completely free to choose.'

'I see.'

Kotkas listed the options on his fingers. 'We can continue on to Denmark and see if we can't get to Norway, which was our original instruction. Though, in my opinion, that has been overtaken by events. So, we can perhaps sail to Germany where, I suspect, we might in due course be required to surrender to the Allies ...'

'Better than surrendering to the Soviets.'

'Agreed ... or we can go back to Libau and see if we can't get just a few more people away from that abattoir before whoever's left – poor souls – are engulfed by the Red Army.'

He paused.

Busch could tell he was wrestling with another option.

'Or, sir?'

'Or we can sail north and throw ourselves on the mercy of the Swedes.'

Busch nodded.

They sat in silence for a moment, looking at one another.

It was the lieutenant who spoke first. 'Whatever you decide, sir, we are with you. Every last man.'

'Thank you, Viktor. That is greatly appreciated.'

A further silence followed.

Then Kotkas rose and took up his cap to leave.

Busch followed suit.

'Libau it is,' said Kotkas.

'Thank you, sir,' said Busch.

II

The next morning, Busch and Kotkas were on deck supervising refuelling and revictualling when the lieutenant from the harbour office appeared. Kotkas invited him on board and, at the lieutenant's request, the two of them went into the Commander's cabin.

'So, what's this about?' said Kotkas.

'I'll get straight to the point, sir. You know Bornholm's primary purpose?'

'A listening post.'

'Exactly. Radio intercepts and intelligence gathering. In effect, your speciality.'

'Who told you that?'

'One of the intelligence unit. A chief petty officer from Berlin, posted here around eighteen months ago. I wasn't sure about you. So I asked around the unit and he told me. Said you were highly respected.'

'Flattered. But now, let me guess. You want me to stay here on the island? Join the unit?'

'Lead one of the sections. The island commander's suggestion.'

'Suggestion or order?'

'Suggestion, sir. At least, in the first instance.'

Kotkas looked around at his little cabin. 'What about my ship? My men?'

'They can carry on. I think someone said that when they came to requisition the fuel, you were planning to go back to Libau?'

'Correct.'

'Nothing to stop them.' The lieutenant unbuttoned a breast

pocket, drew out a folded piece of paper and handed it across to Kotkas. 'The island commander has ordered your lieutenant – Busch, I believe – to assume command.'

*

The farewell between Kotkas, Busch and the crew followed a pattern familiar to all sailors since humans first ventured out onto the sea. They exchanged handshakes and salutes and vowed to meet again in some godforsaken bar in some godforsaken harbour in some godforsaken corner of the world somewhere, sometime.

Kotkas watched as the minesweeper's engines grumbled into life. The lines and hawsers binding her to the land were released. They splashed into the murky water and were gathered in. The screws churned, causing the grey sea to gush and roil beneath her stern.

He did not wait. He turned without looking back and made his way to the harbour buildings. He felt like Robinson Crusoe.

Mercifully, the familiarity of wireless intercepts and intelligence work was soon distracting him. He was surprised how easily he slipped back into the rhythms and intellectual challenges of that world.

Two days passed. Apart from the increasing evidence of the presence of the Red Fleet in the Western Baltic, there was little or no news from anywhere else. It was as if nobody knew what to do with them, stuck out in the middle of nowhere on that stubborn little island.

Kotkas and officers and men from the twelve thousand personnel stationed across the island met together in the mess halls for breakfast, lunch and dinner. Once in a while, he encountered his former flotilla commander; struggling to get his ship seaworthy again. No one knew anything. They might as well have been prisoners of war. While the initial plan to concentrate a significant German force on Denmark and

Norway was the last general directive anyone had received, inertia now seemed to be the order of the day.

Rumours abounded. There was the one about how the Red Army had invaded over the roof of the world and down into Finnmark at the top of Norway. Another contained the not unrealistic expectation that surrender was near. Doubtless, this would be something to do with Admiral Dönitz and the new High Command.

It was a few days after Kotkas's arrival that the island commander finally summoned his senior officers to the headquarters building for an announcement. Kotkas, for his part, knew what it was going to be; it was he who had brought the relevant message from one of the radio huts straight to the commander personally.

It was the notification of the complete and immediate cessation of hostilities. The commander told the room. The German Army, Navy, Air Force and ancillary personnel had been ordered to lay down their arms immediately. They were to either wait for further orders or make their way to the nearest Allied or Soviet unit to hand themselves over.

In other words – a general unconditional surrender.

'However,' the island commander said, 'due to the nature of our work and the strategic importance of Bornholm, I have made it clear to the Soviets rapping at our door – and anyone back in Berlin who will listen – that we shall not be surrendering to Ivan.'

Neither Kotkas nor anyone else in that room could conceal their relief. Feet shifted, shoulders relaxed and, despite the humiliation of defeat, a smile or two twitched on a face here and there. They'd all been dreading falling into Soviet hands – and the consequences of this – ever since rumours of surrender had started to circulate.

'Consequently,' the island commander said, 'I have made a request at the highest level that a member of the Allied forces – whether a general in the Marine Corps or a private in the

Latrine Corps – be flown to Bornholm immediately, so that we might surrender to him, and the governments and armed services he represents.'

There was a mixture of light applause and muted cheers. The meeting was then dismissed, with the officers instructed to pass the details on to the people for whom they were responsible.

The Soviet onslaught began barely twenty-four hours later.

All areas of the island were subjected to heavy, relentless air raids.

After yet another such raid, and the subsequent all-clear on the sirens, Kotkas made his way once more to his bed.

The room was a dormitory which he shared with eight other senior officers.

They were woken in the early hours of the morning by the door bursting open and the lights being switched on. Kotkas blinked and shielded his eyes. He could not make out who it was that had so rudely intruded. Then it became clear.

Two Red Army soldiers.

They were jabbing their rifles at the officers. Telling them to get up and get dressed.

The men were chivvied to the main building, where scores of other German officers were being addressed by a Soviet colonel.

'I am pleased to inform you, gentlemen, that you are now in the care of the Red Army. You are to be processed and dealt with accordingly,' he said. 'First, we will take your names and your papers ...'

'Our papers ...?' one of the naval officers said.

'Which will be filed along with your names and kept safe. You do not need to worry.'

Which, the officer who spoke and all the others present knew, was far from true. They absolutely did need to worry.

They were herded into a further hall, where they were left to stand, to sit, to smoke, to talk, and to await their fate.

Occasionally, perhaps in some courtyard somewhere, the brief rattle of automatic weapons could be heard. The Soviets were not great conversationalists, it seemed, and preferred to conduct their enquiries with machine guns.

Then it was Kotkas's turn.

He was brought before an officer, with red and gold epaulettes, seated at a table. The soldier escorting him produced Kotkas's identity papers, which had been removed from him – *for safekeeping* – earlier. At least Kotkas had kept his papers on him. Those who had concealed or destroyed them had been immediately taken away. Perhaps they were the subjects of the machine- gun fire.

The officer at the table had a large file. It contained a ream of papers with names on it. The officer consulted Kotkas's ID papers and turned to the section headed 'K'. He ran his finger down the list. It stopped at one name in particular.

'Hendrik Kotkas?'

'Yes.'

'Wait over there, please.'

The soldier led him to a corner of the room.

A few moments later, a further armed guard took Kotkas off his comrade's hands and led him away.

He was marched along a corridor through a door that led to a cellar. They descended, stone steps echoing with every footstep.

They found him a room and threw him in, bolting the door behind him.

*

'Here ... I managed to snaffle us a little extra milk.' Emilie had come in from a full day working for the district milk cooperative. She always took a jug with her in case she was allowed to take a *little something* home for the children. They hadn't eaten properly for days, and the rich creamy liquid was the only treat they got. The smell of fresh milk, in those days, was the most delicious, enticing aroma. Their diet otherwise was, as it had mostly been of late, stale bread and thinly sliced sausage. For Emilie, the only highlight in a bland diet was ersatz coffee, and that wasn't saying much.

Emilie's sisters had gone to live with a cousin twenty kilometres away, to enable Emilie more easily to eke out the rations at the house in Lehrte.

'Anyone home?' a voice called from the front door. It was the postman. 'Hello, all. How are we?' he said.

'Very well, thank you,' said Juhan, keeping track of his manners.

'I have something for you.'

'A letter?' said Juhan.

'A letter,' beamed the postman. He presented it to Emilie and withdrew.

'It's … it's from your father …!' said Emilie, trembling as she opened it.

'He's alive!' said Maret.

'He's alive!' said Juhan.

They jumped up, grabbed each other by the wrists and began to dance.

'He's coming to get us. He's coming to take us home!' they sang.

Emilie had begun reading. The smile that bathed her face a moment before faded. The children noticed. Their song and dance subsided.

'What's the matter?'

'What does it say?'

'My dear children, look at the date.' She showed them. 'It was written weeks ago. It's addressed to your mother. I should have noticed that on the envelope. When he wrote it, perhaps he thought she was still alive.' She looked at the official rubber stamp at the bottom of the page, the one that meant it had been passed by the official censor as acceptable. 'It was sent from Königsberg. That's now in Russian hands.'

'Everything's always in Russian hands,' said Juhan.

'What does it mean?' said Maret.

'I don't know,' said Emile, and sat down heavily in a chair.

'Read it to us, anyway, please.'

She read it to them.

Maret and Juhan brightened slightly when he mentioned them towards the end, but then all was solemn again as they listened to their father's final words of farewell.

Emilie finished reading. She let her hands drop into her lap, still holding the letter.

All three sat in silence.

Emilie began to cry.

*

Kotkas lost track of how many hours he had waited in the basement room. He had no light, no water, no food. He dozed on and off and had to remind himself, when he woke, of where he was and of the nightmare he had been caught up in. He recalled that cell long ago in Berlin. In the early days.

Now in this present captivity, he could still hear the sound of that machine gun being fired, somewhere beyond the walls. He hoped it was just practice. He knew it probably was not.

Eventually – perhaps it was twelve hours later, perhaps it was eighteen, perhaps it was twenty-four – footsteps approached. A key ground the lock open. A Russian soldier lifted him from where he was sat cross-legged on the stone floor and pulled him, blinking, unshaven, out into the corridor.

He was marched along, up some stairs, and into a cobbled courtyard of shadows. The cold air made him shiver. He pulled his collar tight around his throat. He wondered which wall he would be put up against.

However, they continued across and in through another door.

They went along a further corridor and, eventually, into a room with chairs, a desk and a lamp.

'Sit,' the soldier said, and took up a position by the door.

Kotkas sat.

He sat. For an hour; possibly two.

He was just thinking about asking the soldier what was going to happen next, and when it would happen, when he heard more footsteps.

The door opened.

A man in British Army-issue leather jerkin, blue beret and lieutenant's pips appeared. He was accompanied by a Soviet Army captain, who did not look in the least pleased.

'Hello, old man,' the British officer said to Kotkas. 'Bit of a pickle, eh? Let's see what we can do to unpickle you, shall we?'

It was Tamm.

*

The argument had been going on most of the afternoon: Maret finding fault with everything Emilie had done or was trying to do; Emilie finding fault in Maret's whole attitude – she never helped around the house; she was never grateful; she was always rude. After the evening meal, Emilie having once again failed to get Maret to help tidy and wash up, Maret had chosen instead to go up to her room to read. So Emilie followed her and stood in the bedroom doorway.

'Did you learn nothing at Young Maidens Group, Maret?' Maret, lying on her bed, did not reply. 'Where is the helpfulness? Where is the doing whatever you can for others?'

'When someone deserves help, I will give it. But you do not care for the State. If you did, you wouldn't be here,' Maret said.

'The State you are speaking about is finished. I told you about the surrender. And I am here to look after you two.'

'Yes, convenient, that, isn't it? Instead of helping in a

factory or a hospital. Nice easy excuse to live in a fine house with a quiet life, while Adi cried out for your help on the front lines, where the real need was. It's your fault we had to surrender.'

'This was just as much a front line. It still is. Have you forgotten everything that's happened to us? Everything I have done for you?'

'Nobody asked you to.'

'Your father asked me to.'

'He's probably dead.'

'Just because we haven't heard from him ...'

'Might as well be dead for all he cares about us. I bet he hasn't given us a single thought since he left.'

'That's not fair, Maret,' said Juhan, joining them.

'Well, it's true. He cares more about the navy than us.'

'That's not true, Maret,' said Emilie. 'He really is doing the best he can for you. I know he is.'

'How do you know? Have you heard from him? Heard from him now. Not old letters.'

'No, but when I was with him last, he let me know how much everything he was doing was for you. Both of you. Only for you.'

'What kinds of things?' said Juhan.

'Things like trying to end the war, so you can all go back home to Estonia.'

'How could he have ended the war? He's only one person,' said Maret.

'You'd be surprised what he was trying to do.'

'Like what? Tell me.'

'Well ...' *Can it really do any harm, now it is all over? Now the Americans are here, and the Russians are dismantling Berlin brick by brick.* 'You see,' she said, 'he was one of a number of people that were trying to stop the war from the beginning. Or at least make it end as soon as possible.'

'Yes, by winning it,' said Juhan.

'By stopping it from the inside.'

'What do you mean?' said Maret.

Emilie sat down on the edge of Maret's bed. 'Well, you see, your father believes that this war should never have happened. That the people who started it were wrong, and that as a result of it being wrong, Estonia got caught up in something that wasn't their business. So he decided to try and make it stop by preventing the wrong people from being in charge anymore.'

'The wrong people?' said Juhan. 'You mean like the people in Berlin?'

'Among others, yes.'

'But he's one of them.'

'Well, yes and no ... Even though he was in the navy, he wanted to stop the people who wanted to carry on fighting the war.'

Maret spoke slowly. 'You mean he's a traitor? He betrayed the people of Germany? Betrayed Adi?'

'No. Exactly the opposite. He believed the people in power betrayed the people of Germany, and he was working to put things right. Right especially for Estonia.'

The children looked at Emilie in silence.

'No,' said Juhan. 'No. My father's a hero.'

'Yes, he is a hero, Juhan,' said Emilie. 'Just not the kind of hero you mean.'

'I don't believe you. You are lying,' said Maret. 'You are just saying these filthy things to get us to hate our father so you can control us.'

'I'm telling you the truth. All the time you've been here in Germany, all the years that you and Juhan have gone to your groups, you have been told lie after lie after lie. It's time you knew the real truth.'

'No! You're the liar!' screamed Maret. 'Liar, liar, liar!' She leapt off her bed and ran downstairs.

'Come back, Maret!' Emilie and Juhan chased after her.

Maret reached the front door and snatched at the latch. Emilie grabbed her hand and pulled it away.

'Let go!'

'Juhan, help!' Emilie said.

Juhan grabbed Maret around the waist. Terrified that if his sister went through the door, she might never come back. 'Don't go!' he cried.

'No! I don't want to stay here in this terrible place with her filthy lies.'

Emilie managed to lever Maret back into the hall. She stood between her and the front door.

Maret ran to the back door. Juhan ran after her, pulled her aside and locked it, thrusting the key into his pocket.

Emilie joined them.

Maret stood glaring at the floor. 'Leave me alone ...'

'Maret, you've had a terrible time. I understand that. I want to make things better for you ...'

'You want to make things better for me? Then why don't you die? Why don't you all just go off and die and leave me in peace? You liars. Traitors. Criminals.'

'Your father is not a traitor. I know it's hard to accept. But one day you will understand. And you will be proud of him.'

Maret held her hands to her ears. 'I'm not listening. I'll report you. You are holding me prisoner. I'll see you get arrested for this.'

'Maret, it will get better. I promise.'

'How can it get better? My mother's dead. I don't know where my father is. And even if I did, I don't care. He's a traitor.'

Emilie's voice softened. 'Believe me. I understand how you are feeling ...'

'You have no idea how I feel.'

'I have every idea ... My mother died when I was eight. My father remarried. Then he died. I was left in a strange town with a stepmother and two sisters, who hated me coming into their lives, and who I wanted nothing to do with. Yes, they aren't my sisters. They are my stepsisters, really. You see? I know how you feel. How lonely and frightened you are. But we made it work, my sisters and me. And you and I, and Juhan, we can make it work ... you'll see ... just let me try. Let me help.'

Maret went back up to her room and slammed the door.

*

They were in the air; a Lysander, leaving Bornholm behind. Tamm was trying to make himself heard above the clatter of the engine.

'As I say, it was the very devil to prise you from their grasp. Thank goodness a bright Allied intelligence liaison officer on Bornholm recognised your name on the detainee list. He put a hold on your being processed by our Soviet friends, and then told Hamburg. That's where I was. I flew straight up here to get you. Uncle Joe's chums wanted to keep you, do goodness knows what with you – or *to* you. They just hadn't got around to interrogating you yet; so many captives, so few Soviet intelligence officers who spoke German. Thankfully, our people had enough clout with their people to suggest we should be very unhappy were we not, at the very least, able to have a few hours alone with you.'

'So they released me to you?'

'In a manner of speaking. I flew in. Had a bit of a hand-waving argument with my opposite number and thankfully won the point, if not the match. They want you back tomorrow. I've got you for twenty-four hours.'

'But ...'

'Yes, we appear to be in an aeroplane flying out of the country, don't we? Next stop, Hamburg; refuel, and then get you to England. Sadly, as far as Ivan's concerned, we will mislay you. Fog of war. Fog of postwar. Though, I should say, our own people back in London took a lot of convincing. After all, you ditched them.'

'I had to. I had to keep one step ahead. I had to make sure no one had anything on me. The Germans, the Russians, the British. Be as invisible, as inconsequential as possible. So I severed all my ties. Germany, Estonia ... even you. I would become a simple naval officer prosecuting the war in his own simple navy way. No double-dealing. No secret meetings. No intelligence work for anyone.'

'And what then? Hide under the table until the nasty war went away?'

'I did what little I could to help my people in such circumstances without tipping my hand. Then, once everyone had forgotten me, who I used to be, I hoped I'd be more free to act. My plan was that I'd get command of a ship. Go out and come back a few times like a good fellow. Then, one day, sooner or later, I would be tasked with something in the Western Baltic. Not a vain hope – it was clear the Red Fleet would soon push us all that way anyway.'

'So you expected at some point to end up in Königsberg?'

'Or near enough. And then ... well, I would see what was what, and do what I could. Gather up my family, make a run for Sweden perhaps? Or at least find a neutral fishing fleet I could hand them over to, for safekeeping.'

'But your crew – would they have allowed it?'

'Perhaps. It remained to be seen. It was a plan at least. Something to keep me hoping. Hope ends up being all you have in war. Everything else gets destroyed. But the opportunity never came. And then it was too late. My family had gone deeper into Germany and everything was collapsing. I suppose I could still have cut and run for Sweden, but I couldn't do it. Not if it meant leaving my family behind all over again. Not sure how I'd have got them away, but I would have thought of something. Once the war was ending, well, that was different. Then I had no option but to try. Something. Anything ...' He sighed. 'Have you heard anything from my family, by the way?'

'Your children? They are well, as far as we know. Some place just east of Hannover.'

'Lehrte. Good. And Leena?'

'Leena?' Tamm paused. 'Hendrik ... I'm so sorry ... haven't you heard?' Tamm hated this. How could one get across how truly sympathetic one was when one had to make oneself heard above the clatter of a Lysander? 'Leena didn't make it.'

Hendrik looked away. Anguish surged in his breast. The straps pinning him back in his seat seemed to suffocate him. He wanted to tear at them with his bare hands. Claw them until his fingernails bled, until they or the straps were shredded. He wanted to pound Tamm, or the uncaring, unfeeling pilot in front of him, with his fists. Anyone. He wanted to kick a hole into the aircraft's floor until they all fell through it; plummeting down into the unforgiving sea and disappearing forever. He looked out of the window. Tears were cascading down his cheeks. Far below, an iron cold sea was turning the colour of night.

Tamm held the silence for some minutes; looking steadily ahead but feeling the shuddering of his friend's grief beside him. Then, when he felt the time was right – *when could it really ever be right?* – he rested a hand on his friend's shoulder. 'She was very ill, wasn't she?'

'Yes. But – I don't know – I'd hoped that perhaps ...' Hendrik wiped his eyes with his sleeve.

'I know.'

'How did you find out?'

'Message through from our American cousins. Someone called Emilie Meyer's been trying to get in touch. Tried everything. Including, it seems, via the US military. The name *Kotkas* rang a bell; someone found it on US intelligence's wanted list. Person of Interest to us. Gave our people a tinkle and that was that. Funny old war, eh? Can't use the telephone in your own country but can get a message through an obliging enemy unit, then halfway across the

371

continent of Europe.' Tamm was babbling to give his friend time to gather himself.

Kotkas nodded. He wasn't really listening. He was winding the wedding ring round on his finger; the one she'd put there eighteen years before. 'I need a cigarette,' he said, eventually.

'Sure.'

'Any news from any other of my family?'

'Are you sure you want to hear it?' Kotkas nodded. 'Your brother-in-law, Feliks, was caught by the Soviets.'

'And ...?'

'What do you imagine they do to partisans?'

'I see. Peeter?'

'Last heard ... still working in Tallinn. Munitions factory. The Reds seem to like him.'

'That's Peeter for you. Gets on with anybody.' Kotkas made a noise; half-sob, half-laugh. After a moment, he spoke again. 'How about Lieutenant Busch and my crew? Do you know anything of them? They went back to Libau.'

'Sorry, old boy. No idea. If they were anywhere near Libau when Germany capitulated ...' He shrugged. 'The ship, if not destroyed, will be commissioned into the Baltic Red Fleet.'

'And the men?'

'Your guess is as good as mine. Shot in the head or marched across the continent to disappear into the vastness. I'm sorry. If you want, I can see what I can find out.'

There was a pause as Kotkas looked out of the shuddering window into the night. 'Well ...' He dusted some stray cigarette ash from his trousers. 'I haven't thanked you.'

'For what?'

Kotkas waved a hand to indicate the aircraft. 'All of this.'

'Hendrik. We can talk about *all of this* another time...'

'No – let's talk about it now. I need to. Please. As you rightly say, I am not trusted by the British. They can't possibly have known whose side I was on. How did you convince them to get me out?'

'After everything I'd done for them – all the risks – I called in a favour. Probably one of my last.'

'Thanks.'

'Don't thank me. You're right, they don't trust you. They have no idea whose side you're on. Neither, frankly, have I. Even now, if I'm honest. To get them to finally agree, I had to tell them I was bringing you back as my prisoner.'

'Oh.'

'Just before we land, I am going to have to handcuff you. And surrender you to the Prisoner of War Interrogation Section. Then, I am afraid, it's out of my hands.'

Autumn 1946

Whirling russet leaves, torn from the tyranny of the branches by the wind, piled themselves into drifts around the front of the house. To Maret and Juhan, Emilie seemed to have been in a strange mood all day. Ever since she'd received a telegram that morning. The postman had even winked when he handed it over to Maret on the doorstep just as she left for school.

And now, she and her brother were home again. They both went to high school. Juhan in the second year; Maret was completing her sixth. It was not like the junior school they'd grown used to in Königsberg. A mixed school out of necessity, Lehrte's was smaller, friendlier. Maret had particularly taken to it. The boys were funny and interesting. Especially Jens. He was the joker. He would make fun of the way the former government had tried to Germanise every word in the language; excising any un-Aryan word. The other day, he had suggested the word for nose could be *dachfensterdesgesichts:* the dormer window of the face. She liked his dark side too; suggesting the war had been good for depopulating an already crowded planet. She was looking forward to one day graduating with him and them going on to university together.

Maret and Emilie lived an uneasy truce; a dignified detachment. Making do. Getting on with things. The country was in such a mess; scarcity and simple survival the norm – where else could either of them go?

They were in the kitchen. Maret doing her homework, Emilie at the stove, Juhan preparing the table.

'Would you lay four places, please, Juhan?' Emilie said.

'Four places?'

'Yes, we shall have a guest for our evening meal. Maret, you will have to move your books.'

The sentence had barely left her lips when there was a knock at the door. 'Wait here,' she said, wiping her hands on her apron. She couldn't keep herself from scurrying into the hall. There was the sound of the front door opening, some indistinguishable conversation, then the sound of the door closing again. Footsteps back along the hall.

Emilie returned and stood in the doorway, hands clasped in front of her apron. She was glowing. 'Children,' she announced, 'there is someone here to see you.' At which, she stepped aside.

Hendrik appeared.

The children looked up. For a moment, they could not take it in.

Their father's face was grey and drawn. He was unshaven, grizzled. His hair wild. He wore a battered navy-issue jacket with brass buttons – but no insignia – corduroy trousers and sea boots.

'Hello, Maret ... Juhan,' he said.

He had been nervous all day. Unsure how they would receive him. Their silence confirmed his worst fears.

Juhan broke ranks first.

'Father!' he cried, and hurled himself into the waiting arms.

They hugged and laughed and Hendrik spun his son round.

He set the boy down and looked across at Maret.

She still sat among her books at the far end of the kitchen table. She was trembling.

'Maret,' said Emilie. 'Your father. He's come home.'

'Maret?' said Hendrik.

With a howl, Maret swept the books from the table, kicked over her chair, hurled herself at her father and began to cudgel him with her fists.

'I hate you! I hate you! I hate you!' she screamed.

Hendrik fended her off as best he could, but still she

sustained her assault. A storm. A rage. Fists flailing.

Eventually, Hendrik managed to grasp both her wrists. He lowered his head so his face was close to hers.

'My baby,' he said, 'my poor darling baby …' He started to cry.

Maret subsided; she sank to her knees, crying too.

He got down on the floor with her. Then he reached into his jacket pocket. He pulled something out. It was a once-white handkerchief, now muddy and grey. He laid it on the floor and, little by little, unfolded it. There was something wrapped inside. Despite herself, Maret, tears still coursing down her cheeks, looked to see what he was doing.

'I have a present for you, Maret. I found it outside and thought of my clever, brave little girl.'

The contents of the handkerchief now revealed itself.

It was a piece of velvety green moss.

She grabbed it, howled again, buried her face in her father's chest, and they cried together.

'It's over.' He stroked her hair. 'It's all over, now. Everything.'

*

It was nearly midnight. Hendrik and Emilie sat in the living room, he in a chair, she on a sofa. There was a modest fire in the grate; the whiff of burning coal was somehow comforting. They both looked into the flames; the light from them playing on their faces.

'How have they been?' he said.

'Awful,' she said. 'Understandable, but awful.'

'Towards you?'

'They miss their mother.'

'I will speak with them.'

'I don't mind.'

He looked at her. 'Yes, but I do. I can't thank you enough for all that you have done. For Leena, for the children. For me. Words won't cover it. But now, I know, we must get out of your way. Find our own place. Start putting ourselves back together as a family. Without Leena.' He suppressed a sob and looked away. 'I'm sorry ...'

She looked across at him. She sat still, back straight, with her hands in her lap, like her father had taught her. She waited for him to collect herself. *Poor dear man.*

'Why not stay here?' she said, when he was ready.

'You have done more than enough. You have your life to live now. Your own people.'

'What people? My parents are dead. My stepsisters are settled. Now the Americans have moved out, they have been able to get back their family home in Schwüblingsen. There is nothing for me.' She paused. 'Except the children.'

'But you said—'

'That they were awful, yes. But we've been through everything together. That's a bond of a sort. I don't mean that they've become like my own children. But I've, well, got used to looking after them. And, I think, despite the way they've been towards me, they've got used to me.'

'Well ... here's the thing. Unfortunately ... I've been offered a post.'

'Where?'

'Stockholm. The Allied Control Council have asked me to help oversee their displaced persons work there. Finding exiled Estonians new homelands: Canada, America, Australia ...'

'Working for the Allies? Where you belong, I suppose.'

'That's what they came to accept, yes,' he said. 'After I was arrested, I had a lengthy, painful debriefing over many weeks, but then I was cleared. After which, I was brought down to London and put to work with their intelligence people. A nice woman took me through all sorts of reports and intercepts. Marjorie, I think her name was. What did I know? Who was who? What does this mean? Why are they saying that? Which side did I think this one was on, which side that … and so on. The same old game, I suppose. Just different contexts.'

'And Stockholm? Will you be back in the same old game there, too?'

'Alongside the repatriation work? Yes. I'm afraid so. We need to weed out those who have to answer for their crimes. They're hiding everywhere – among the innocents, the lost, the discarded. And we have to keep our eye on Uncle Joe. No matter who we think we want to be, the world, circumstances, always choose who we are for us.'

'And you want to do this?'

'It's all I know. There's nothing for me here. And we can't go home to Estonia. Not yet, at any rate. Perhaps not for a very long time.'

'What about the children? They are happy here. At least, as happy as any child can be with what they've been through.'

'Have you been to Sweden?'

'No.'

'I saw you eating this evening. How often do you and the children have meat on your plate?'

'Not very.'

'I could see that. You left a morsel till last. So you could savour it. In case it's the last piece of meat you'll ever taste again. You're scrabbling around for coal for the fire. I imagine, often, there's no eggs, no milk, no cheese, no bread. In Sweden, there's all of that and more. Besides, without us here, imposing on you, you'll have more food for yourself. Plus there's a clean, warm apartment they've promised to give me and the children just down from Östrastation on Valhallav-ägen. There are schools in Stockholm. Good schools. I don't want to tear them away from their friends, but their lives there could be so much better. A new beginning; a fresh start. And then there are Estonians in Sweden. Thousands of them. They'll be among their own people, even if it isn't their own country …'

Emilie nodded. 'Of course. It makes the best sense.'

'Will you be all right?' he said.

'I'll manage.'

He paused. They both looked back at the fire. After a moment, he spoke again. 'You could come with us?'

She looked at him.

*

It was the evening train to Stockholm. The carriage windows were misted inside, frosted outside. The world whirled past: houses, cottages, cabins; the reassuring sight of people's homes lit from within. There was the clanging of level crossings and the mesmerising clattering over points. Kilometre after kilometre, hour after hour.

In the low-lit carriages, the corridors, the dining car, there were the murmured conversations of long-distance travellers.

They'd already left Germany behind, crossing over on the ferry from Fehmarn.

They were now rattling through the Danish countryside en route for the Helsingør-Helsingborg crossing; the narrow strip of water dividing Hamlet's Danish castle from the Swedish mainland.

He looked out of the window. The sun had set, but the sky was still blue; it was deepening by the minute. There was a row of squat firs, the sweep of an artist's brush; charcoal against the evening. The first snow of the year had fallen and was settling; pure and clean. Blue, black, white, he thought, the colours of the Estonian flag.

Across the compartment, on the seat opposite, Juhan slept.

Emilie was beside him.

They rested their heads on each other, swaying with the rocking of the carriage.

Maret sat with her father, holding his hand. He looked at her. *Sixteen years old; a young woman already and yet still the vulnerable little girl I used to know.*

She gazed out of the window as the night closed in. She wiped the condensation from the window from time to time with her elbow. Just as she had done with the porthole when she, her mother and her brother left Tallinn in the cargo ship five years before. Hendrik knew she was missing that boy Jens. Missing school. Missing Germany, even. He squeezed her hand. She looked at him. 'We did the best we could, we'll do the best we can,' he said.

'When will it all end?'

'I have no idea.'

She settled against him and rested her head on his shoulder.

'Father?'

'Yes, Maret?'

'When will we go home? To Estonia.'

'Soon, darling. Soon.'

Acknowledgements

A Note on the Maritime Imagery

The departure from Tallinn in 1940 marked the end of an era for my family and for Estonia itself. In describing the Kotkas departure, I have leaned into the grit of the early 20th-century maritime tradition, specifically drawing upon the evocative "salt-caked smoke stack" of John Masefield's Cargoes. I intended this as a deliberate nod to a poem that has stayed with me since my schooldays—a way of anchoring my family's specific history within the broader, rugged textures of Northern European seafaring life, and indeed, my own story.

I am especially grateful to Jörgen and Karin Linneberg for the long conversations that often lasted into the night and which gave me insights into the many extraordinary events that the Linneberg and Tofer families experienced. I am also very grateful to Harriet Tofer, who in turn kindly gave me rich background material.

My thanks go to my good friends in the Estonian Evangelical Lutheran Church (EELK) Gustav Piir and Annika Laats; both of whom helped me in my search for information related to relatives and places important to my family's story. I am also grateful to Archbishop Urmas Viilma and Bishop Tiit Salumäe, also of EELK, who showed interest throughout this project and supported me in every way.

The wonderful Arvet Tetsmann from the Tallinn Yacht Club was indispensable in supplying important background information.

The invaluable Arto Oll from the Estonian Maritime Museum has been both a good friend and an excellent source of information. I am deeply grateful to him for taking the trouble to review the first draft of the book, often drawing attention to errors and inaccuracies, especially regarding the naval activities that took place in the Baltic countries in 1939–45. Mistakes that have gone unnoticed or have been left in the book for the purpose of shaping the plot – after all, it is still a novel – remain completely my fault.

Special thanks go to Tiit Treimuth and Aili Saks, who considered my story worthy of inclusion in the extensive range of books published by the highly regarded Eesti Raamat.

I am especially grateful to Piret Lemetti for her translation and literary skills. I am very proud to call her both friend and colleague. Thanks, too, to Mari Tuuling for casting her glittering editorial eye over the manuscripts and to Jaan Tammsaar for his cover art. Thanks, too, go to Rachel, Ann-Marie and Adrian of The Choir Press.

Finding the facts turned out to be surprisingly difficult in certain areas, as there are few research materials in English. In addition, my Estonian leaves a lot to be desired. In terms of historical information, I found the following books particularly helpful: *Naval Warfare in the Baltic 1939–1945* by C.W. Koburger Jr.; Earl F. Ziemke's *The German Northern Theater of Operations 1940–1945* and Robert Jackson's *Battle of the Baltic: The Wars 1918–1945.*

During the final stages of my family's life in Germany, Isabel Denny's poignant and moving *The Fall of Hitler's Fortress City: the Battle for Königsberg, 1945* helped to shape the relevant scenes.

My deepest apologies if I have forgotten to mention someone who also deserves my thanks. I didn't do it on purpose. Please let me know if I have omitted to mention your contribution to this novel and I will correct my mistake as best I can.

Martin Allison Booth

www.ingramcontent.com/pod-product-compliance
Lightning Source LLC
Chambersburg PA
CBHW030553020726
47494CB00005B/1589